CRITI

"Maynar
ly entert
reflects classic old-school style themes told with a decidedly modern perspective."

—Brian Keene, author of *Darkness on the Edge of Town*

"Maynard and Sims make readers accept terrible denizens from nightmare as casual fact."

—*Cemetery Dance*

"Maynard and Sims write with a fluid graceful style and know how to involve the reader in their story."

—Masters of Terror

"Reminiscent of the work of Ramsey Campbell."

—Gothic Net

"Maynard and Sims know what makes a horror story tick."

—*Shivers*

"L. H. Maynard and M. P. N. Sims are a duo of talent to be reckoned with."

—The Horror Review

"L. H. Maynard and M. P. N. Sims write a true horror story that will scare the heck out of readers."

—The Best Reviews

"Maynard and Sims are erudite horror stylists whose stories leave a lingering shiver of delicious terror that leave the reader wanting more."

—Author Link

"[Maynard & Sims] know when to take a quiet tack, using the carefully chosen line to disturb, to evoke a feeling of dread anticipation, the hint of something seen out of the corner of an eye, and when to render limbs and buckets of blood all over the text so that the reader is shocked and the odds against the characters heightened."

—Case Notes

THE LIVING SHADOWS

The sense of danger was becoming oppressive and Lucja quickened her pace. The bracken seemed alive now. There were black shapes everywhere, dancing on the path in front of her, skimming across the water of the canal, making the undergrowth rustle and move. She took one more look behind her and a cry burst from her lips. Not more than three paces behind her was a man, at least it looked like a man, but most of his face and body were in shadow.

Her heels were hampering her flight and as she ran she kicked them off, ignoring the pain of the sharp gravel as it drove into the soles of her feet. Her breath was coming in short stabbing gasps and her lungs were on fire. She glanced back. The figure was still behind her, at exactly the same distance—it hadn't gained or receded from her. She could see a gate in the fence ahead. Beyond the gate was the road and comparative safety.

She was about to veer towards the gate when the flitting shadows came at her, rushing at her legs, entangling themselves around her ankles. With a choking cry she pitched forward into the freezing, filthy water of the canal. . . .

Other *Leisure* books by L. H. Maynard and M. P. N. Sims:

THE BLACK CATHEDRAL
DEMON EYES
SHELTER

NIGHT SOULS

L. H. Maynard
M. P. N. Sims

LEISURE BOOKS  NEW YORK CITY

Mick: This book is dedicated to Clare Sims and Emily Rose Sims, eternal loves.
Len: This is for Bev Manders. Old love, new love.

A LEISURE BOOK®

June 2010

Published by

Dorchester Publishing Co., Inc.
200 Madison Avenue
New York, NY 10016

ISBN 10: 0-8439-6378-6
ISBN 13: 978-0-8439-6378-6
E-ISBN: 978-1-4285-0878-1

Printed in the United States of America.

10 9 8 7 6 5 4 3 2 1

ACKNOWLEDGMENTS

We offer grateful thanks to Don D'Auria and the entire Leisure team who present our books to the world with style and grace. The patient encouragement of Clare Sims is acknowledged, and the youthful inspiration of Emily Rose Sims is appreciated. Sally Melton offers her American retreat for essential battery recharging. All the people who took the time and trouble to give criticism in reviews, blogs, or verbally are thanked because they provoke a reaction that makes us want to do it all again with the next book. We thank Ian Drury for taking us on and offering us hope for the future. Hugh Lamb has always been a quiet encourager, and Stephen Jones has been a modest mentor. We acknowledge unreservedly that if you, the reader, didn't buy the book and read it and have an opinion on it, we wouldn't have the opportunity to be published in the first place.

Night Souls

Day One

A thing of beauty is a joy forever: Its loveliness increases;
it will never pass into nothingness; but still will keep a
bower quiet for us, and a sleep full of sweet dreams,
and health, and quiet breathing . . .
—John Keats

Barbarous nations breathing pure air and eating simple food enjoy immunity from its ravages.
—Ambrose Bierce

Chapter One

Dunster House, Docklands, London, England

Robert Carter pulled up behind Department 18's black SUV and switched off the engine of the Toyota. He was thirty-five, tall and slim with an athletic physique he owed to the four hours a week he spent at the gym, combined with regular games of squash. The exercise was complemented by a healthy diet, apart from far too many cigarettes, a light intake of alcohol, and occasional sex with willing partners.

The rain was beginning to ease. As Carter stepped out of the car, he saw Frankie Morgan sheltering in the doorway of Dunster House, the very exclusive apartment building he'd been asked to investigate.

He sketched a wave and stared up at the building. Twenty-six floors of cold concrete and glass. Carter remembered a time when this area of London was a rundown part of the city, with streets filled with slum dwellings backing onto the River Thames. But that was before the London Docklands redevelopment program transformed the place. Millions of pounds injected by astute businessmen who saw the potential of riverside dwellings for the upwardly mobile men and women flooding into the area to be closer to their workplaces in the city and Canary Wharf.

Now the area was unrecognizable from the dark side of town he'd known as a child.

"Frankie, what have we got?"

"Didn't Crozier brief you?" Frankie Morgan was thirty, pretty, with fair hair tied back in a ponytail from her round, open face.

"He left a message on my answering service asking me to get down here. He mentioned poltergeist activity, said you'd fill me in."

"Not very helpful," she said.

"When is he ever?"

"You look flushed," she said.

"I came straight from the squash club. Are the others inside?"

"Yes. And I think it's a little bit more than poltergeist activity. The police evacuated the place yesterday after the third fatality."

"On whose authority?"

"The Home Office."

"So the whole building is empty?"

"Apart from the ghosts," she said with a smile.

"Let's get out of this rain," Carter said and pushed open the door to the apartment building.

The three others in Frankie's team were waiting inside, all of them young and fairly inexperienced. Adam Black, Chris Baines, and Ellen McCrory. Frankie made the introductions.

"So Crozier thinks we can't handle this on our own. Great vote of confidence," Baines said petulantly, glaring at Carter. Baines was in his early twenties and had an attitude that bristled with antagonism.

"It's not like that," Frankie said.

"I've handled poltergeist cases before," Baines said.

"So have I," Ellen McCrory said. "And I really don't think we need a babysitter." At thirty-two, Ellen was the oldest of the group.

"In my experience, poltergeists don't kill people," Carter said. "How many fatalities have there been, Frankie?"

"Three."

"So it's unlikely we're dealing with a poltergeist," Adam Black said. Black was in his midtwenties but looked like a teenager. Carter had read his file and had been looking forward to meeting him. Adam Black's upbringing was similar to his own. A child prodigy when it came to clairvoyance, giving readings from the age of eight. A domineering father with a God fixation who pushed his son relentlessly to the point of a nervous breakdown. Carter could empathize.

"Unlikely, but not impossible."

"So what do you think it is?" Baines said.

"No idea. I've only just arrived. Frankie, where was the first fatality?"

"Apartment 53. Fifth floor."

"Ok. We'll start there. I suggest that, until we have a clearer idea of what we're dealing with here, we all stick together."

"Oh, for Christ's sake!" Ellen McCrory said. "We know what we're doing."

"And we have the details of your next of kin on file, do we? Just so we know who to contact if you get killed," Carter said.

Ellen McCrory glared at him.

Carter held her gaze until she looked away. "Right. Let's get on. Are the elevators working, Frankie?"

"Yes. All utilities are functioning. The police just cleared the residents out and left everything else alone."

"What were the residents told?" Carter asked her as they walked toward the two elevators set into the south wall.

"Asbestos alert," Frankie said. "They were told that routine maintenance had uncovered asbestos in the roof and they had to be evacuated until it was cleared. We fed the same story to the local media. Didn't want a circus down here."

"Good idea. And all the residents swallowed it?"

"Most of them," Frankie said. "There were one or two who didn't believe a word of it, but they were the ones who'd had *other* experiences here, and they were only too happy to have an excuse to leave."

With a hiss, one set of doors opened. "Okay. Fill me in on the details on the way up," Carter said and was about to step into the elevator when the main door of the building opened and a young man wearing an Armani suit and an angry expression strode into the foyer. "Would one of you mind telling me what the hell is going on here?"

Frankie Morgan stepped forward to intercept. "I'm sorry, sir, I'm going to have to ask you to leave. For your own safety."

The young man raised his chin pugnaciously. "And who the fuck are you?"

"Dr. Frances Morgan, Environmental Heath. And you are?"

"Jonathan Lassiter, Braxton Developments, the company that built this building. What's all this crap about asbestos? There's no asbestos here. The building's only a year old."

"Be that as it may, Mr. Lassiter, but I'll have to ask you to leave until the matter has been properly investigated."

"Tough. I'm not going anywhere. Let me see some identification."

Frankie glanced back at Carter, uncertain how to proceed.

Robert Carter sighed and walked across to join them. "Do we have a problem, Dr. Morgan?"

"Identification," Lassiter said. "Now, or I call the police."

Carter reached into his jacket pocket and pulled out his pocketbook, flipping it open and letting Lassiter read his ID card.

"And what's Department 18?" Lassiter said, looking at Carter quizzically.

"Part of the government. We've been called in by the Home Office to investigate three suspicious deaths that have occurred here in the past week."

The color drained from Lassiter's face. "Three deaths? Nobody told me. What are you, police?"

"We work in conjunction with the police and the security services and, as Dr. Morgan said, the Home Office. So, if there's nothing else, for your own safety, you should leave now."

Confusion clouded Lassiter's eyes. "I'm not happy about this," he said.

"I don't care," Carter said. "Go away, and leave us to do our job."

Lassiter hesitated for a moment, then spun on his heel and stalked from the building.

"Thanks," Frankie said. "I wasn't sure what to do when he asked for identification."

"Always tell the truth, Frankie," Carter said. "Within reason," he added with a smile. "Come on, let's get to work."

Frankie turned the key in the door of apartment 53 and pushed it open, reeling back as the stench hit her like a physical blow. She clamped her hand over her nose and mouth and struggled to prevent herself from gagging. "Jesus! What *is* that?" she said.

"I can't smell anything," Baines said.

Ellen McCrory shook her head. "Nothing."

Robert Carter was watching them. He worried about Frankie Morgan sometimes. She was too open, her senses too attuned. She needed to protect herself more. He lowered his defenses slightly and sniffed the air. Yes, she was right. There *was* an odor; something rank and fetid, something long dead. He stepped through the doorway.

"Very nice," Chris Baines said as he followed the others into the room. "Wouldn't mind a place like this myself. Look at the size of that TV."

"Concentrate," Carter snapped at him. "Frankie, are you okay?"

She was last into the room and now had a handkerchief pressed against her nose. "It's fading," she said. "The smell's nowhere near so strong once you're inside."

From his pocket Carter took a small black box with a dial at its center and a small white dome on one end. There was a switch on the side. He flicked it on. The needle jumped across the dial. "Strong electromagnetic residue," he said. "Be careful."

"The death occurred in the bedroom. Melanie Fry, thirty-two, commodities analyst," Frankie said.

"How did she die?"

"The autopsy was inconclusive. Four puncture wounds to her thorax, but small, not enough on their own to kill her. The pathologist could find no other injuries. In his words, it was as if she had just been switched off. As if someone had thrown a switch and she just died."

Carter walked through to the bedroom and looked around. It was smart and neat with a low, oak-framed, king-size bed taking up the center of the room. The rest of the furniture was modern and plain, Shaker style. "There's nothing here," he said. "I'm not picking anything up."

"How do you explain the smell?" Frankie said.

"An echo, I suspect. Nothing more." He held the meter out in front of him and scanned the room. "Are you sure this is where she died?"

"She was found in bed. Naked, spread-eagled. Looked like she'd been having sex when she died."

Carter shrugged. "I'd expect there to be more residual energy than I'm picking up." He slipped the meter back into his pocket. "Okay. The second death. Which floor?"

"We go up," Frankie said. "Apartment 120. Twelfth floor."

"Right, let's get on," Carter said.

* * *

Chris Baines had already left apartment 53 and was making his way to the stairwell. Ellen McCrory was close behind him. "Where are you going?" she said.

"Up," Baines said. "I'm getting nothing on this floor, but something's nagging me to climb. Coming?"

"And you don't care if you upset Carter." It wasn't a question, and the grin on her face encouraged him.

"Come on then." He pulled open the door to the stairwell and started to climb the stairs two at a time.

By the time they reached the tenth floor, Ellen McCrory was panting for breath.

"It's time you quit smoking," Baines said.

"What are you, my father? Why didn't we take the elevator?"

"Not safe," Baines said, every nerve in his body tingling.

"But we just used it."

"Well it's not safe now. Trust me. Come on." He pushed open the door to the tenth floor. He stood for a moment, eyes closed, letting the random impressions flood into his mind. *Black shapes slithering across the floor, coalescing, becoming a much larger mass, rising up and moving through the apartments.* A *woman's scream. Pain. Death.* "This way," he said, his eyes snapping open.

Ellen watched him nervously, her maverick spirit starting to dissipate. She'd worked with Baines before and knew he was a risk taker. She found it an attractive attribute and, if she was honest with herself, a bit of a turn on, but she was beginning to have second thoughts about leaving the others behind.

She was getting her own impressions of the place, and they weren't good. Not good at all.

"Did you see that?" she said, squinting and peering along the plush, carpeted corridor.

"See what?" Baines said. He was looking from door to door, trying to focus, to feel where he should lead them next.

"Something black, moving, down at the end of the corridor. It went into one of the rooms."

"Can you try to describe it?" he said, turning his attention back to her.

"Like a black sheet, blown in the wind, but not as substantial. Like gauze."

He frowned at her. "Come on. Show me the room." He strode off down the corridor, Ellen following tentatively a few paces behind.

"Where are McCrory and Baines?" Carter asked as he came out of the bedroom and saw Adam Black standing alone in the lounge.

Black shrugged. "One minute they were here, the next they'd gone."

Carter swore and wheeled on Frankie. "Is your team always this undisciplined?"

"No, Robert," she said bridling. "But they're used to carrying out these investigations unsupervised. They're both strong psychics so they're more than capable of looking after themselves."

"Let me be the judge of that," Carter said. "We don't know what we're dealing with here yet, and until we know what the danger is, I don't want anyone taking unnecessary risks. Come on, let's find them."

"We'd better check floor by floor," Frankie said, trying to wrest back some element of control from Carter. She knew why he was so angry. A routine investigation he'd headed a few months ago had ended tragically with the disappearance of his assistant, Sian Davies. Some members of the department were convinced he'd never really gotten over it. "We'll take the stairs and search thoroughly."

"Up or down?" Adam Black said.

Carter turned to the young man, who was scuffing the toe

of his shoe on the deep-piled carpet in a mixture of anxiety and embarrassment, and avoiding eye contact. "Pardon?"

"Up or down," Black said again. "We don't know which way to go."

"Up," Carter said.

"Why?"

Carter fixed him with a cold hard stare. "Because I say so."

"You're the boss," Black said without malice.

"And I just wish people would remember that," Carter said and walked from the apartment.

Jonathan Lassiter was seething. He paced on the street outside Dunster House, punching numbers into his cell phone and wallowing in the frustration of not being able to raise anyone significant at this time of day. The frustration was feeding his anger. He couldn't believe he'd been dismissed from the building in such a high-handed way, as if he were nothing more than an errant schoolboy caught loitering indoors during recess.

He snapped his phone shut and dropped it back into the pocket of his suit jacket. He suddenly became aware of the rain, soaking his hair, his Armani, and his Gucci loafers. This was intolerable. He turned on his heel and pushed open the door of Dunster House and walked out of the rain.

Once inside he looked around for someone to vent his anger on, but the foyer was deserted. He swore savagely and crossed the marble-tiled floor to the elevator, punching the call button, tapping his foot impatiently as he waited for the elevator to descend. Once the doors slid open, he stepped inside, staring at the panel of buttons for a long moment before making a decision. Finally he pulled his bunch of keys from his pocket, inserted one into the panel and twisted it, at the same time hitting the button for the penthouse.

As the car started to ascend, he leaned back against the

wall, taking out a handkerchief and dabbing away the rain from his face. He'd been up to the penthouse only twice before and that was pre-occupation. Now the luxurious apartment was owned by an Asian businessman who had made his fortune in the clothing trade.

It would be interesting to see how the mega-rich lived. It was a lifestyle he aspired to but knew he was a long way from attaining. He also wanted to be up at the top of the building when the bunch of morons from the Home Office, or wherever they were from, arrived there. He'd show them he wasn't fazed by their scare mongering and that Braxton stood by the quality of its developments.

The elevator juddered to a halt between the twenty-first and twenty-second floor. He twisted the key and pressed the button again, but the car didn't budge. He ran his hand over the panel, hitting all the buttons, but nothing happened.

He was suddenly aware that the temperature in the car was dropping. A few seconds later, his breath started to mist in front of his face and he shivered. He sniffed the air and recoiled as the stench of rotting meat filled his nostrils.

As the first black shape slithered in under the door Jonathan Lassiter felt a tremor of disquiet. *What the hell was going on?*

Chris Baines hesitated outside apartment 105 and rested his hand on the door. There was something inside. He could sense it.

"Well?" Ellen said, catching up with him.

"Can't you feel it?"

She shook her head, chewing pensively at her bottom lip.

"You're blocking."

"You betcha," she said. "I'm not leaving myself open to attack. Three people have *died*, Chris."

"Okay," he said. "Stay behind me." He slipped the key card into the lock and turned the handle.

It was dark inside the apartment, despite the onset of early morning. He slid his hand across the wall and located the light switch. He flipped it, but the room stayed dark.

"The lights should be working," Ellen said, a tremor to her voice. "We shouldn't need them anyway, it's light outside."

"Relax," he said and pulled a flashlight from the bag he had slung over his shoulder. He switched it on and swung the beam around the room, drawing in his breath when the light flickered over a figure sitting in a chair by the window. He pulled the beam back, aiming it directly at the chair, but he couldn't see any more clearly. There was a figure there, but it seemed to be absorbing the light, sucking it in like a black hole.

"We should go back and get Carter," Ellen said, clutching the sleeve of his jacket,

"Shh! Hello!" he called to the figure in the chair. "I'm Chris Baines. This is my colleague, Ellen McCrory."

The figure remained silent and unmoving.

"We were told this building was empty. Would you mind telling us what you're doing here?"

Ellen tugged at his sleeve. "Chris? Chris! Let's get out of here."

As she spoke, the figure started to rise. They still couldn't see properly. It was just a shape, the build of a large man, darker than the surrounding darkness.

They took a step backward. Ellen clamped a hand across her nose as a foul odor hit her like a physical blow.

"God! I think I'm going to be sick." She started to retch.

Baines focused the flashlight, willing the beam to glow brighter, but it was useless. The light was being swallowed. There was a sound, like dry autumn leaves blown across concrete, and the shape exploded, fragmenting into a hundred smaller shapes that skittered across the floor, flapping and flailing like disembodied blackbird wings. The shapes moved past them, plucking at their clothes, slithering over their skin.

Ellen screamed.

Baines dropped the flashlight and sank to his knees, folding his arms over his head as he was buffeted by the shapes.

The apartment door slammed, and it was all over. The stench and the shapes had gone.

Baines gradually uncurled his arms from his head, picked up the flashlight, and stood. He shined the beam around the room. Ellen was standing at the window with her back to him as if staring out at the street below. "Ellen? Ellie?"

She didn't move, didn't acknowledge him at all.

He took a few steps forward, reached out, and touched her shoulder. "Ellie?"

At his touch, she crumpled to the floor, deflating like a burst balloon.

The flashlight's beam took in the withered skin of her face, the bleached white, cotton-candy texture of her hair. Her mouth sagged open, and he watched as her teeth crumbled to dust and fell away.

And then he screamed too.

He was still screaming when the others found him five minutes later.

In the elevator, Jonathan Lassiter was brushing frantically at his clothes, trying to dislodge the black shapes as they crawled up his neat Armani suit toward his face, but it was no use. It was like trying to sweep away shadows.

He could feel his heart pounding in his chest. Panic, pure blind panic.

The shadow shapes reached his throat, and he felt himself suffocating as they constricted his breathing. He opened his mouth wide, trying to suck in the fetid air of the elevator car, but succeeded only in sucking in the slithering black shapes.

They poured down his throat in a shadowy wave, filling him up, swelling in his stomach. And then they were moving through his body; settling in his legs and arms, nestling in his genitals, making his penis swell into a huge erection.

Suddenly he felt exhilarated, more alive than he had for years. He stretched his arms wide, inviting the shapes to enter him; all panic gone, just a sense of peace, of power. He felt he could do anything, anything at all.

Anything, that is, except remember who he was.

The elevator car lurched and restarted its ascent. As it reached the penthouse, the doors opened and he stepped out into the plush, luxurious apartment. He looked about him, taking in the hugely expensive antique furniture, the massive plasma-screen television, the Picasso hanging on one wall and the Degas on another, and he felt nothing. No sense of envy, no sense of desire. Everything he had ever needed, he now possessed. Buried deep inside him was the key, the essence of life itself. He flopped down onto a Louis XIV chair, surveyed his new kingdom, and started to laugh.

"Frankie, take Baines downstairs and get him out of the building. Wait by the car."

Frankie was staring down at Ellen's desiccated body, a look of sheer horror on her face. Carter's words washed over her but didn't sink in.

"Frankie!" Carter gripped her by the shoulders and shook her. "Get Baines outside, now!"

Her eyes refocused and she stared at Carter as if seeing him for the first time. "What?"

Carter turned to Chris Baines, who was slumped against the wall, tears coursing down his face. "Chris, go with Frankie."

Adam Black said, "I'll take them."

"No, I want you with me."

"It's okay," Frankie Morgan said, gathering herself. "I'll take him. I'm fine now." She crossed to where Baines was leaning against the wall and wrapped her arm around his shoulders. "Come on, Chris. Let's get you out of here."

Baines responded by burying his face into Frankie's shoulder and sobbing, his whole body heaving with the shock of losing Ellen.

Carter watched them go. He was as relieved to get rid of Frankie as he was to be rid of Baines. He'd seen the fear in her eyes, and fear was dangerous in a situation like this. He walked from the apartment, out into the corridor, Black trailing close behind him.

"Any ideas?" he said to the younger man.

Black was staring at the indicator panels for the elevator. "There's a clue," he said, pointing to the right-hand panel. A red letter P was glowing under the black plastic casing. "The penthouse," he said.

"How can you be so sure?"

"Because it should be showing the ground floor, not the penthouse. We called both elevators *down*, remember? Someone, or something's, taken it up to the top of the building."

Carter crossed to the elevators and pressed the call button. Moments later the left-hand doors opened and they stepped inside.

Black studied the buttons. "We need a key to get up to the penthouse. This only takes us to the twenty-fifth floor."

"It will have to do," Carter said. "There must be service stairs, or maybe even a fire escape that will take us up there." He hit the button to floor twenty-five and watched as the doors slid shut.

Black tapped his foot nervously as the car began to move. There was a fine sheen of perspiration coating his face.

"Are you up to this?" Carter said to him.

Black nodded. "What do you think happened to Ellie?" he said.

Carter shook his head. "I've never seen anything like it

before. What I don't understand is how Baines escaped the same fate."

"Maybe he was better able to protect himself," Black offered.

"Possibly. But I don't want to lose anyone else, so be careful."

"You mustn't blame yourself," Black said.

"I don't," Carter said bluntly. "I said we should all stick together. If they'd listened, Ellen McCrory might still be alive."

Black fell silent and watched the floor numbers pass with a mounting sense of trepidation.

When they reached twenty-five, the elevator stopped moving, the doors opened, and the two men stepped out.

Frankie settled Chris Baines into the back of the SUV, closed and locked the door. He was too distraught to go anywhere so it would be safe enough to leave him. She'd caught the look of concern in Carter's eyes, and it was bothering her. He'd submit a report to Simon Crozier, Director General of Department 18, and, however he phrased the words, it would show her in a bad light.

She had spent the last two years pushing for the promotion that would enable her to lead her own investigative team and finally she had achieved her ambition. It would be nothing short of a travesty if, on her first serious assignment, she was perceived to be lacking the necessary leadership skills. The fact that Crozier had called in Carter to oversee the operation showed that he still had no confidence in her abilities. She couldn't afford to be seen as weak, or worse, incapable.

She pulled up the collar of her jacket against the rain and walked quickly back to Dunster House, pushing open the doors and slipping inside.

Every member of Department 18 had one psychic ability

or another. Frankie Morgan was a highly adept physical medium. She had held séances where whole rooms had come alive as psychic energy channeled through her. There was one memorable instance where a stone elephant weighing several hundred pounds had risen three feet into the air, floated the entire length of the room, and then landed gracefully in the fireplace.

She wondered now how best to put her special skill to work. First she had to ascertain just what they were up against. Chris Baines had described shadow shapes swarming over them. The description rang bells in the back of her mind. She'd read something about similar phenomenon, but it had been a long time ago and she couldn't bring the exact details to the forefront of her mind.

She sat down on the cold hard tiles in the middle of the foyer and closed her eyes. Letting her breathing settle into a steady rise and fall, she lowered her defenses little by little and opened her mind, letting the store of random images floating about the place register in the deepest part of her subconscious.

Come on, show me what you are. She spoke the words in her mind, calling out to the entities that inhabited Dunster House.

You're very brave, Dr. Morgan. You really don't want to know what we are.

The words entered her head. She recognized the voice immediately. The young man who had barged into the building earlier spitting piss and vinegar. Lassiter. Jonathan Lassiter.

She flicked open her eyes, but there was nothing to see. Nothing at all . . . except . . .

She focused on the elevators. The indicator panels were glowing red, letters instead of numbers.

Up here.

Up where? she thought and the answer came to her in another psychic flash.

The penthouse. Come and join the party.

She got to her feet and crossed the marble floor to the elevators. *Okay,* she thought. *You want to play, we'll play.* She punched the call button and waited for the elevator to descend. The doors opened and she stepped inside. The doors closed and the elevator began its upward journey.

It was only when it reached the halfway point that she realized she hadn't selected a floor.

Ellen McCrory.

When he opened his eyes, Chris Baines could see Ellen McCrory.

That couldn't be, but she was there, in the doorway to the apartment building. Standing behind the ornate glass doors.

She was smiling at him. She raised her hand and waved. No, she beckoned him.

Beware the beckoning stranger.

The words vibrated in his brain.

Ellen isn't a stranger. She's a colleague, a friend. I thought she was dead, but she can't be.

Baines opened the door to the SUV and slammed it closed behind him. His feet on the pavement felt a bit shaky, but he made himself cover the distance between the vehicle and the doors.

The glass felt cold to the touch, and when he took his fingers away they left an imprint. He touched the mark and thought the imprint was slightly indented, as though the pressure of his touch had pushed the glass inward a little.

Ellen was beckoning him more now.

It looked as if she was naked. That must be a trick of the light.

Baines took the handle of one of the heavy glass doors and pulled it toward him. It opened and it felt like a hand tugged at his clothes to encourage him inside.

There was no sign of Ellen.

He looked around the foyer, but it was empty.

Then he felt moisture on his head, as if water had dripped onto him.

He looked up and wished he hadn't. He wished he had stayed in the SUV.

He had found Ellen.

She was hanging from the ceiling by her hands and feet. Her arms and legs were bent behind her so her body was arched forward, as if waiting to pounce.

Surrounding her, forming a blanket of black around her, were dozens of what seemed to be shadows. When Baines looked more closely, he saw they were more than shadows; they had more substance. They were different shapes and sizes but coalesced into a smooth sea of darkness. The smaller ones looked like beetles with arched backs, while some of the larger ones had appendages poking from misshapen bodies in a parody of limbs.

Baines wanted to run, but he wasn't fast enough.

With a scream that was as shrill as it was fierce, Ellen fell onto him and enveloped him like a huge eiderdown of skin. She wrapped herself around him, folding into every crevice and orifice until she was invading him.

When he was totally entrapped, the black shapes dropped from the ceiling and entered him.

The service stairs up to the penthouse were poorly lit, just two low-wattage emergency lights lit their path as Carter and Black climbed. They reached the top of the staircase and were confronted by a steel-clad door. Carter twisted the handle, but the door didn't budge. "Damn it!" he said softly and as the words left his lips, there was a click and the door swung inward.

"Looks like we're expected," Black said.

"That's worrying," Carter said. "Come on. Stay close."

The penthouse apartment was in semidarkness as they

slipped in through the doorway. What scant illumination there was came from a large glass tank in the corner of the room, where multicolored tropical fish darted back and forth. Music was playing softly on the stereo; jazz—Miles Davis, *Blue in Green*. It would have been soothing had the circumstances not made it so incongruous.

"Welcome, Mr. Carter. And you too, Mr. Black. Welcome to my humble abode."

The voice seemed to come from everywhere. Gliding on top of Miles Davis's mellow horn.

"Show yourself," Carter said.

"And spoil the surprise? Besides, it would be rude to start the party before the final guest has arrived."

A small bell sounded as the elevator reached the penthouse. There was a hiss as the doors opened, and Frankie Morgan stepped out of the car.

"Ah, right on cue."

Carter ran forward. "Frankie! Get back in the elevator. Get out of here!"

A shadow passed in front of his face and something wet and heavy crashed into him, knocking him to the ground.

"Carter!" Black yelled and rushed toward him, but more shadows appeared, crawling from the darkened corners of the room, slipping out from beneath the furniture. They circled Carter as he struggled to push himself to his feet. Black stopped in his tracks as one of the shadows reared up in front of him. He felt himself being lifted from his feet, and then he was thrown backward, crashing into the fish tank. The glass shattered, sending water cascading over the Persian rug.

Frankie Morgan stood at the threshold of the room, trying to focus her thoughts, to channel her energy. She could feel the evil all around her. She tried to push it back but it was pervasive.

The evil was in every shadow that moved through the

room. A tangible evil, cloying, pressing down on her like a suffocating wet rag. She tried to call out to Carter, who had made it to his feet and was standing, swaying in the center of the room, but the shadows had reached her now and were starting to move up her body. Her chest was constricted, and it was becoming more and more difficult to breathe.

Suddenly the whole apartment was flooded with light as every lamp in the place burst into blinding life.

Standing there was Jonathan Lassiter, illuminated by an overhead spotlight, behind him the open French doors to the balcony. The Armani suit was immaculate, the Gucci loafers gleaming, and he was smiling. Around him shadows danced with a life of their own.

"Lassiter?" Carter said.

The man's smile broadened into a grin. "Yes," he said. "And no. The inadequate young man who entered this building is no more. We have entered him, improved him."

"And who are you?" Carter said. "What are you?"

"You're about to find out," Lassiter said. He raised his arms, and the shadows around him rushed forward.

Carter spread his arms out in front of him as if welcoming the shadows, as if he was going to embrace them, but as they were about to swarm over him he crossed his arms over his chest and yelled, "No!"

The shadows faltered and then started to retreat, slithering back to their hiding places.

Lassiter's smile faltered, and he took a step backward. A frown creased his forehead.

Carter glanced round at Frankie and Adam. Frankie was on her knees, almost engulfed by the shadows. Adam was wet and bleeding. He was clutching his left arm, which had been sliced open by a shard of glass from the shattered aquarium. From the way blood was pumping out through his fingers, it was likely an artery had been severed.

"You and me!" he shouted at Lassiter. "Let the others go."

"And why in God's name should I do that?" the young man replied.

"Because if you don't, I'll know you're still the inadequate, pathetic little prick I met down in the foyer. Delusions of grandeur. Is that it, Lassiter? Show me the kind of man you are now."

"You'll regret it," Lassiter said, the smile returning.

"I doubt it."

Lassiter snapped his fingers, and the shadows slipped from Frankie's body and slinked away into the corner of the room.

"Robert, no!" Frankie said.

"Frankie, take Adam down in the elevator and get him to a hospital before he bleeds to death."

"I'm not leaving you," she said.

"Neither am I." Adam staggered forward, then sank to his knees, weakened by the loss of blood.

"Do as you're bloody told! Both of you!"

Frankie looked from Carter to Black, who looked as if he was about to pass out. Then she rushed forward, helped him to his feet, and hauled him across to the elevator. With one desperate glance back at the apartment, she hit a button.

As the doors closed, Lassiter laughed. "They don't have as much faith in you as you do yourself."

"Go to hell!" Carter said.

Lassiter snapped his fingers again, and the shadows surged forward. This time Carter was too slow, much too slow. The shadows swarmed over him, shredding his clothes, ripping at his skin. They had weight, so much weight. He felt his knees begin to buckle. With a supreme effort of will, he focused his thoughts, concentrating fiercely, trying to repel the onslaught. But he'd miscalculated badly. There were too many of them, and they were pulling him down.

He could feel claws raking his body, sharp pains as spindle thin spikes were driven into his side. The spikes moved inside him, searching out his vital organs, hungry, probing. As he was pulled down by the weight of the shadows, he felt his life begin to slip away. The room was growing dark, the light being sucked into the shadows. He was aware of Lassiter laughing obscenely, triumphant, victorious.

His neck was wrenched one way then the other. Hard blows smashed into his chest and he felt ribs crack.

And then the elevator doors opened, and Adam Black was back in the room, running, throwing himself at Lassiter. The two men tumbled backward, crashing onto the balcony. For a moment it seemed like they would stay propped together against the metal railings. Then there was a shout like a pistol shot, and they tumbled, Lassiter wrapped in Adam's embrace, out into the night and down to the cold hard ground below.

As he lay there, unable to move, Carter felt the weight of the shadows lift from his body as they slithered away. And then Frankie's face swam into focus. "Shh. Don't move. I've called for an ambulance."

"Too late," he said. "Much too late."

And darkness crashed in to claim him.

Chapter Two

Clerkenwell, London, England

They'd found him again.

Daniel Milton's senses were rattling. He couldn't see his pursuers yet, or even hear them, but he knew they were there. He could feel them close by and knew they were in the derelict office block that had been his home for the past two weeks. Somewhere beneath him, they were moving stealthily through the abandoned lower floors; maybe a few were even now climbing the stone stairs to reach his sanctuary.

Earlier he had broken cover, traveling up to the West End, knowing it was a risk but a necessary one. His meeting with Simon Crozier of Department 18 was important, vital. Thankfully the man had taken him seriously. Crozier even offered to feed him at his club. The gnawing hunger pains in his stomach made the offer too tempting to turn down, but it was a mistake. The good food and wine made him drowsy and sluggish and dulled his instincts, which allowed them to get close without him sensing them.

And now they were here.

He slipped out of the sleeping bag, shucking it off like a bug emerging from a larval sac, picked up the thin, needle-pointed knife, and hefted it in his hand. The weapon was a constant companion now, and he was never more than an arm's length away from it. He slipped it into his belt and crept silently to the door, opening it a crack and listening.

For a long moment there was nothing, a pregnant silence broken only by the sound of the engine of a passing car.

A *creak*.

A floorboard being stepped on.

Two, three floors down.

Even closer than he'd anticipated.

He looked back into the room. The scruffy green rucksack lay against the wall. It contained a few of his possessions, but nothing he couldn't leave behind. He slept fully clothed these days—a habit since the last nocturnal attack—and everything important to him, credit cards, cell phone, money, was stashed in the numerous pockets of his combats. He was ready to run, to flee at a second's notice.

Another creak. Closer this time.

He edged out into the corridor, his eyes accustomed to the darkness, but his vision was nowhere near as good as theirs in this gloom. This was like daylight to them. They could see as well as cats in the dark, so they had him at a disadvantage. The only thing on his side was his knowledge of the building and, after a fortnight using this as his refuge, the building was now very familiar to him, as familiar as an old friend. He'd started to feel safe here, and that was another mistake. Safety equaled complacency, and that was something he couldn't afford anymore.

He crossed the corridor to the stairwell and pulled back the door, slipping through to the concrete stairs and climbing them silently. There were four floors above him and above them the roof, flat concrete with a steel fire escape reaching all the way down to Clerkenwell Road, and a spectacular view of St. Paul's Cathedral. A few streets away was the traditional meat market of London, Smithfield's, open day and night. Watching butchers in blood-soaked aprons drinking pints of Guinness in the early hours of the morning was a surreal sight.

He could hear noises below him on the stairs. They were climbing and were only two floors down. He had to move quickly.

As he turned the corner at the top of the next flight, someone cannoned into him. A man, six three, six four, two hundred and forty pounds. A big man dressed in jeans and a T-shirt, biceps and pectorals straining at the thin cotton.

Stupid!

He'd come down from the roof. Daniel had been so preoccupied with the pursuers below it hadn't occurred to him they might try an attack from above.

Stupid, stupid, stupid!

The big man seemed as surprised as Daniel and rocked back on his feet, mouth working but unable to find the appropriate words. It was only when recognition registered in his eyes that his hand came up holding a gun and he called out. "He's here. I've got him!"

That's what you bloody think, Daniel thought, pulling the

knife from his belt and stabbing the man through the eye in one fluid movement. The eyeball popped like a ripe grape, blood and a jellylike fluid pouring from it.

The gun cracked as a muscle spasm jerked the man's finger, but the bullet whistled past Daniel's shoulder and embedded in the wall behind him. The man dropped the gun and staggered backward, his hands to his face, a wailing cry following the explosion of the gunshot. He was already starting to change, to revert; the skin thickening, becoming scaly, the fingers stretching, thinning, the nails tapering to points, the slits in the fingertips opening and closing, tiny mouths searching for food.

As the man crumpled to the floor and started to disintegrate, Daniel heard more footsteps below him and still more coming down the stairs from the upper floor.

A *pincer movement*.

The phrase floated through his mind, and he smiled grimly. They'd outflanked him with almost military precision. There was only one way out now, only one escape. He retraced his steps and went back to the corridor. Halfway along was an elevator shaft gaping open, the brass concertina gates long gone, stolen for their scrap value. Steel cables hung from the machinery above, black with grease and dirt. Below, and a long way down, he could see the roof of the elevator car stuck between floors.

The doors at the stairwell end of the corridor opened, and suddenly the corridor was filled with bodies; men and women advanced on him. There was nothing special about them. They could have been a bunch of people lifted from any busy shopping street and transplanted here. They ranged in age from their twenties to their sixties. One of the men was wearing a smart pinstriped suit, another a leather jacket and oil-stained jeans, the long hair and beard suggesting that he'd left his Harley Davidson chopper out on the street below. A woman in a tweed suit, her gray hair permed and lacquered, grinned at him malevolently, while a younger woman wearing a skimpy black skirt and cream blouse fluttered her eyelashes at him in a parody of seduction. A few of the other faces were contorted with rage, angry that he'd evaded them for so long. A few were smiling in triumph that they had finally cornered him, had him trapped.

They all looked hungry.

He counted. Twelve of them. He could take two easily, three at a push, but the others would be on him before he could eliminate any more.

The corridor was eerily silent as they advanced on him. No one spoke. The only sounds were the shuffling of their feet, and the sibilant sounds of skin and bone stretching as their fingers elongated, fingernails lengthened into deadly points.

They wouldn't take him. He'd promised himself that a long time ago. They wouldn't have the satisfaction of feeding from him, or worse still, making him as they were.

He grinned, threw a salute, and stepped backward into the empty elevator shaft.

Smiling is very important. If we are not able to smile, then the world will not have peace. It is not by going out for a demonstration against nuclear missiles that we can bring about peace. It is with our capacity of smiling, breathing, and being peace that we can make peace.
—Thich Nhat Hanh

Chapter Three

Krakow, Poland

In a room at the Prince Albert Hotel, situated in the center of Krakow, Jason Pike gave a small gasp and sat bolt upright in bed. The young woman next to him sighed softly and rolled over onto her side, but she didn't wake. He glanced down at her, watching her long brown hair slip like silk over her shoulders. Anna? Was that her name? He couldn't remember now. He tried to concentrate, dismissing her from his mind and focusing on the wave of despair that had woken him.

Daniel.

Daniel Milton was in trouble.

As he opened up his mind, a jumble of images flashed across his consciousness.

Gray-painted walls. Long, empty corridors. A deep, dark pit. Falling. Faces staring down at him. Evil faces grinning.

Them.

He picked up his cell phone from the bedside table and punched in Milton's number. Even as he waited for the phone connection, the images in his mind started to fade, evaporating like a splash of water on a hot plate. He focused more deeply, grinding his teeth, trying to hold on to the images, trying to get a fix on Milton's location.

The girl beside him murmured again, and that small distraction was enough to blow the images away. He swore under his breath, threw back the covers, and pressed the phone closer to his ear, listening to the cell ringing at the other end of the line.

No answer.

Still holding the phone to his ear he padded through to the en suite to relieve himself. Finally he switched the phone off. Daniel wasn't answering or, more probably, *couldn't* answer.

There was little Pike could do for him now. Daniel Milton was several hundred miles away in England. Here in Poland, Pike had important work to do and couldn't afford to bail out and leave the country. Besides, it was probably too late to do anything to help his friend. It seemed likely that they had finally tracked him down, as they had with others before him. Pike hadn't been in England then either; though he had gone back to attend most of the funerals.

He laid the phone on the marble surrounding the sink and washed his hands, cupping the water and splashing it over his face. He could see the bedroom reflected in mirror above the sink; could see Anna, or whatever her name was, still sleeping peacefully.

There were four small wounds in the ivory skin of her back where his fingers had penetrated her. They would heal in a matter of days and leave no scars. He had taken from her only what he needed—just enough to sustain him for a week or so. When she eventually woke, she would feel slightly under the weather and, for two days, three at most, think she was coming down with the flu. And then it would pass and she would be well again with no aftereffects. Unlike Holly and his kind, Pike never killed when he took what he needed.

She'd felt no pain as his fingers burrowed into her, but then the digits had tapered to stiletto-like points, so the entry wounds were small. The other reason she'd felt no pain was the posthypnotic suggestion he'd planted in her mind, and in a few hours she would have forgotten she'd ever met him—another suggestion.

He finally looked at his face and hated what he saw there.

He hadn't been born like this. He'd been created, turned into a freak by one of the many freaks he'd met in his fifty-eight years.

He showered quickly, threw on some clothes, and went down to the lobby to get a coffee, irritated when he found the restaurant closed. He checked his watch. 3:20 AM. Hell! What did he expect?

He walked out into the night and for the next two hours pounded the streets of Krakow, trying to clear his head and get his thoughts into some kind of order.

Slawkowska, Florianska, Grodzka, most of the streets in the old part of the city. The red stone buildings, many with arched windows, three or four stories above them, with intricate carvings on the roofs.

For centuries Krakow was the capital of Poland, the seat of kings, attracting scholars and artists from all over the world. Their legacy shaped much of the past that can be seen today. The renaissance Royal Castle at Wawel, the gothic St. Mary's Basilica, the historical trade pavilions of the Cloth Hall, the former separate Jewish city of Kazimierz.

Krakow connects Polish tradition with modernity.

Pike's thoughts were of a different tradition. A violent past that still existed today.

A past and a violence he was determined to stop.

Chapter Four

Kings College Hospital, London, England

Crozier had always had a fantasy about hospitals.

In truth it was a contrived one, created from his perceptions of hospitals as he imagined they should be. Drawn from TV programs such as *ER*, *Chicago Hope*, and *Casualty*.

The doctors were busy but never too busy to flirt and more with the beautiful nurses. The patients always had some deep psychological problem or family issue that the wise interns could solve while discovering a previously undetected tumor, or heart murmur. The patients were always grateful for the interference. The nurses always grateful for the romantic attention.

There was another reason why Crozier liked hospitals. They were full of confident, educated men in doctor's garb, and in his fantasies it was they who were grateful.

He parked his car in a two-hour bay outside the Maudsley psychiatric hospital on Denmark Hill. He glanced across as he navigated crossing the busy road. *That's likely where I'll end up, dealing with people like Carter.*

The iron arch heralding the *King's* name stood proud in the light morning sun. The vast glass frontage of the hospital reflected tops of ambulances, occasional trees, and the tall, elegant figure of Crozier as he walked across to the front entrance and went inside.

King's College Hospital is now an acute-care facility, referred to locally and by staff simply as "King's" or abbreviated internally to "KCH." It serves an inner-city population of 700,000 in the London boroughs but is also a specialist center for millions of people in southern England.

Crozier took off his raincoat and placed it over his arm. The foyer was large and modern. It spoke of cleanliness and efficiency. He walked to the reception desk and asked where he needed to go to see Carter. It was several floors up, the elevators were to the left, and it was a neurological ward, he was told.

King's was originally opened in 1840 in the disused St. Clements Dane workhouse on Portugal Street close to Lincoln's Inn Fields. It was used as a training facility, where medical students of King's College London could practice and receive instruction. The surrounding area was overcrowded slums full of poverty and disease.

Whether in a fantasy or in reality, hospitals are always busy. There is an underlying swell of noise from voices. The emotions contained within the walls cover every aspect of human experience. Good news, bad news, a lifeline or a death sentence. The patients emit almost visible waves of fear, hope, desperation.

The elevator was quiet and efficient, much like the majority of the staff. Unlike Crozier's fantasies, they were too busy and too professional for anything like the atmosphere of suppressed sexual excitement he imagined.

Simon Crozier, who had an active social life, lost patience with people when they let their lives outside Department 18 get in the way of their work. He was a large man in his early fifties, with iron gray hair cut close to his skull. His eyes were deep brown and penetrating, and his hawk nose gave him a predatory aspect that was reflected in his manner. Simon Crozier was not a man to suffer fools gladly and made no pretense that he did.

Carter was in a private side room along a sterile corridor where white walls were punctuated by modern and abstract prints of bright colors.

The first thing Crozier noticed was that the room was dark. The blinds were drawn, and the only light was from an under-shelf unit over the bed. Once his eyes became accustomed to the gloom, he realized there were several vases of flowers dotted about. He hadn't brought flowers, or grapes, or anything to read. He hadn't brought anything.

In truth he didn't really know why he had come. He didn't like Carter, and he knew Carter did not like him. It was obvious other people had visited, and many of them would be from the department. So far as Crozier was aware, Carter had no social life beyond the department, and that hold had tightened through his relationship with Jane Talbot.

Something moved behind him, and he turned casually, expecting it to be the blinking light of a monitor or similar. There was nothing there.

Then the nothing shifted.

In the corner of the room was a pool of black shadow that seemed to ripple. Crozier tutted. The appearance of cleanliness in the hospital obviously didn't extend to the side rooms if that pile of dirt was anything to judge by.

Eventually he looked at the figure lying in the bed. Carter was asleep, probably drugged to the eyeballs. There were two drips feeding into his arms, one would be saline for fluids and the other would be painkillers. His head and shoulders were encased in a brace that prevented movement even when he was sleeping. There was a chart clipped to the end of the bed, but Crozier couldn't discern anything from it. He knew Carter had been badly injured, but the full extent of the damage he didn't know.

He found it surprising that he was a little scared to ask, in case it was serious.

He noticed some more untidy piles of dark dirt under the bed. This was really not good enough. The department's health insurance was paying for this, and the least they could expect was for the room to be cleaned.

It was colder in the room than he would have expected as well. Normally hospitals were kept far too warm. He checked the windows, but they were shut, with unattractive views over a side wall of another part of the building.

Behind him, under the bed, the pile of what he thought was dirt moved and breathed.

To live is not breathing it is action.
—Jean-Jacques Rousseau

Chapter Five

Clerkenwell, London, England

Oh Christ, it hurt!

Of course it bloody hurt! He'd fallen thirty feet onto the unyielding roof of the elevator car and landed on his back, snapping his spine. His left arm and collar bone were broken as well. With a monumental effort of will, he opened his eyes and stared up. A few faces were peering down at him. The woman with the perm, not grinning now but dabbing her tearful eyes with a tissue. The teenage seductress, her pink tongue flicking across her lips because, to her, death was a turn on.

His eyelids drooped, and he lost consciousness, drifting into a comfortable black void where pain was just a memory. He was vaguely aware of being lifted; hands under his shoulders, fingers curling around his ankles. When he drifted back to the world of pain, he found he was lying on the cold hard linoleum of the corridor. There were three of them still there, crouching over him, concerned looks on their faces. The biker, the pinstripe, and the perm, all staring down at him anxiously.

"Yes, I know you said he wasn't to be harmed, but the stupid fucker jumped down a bloody elevator shaft before we could get to him."

There was someone else there too; another man, standing out of Daniel's eye line, speaking into a cell phone, his voice echoing in the bare concrete corridor.

"I think his back's broken. He's barely alive. What shall we do with him?"

There was a pause. The three faces transferred their attention to the man with the phone. He was standing some way away, and Daniel couldn't move his head to see him.

"Okay. Will do."

The conversation ended.

"Well?" the perm spoke; a nicely modulated voice, a Home Counties accent, a woman more used to addressing the weekly meeting of her local Women's Institute than hunting fugitives in derelict office buildings.

"We leave him here," cell phone said. "From the look of him, he won't last much longer."

"Oh dear," the perm said. "Such a shame. All that effort to bring him up here, and we could have left him down the shaft. What a waste of time."

And then they were gone.

Daniel Milton started to shiver.

Chapter Six

Krakow, Poland

The depressing concrete apartment building stood in a row of similar buildings on the outskirts of Krakow, decaying quietly, its metal casement windows corroding, the moss-covered roof hemorrhaging tiles, leaving gaps for rain and pigeons to enter the roof space and destroy its integrity.

It was a building in waiting, holding its breath until some sharp-eyed developer recognized its potential and transformed it into a retro-chic block of living spaces for the wealthier city workers to occupy. It would happen eventually, as it had happened elsewhere in the city limits, but at the moment it offered cheap, if less than salubrious, accommodation, and it was the best Jacek Czerwinski could afford.

The apartment he was renting was on the third floor. The elevator had died six weeks ago and as yet no one had been around to fix it, despite several increasingly bad-tempered complaints to the landlord. The only way up to his apartment now was via a series of echoing stone staircases and cracked-tiled corridors. Walking along the corridors was like listening to a radio whose tuning knob was being twisted and turned. Sounds issued from each apartment he passed. A snatch of an argument here, a blaring stereo there. In one apartment, someone was practicing the clarinet; in another, a baby cried, fractious and forlorn. The sounds were as random as the smells that drifted through the building. Wafts of curry and other spicy foods mingled with the sweet smell of marijuana and the rancid tang of stale cooking oil.

But underpinning the various aromas was another, stronger odor, acrid and sour, as if someone had been pissing on the radiators.

As he walked the corridors and climbed the stairs, he kept stopping to glance behind him. The feeling he was being followed had started the moment he had climbed from his ancient and battered Renault and walked across the road to his building. By the time he was turning the key in the front door, he'd stopped glancing and was staring intently along the corridor, convinced that any moment whoever was following would reveal themselves. He stood, staring for a full sixty seconds before pushing the door open and letting himself into the apartment.

He closed and locked the door behind him, dropped the heavy leather bag he was carrying, and switched on the light. The bulb hanging down from a cracked plastic rose in the center of the room spread a dingy light over his meager belongings. He'd rented the rooms furnished, so at least he had a couch to sit on and a bed to sleep in, but there wasn't much else in the way of furniture, and what there was had been wrecked.

The apartment had been trashed.

"Shit!" he said, looking about him.

His ancient television was lying on its side, the screen smashed, the back ripped off and tossed into the far corner. The faux-leather couch had been slashed and ripped apart. Drawers had been pulled from the plywood sideboard, their contents scattered over the floor. He walked through to the bedroom. It was the same story in here. The duvet had been stripped from the bed and was piled in a heap in the corner of the room. The wardrobe doors were hanging open, and his clothes were shredded. This wasn't an ordinary break-in. There was fury and rage here. Whoever did this had systematically wrecked the place.

This was a warning.

He wandered back to the lounge and, like a magician pulling a bouquet of flowers from his sleeve, he fished in the pocket of his overcoat and produced a half bottle of vodka. Setting the couch back on its feet, he unscrewed the cap from the vodka bottle and took a long pull, then flopped down on the ruined vinyl, dragging his leather bag toward him. He unzipped it and reached inside, using both hands to lift out three box files, each overflowing with documents and photographs, the lids of the files held in place by thick rubber bands. Setting them on the couch next to him, he took another swig from the bottle, then laid his head back and closed his eyes.

A few seconds later someone knocked on the door. Perhaps whoever had been following him had finally plucked up the courage to make an approach. Or maybe the same person who had trashed the apartment had come back to trash *him*. He was taking no chances. He reached into the bag again and took out a small Beretta. Holding the gun against his leg, he went to the door.

"Who is it?" he called through the flimsy wood.

There was a pause and then a quiet male voice called softly. "Mr. Czerwinski, I need to talk to you."

"Why?"

"It's very important. Please open the door."

Jacek put his eye to the spy hole. Through the tiny fish-eye lens he could see his caller; a small man, about his own age, balding, with rimless glasses and a pasty complexion. If he was a threat, then Jacek was pretty sure he could neutralize him.

He stuck the Beretta into the waistband of his trousers and opened the door.

The earth upon which the sea, and the rivers and the waters,
upon which food and the tribes of men have arisen,
upon which this breathing, moving life exists,
shall afford us precedence in drinking!
—Atharva Veda

Chapter Seven

King's College Hospital, London, England

The lake was a still sheet of glass, broken only by the occasional stream of bubbles from the fish that swam beneath the surface. Robert Carter sat on an old wooden jetty, his legs dangling over the edge, his boots inches above the water. A fishing rod was propped on a wire stand to the left of him, to the right a bait box, its plastic tray filled with hooks, spools of line, spherical lead weights, and a polythene container with hundreds of ivory-colored maggots, writhing and wriggling on a bed of sawdust. Hanging from one of the jetty's stanchions was a keep net, mostly submerged, containing half a dozen perch swimming listlessly in circles—the day's catch.

He sat smoking a cigarette, watching the fluorescent orange float bobbing gently twenty yards away, waiting for a fish to strike. The day was the best summer had to offer; a clear blue sky, streaked with thin wisps of cirrus; a gentle breeze tempering the heat of the sun before it could become oppressive. High above him in the trees, jays, thrushes, and blackbirds serenaded him with their summer songs, and once in a while a kingfisher swooped low over the water, looking for its next meal.

The Lake District of England was a beautiful natural wonderland of lake and forest. The different lakes, Ulleswater, Derwent, all had their own unique attraction, and the entire area was a magnet for tourists all through the year.

Jane would be coming to see him. He had to get some coffee on, prepare some lunch.

He put down the fishing rod and tried to stand. He couldn't. His arms were trapped. He tried to open his eyes, but they were refusing. There was a throbbing in his head as if all the songbirds were singing at once, loudly, out of tune, discordant and insistent—shouting at him.

In 1909, King's moved to its present site at Denmark Hill, south of the River Thames. During World War I, the hospital was used for military purposes. A dental school was established at the same site in 1923. During this time, most patients were still poor, and in 1937 the private Guthrie Wing was established with a donation from the Stock Exchange Dramatic and Operatic Society for wealthier patients to have less crowded wards. During the Second World War, the hospital was used for treating casualties of air raids and was fortunate never to be bombed during the blitz. With the creation of the National Health Service in 1948, the hospital was given Teaching Hospital status.

At the entrance, two people walked through the glass doors and glanced up at the signs, seeking out the ward they wanted. It was clear they couldn't see it straightaway, so just as Crozier had done, they went across to reception and asked after Robert Carter.

They were directed to neurology. The elevators, the short journey up. Between them they were bringing gifts. Magazines, some chocolate, an iPod, and some fruit. They didn't know Crozier had already visited; he had kept that as one of his little secrets.

* * *

Carter's eyes opened. He looked for the trees, the lake, tried to feel for his cigarettes but found his arms still bound.

His brain fumbled to explain where he was. This wasn't his home in the Lake District. This wasn't outdoors at all.

He was in a brightly lit room with machines bleeping. His arms were connected by wires to bags of fluid above his head.

He gradually realized he was in a hospital. The dull aching pain told him he had been injured in some way.

His head, his neck, most of his shoulders, were encased in a plastic-coated brace so he couldn't move his upper body at all.

Only his eyes. He could move his eyes.

He wished he couldn't.

The room may have been brightly lit, but pools of black punctuated the corners. The pools were rippling as if they were a parody of the surface of the lake he had been dreaming about.

The elevator eased to a halt, and the two people got out, the man holding back so the woman could exit first. She smiled a thanks to him. Their body language showed they weren't a couple, weren't involved romantically, but they knew each other, were most likely friends.

They looked both ways along a white corridor, unsure which direction to take. The man pointed left, and they went that way, signs hanging from the ceiling eventually confirming they were on the correct course. Neurology.

The woman shifted the bag she carried from one hand to the other. It wasn't heavy, the movement was more a nervous reaction to hospitals. Like many people, she was uncomfortable around so much suffering. The healing process was such a mystery it left her uncertain.

The man looked at ease, but the way he held his posture, the way his mouth was set in a determined line, revealed the tension he was feeling.

They reached the nurses' station and waited while a blue uniformed nurse finished a telephone conversation that seemed to be about reassuring a relative with vague platitudes.

They asked about Robert Carter, and the nurse pressed a key on the computer keyboard.

At that moment alarm bells and monitor buzzers went off and were worryingly loud.

The blackness was moving.

Carter flicked his eyes from side to side trying to see both sides of the room as well as beyond the foot of the bed.

The darkness was sliding across the floor. Both corners of the room at each side of the bed were slithering forward, the inky black absorbing the lights from the ceiling. As each mass of dark reached below the bed, it merged with another pool that was rippling there.

The darkness disappeared beneath the bed and out of sight.

There was a stench in the room. As if something that had been dead a long time had resurfaced. Rotting fish, diseased flesh.

Carter held his breath. By straining his neck up a couple of inches he could see over the end of the bed. He could see the layer of darkness there, thin and misty, like piles of dust swept against the wall. As he watched, the layer began to rise like a pillar at first. But then as it was about six feet in the air, it opened out, like a flower in summer. It opened until it had a density about it. It opened until it had a recognizable shape. The shape of a man but not as distinct.

From the ceiling black shapes were pulling free from the white tiles. They looked like more than scraps of black rag, though less substantial than cloth, and they dropped onto the bed, scuttling like beetles.

The shadow was moving slowly toward him. His fingers fumbled frantically for the alarm monitor to summon the nurse, but it had slipped away from him.

From under the bed another shadow emerged. Talons gripped the edge of the bed, ripping into the sheets as the shadow pulled itself out into the light.

Carter was helpless. His upper body immobile, his lower body encased in the bedsheets.

The shadow was leaning over the bottom of the bed, palms outstretched as if directing the beetle shapes. The small black shapes crawled over the sheets, burrowing beneath them. The shape from under the bed pulled itself upright, the gray skin pulsing in the light.

His only hope was his power, his gift.

Carter summoned the strength he had, his mind clouded by the painkillers and medicines. He drew his concentration into a ball of focus. He tried to call for help.

"What is that?" the man asked.

The nurse behind the desk ran toward Carter's room. Other nurses and a couple of doctors suddenly materialized and ran that way as well.

The man and woman did the same.

The nurse who opened the door to the room stayed in the doorway. The others crowded behind her.

Their duty was to enter the room and help the patient. What they were seeing was stopping them.

Leaning over the end of the bed, being absorbed into the bedclothes, a black man-shape was half buried into Carter's legs.

Mounds of small creatures had burrowed beneath the sheets and were tearing at the flesh of his chest.

The gray shape from under the bed looked as if it was formed out of tentacles and scraps of torn material. The fingers were long and pointed. They gripped Carter's head, shaking it from side to side, pulling loose the plastic neck brace.

Pushing through the shocked crowd of medical personnel, the man and woman took a few seconds to appraise the situation. Then their hands locked together, and they closed their eyes.

They probed with their minds and through pain and fear they found the essence of Carter. He had sent out a cry for help that had somehow set off dozens of alarms. As they swept the room with their power they found resistance. They pushed harder.

The lights went out.

In the darkness it was impossible to see the black shadows. Gripping their hands together even tighter, the man and woman concentrated on the gray shape at Carter's head. It represented the most immediate danger, and instinctively they knew it was the leader. They shoved it, aiming in the general direction they guessed it would be. As its fingers loosened on Carter, he was able to add his power to theirs. Despite the pain from his injuries and the damage being inflicted on his body, he summoned a supreme effort of will and mentally pushed at the shape.

With all three wills being directed in unison, it worked. The lights flickered back on. The gray shape dissolved, like a morning mist.

With the room bathed again in light, the man and woman were emboldened. They moved to the end of the bed, directly behind the large shadow. Gradually, with joint effort, the shape became less dense. It wavered like heat haze on a road, almost liquefying as it washed harmlessly onto the bedclothes.

A nurse ran to Carter's side and checked his drips. A doctor began adjusting the monitor. Two other nurses stripped the sheets from the bed. They all expected to see small black shapes scurry out from the sheets, but there was nothing there.

The man and woman looked at each other and dropped their hands.

Carter was being propped up on the pillows by a nurse.

The pain was etched onto his face, but he managed a weak smile.

It was good to see John McKinley again, even better to see Jane Talbot.

Chapter Eight

Clerkenwell, London, England

He jolted awake.

Morning had broken while he was sleeping, and now the corridor was bathed in pale amber light that barely chased away the shivering shadows.

Christ, he was cold!

His whole body felt as if it were encased in a block of ice. He couldn't feel his legs at all, and his hands were aching from the chill.

This was where he was going to die; he'd resigned himself to that. All he hoped for now was that death came quickly. It was stupid to have thought he could elude them forever. In the back of his mind he always knew that they would catch up with him one day. *Well*, he thought, *at least the chase is over now.*

A noise. A footfall. Perhaps they had come back to finish the job. He held his breath and listened intently.

Maybe someone had come to rescue him. At that thought a small flame of hope flickered in his mind. The game may not be over, not just yet.

Footsteps were padding along the corridor, but he couldn't raise his head to see who was there. And then someone was crouching down by his side.

"Well, Daniel, you seem to have gotten yourself in a bit of a mess, don't you?"

He stared at the familiar face smiling down at him. "Jason?" He managed to croak out the name.

He was confused. He'd spoken to Jason Pike only a few hours earlier to tell him about the meeting with Simon Crozier of Department 18. Pike had been in Poland.

"Czerwinski," he said. If only his lips and throat weren't so dry. Speaking was torture, like swallowing barbed wire.

"Czerwinski, yes," Pike said.

"Water. Thirsty, so thirsty."

A large hand cupped his head, raising it slightly, and a bottle was put to his lips. As the water trickled over his lips he drank greedily, making himself cough, sending paroxysms of pain coursing through his body, pain so fierce he cried out.

"Easy," Pike said gently. "Tell me about Czerwinski."

"Our last hope of finding Julia," Milton said, his thoughts woolly. "You said he could be the last hope of tracking her down."

"Ah, yes. Of course I did."

Daniel Milton tried to move his body, tried to sit up, but it was no use. His arms and legs were not taking orders from his brain. The effort was making sweat bead on his brow and bringing tears to his eyes. "You have to help me, Jason," he said.

"Of course, Daniel. An ambulance is on its way. You'll soon be in safe hands."

Daniel managed a weak smile. "Thank you."

"Tell me more about Czerwinski."

Daniel licked his lips. The water bottle was there again, but this time he sipped slowly. "You should be in Poland," he said. "What are you doing here?"

"You called me. I came."

"I don't understand." Daniel could feel his tenuous line to consciousness starting to fray. Sleep was waiting in the shadows, cajoling him; its voice alluring, seductive. The strain of keeping his eyes open was almost too much.

"Poland," Pike said. "Tell me about Poland."

"You know. It was your idea."

And then something shifted in Daniel Milton's mind.

Tell me about Poland.

This time the words were spoken in his head. But it wasn't Jason Pike's mellifluous voice intoning the words. It was an urgent, insistent voice, vaguely familiar.

He searched his memory, trying to match the voice. He opened his eyes and looked up at Pike.

The face in front of him looked serene; kindly eyes looking deeply into his, lips curled into a reassuring smile.

And then the image juddered, like film slipping on a spool. For a split second the face changed, but that was all Daniel needed. Summoning all that remained of his strength, he focused his mind, trying to force out the insistent voice.

Jesus Christ! It's strong.

He was holding his breath, straining, his muscles bunched. Blood vessels popped in his eyes, and his ears and nose started to bleed. Finally the voice was gone and through the red mist clouding his vision he saw the illusion.

Jason Pike had disappeared like the smoke ghost he was. Crouching next to Daniel instead, with a look of fury on his face, was a man he hadn't seen for a long time.

"Holly!" he hissed.

The anger dropped from John Holly's face to be replaced by a condescending smile. "I underestimated you, Milton.

You're stronger than you look. But never mind. You've given me enough."

Daniel Milton glared up at him, but the effort of forcing Holly's illusion from his mind had weakened him still further.

"I could snuff you out," Holly said. "I could kill you in the blink of an eye if I wanted to."

"Just do it then, you bastard," Daniel gasped.

Holly stood and stared down at him disdainfully. "I wouldn't waste my time with something so pathetic." Then he spun on his heel and stalked back down the corridor to the stairs.

Daniel listened to Holly's footsteps receding. He took a deep breath and squeezed his eyes shut. A single tear forced its way out from between his closed lids and slid down his cheek.

When the breath wanders the mind also is unsteady.
But when the breath is calmed the mind too will be
still, and the yogi achieves long life. Therefore,
one should learn to control the breath.
—Svatmarama, Hatha Yoga Pradipika

Chapter Nine

Krakow, Poland

"Thank you," the man said and bustled inside. He was breathing hard, as if he'd been running a race, but it was probably just exhaustion from climbing the stairs. He didn't look very fit.

"Excuse the mess," Jacek said with a sweep of his arm. "I haven't got round to tidying up today."

The small man looked at him, confusion in his eyes. Jacek walked past him and swept up the bottle of vodka from the floor where he'd left it. "Vodka?"

The man hesitated. "Yes . . . please . . . a small one."

Jacek went through to the kitchen, found two glasses that hadn't been smashed and took them back to the lounge.

"What's your name?" Jacek said, handing the man a shot of vodka. "And what do you want with me?"

"Can I sit? Those stairs . . ." the small man said, cupping the glass in both hands and staring down into the crystal liquid as if it were poison.

"Sure," Jacek said.

"My name's Adamczyk, Cyril Adamczyk. I was given your name by an acquaintance. He seemed to think you might be able to help me."

Jacek pulled up a hard chair and straddled it. "This acquaintance, does he have a name?"

"Pike. He's American, I think. Jason Pike."

Jacek shrugged. "Means nothing to me."

Adamczyk looked troubled. "So you won't help?"

Jacek frowned and knocked back his vodka. Wiping his lips on his sleeve, he said, "I didn't say that. Just that I haven't heard of this Pike character."

Adamczyk clutched at the straw that was apparently being offered. "So you'll help?"

Jacek shook his head. "I didn't say that either. What's the problem you need help with?"

"My daughter . . . she's missing. I have to find her." Finally Adamczyk put the glass to his lips, tilted his head back, and sipped at the vodka. His whole body shuddered as the spirit did its work.

Jacek watched him closely. The eyes behind the glasses were glazed with tears and his face was pallid, washed out, a film of sweat covering his brow. He appeared to be telling the truth, but Jacek had learned from bitter experience that things were not always as they appeared. He leaned forward in his seat. "Tell me about her," he said.

Adamczyk took another tentative sip of his drink. "Her name is Karolina. She's nineteen and she went missing from university about three weeks ago. Disappeared into thin air."

"Boyfriends?"

"That's what the police asked, and I'll tell you what I told them. There were a few, nothing serious. No one special."

"As far as you know."

"We know. Olga and I—Olga's my wife—Olga and I have a wonderful relationship with our daughter, Mr. Czerwinski. She tells us everything."

A slight smile played on Jacek's lips. "Mr. Adamczyk, no child tells her parents *everything*."

For the first time Cyril Adamczyk showed something other than forlorn desperation. He bridled. "Karolina isn't like other children. She's honest, open. In all her nineteen years we've never had a moment's concern about her. She comes to us with her problems, no matter how intimate. We sit, we discuss, and then we decide on a course of action that will solve any difficulty she's having. It's always been that way. And now this. I just don't understand it, and I'm afraid I'm starting to think the worst. I fear something dreadful has happened to her. You must help me."

"How far have the police taken this?"

"They're useless. They won't take the disappearance seriously. They're convinced Karolina has met someone and gone off with him."

"Anything to support that?"

Adamczyk stared down into his glass and said nothing.

Jacek drummed his fingers impatiently on the chair back. "Well?"

Adamczyk looked up at him. "Could I have a cup of tea? I really can't stomach vodka."

Jacek stood. "Sure. Lemon?"

Adamczyk nodded. "Two sugars."

Jacek reached into his pocket and fished out a small digital recorder and set it down on the chair. "I want you to tell me everything. Leave nothing out. This will record your voice. I'll put the kettle on."

In the kitchen he filled the kettle, then took a lemon from the fridge. With a very sharp, long-bladed knife he began to slice the lemon, concentrating on making each slice no more than four millimeters thick. While he sliced, the more analytical side of his mind thought about Adamczyk's missing daughter, lining her up side by side with the twenty or more young people who had gone missing in the last few months.

When he returned from the kitchen, he set the tea down and switched on the recorder. "Now, in your own time, I want you to search your memory for anything, however trivial you might think it is, that could possibly relate to Karolina's disappearance. Including the name of the man she was seeing shortly before she vanished."

"But . . ."

Jacek pushed him. "She *was* seeing someone, wasn't she? That's why the police aren't interested."

"Yes, but . . ."

"You need to tell me *everything.* I won't think any less of your daughter, no matter what you tell me, but you must be honest. If you want me to help you, there can be no secrets between us."

Cyril Adamczyk sighed deeply as if dredging the truth up from a dark place hidden deep within himself. "His name is Kaminski. Wladyslaw Kaminski. That's all she told us," Cyril Adamczyk said and took a mouthful of the scalding hot tea, feeling the heat of it around his teeth before swallowing, as if to wash the name away. "She met him at a student party."

"No other details?"

Adamczyk shook his head. "She told us very little about him, though I gathered he wasn't a student. She did tell us he was older, early thirties." He paused, sipping at his tea, as if he was steeling himself to speak again. "And . . . and that she loved him."

Jacek looked at him steadily. "Anything else?"

"That's everything I can remember."

"How long had it been going on?"

Adamczyk shook his head. "I don't know. Weeks . . . a month maybe."

"And yet she claimed to be in love with him. Is he married?"

"No! Karolina wouldn't do such a thing."

Jacek shrugged. There was growing evidence that the Adamczyks didn't know their daughter anywhere near as well as they thought they did. "Did you or your wife object to Karolina's relationship with this Kaminski?"

"We weren't happy about it, if that's what you mean. Her studies were starting to suffer. Her marks were falling, and her attitude toward her exams was lax, to say the least."

"And did you let her know you disapproved?"

"I didn't. I held my tongue, hoping this was just a phase she was going through. I trusted that she'd come to her senses eventually, hopefully before it was too late to salvage her education."

"But your wife?"

"I'm afraid Olga is not a tolerant woman."

"So your wife confronted Karolina about it. With what result?"

Adamczyk flushed, bringing two spots of color to his pasty cheeks. "There was a lot of shouting. A lot of tears."

"And how long was this before Karolina disappeared?"

"Two days."

Jacek reached down and switched off the recorder and slipped it back into his pocket. "It seems pretty obvious what's happened here. Karolina is smitten with this man, and your disapproval has forced her into an extreme reaction. It seems likely that she has simply run off with him."

Tears sprang to Cyril Adamczyk's eyes. He slumped in the chair, defeated. "That's what the police said."

"Then I'm afraid I must agree with them."

"So you won't help me?"

Jacek shook his head. This was so difficult, looking into Cyril Adamczyk's watery eyes and knowing that he, Jacek Czerwinski, was the poor man's last hope. "I didn't say that," he said gently. "I can try to track her down for you. But I can't guarantee I can reunite your family." He felt guilty saying it. He knew he was offering the man false hope, but he couldn't bear to crush him, not right at this moment.

Adamczyk swallowed the last of his rapidly cooling tea. "Anything you can do . . ." he said, before lapsing into a depressed silence.

"Do you have a photograph of Karolina?"

Adamczyk nodded. From the inside pocket of his jacket, he produced a six-by-four-inch glossy color photo and handed it to Jacek.

Jacek stared at it for a long moment. The girl who'd been captured by the camera's lens was pretty: honey-colored almond-shaped eyes; shoulder-length black hair cut into an indifferent, unflattering style; and a generous mouth set in a shy smile.

It was a heart-wrenching moment for him. One day he'd have to tell Cyril Adamczyk that it was very unlikely he would ever see his daughter again; never see her honey eyes or her full-lipped smile.

The box files sitting on the couch next to Adamczyk were filled to overflowing with similar photographs and similar stories. So far only a small percentage of those missing had been reunited with their parents, but there was every reason to believe that Karolina Adamczyk would never be found. In more than half of the cases he had so far documented, the name Wladyslaw Kaminski had been mentioned in circumstances almost identical to the Adamczyk's. It was becoming a depressingly familiar scenario.

He swallowed the last of his vodka and poured himself another. His hand shook slightly as it tilted the bottle. Perhaps he should just get it over with now; kill the hope before it had time to flourish. He looked at Adamczyk bleakly. "Mr. Adamczyk . . . Cyril . . ."

Adamczyk seemed to sense what might be coming and reared up in his seat. "No! No! I refuse to give up. If it's a question of money . . . Well, I have money. Enough to pay for your time and your expenses."

"It's not a question of money. It's a question of probability. I doubt Karolina's even in Poland now. She'll be in the United States, Britain, or even Scandinavia, that's if she's still alive."

"NO!" The word seemed to be dredged up from Adamczyk's very soul. It was a wail, a primal scream. "You must help me! You must . . ." The words trailed off into a whimper, and suddenly he was sobbing, hands clasped over his face, shoulders heaving.

Jacek let him cry himself out. "I'll do what I can," he said wearily, slumping in his seat. "But I make no promises."

A glimmer of hope appeared in Adamczyk's red-rimmed eyes. "Pike told me you were a good man. I knew you wouldn't let me down." He dabbed at his eyes with a white linen handkerchief.

"Two more questions," Jacek said.

"Anything."

"Why did you follow me into the building instead of approaching me when I got out of my car?"

"I'm sorry. I'm not sure I understand. I didn't follow you. I got off the bus and came straight here. I didn't see you until you opened the door to me." The look of incomprehension in Adamczyk's eyes was genuine enough.

Jacek shook his head. "It doesn't matter."

"You said *two* questions."

"Who is Jason Pike?"

"He came to see Olga and me a week ago. He'd heard about Karolina and said he wanted to help. He listened while we told him what we knew, and then he gave me a card with your name and address printed on it. He said to come and see you, that you had experience in these matters."

"Describe him," Jacek said.

"Very tall, black. As I said, possibly American . . . the accent certainly was. A big, powerful-looking man. Oh, and his face . . . he had tribal markings, vivid scars on his cheeks."

"Scars? Scarification?"

"Yes, in certain parts of Africa they still use tribal markings as a distinction. Many do it as a rite of passage into adulthood, and some believe doing it on newborn children helps prevents illness. Olga seemed quite scared of him at first, but gradually, as he spoke to us, she realized that he had great compassion. Olga kissed him when he went, and I assure you, Mr. Czerwinski, my wife is not prone to displays of affection with total strangers."

"Okay," Jacek said. "That will be all for now." He walked to the door and opened it. "I've got to get on," he said. "Write your telephone number on the back of the photograph and leave it with me. I'll be in touch when I have any news."

"And your fee?" Cyril Adamczyk said as he scribbled his number down.

"Only payable if I get a positive result."

Adamczyk nodded, handed Jacek the photograph and

shook his hand. "I'll wait to hear from you," he said, the hope still chiming in his voice like a bell.

The door closed, and Jacek listened to the receding footfalls along the hall. Then he opened one of the box files, dropped the photograph on top of the bulging folders, and closed the lid.

The bottle of vodka was nearly empty. He put it to his lips and drained it, questions tumbling over and over in his mind. Who had broken into his apartment and trashed it? Who the hell was Jason Pike and why had he told Adamczyk to bring his problems here? And, if it wasn't Adamczyk following him earlier, who was it?

He slid open the door to the small balcony and breathed in the morning air. There was a hint of jasmine on the warm breeze that drifted across from the gardens overlooked by the apartment building. It reminded him of his childhood, time spent at his grandmother's in a small village just outside Gdansk. Happier times.

He pushed the memories to the back of his mind. He had no time for nostalgia. Life for him was the here and now, and a progression toward a brighter future. If he allowed himself to dwell on the past, he'd go mad.

Chapter Ten

30 St. Mary Axe, London, England

The couple pushed through the heavy glass doors of the Gherkin and walked briskly across the marble floor of the lobby to the reception desk. "My name is John Holly," the man said. "This is Alice Spur. We're here to see Mr. Goldberg."

The receptionist looked up at them and smiled, picked up a clipboard from the desk and checked their name against those listed there. He looked up at them again, nodded, and slid the clipboard across the desk. "Sign and print your names please, Mr. Holly," he said, then reached into the desk drawer and took out two laminated visitor passes, pushing those across the desk as well. "Kindly wear those at all times while you're in the building, sir," he said. "Room 319. Third floor. The elevators are over there."

Holly took the passes and handed one to Alice, who clipped it to the lapel of her jacket. He thanked the receptionist and, taking Alice's arm, steered her toward the elevator.

The building was a marvel of marble, glass, and tubular steel; the elevators, simple glass bubbles that rose from the ground floor to the atrium above. Alice was unimpressed. To her the place had all the appeal of a laboratory, and she had seen enough of those to last a lifetime.

The elevator rose to the third floor. The doors slid open silently, and they stepped out into a plush, brightly lit corridor. Light was obviously a design conceit; it was like being trapped inside a two hundred-watt bulb.

30 St. Mary Axe, also known as the Gherkin and the Swiss Re Building, is a skyscraper in the financial district of central London with an extremely distinctive design. The building is on the site of the former Baltic Exchange building. On April 10, 1992, the Provisional IRA detonated a bomb close to the Exchange, severely damaging the historic Exchange building and neighboring structures. The new building was built in December 2003 and opened on April 28, 2004. Five hundred ninety-one feet tall, with forty floors. Despite its overall curved glass shape, there is only one piece of curved glass on the building—the lens-shaped cap at the very top.

Room 319 was two-thirds along, a simple brown wood

door with the numbers picked out in chrome. At the side of the door was an intercom and above the doorframe a discreet camera. Holly pressed the button on the intercom and stared up into the lens.

A crackly voice said, "Yes?"

"It's John Holly."

Silence was followed by an electronic buzz and the door opened an inch. Holly pushed it wider and they found themselves in a small, plain anteroom with another door leading off from it. The anteroom was decorated with pictures of diamonds and precious stones. Taking up half a wall was a poster advertising the Tucson Gem Fair 1998, depicting a huge topaz crystal surrounded by half a dozen exquisitely cut stones. Diamond and precious stone dealing was how Saul Goldberg made his legitimate money. If his clients only knew the truth. Holly smiled and closed the main door and, as it clicked shut, the secondary door opened.

The office they entered was small and cramped. A floor-to-ceiling safe, three filing cabinets, and a large oak desk took up most of the floor space. On the desk was a phone, a blotter, and a set of futuristic-looking weighing scales. Behind the desk sat a very old man, almost swallowed by a brown leather chair. As Holly opened the door, the man looked up and stared at them through the thick half-rimmed glasses perched on the end of his hooked nose. As they took a step into the room, he reached into the desk drawer and pulled out a snub-nosed Smith & Wesson revolver. He pointed it at them.

"Is that really necessary, Saul?" Holly said.

The old man cleared his throat. It sounded like a crocodile breathing. "I'm eighty-three years old," he said in the same crackly voice they'd heard through the intercom. "I've lived this long by taking precautions. This"—he gestured to the gun with his free hand—"is a precaution."

They sat down on the two tubular steel-and-leather chairs

on their side of the desk. The gun followed their movements, shaking a little but never letting them out of its sight.

"I didn't come here to harm you, Saul," Holly said.

"So *you* say," Goldberg said, something like amusement in his eyes.

"Lower the gun. Firearms make me nervous."

"Ha!" It was a laugh of sorts. "You and your kind make me nervous. Say what you've come here to say, then get out."

Alice took a breath; she'd never been held at gunpoint before and she found the experience terrifying, especially the way Goldberg's palsied hand shook. She wondered how sensitive the trigger was. Holly had warned her that Saul Goldberg could be a cantankerous old bastard. Now she believed him. She glanced round at John, whose face betrayed nothing. If anything, there was a slight smile on his lips.

"Okay," Holly said. "I'm concerned about the supply line. We were due a shipment last month, which never materialized, and the shipment before that was fifty percent down."

Saul Goldberg shrugged. "So?"

"I thought we had an agreement. We have a lot of angry customers demanding to know what's going on. Our restaurants are half empty and we're running out of product. I calculate another month and our stocks will be so depleted our customers will be looking elsewhere for satisfaction, and we both know what that means."

"Tell me anyway," Goldberg said.

Alice watched Holly's back stiffen slightly as the muscles bunched. The old man was playing a dangerous game of cat and mouse, trying to humiliate Holly in front of her. She hoped he would live to regret it.

"The whole idea of bringing untraceables into the country was to avoid the situation we are now facing," Holly continued smoothly, not a sign of the irritation he must have been feeling evident in his voice. "If our patrons are forced to look elsewhere for sustenance, it will create havoc."

"You're worried that they will have to go out onto the streets and start hunting again."

"I'm concerned that might be the outcome. And you know as well as I do that it will inevitably lead to discovery."

Saul Goldberg leaned back in his seat, the revolver poised. "I made that agreement with your father a long, long time ago. When Abe died, the deal died with him. But let me reassure you, your fears of discovery are groundless."

"Then why has the supply stopped?"

Goldberg grinned. He was enjoying this. "It hasn't. In fact I'd go so far as to say it's increased. We have now established a base in South Africa, and as such have access to the entire African continent. A limitless supply."

Holly frowned. "I don't understand, Saul. If you're still bringing in untraceables, what's happening to them? Where are they goi—" And suddenly understanding dawned on him. "You're supplying someone else?" he said, disbelief in his voice.

Saul Goldberg inclined his head in acknowledgment.

"Who?"

"I'm afraid I'm not at liberty to say. What I will say, though, is this: I always thought that your father was a man of honor. Unfortunately, I was proved to be mistaken in that belief. The research he embarked upon in his later years—the research I believe you are continuing—will change things. I have it on very good authority that this research, if successful, is going to upset the status quo. It will put me out of business. And this is not just my concern. There are others who, unlike you, are not looking for change, others who like things just the way they are. I'm just one of them."

Holly looked at him steadily. "Then there's no way I'm going to get you to change your mind, is there?"

"No. No there isn't."

"Then there's only one thing left to do," he said, getting to his feet.

The next movement he made was faster than Saul Goldberg's arthritic trigger finger. The gun was swept from the old man's grasp and went clattering across the desk, landing with a metallic thud on the vinyl-tiled floor. Holly bent and picked it up and slipped it into the pocket of his jacket. "I don't like being threatened, Saul, especially by a treacherous little maggot like you. The question is, what am I going to do? I should really make an example of you, to dissuade others from following your lead."

Goldberg sat like a startled rabbit, staring up myopically at Holly. The color had drained from his face, and he was shaking. His eyes met Alice's. There was a plea for help there.

"John. Leave it," she said.

Holly glanced at her, something close to contempt in his eyes.

Goldberg's hand was inching along under the desk, reaching for the button that, when pushed, would bring the floor's security detail running. They had pass keys for the doors. They could liberate him within seconds. His finger found the button and pressed it.

"So what would *you* like me to do with him?" Holly said to Alice.

"Let's just go," she said.

Holly shook his head slightly, and then took a step toward the door. "Very well," he said. "Come on." He turned to Goldberg and leaned in close. In something approaching a whisper he said, "You'll be hearing from me." Then as almost an afterthought, "Sooner than you think."

"What does that mean?" Goldberg said.

Holly gave him a harsh smile. "Use your imagination," he said and slipped from the office, Alice half a step behind him. They were three paces along the corridor when two uniformed men ran past them and started unlocking the door to room 319. The elevator doors opened as soon as Holly touched the button.

Alice stepped inside, but Holly hung back. He reached into his pocket and produced his car keys, handing them to her. "Go back to the car and wait for me," he said,

Panic flared in her eyes. "What are you going to do?" she said.

"Go back to the car," Holly said firmly. "I'll join you shortly."

The doors were closing. "John . . ." she said, and then the doors closed. She leaned against the wall of the elevator and hit the button for the ground floor. There was nothing she could do. John was too stubborn, too strong.

Within two minutes she was out of the Gherkin building and walking along Cheapside toward Gresham Street, where John Holly had parked the car.

The nose is for breathing, the mouth is for eating.
—Proverb

Chapter Eleven

Department 18 Headquarters, Whitehall, London, England

Simon Crozier sat at his desk drinking his fifth cup of coffee of the day. The caffeine was making him twitchy, but he needed the hit; he'd been awake for much of the previous night. There was a knock on his door, and Martin Impey came into his office and dropped a file onto the table.

For a Georgian building in the center of London's Whitehall area, the office was loudly modern. There was the ambiance of a newly opened and longing to be fashionable restaurant about it. Though discreetly set on the desk was all the apparatus of a high-powered executive. Which in many ways was exactly what Crozier was. Few chief executives could boast an intellect to equal Crozier's sharp and well-ordered mind.

"That's everything I've been able to find on the Hollys so far," Martin said. "Quite a family."

Crozier pulled the file toward him, flipped it open, and started leafing through it. "How comprehensive is this?" he said, not looking up.

Martin pulled up a chair and sat down opposite his boss. "As far as I can see, it contains everything written about them that's available to the public. Of course, I've edited it down to get rid of duplications, but it's as complete as we can get, given the time you've allowed us to compile it." There was an edge to his voice. Simon Crozier expected miracles sometimes, and this was no exception. A summons to Crozier's office as soon he arrived this morning and a barked request.

Martin was thirty-nine and had been with the department for the best part of ten years. He was a small, energetic man who reminded people of a Jack Russell terrier. Fiercely intelligent and possessed of a cutting wit that more than compensated for his lack of physical stature, he was one of the most popular members of the department. His brown eyes always seemed to be smiling, as if he had looked at the world and decided it was one huge joke, but today he seemed unusually tired. His wife had recently given birth to their first child and midnight feeds and disrupted sleep patterns were taking their toll.

"Get me everything you can find on John Holly. Family details, businesses he's involved in, people he socializes with. The lot. As soon as you can."

That was hours ago, and Martin got straight to it. The two girls on his team, Maggie and Christine—his right and left hands—trawled the internet, while he scorched the phone lines, calling his contacts in Fleet Street, the Stock Exchange, MI5 and 6, Interpol, and other agencies across the globe.

Cold, hard, and brittle; those were the words often used to describe the chrome-and-white decor and the antiseptic, almost futuristic look of the desk, the chairs and other office furniture. It was also the epithet sometimes used to describe Crozier. Guests to the office sat on a white leather and chrome chair, designed for elegance rather than comfort, facing Crozier across the glass-topped desk. The desk was another design conceit—smoked glass supported by a chrome-plated tubular steel frame, and Crozier kept the desk clutter to a minimum. There were two white telephones, a small laptop computer and a black leather file, positioned at right angles to the edge of the desk, and nothing more. The glass was polished to within an inch of its life and nothing, not even a thumb print or a flake of dandruff, marred its pristine surface.

As head of research for Department 18, Martin Impey's contacts fed him information based on little more than the strength of his personality. Everyone knew he was about the best in the field at what he did. But more than this was his willingness to reciprocate, using the massive Department 18 database.

"Okay," Crozier said, glancing up. "Don't get comfortable. I've got another job for you."

Martin raised his eyebrows.

"I want you to look into something that happened a while ago. A girl called Alice Spur was involved in an apparent auto accident in Cambridge. Miss Spur was in intensive care, but one night she just upped and vanished. Hasn't been heard from since. Go through the police records, local papers, that sort of thing and see what you can find. And while you're at it, she had a boyfriend, Daniel Milton. Dig up anything you can find out about him."

"And do you want this yesterday as well?" Martin said, a hint of sarcasm in his voice.

"No, I'll have it the day before."

Martin smiled tightly. Crozier didn't smile at all.

Crozier waited until Martin had left the office, then picked up the phone. He punched in a number and waited. After three rings, the phone at the other end was picked up.

"Yes?"

"Dylan, its Simon."

Silence.

"Dylan? Are you there?"

"I'm here. I'm just surprised to hear you on the other end of my phone." Michael Dylan spoke with a softly lilting Irish brogue. It was a voice impossible to read. "I'm still on leave. What do you want?" Dylan was one of the department's senior operatives. A psychic with phenomenal powers who didn't take himself too seriously, unlike some of the others on the roster. Crozier immediately thought of Carter.

"How's Ireland? I must admit, I've always had a soft spot for Dublin. One of my favorite cities . . ."

"Simon, now, you didn't ring me to discuss geography. What do you want?"

"I have a job for you," Crozier said without further preamble. His fingers pulled a paperclip from the pages of a file on his desk. Cradling the phone against his shoulder, he started to straighten it out.

"As I said, I'm still on leave."

"I know you better than that, Dylan. The job's in your blood. You live and breathe it. Once you hear what I have to tell you, you won't be able to resist. Leave or no leave."

Crozier used the straightened out paperclip to dislodge a small piece of salmon that had wedged itself between his teeth at lunchtime. He patted his lips with a handkerchief and dropped the paperclip into the bin. "Something's fallen into my lap, Dylan, and I need my best people to investigate it. Unfortunately I'm running short of bodies here. Jane Talbot's on semipermanent *gardening* leave and Carter's hospitalized, though it's nothing too serious, unfortunately. That Kulsay business screwed up both of them."

"And McKinley's told you to stuff it."

Crozier winced, remembering the heated conversation he'd had with McKinley early this morning. "More or less. At least let me run it by you. Once you hear what I have to say, I think you might reconsider."

"Okay, talk. It's your phone bill."

"No, not on the phone. I'd like to meet in person."

"I'm in Ireland on vacation, and I'm not coming back unless there's a bloody good reason."

"I can come to you," Crozier said, flipping open his desk diary and scanning the pages.

"When?"

"I can fly out this evening. We could meet tomorrow morning."

"It's that vital?"

"I think so, yes, otherwise I wouldn't have called you."

There was a pause, and then Dylan said, "Okay. How well do you know this part of the world?"

"A passing knowledge of Dublin, but I wouldn't say I know it intimately."

"I'm not in the city. There's a village about ten miles to the north. Dunkerry. In the center of the village, there's a pub, The Republican Arms. I'll be there at ten."

Despite the indignity of being in a pub that early in the morning, Crozier smiled. "Splendid. I'll see you there." He hung up the phone, then flicked a button on his intercom. "Trudy, book me the first available return flight to Shannon, and order me a hire car."

"Anything else, sir?"

"Not at the moment."

He flicked off the intercom and picked up the phone again.

"Harry, it's Simon. I'm coming to Dublin this evening and I was wondering if I could prevail upon your hospitality and beg a bed for the night."

The voice on the other end of the line was gruff and thick with whiskey. "You old sod," Harry Bailey said. "Don't phone me for years, then, out of the blue, call me up and invite yourself to stay. Typical."

"You know how it is, Harry, scarcely a moment to catch my breath. Besides, isn't that the mark of true friendship that you can lose touch for ages, then make contact and pick up from where you left off?"

There was a fit of coughing. Then Harry Bailey said, "I suppose."

"You sound well," Crozier said. "Still smoking forty a day of those filthy things?"

"More like sixty."

Crozier chuckled. "You never learn, do you?"

"Not only invites himself to stay, but then has the gall to start lecturing me. I should tell you to fuck off."

Crozier smiled at the memories of their constant sparring matches. Unlike the antipathy between himself and Robert Carter, Bailey's replacement, there had never been any animosity between them. He was looking forward to seeing him again. "But you won't, will you?"

There was a long pause followed by more coughing. Finally Harry said, "No . . . not this time."

"Good. I'll see you later. I'll call from the airport."

"I suppose you want me to pick you up."

"No. I think a hire car's a safer bet. I can smell the whiskey fumes from here." When he was promoted to director deneral of the department, one of the first and most difficult decisions he had to make was to retire Harry Bailey, even though the man had not long entered his forties. Thankfully there was no bitterness. Crozier's decision was based more on friendship and his liking of the man than for any other reason, and Harry Bailey himself was relieved to get out of the game. He needed to escape while he still had his sanity, and Simon Crozier recognized the signs and facilitated the retirement on full pension.

"Bastard!"

"I'll bring you a bottle of Jameson's." Crozier smiled and hung up the phone. It would be good to see his old friend again. Harry Bailey had been a fixture in Department 18 when Simon Crozier joined and was one of their biggest assets. A *sensitive* of extraordinary capabilities and the head of many top-level investigations. But over the years his effectiveness had been slowly diminished by his marriage to the bottle, his way of fighting the demons that raged inside his mind.

The intercom buzzed. "Yes."

"Your flight's at six. Heathrow," Trudy said. "I've been in touch with the rental company. There'll be a car waiting for you at the other end."

"Good girl," Crozier said and glanced at his watch. He needed to step up a gear if he was to catch his flight. He closed down his computer, got his coat from the stand, and walked out of the office. At Trudy's desk he paused. "Martin Impey will have some information for me. Get him to send it through to my PDA."

"It's urgent then?" she said.

"Yes," he said. "Very."

Chapter Twelve

King's College Hospital, London, England

McKinley was a tall black American whose large frame seemed uncomfortable being forced onto the tiny plastic chair the hospital provided to ensure visitors didn't overstay their welcome. His deep voice resonated like the bass lines in a complex jazz composition. His demeanor was often mistaken for a morose character, until his sardonic wit came into play and his face lit up in smiles or innocent grins.

He wasn't smiling now. It was obvious Carter was in great pain. He was propped up against the pillow as the nurses checked his drips and administered an injection into his upper arm. They had taken away his neck brace but ordered him to lie still, "Until you've been checked over thoroughly."

Jane was at the head of the bed, standing over Carter, holding his hand and talking quietly to him. They may have been alone in the room, such was their intense attention on each other.

McKinley had witnessed the time they got together. It hadn't been easy for them, especially Jane. Married with two young children, she had gone through agonies of guilt about what she was doing. Over the past couple of days, when he had been in her company, McKinley would have said she was still going through a torment.

If he were a betting man, he would not have laid money on Carter being pleased with what Jane might tell him. Love was a long and winding road.

A doctor came into the room; dressed in a Savile Row

suit with an expensive shirt and tie, he was clearly a senior man, a consultant called away from whatever surgery he had planned in order to check on this extreme patient. The three junior doctors in white housecoats who seemed to hang on his every word was the other clue that this was an important man in the hospital.

"Well, Mr. Carter," he said, and if he could have placed more emphasis on the *mister* it would have bordered on sarcasm. "My name is Dr. Bernard. What seems to have occurred here today in my hospital?"

Carter still had his eyes closed when he replied. "*Your* hospital? I thought it was the King's."

McKinley guessed Carter was struggling to keep his voice even. The nurses were satisfied with the tubes feeding into Carter's arms and after looking around the room as if expecting to see . . . whatever it was they had seen earlier . . . they left.

Dr. Bernard, conscious of the three young doctors' attention, nevertheless seemed amused. "There hasn't been a king since he died in 1952, Mr. Carter, the year I was born and before Queen Elizabeth ascended to the throne. I often wonder which event was the most significant. Around here, in as much as a hierarchy exists, I *am* king."

Carter opened his eyes, slowly and painfully. Bernard was smiling down at him. "Never been much of a monarchist," Carter said.

"Pity, as I am about to administer some medicinal care and attention to you. I'd hate to think you were a nonbeliever."

Jane moved away from the bed to allow the quartet of doctors to do their work. Each time they moved one of Carter's arms, his face screwed up in pain; each time they moved his head, he let out a low grunt that was a silent scream inside.

"So," Bernard said as he shone a light into Carter's eyes. "What exactly were those things?"

"Something that would make our kings and queens, even our hospital consultants, look like newborn kittens."

Bernard may have murmured a response, but his heart wasn't in it. He had never experienced anything like what had happened in this room, and he needed the reassurance of medical science to give him back a modicum of normality.

"He is going to be all right, isn't he?" Jane asked.

Bernard looked at her as if realizing for the first time she was in the room. "Ah, Mrs. Carter?"

"She's not got that misfortune," Carter said.

"How providential for you," Bernard said to Jane.

Jane tutted. "I'm a friend." She indicated McKinley. "We both are."

Bernard looked at the most nervous of the three doctors in white coats. "Is Mr. Carter 'going to be all right,' Dr. Patel?"

The young doctor looked at Carter as if the answer was written on his forehead. He was smart, though, had read the charts and had a strength of character that would one day make him a successful cardiac surgeon. "The original prognosis on initial admission was suspected concussion, but I think we can dismiss that, although there is bruising and some trauma to the neck area. Broken ribs, a dislocation to the knee, a few superficial scratches and bruises to the face and upper torso."

"That seems to cover the injuries that first caused Mr. Carter to join our happy band here. What about the recent events? Have they caused anything we should become concerned about?"

Patel looked around at the others. "I would have to do a thorough . . ."

"No matter, Dr. Patel, unfair question. Like you, I haven't the faintest idea what just happened so cannot expound a theory about how it may affect the patient physically. Vital signs are strong, heart rate, blood levels, temperature, all normal. There are no scars that we can see, no entry wounds, even though it appeared as if . . . well, at any rate, no damage done."

"So he is going to be all right?" Jane persisted.

"Routine X-ray, MRI scan, check all is normal on the inside. I suspect it is."

"I'm still here you know," Carter said.

"But not for much longer I would hazard a guess," Bernard said.

"So when can I go home?"

"All being well with the tests, tomorrow or the day after."

A few moments later the doctors left, and McKinley was in the tiny plastic chair. "So how *do* you feel, man?"

"Like shit strained through a sock."

"Charming!" Jane said, but she was smiling.

McKinley looked serious. "That was a hell of a thing you know. Any idea what those things were?"

Carter had an idea, but he wasn't ready to share it yet. He started to shake his head but stopped when it felt as if his brain was break dancing against his skull.

Jane put her hands on his shoulders. "Don't move your head. Not until they've X-rayed it."

"I've read the report on the apartment building. Sounds like a similar phenomenon."

Carter asked Jane for some water. There was none in the room, so she said she'd get some from the machine along the corridor. As soon as she was gone, Carter said, "Listen, I'm not being rude, but I need some time with Jane. I've hardly seen her recently and . . . well you know how it is."

"Sure thing. If I sit in this chair much longer I'll get molded to it."

Jane had three bottles of water.

"Heh, I'm going to take mine and drink it on the way out."

"Are you sure?" Jane said. "You can stay as long as you want you know, visiting times are pretty flexible."

McKinley was already out of the chair. "No, you're okay.

I've seen enough of this guy to know he's going to keep on being a nuisance for a while longer yet." He squeezed Carter's shoulder. "Take it easy. Crozier will get you back on the job to suit him so you make sure it suits you too. Hear me?"

"I hear you. Thanks for coming."

As the door shut behind him, a silence descended on the room. The monitor ticked away quietly, and Jane scraped the chair across the floor to get nearer to the bed.

Carter waited for her to speak. When she didn't, he said, "It's good to see you, Jane. I've missed you."

Jane closed her eyes and sighed.

Carter took her hand and held it lightly. "Tell me."

"David has asked me to go back to him."

If you woke up breathing, congratulations!
You have another chance.
—Andrea Boydston

Chapter Thirteen

30 St. Mary Axe, London, England

Holly waited until the elevator doors closed and then went back down the corridor to Room 319. Once outside he stopped, put his ear to the door, and listened. Then he took a step back and rested his palms against the smooth wood, closing his eyes and concentrating fiercely.

In his office Saul Goldberg was explaining to the two security men that he'd hit the emergency button by mistake.

They listened patiently and were about to leave when Goldberg clutched his head and screamed. Sinking to his knees, he ripped his glasses from his face, fell forward and lay there twitching.

The security guards exchanged looks and moved as one to assist him. As they took a pace forward, invisible hands grabbed them, and they were thrown backward against the filing cabinets. Winded and bruised, they picked themselves off the floor and tried again, with the same result. Only this time they were thrown back more violently.

Eddie Hampshire, the older and more experienced of the two, cried out as his shoulder dislocated; Steve Fisher, who had only been on this job for three weeks, was knocked out cold as his head collided with the reinforced steel wall of the safe. A two-inch gash opened at his temple, and blood gushed onto the tiles where he fell.

Goldberg had stopped twitching and was hauling himself to his feet, using the edge of the desk for support. His mind was clouded, his thoughts muddled. He found himself looking into the eyes of his wife, captured in the framed photograph that sat on the desk. He gripped the edge of the silver frame with an arthritic hand and smashed it down on the desk, shattering the glass and twisting the metal. His fingers were cut and embedded with splinters of glass, but finally they closed over a shard three inches long and curved into a wicked point. He edged around the desk and collapsed into his chair.

Over by the filing cabinets, Eddie Hampshire was clutching his shoulder and rocking back and forth, hot tears of agony dribbling down his face. He was locked in his own private hell of pain and was taking no notice of Saul Goldberg behind the desk. Goldberg was pulling the shirt from the waistband of his trousers and undoing the buttons.

When the wrinkled white skin of his stomach was exposed Goldberg gripped the shard of glass tightly and drew it across his flaccid belly. For a second nothing happened, and then small beads of blood appeared at the edges of the cut. Using the glistening red dots as a guide Goldberg slashed himself again, cutting deeper this time, carving through the skin and reaching the layer of fat beneath.

He felt no pain and no fear, even when the blood started to pour from the wound. He gripped the glass and cut again.

"Hey!" Eddie Hampshire finally noticed what was going on behind the desk. He pushed himself to his feet and staggered across the office. "Holy shit! What do you think you're doing?"

As Hampshire leaned forward to peer at the self-inflicted wound, Goldberg made a noise in his throat that sounded like a growl. He was staring up at Hampshire but was not seeing him. Instead he could see only John Holly. It was Holly who was staring back at him; Holly's eyes boring into his; Holly's lips curling into a twisted smile. "Good-bye, Saul."

"Fuck you, John," Goldberg said, and the hand holding the glass arced upward, catching Eddie Hampshire under the chin and slicing up through his mouth. As his tongue was speared, his eyes widened in shock. Goldberg yanked back on the glass and slashed Hampshire's neck, severing the carotid artery. Blood spurted from the wound, and Hampshire toppled backward, falling to the floor, hands clutching his neck in a futile attempt to stem the flow of blood from his body.

Goldberg took no more notice of him. He lay the glass on the desk and examined the wound in his stomach. It was pouring blood but was deep enough now to insert his fingers. Using both hands he burrowed into the wound and started to open it wider. Still there was no pain, even when the wound was gaping open and he stared at the white coils of his intestines.

He gave a small giggle and plunged his hand into the

coils, feeling them slip and slide around. His fingers closed over a white, slimy tube and he wrenched it out, dragging it up to his lips. As his teeth bit through the tough membrane, bitter fluid flowed into his mouth.

It was then his mind cleared, the fog clouding his thoughts being blown away as though caught in a gale. He started to gag, and then, when he realized what he had done to himself, started to scream. The scream lasted until his eighty-three-year-old heart exploded and he collapsed dead across the desk.

In the corridor, John Holly took his hands away from the door, pulled a handkerchief from his pocket, wiped his brow, and walked slowly back to the elevator.

Alice glanced round as John Holly opened the door of the BMW and slid into the driver's seat.

"Well?" she said.

John Holly sat behind the wheel, dark glasses hiding his eyes, black hair swept back from his handsome face. "It's a shame. I thought he might be more amenable with you there, but I guessed I wouldn't get anywhere with him, even before we walked into his office. As things stand now, Saul Goldberg will not be making any more deals." He said the last with a smile.

"You killed him?"

"He left me no choice."

"I see."

He laid his hand on her arm. "No, you don't. You don't see at all. My methods repulse you. I can see it in your eyes. They're more eloquent than your words could ever be."

She stared out through the car's windshield. On the busy London streets people were going about their daily business lives: carrying laptop cases, dressed in smart suits with one hand permanently welded to their ears as they conducted cell phone calls while walking along, dashing to get to their next important meeting. By the entrance of the underground station, a busker was strumming a battered guitar and singing a bad version of Oasis's "Champagne Supernova." Normal lives—forbidden fruit to her now.

She wished she'd had the presence of mind to grab Goldberg's gun when it fell to the floor. She could have used it to blast a hole in John Holly's saturnine face. She could have ended this nightmare right there, in that moment. But then this particular nightmare would only be replaced by another. "Where now?" she said.

"Harrow," Holly said and twisted the key in the ignition.

"What's in Harrow?"

"You'll see when we get there," he said, then eased the BMW out into traffic.

Chapter Fourteen

Harrow, London, England

Karolina Adamczyk sat watching the news on a large plasma TV. Fighting and bombings in Afghanistan and Iraq; trouble on the world's stock markets; the abduction and murder of a child in the north of the country.

Bad news. It was the same the world over.

The man emerged from the kitchen carrying a tray of food. He was short, muscular, and dangerous looking, with a scar on his face that ran from just under his left eye, down his unshaven cheek to the corner of his mouth, where it hitched up his top lip in a permanent Elvis sneer. He set the tray down on a small table to the left of her. "*Jedza*," he said. *Eat.*

She lifted her arm. Her wrists were shackled by steel cuffs attached to a chain that was bolted to the floor. "Unlock these and I might."

He glared at her. "You must eat," he said.

She glanced at the food. A rich, meaty stew; beef with carrots, onions, and pearl barley, topped with white, fluffy dumplings. She was ravenous but determined to pursue her hunger strike because she knew it rattled him. "*Fuck you!*" she said.

His face flushed and his nostrils flared as he raised his hand to strike her.

"I dare you," she said defiantly, but suddenly terrified she had pushed him too far.

"Little bitch!" He took a threatening step forward.

"Jozef, enough!"

Wladyslaw Kaminski walked into the room. His entry into the house had been so quiet neither Karolina nor Jozef had heard him.

Jozef dropped his arm and scurried out.

Wladyslaw smiled and sat down on the couch next to Karolina. "You shouldn't tease Jozef so," he said. "He hasn't my self-restraint."

Karolina glared at him. This was the man who'd swept her off her feet, persuaded her to quit her university studies and accompany him on a mad, impulsive trip to England. The man who had, in fact, abducted her and brought her to London, making her a prisoner in this uncomfortable old house on one of Harrow's busiest streets.

Despite his deception, Karolina still found him attractive. His fair hair was long, as were the lashes that framed eyes of the deepest blue. She could drown in those eyes. Just being in the same room as him made her heart race. She struggled to keep her feelings under control, using her anger to neutralize the spell he cast over her, but it was fairly futile. He was the first man she had ever really fallen in love with, and it was difficult to deal with the fact that he had only been using her. What made it more difficult was the fact that she didn't know what he wanted with her.

"How much longer are you going to keep me here?" she said

He rested a hand on her thigh, making her flesh tingle. "Not very much longer. In fact you could be out of here soon. Sooner than you think."

Something cold slipped down her spine. *Soon*? She was aware he couldn't let her go. She would go straight to the police and he knew this. What then? Was he planning to kill her? She'd seen too much; she knew too much. It was the only course of action left open to him. Warm tears slid down her cheeks. The thought she would never see her parents or home again was suddenly unbearable.

"Why are you crying?" he said.

"You're planning to kill me, like the others." When she'd first arrived at the house, there were six other girls there. Now there was only her. She'd heard the screams, the comings and goings in the night.

He looked at her steadily and took her hand in his. "You're not going to die," he said. "That was never part of the plan. There are some people coming here this evening who want to meet you, and there's every likelihood that you will be leaving with them."

She searched for the truth in his eyes. "Why me? Why did you choose me?"

"You were chosen a long time ago, Karolina, because you're special," he said. "Now, eat your food. You need your strength."

He left her, closing the door behind him. She leaned forward and sniffed the stew. It really did smell delicious. She picked up the spoon and took a tentative mouthful, chewing the tender meat and carrots, flavors exploding in her mouth. She took another mouthful, and then another, until the bowl was empty.

Inhale, and God approaches you. Hold the inhalation, and God remains with you. Exhale, and you approach God. Hold the exhalation, and surrender to God.
—Krishnamacharya

Chapter Fifteen

Krakow, Poland

The double espresso was good, as good as he'd ever tasted. Jacek Czerwinski sat at an outside table overlooking the Rynek Glowny Central Square.

The Szara was his favorite restaurant. He knew the waiters and they knew him—hence the fantastic espresso. The restaurant was also a great place to people watch, one of his favorite pastimes. It was a mindless occupation that gave him a chance to organize his thoughts. The restaurant was his little oasis of peace in an otherwise frenetic life.

So when someone pulled up a chair and sat down next to him, he was less than pleased at the intrusion. He turned and was about to say something to the interloper when he stopped, his mouth working but no sound issuing from his lips.

The man who was now sharing his table was huge, black, and his face was marked with distinctive cuts, long healed, though they stretched when he flashed a friendly smile.

"Can I help you?" Jacek managed at last.

"You've already helped me," the stranger said in faultless Polish shaded by an American accent. "More than you know." He stuck out a huge hand. "Jason Pike," he said.

Jacek narrowed his eyes. "Yes, I assumed so," he said and shook the hand. The grip was strong, giving Jacek the impression that if Pike had it in mind to crush his fingers, he could. With ease.

"You know who I am?"

"You were described to me. You told Cyril Adamczyk to come and see me."

"Ah, yes. Mr. Adamczyk. Another tragic case," Pike said, staring at a horse-drawn carriage as it made its sightseeing circuit of the square. "You have a beautiful city," he said.

Jacek refused to be sidetracked. "You sent him to see me. Why?"

"I thought you may be able to help him," Pike said. "You've had experience. You've taken on several missing-person cases in the last few years, and, as I'm led to believe, solved a number of them."

Jacek leaned back in his chair and ran his hands through his hair. "Considering how many I've taken on, those results are pretty negligible. The ones I *have* solved have been simple runaways. They're pretty easy. The others . . . well, divorce cases are much simpler, believe me. And I've had my fair share of those. Bread and butter."

"Yes, I know. In fact I know a lot about you, Jacek," he said. "Jacek Czerwinski. Forty-four. Educated at Warsaw University. Graduated with degrees in law and psychology. Joined the police in 1986. Rose through the ranks quickly to Inspector. Left them and started your own detective agency. Why did you leave the police?"

Jacek picked up his coffee and took a sip, staring at Pike over the rim of the cup. "You tell me. You seem to know enough about me."

Pike smiled. "I suspect it was because your niece, Julia, disappeared, and you felt the police weren't doing enough to find out where she'd gone. So you decided to quit and track her down yourself. Correct?"

Jacek shrugged. “Close enough.”

“But you never found her.” It wasn’t a question.

“No,” Jacek said. “I never did.”

“Taking on missing-person cases has become something of a crusade for you now, hasn’t it? You only take expenses on these cases. Otherwise you waive your fee. In my book, that’s a crusade. A man driven by passion.” He smiled. “I suppose that explains the other work you do.”

“As I said, bread and butter. Divorce cases pay my rent.”

There was a silence between the two men.

“Have you been following me?” Jacek said at last.

Pike nodded.

“For how long?”

“A few days.”

“Why?”

“I needed to know if I could trust you. When I saw them break into your apartment yesterday, I guessed you must be okay.” He summoned a waiter and ordered two more coffees.

“You know who they are? The people who broke in?”

Pike nodded his head slowly. “Oh yes, I know them. Bad people. The worst. It was lucky you weren’t there. I think they might have killed you. In fact, I’m surprised they haven’t killed you already. You’re getting too close to them.”

“The police don’t believe me.”

“Can you blame them?”

Jacek sighed. “I suppose not.” He uncrossed his legs and leaned forward, resting his elbows on the table. “Okay, enough pissing around. What do you want from me?”

Pike glanced round as the waiter reappeared. “Ah, the coffee.”

He said nothing until the waiter had moved on to another table. “I want you to help me bring them down.”

Jacek’s eyes opened in surprise. “What makes you think I can do that? I’ve been trying for the last few years, and I’ve gotten nowhere. Almost all my investigations have ended in failure. I get so far and then hit a brick wall. It's the classic, *as one door closes, another slams in your face* scenario. All I've managed to find out so far is that their influence runs deep, through every strata of society."

"Yes, you're right. You're up against some very powerful people. But there's more to it than that."

"What do you mean?"

Pike took a mouthful of coffee, then sat back in his seat. "Tell me, Jacek, do you believe in the supernatural, the paranormal?"

The question came from left field, and Jacek was unprepared for it. "If you're talking about ghosts and séances and things like that, then no. No, I don't think I do. Nor do I believe in an afterlife, despite being born and raised a Catholic. I do think though we, as a race, are sometimes influenced by forces we don't really understand. Whether or not they're supernatural, I wouldn't like to say. Why do you ask?"

"Because I want to know if you have an open mind or a closed mind. Because what I'm about to tell you falls outside what we call common experience. Your answer demonstrates that your mind is more open than some. What would you say if I were to tell you that the human race is not the superior species on this planet? What would you say if I were to tell you that there is a race of beings on this earth who, if circumstances were right, could wipe us out, erase us from existence?"

Jacek looked at him steadily. "I'd say you did too much ganja in the past." He smiled. "I'd say you were crazy. Demented. A nut job." He got to his feet. "I'd say this conversation is over. Good-bye, Mr. Pike. I hope we never have occasion to meet again." He walked away from the restaurant. He'd gone a few yards when he looked back. "Oh, and stop following me."

"I can prove it, if you like. But then I don't think I have to. At least, not to you," Pike called after him.

"Some other time maybe," Jacek said and continued walking.

Pike watched him go, then reached across the table and picked up his cup. *Good coffee*, he thought as he sipped at his double espresso and waited. He signaled to the waiter to bring a bottle of vodka. After fifty yards Jacek stopped walking, turned, and came back to the table.

He pulled out the chair and sat, dragging his half-drunk coffee toward him. "Okay," he said, taking a sip. "I'm listening."

"What made you change your mind?"

"Curiosity . . . and stupidity probably. And the fact that I don't like being played, and that's what you're doing, isn't it?"

Pike smiled. "Yes, I am, in a way. But only for the greater good."

"Which is?"

"As I said, the survival of the human race."

Jacek looked at him for a long moment. "You're serious, aren't you?"

"Deadly," Pike said.

Jacek poured some vodka into their glasses. "Then let me go first and tell you whether I believe in the supernatural, the paranormal."

Chapter Sixteen

Harrow, London, England

"So why have you brought me here?" Alice said as the BMW pulled up outside the redbrick Edwardian house in Harrow View.

"All in good time," Holly said.

Alice peered through the side window. The house looked semiderelict. Strips of paint hung from the front door like peeling skin, showing the rotting wood beneath, and on the walls clung patches of lichen, cancerous growths eating into the fabric of the brickwork. Listless net curtains hung from the windows, so filthy they looked nearly black, and the windows themselves were coated in road grime and hadn't been cleaned for years.

"It doesn't look very inviting, I'll grant you. It's better inside," Holly said.

"You haven't answered my question."

"Patience. You'll see soon enough."

At the front door, Holly took a key from his pocket and slid it into the lock. The door opened smoothly. Alice had expected it to creak on rusty hinges. He'd been telling the truth; it was better inside but only marginally. The carpet in the hallway looked new, but the paper on the walls looked tired and probably early 1990s in design. A stairway led off from the hall, the treads carpeted in the same brown as the hallway, but a single, naked bulb offered scant illumination, making the stairway dark and foreboding.

A door farther along the hallway opened, and a young

man stepped out, a look of something close to panic on his face. "Mr. Holly, you're early. You should have phoned to let me know."

Holly appraised the young man, a look of irritation in his eyes. "Is there a problem, Kaminski?"

Wladyslaw Kaminski was flustered but fighting to hide it. "No. No problem. It's just that we're still getting her . . ."

"Spare me the details. We'll wait in here." He pushed open a door and ushered Alice inside.

The room Alice entered was the lounge. She spotted the chain and shackles immediately and spun on her heel. "What is this place?"

Holly came into the room and shut the door behind him. "It's one of our restaurants. It's also where we bring the new arrivals from Poland for processing. It's in an ideal position. Harrow has a large Polish immigrant population, a constant ebb and flow, so new faces don't attract much attention here. Also, within the population, there are a number of borderline poverty cases who are only too happy to supply us with names of potential candidates, in return for a fat fee of course."

"*Candidates*," Alice said scornfully. "It nauseates me the way you dress things up. 'Restaurants, candidates' . . . It's all subterfuge. Do you think that if you use anodyne names you somehow sweeten the sick business you're engaged in?"

Holly looked at her patiently. "The 'sick business,' as you call it, is our way of surviving. And don't kid yourself that I like it any more than you do. My father was working for a way forward, a way of ending our reliance on the . . . *candidates*. When he died, it set us back years. So don't preach to me, because you know nothing about it. You and your bad driving are to blame for his death, and for the steps I have to take."

"That's a lie, and you know it. Your kind will never give up these places. It's a way of life, a tradition. You might think that by carrying on your father's research you're working toward a bright new future, but there are those who'll never accept your ideas. People like Saul Goldberg. What are you going to do, John? Roll over them? Kill all those who don't share your vision, who don't play by your rules?"

He looked at her steadily. When he spoke his voice was soft, barely a whisper. "Yes, if I have to."

She opened her mouth to say something else, then snapped it shut. What was the point? She'd had countless arguments with him over the past few months, and it had gotten her nowhere.

She hated the man standing in front of her, hated him with every fiber of her being. The hatred was like a physical ache, cramping her arms and legs and making her head throb. But she knew she was tied to him for as long as he wanted her to be. She had tried to escape him a number of times, and each time he'd found her and brought her back. How can you hide from someone who can read your thoughts, who can see what you see, hear what you hear, and feel what you feel? It was hopeless. And it could be argued that hate was another useless, impotent emotion, but she refused to let it go. It was the hatred that kept her moving forward.

Hatred and the need for revenge. John Holly had destroyed her life. He took her away from the one person she had ever truly loved. Daniel Milton had been her life partner and soul mate. John Holly had snatched her from the hospital because what she knew was an obstacle to his plans. It was that loss, the manner in which he kept her away from the life she had known, used her as his assistant, involved her in his grotesque schemes that fueled Alice's need to avenge, that gave her the strength to keep going. She'd promised herself, and promised Daniel, wherever he was, that one day she would make John Holly pay for what he'd done.

The door opened, and Wladyslaw Kaminski sidled into the room. "Five minutes," he said.

Holly glared at him. "You should have been ready. This isn't good enough." He turned to Alice. "You might as well sit down," he said as Kaminski scurried from the room and ran up the stairs.

Alice looked across at the couch, at the chain and shackles and suppressed a shudder. "I'll stand."

"As you wish." He glanced at his watch and tapped his foot impatiently.

Alice walked across to the window and stared out through the grimy net curtains at the road beyond. There were people hurrying along but, on the road, cars, buses, and trucks sat nose to tail, barely moving; the usual urban rush-hour crawl. She wondered if curious eyes ever tried to peer in through the curtains from the outside; wondered if anyone out there ever thought about what was happening behind the mildewed facade of the house. She guessed not. They were all too busy going about their lives, too wrapped up in themselves to care about the plight of others.

In London anonymity was king.

In the room above the lounge, Karolina was sitting on a hard-backed chair while a hairdresser, a young Polish woman with too much makeup, gelled her hair and teased it into spikes.

Jozef was standing in front of the door, watching the procedure with disinterest.

The hairdresser had said little since her arrival an hour before; the woman hadn't even met Karolina's eyes. On the mantelpiece above the fireplace she'd propped a small photograph and as she worked on Karolina's hair, she kept glancing at it, as if using it for reference.

Finally she came round, stood in front of Karolina, and looked at her, nodding slowly. "Good," she said, walking across to Jozef. She showed him the photograph. Jozef studied it for a moment, then stared hard at Karolina.

"What do you think?" the hairdresser said.

Jozef shrugged.

The hairdresser made a noise of disgust in the back of her throat. "Your enthusiasm is overwhelming."

"I should care," Jozef said.

She pushed past him and opened the door to call Kaminski.

Karolina felt numb. Ever since Wladyslaw told her she could be leaving here tonight, she had felt sick with dread. Her thoughts were in turmoil. What started out in Poland as a great adventure had turned into a bad dream. One from which she thought she'd never wake. She couldn't believe how much Wladyslaw Kaminski had changed since they arrived in England. Her kind, attentive lover, the gentle soul who had swept her off her feet, buying her flowers and taking her for candlelit dinners, had turned into a monster.

When they arrived at the house in Harrow View, he'd taken her upstairs to this very room to unpack her belongings. Then he started undressing her, pushing her down onto the bed. Even when he produced the cord and started binding her wrists, the alarm bells failed to sound; they'd played mild bondage games in her room back in Poland. When he then tied her ankles tightly together and left the room, she realized she was in very serious trouble. *How could I have been so stupid?* The question kept playing over and over in her mind. As yet she'd failed to find an answer.

And now the day had taken a step into the bizarre. Why had they brought a hairdresser in to cut her hair? She caught a glimpse of her reflection in the dressing-table mirror and barely recognized herself. The hair was much shorter than she usually wore it, and she would never style it like this. It made her look older. In fact, it made her look like the woman in the photograph.

She turned as Kaminski came into the room. "Come on," he said. "They're waiting."

Karolina didn't move from her seat.

"I said *come on!* We've kept them waiting long enough, and John Holly is not a man you want to keep waiting."

He crossed the room and grabbed her by the wrist, yanking her to her feet. This was frustrating. He wanted to slap her but was under strict instructions from Holly that she mustn't be harmed in any way. He pulled her to the door, pushed Jozef out of the way, and then put a hand in the small of Karolina's back, thrusting her out onto the landing. She resisted him all the way as he dragged her toward the stairs.

Finally his temper got the better of him and he spun round, grabbed her by the throat, pinning her against the wall. "Listen, you little bitch, if you don't cooperate, I'll kill you. You don't know what's at stake here."

She stared back at him, defiance in her eyes, and then she spat in his face.

Kaminski made a half-strangled noise. His hand balled into a fist, and he swung his arm.

Before his fist made contact with her face, he was lifted off his feet. For an instant, panic flared in his eyes, and then he was being hurled backward along the length of the landing, his body crashing into the wall at the far end. Karolina heard the sickening thud as his skull hit brickwork. He hung there for a moment, spread-eagled against the wall, like a butterfly skewered by a pin. Then his eyes fluttered shut, and he slid down to land in a heap on the floor.

"Are you all right, my dear? Did he hurt you?"

Karolina turned at the sound of the voice and saw a man walking toward her from the stairway. He was tall, good-looking with dark hair swept back from his face. He moved with all the grace of a panther and looked twice as dangerous.

She struggled to find her voice. "I . . . I'm okay. How did you . . . ? Is he . . . ?"

John Holly wrapped an arm around her shoulders and walked her to the stairs. "Don't worry about him. He's of no consequence, no better than vermin. Wait here. I'll show you how I deal with vermin."

Kaminski groaned and tried to sit. A bomb had gone off in his head, and now he was dealing with the fall-out. Nausea was rising from his stomach, and his eyes were rolling in their sockets. In the distance, at the top of the stairs, he saw Holly turn and start walking back toward him. The door to the bedroom opened. Jozef and the hairdresser stepped onto the landing and saw Kaminski lying crumpled at the foot of the wall with Holly advancing on him. The hairdresser gave a small cry and retreated back into the relative safety of the bedroom, slamming the door behind her and locking it. Jozef pressed his back against the wall and wished he were invisible.

Two yards away from Kaminski, Holly stopped. Kaminski tried to focus on him, trying for a look of defiance but achieving only a slightly vacuous frown.

Holly was smiling. "You are a fool, Kaminski. You had the key to it all. Had her in the palm of your hand, but you sold her as a pet. It took my father years of his life trying to track her down, and a brainless . . ."

He raised his arm, and before Kaminski's befuddled mind could register what was happening, Holly clicked his fingers.

The pain was so excruciating it was almost exquisite. It was as if Wladyslaw Kaminski's head had been clamped in a slowly tightening vise. The blood vessels in his nose were the first to explode, followed closely by those in his eyes and ears. As blood poured from every orifice, he gave a small whimper, like a child left alone in the dark. The vise tightened still further, and Kaminski's brain burst, turning to pulp in his skull. He died half a second later.

John Holly smiled and turned his attention to Jozef. Jozef pressed tighter against the wall, eyes open wide, staring at Holly, his mouth working, lips forming a silent prayer.

"Get rid of that garbage," Holly said to him and walked back along the landing to where Karolina was waiting, staring at him, wide-eyed. As he approached, she shrank back. The day had turned now from a bad dream into her worst nightmare.

Alice was still standing at the window, staring out at the street when Holly led Karolina into the room.

"Alice," John Holly said softly. "A surprise for you."

Alice turned from the window and saw the two of them standing there. It was like being kicked in the stomach. All the air seemed to gush from her lungs in one rapid exhalation, leaving her breathless and gasping for oxygen.

The young woman standing next to John Holly was a mirror image of herself.

Alice stared at her, tears springing to her eyes, wanting to believe that there really was a good reason her double was standing there, even though a cold, rational voice in her head told her that it was impossible. This was a trafficked girl, and the man standing opposite Alice now, smiling, was responsible.

She took an involuntary step backward.

No!

It wasn't a perfect likeness. The girl was younger, little more than a teenager. But the face, the hair, and the way she held herself . . . It was an uncanny resemblance.

The girl was looking at her uncertainly, bafflement in her eyes . . . and something else. Fear.

"A gift for you," Holly said.

Alice gathered herself. "Is this some kind of sick joke?"

John Holly's face was a picture of injured innocence. "I'm sure I don't know what you mean."

"And I'm sure you do, you bastard," Alice said hotly as she felt the anger swelling again.

Holly spread his hands in a gesture of appeasement. "As I said, she's a gift to you. A new pet. It's been so long since you had someone of your own. I thought I'd change that." He gestured to Karolina. "She's yours to do with what you will."

Alice looked at him steadily, ignoring the girl. "No," she said. "This isn't a joke. It's just sick."

Holly turned to Karolina. He said nothing to her, but her right leg started moving, taking a step toward Alice. Karolina screwed her eyes shut, as if concentrating furiously. Alice could see the girl's left leg twitching, the muscles almost going into spasm as she tried to resist Holly's will, but a second later the leg moved, taking her another step toward Alice. At the same time, Karolina's arms opened, preparing for an embrace. Sweat was pouring down the girl's face, tears pressing out from her tightly shut eyelids.

"You see," John Holly said. "She wants you. Doesn't a tiny part of you want her too?"

"Stop it!" Alice cried. It was almost a scream of anguish. "Leave the poor girl alone." Why was Holly doing this? Nothing he did was without a purpose. "Stop it," she said again, her voice quieter this time, barely a whisper.

Holly sighed. "Very well," he said and tore his gaze away from Karolina. The girl's arms flopped to her sides, and her eyes opened with a look of confusion and fear.

"Jozef!" Holly called.

Jozef was standing just outside the door, ready to jump if summoned. Having witnessed what had happened upstairs, he feared a repeat performance, this time with himself as the victim. At the sound of Holly's voice, he was in the room in seconds.

Holly gestured to Karolina. "Dispose of this as well," he said.

Jozef leapt forward and pinned Karolina's arms at her

sides. "Move," he said, propelling her toward the door. As the girl passed Alice her lips mouthed the words, *"Pomagają mnie."*

Alice didn't understand the words, but the meaning was burning in Karolina's eyes. *Help me.* A desperate plea for her life.

"Wait!" Alice said.

"Czekają," Holly repeated in Polish.

Jozef froze on the spot.

"A change of heart?" Holly said to Alice.

She took a breath and nodded.

Holly smiled. "Jozef, bring the young lady back."

Almost grudgingly, Jozef led Karolina back into the center of the room and let her go.

"Leave us," Holly said to him.

Jozef nodded curtly and left the room.

"So she's coming with us?" Holly said.

Alice nodded.

"Right then. Let's get out of this shithole before we catch something."

Alice sat in the back of the car with her arm around the girl's shoulders, trying to stop her trembling. Silent tears were trickling down the girl's cheeks. Alice took her hand, squeezing it reassuringly. "It's okay," Alice said softly, not sure if the girl could understand her. "What's your name?"

"Karolina," the girl whispered. "Karolina Adamczyk. Please. I want to go home."

"This is your home now. Get used to it," Holly said from the front seat without looking round. Alice glared at the back of his head. How had he heard their conversation above the music coming from the stereo? She squeezed Karolina's hand again, attempting to communicate silently that she'd try every way possible to grant the girl's wish. Karolina suppressed a sob and slumped back into her seat.

"I'm glad you approved her, Alice. It would have been tiresome for me if you hadn't."

Alice said, "I would never be tiresome."

Holly glanced at her in the rearview mirror. "Karolina will be conducting some of your public duties for a while."

Warning bells rang in her head. "Why would I need her to do that?"

Holly turned the music off. "You'll be too busy helping me with my project. My . . . what did you call it? My research into a bright new future."

They traveled the rest of the way to Hertfordshire in silence.

Breathing is the greatest pleasure in life.
—Giovanni Papini

Chapter Seventeen

Krakow, Poland

Jacek Czerwinski took a long swallow of his vodka. Pike poured more into his glass without asking. This was shaping up to be a full-bottle story.

"My brother, Tomas, had a daughter, Julia. She was a free spirit who danced to her own tune and gave her parents hell." Another swallow of alcohol.

Pike waited; this would take some time. Clearly Czerwinski was telling an emotional tale.

"Tomas himself was . . . unconventional. He ran a business

that fell into hard times. Poland has had some difficult economic periods. The solution Tomas came up with was fraud. He was caught and . . ."

As Jacek's voice trailed off, Pike leaned back. "Tell it in your own time."

Tomas Czerwinski looked around his cell for the last time. The place that had been his home for the past four years looked squalid and incredibly tawdry now as the prospect of freedom loomed.

Three bunks, three lives; three men sharing a space no more than twelve feet square. Jacob's letters from home that he kept pinned to the wall above his bed were yellowing, and with no new ones to replace them, they shouted out the man's desperate loneliness. Grabowski's Freddie Mercury shrine was looking tired and dog-eared, a testament to the fact that Grabowski had long ago given up on life.

Czerwinski's own bunk was curiously anonymous. He had deliberately made it so. He didn't want to give the guards or the other inmates the slightest clue about what went on in his mind.

He had spent the four years of his sentence isolated inside his own head, and not once, not even for the briefest second, even when things had been so bleak he had contemplated suicide, did he feel the urge to open up and bare himself to somebody else. It was safer that way.

At eleven thirty he would gather his parcel of personal effects, say good-bye to the governor, get himself signed out by the releasing officer, and then make the short walk across the courtyard to the main gates. In the years he had been here, he had seen them open many times, but this time it would be special because they were opening for him.

He wondered if there would be anyone there to meet him, but he doubted it. Within two months of him going down, Helena, his wife, had moved in with Wiktor Polanski, the solicitor who had handled his case, and two years later she asked for a divorce. He granted her request with some relief as the marriage had never been sound, but now he was wondering how he was going to face life outside completely on his own.

That would be an entirely new experience for him. Helena and he had been childhood sweethearts and were married a few days shy of his eighteenth birthday. The marriage had lasted nearly twenty years, good and bad. Mostly bad.

He shook his head to shoo the memory away. This was his new beginning, his fresh start, and he didn't want sour memories spoiling it. He closed the door to the cell for the last time and turned to the warder who stood at his shoulder. "Right," he said to the guard. "Time to go, I think."

The prison gate shut with a whisper behind him, and he took his first lungful of free air in four years. Across the street a car was standing, its engine idling. As the gates closed behind him, the car door opened and his daughter, Julia, stepped out. She said nothing but raised her hand in a semblance of a wave.

He was surprised to see her there. She had not visited him once while he was in prison. He met her halfway across the street and they embraced, stopping the trickle of traffic and eliciting several angry horn blasts, but they were oblivious to the noise.

"You've had your hair cut since I last saw you."

She ran her hand through her auburn crop self-consciously.

"It suits you short."

"That's more than Mother thinks. She hates it."

He shook his head. Four years on and his daughter was still playing the rebellious teenager. If prison had taught him one thing, it was tolerance. "No, really, I mean it. It looks good. Brings out your eyes. How is she, your mother?"

"Still with the asshole Wiktor."

He settled in the passenger seat of her Volvo. "Nice car," he said. "Who does it belong to?"

"A friend. He lets me use it sometimes."

"Has he a name, this friend of yours?"

"His name's Wladyslaw."

"And does Wladyslaw have a job?"

"Dad, don't start. Don't spoil it."

"Point taken. Did you bring my keys with you?"

She reached into the glove compartment and dropped the bunch of keys into his hand. He stared down at them and selected two of them. "Can you take me straight to the workshop?"

Julia started the engine and stared straight ahead. "I thought you'd want to go home first. There's . . ." She hesitated.

"There's what? Go on—spit it out."

"Well, I invited a few people over to your place, just to welcome you back."

He sagged in his seat. "Oh God, Julia, why? A coming-out party's the last thing I need. I don't want to see anyone . . . not just yet. I'm not ready."

"It's not a party," Julia said indignantly. "It's just a few friends. It's no big deal."

He slammed his hand on the dashboard so hard it made her jump, and her foot slipped from the clutch. The car lurched and stalled. "Dad! For God's sake. It's not as if you've got to make a speech or anything. It's just the people who've missed you since you went inside. People from the club. Jacek, of course. I thought it would be nice."

"If they'd missed me that much, they would have taken the trouble to come and visit me, wouldn't they? And did they? Did they, hell!"

Julia shook her head. "I didn't realize you'd grown so bitter."

"Will *she* be there?"

"Mum? Do I look stupid? Of course she won't be there."

He was staring back at the prison, taking one last long look. The wall rippled as a shockwave passed through it, and then the bricks began to bulge outward as if made of rubber. The brickwork stretched, ballooning, splitting, and a black shape pushed out from the wall, forming on the pavement outside the prison into an uneven cloud of shadow. It took the human form of a man but was ill defined around the edges, as if incomplete.

Czerwinski gasped and spun round in his seat. "Drive!" he said to his daughter.

Julia turned to him, confused by the panic in his voice. She followed his gaze but saw nothing except the prison wall, solid, iron-gray brickwork, intimidating and unbreachable.

Her father sat in the passenger seat, his face bleached white, a film of perspiration covering his skin, a look of terror in his eyes. "Dad!"

He rounded on her. "I said, drive!" He reached across her and twisted the key in the ignition.

She batted his hand away. "Calm down! I can do it."

The car started and she pulled away from the curb, glancing at her father, who had turned again in his seat and was staring back at the prison.

They reached the outskirts of town. For the past thirty miles they had driven in virtual silence. Julia tried hard to make conversation, but her father was reticent and close-mouthed, confining his answers to monosyllables.

"I'm not sure I can take much more of this," she said, crunching the gears into second as she pulled away from traffic lights.

"Much more of what?" Czerwinski said, although he knew exactly what she was talking about. Since leaving the prison, he had closed in on himself again. It was a trick he developed first when he was on remand awaiting his trial.

He found it a calming exercise, and at that moment he badly needed calming.

He knew he had seen the black shape emerging from the gray brick wall of the prison. Things couldn't pass through solid matter, and the walls *were* solid matter, impenetrable. Equally logical, he couldn't have seen the shadows because they only existed inside the prison. And he really thought, hoped, he had seen the last of them.

"Look, I'm sorry I invited them, okay? We'll get you home and I'll get rid of them."

Czerwinski sighed, forcing the darkness from his mind. "I just need some time to adjust, that's all. I've been surrounded by people twenty-four hours a day for the past four years. The last thing I need is to get out of that place and be surrounded by more. Understand?"

She nodded. "Okay," she said sullenly. He could almost feel her resentment.

He leaned back in his seat with a sigh. This was going poorly. She was trying hard. Their relationship had never been easy, but today she was trying hard and he was throwing it all back in her face. Perhaps she was maturing, after all, becoming the daughter he never thought he'd have.

"I'm sorry," he said. "I'm being unreasonable. Best behavior from now on. I promise."

It was a promise he soon found impossible to keep.

It was a problem meeting his old friends, and when they sang "*Sto Lat*," he started to feel nauseous. The song was usually sung at birthdays or name days, wishing the recipient good health, good wishes, and a hundred-year-long life. He wasn't worthy of the sentiment. He was a man who had committed a crime, who had been caught and punished. He was a man so neglectful of his wife that she ran off with the first man to pay her serious attention. He was a man who had let himself down. He didn't deserve, or want, their goodwill.

An hour in to the gathering, he sought refuge in the garden. He stood underneath the rose arch, smoking a cigarette, trying to think of a way to escape and laughing at the absurdity of it. Here he was at his old house, freshly cleaned and tidied for the first time in four years, surrounded by his own furniture and belongings, and he found it as confining as the prison he had just left.

"It's good to see you again, Tomas. Got a light?" Lucja Wallenski came up behind him.

He and Lucja had been friends for years, since before she married his best friend, Pawel. She had been single then, and he had nurtured a major crush on her, but at the time he was committed to Helena. "You shouldn't smoke, Lucja. It's bad for your health."

"I'll see you in your box first," she said.

He chuckled. "Yes, you probably will. Have you got your car handy?"

"Why, fancy a drive? Or looking to escape?"

"What do you think?"

"Would you like me to smuggle you out?"

"Think you can?"

"Of course."

Five minutes later they were driving out onto the street. "Where to?" Lucja said with a smile.

Czerwinski took a long final pull on his cigarette and flicked the butt through the window. "Do you remember the workshop?"

"Of course I do. You took me there after the pub one night . . . before Pawel and I got together."

"That's right, I did. God, you've got a good memory."

"I remember you proposed to me."

"Did I?"

"You certainly did. Mind you, you were drunk as a skunk."

"And married to Helena."

"Just as well I didn't accept."

"Lucky for you."

"Maybe," she said.

They drove in silence for a few minutes, both wrapped up in the memories of that night.

Life could have been so very different for both of them had they followed their hearts and not their heads.

"Here we are," Lucja said, breaking out from the reverie and turning the car into a narrow lane that ran parallel to the railway line. The workshop was in one of the arches underneath the bridge. He noticed as they drove along the dingy street that most of the other businesses had gone in the time he had been inside. There had once been a second-hand record shop that specialized in '50s rock and roll, a wood turner who made fruit bowls and table lamps, and an old man whose shop was called Iskier-Sparks and who claimed to be able to repair anything electrical. They were all gone now.

They stopped outside his workshop. There were metal shutters secured by heavy padlocks over the entire frontage. Graffiti artists had exercised their creativity. There wasn't an inch of metal that hadn't been covered with spray paint.

He climbed from the car, pressing his hands into the small of his back to relieve the stiffness. He was very aware he was getting older. One day, perhaps sooner rather than later, he would be too old to make use of the workshop. But that was a few years off yet.

"Would you like me to wait?" Lucja asked.

"No, it's okay."

"Call me later in the week."

He bent down and kissed her cheek. "I will. Promise. And thanks for getting me out of there."

"A friend in need . . ."

". . . is a pain in the . . . Yes, I know. See you soon." He blew her another kiss and watched as she U-turned in the road. She winked at him as she drove away. One in a million, he thought, and fished in his pocket for the keys to the padlocks.

The shutters rose smoothly and quietly. The front of the shop was painted a dark green and still looked quite smart. The sign that ran above the shop was in scrolled gold lettering and proclaimed *Tomas Czerwinski Upholsterer*, no more than that, but anything else was unnecessary. He had enjoyed a reputation as one of the best upholsterers in the area, and several interior design shops had him on their books as their first choice. Under their aegis he had done work for some of the richest and well-known people, and he found it a privilege to work on their fine antique furniture, bringing it back to its former glory.

He smiled ruefully. Memories, that's all they were now. Past glories that he would never again enjoy. It was going to be hard getting the business set up again, and he realized it would be starting from the bottom. And this time he wouldn't enjoy patronage from the interior-design companies. They had very up-market images and wouldn't recommend an ex-con to their rich and famous clients. He turned the key in the lock and let himself into the workshop.

It was just as he remembered. His hammer and staple gun still lying on the bench where he'd left them the morning the police came to arrest him. Even the material he had been using to reupholster the couch was still there on its roll, leaning against the wall. The couch had gone, though, as had all the chairs and other pieces he had booked in. He hadn't expected anything else. Helena would have contacted all his customers and told them to collect their furniture. He wondered what excuse she'd used. He couldn't imagine she would have told them the truth. She couldn't have stood the indignity. Her one relief when the case came to trial was that there had been a huge fire at a local firework factory and the stories of death and disaster had kept *his* story out of the local papers.

He walked across to the compressor, stroking the hoses that fed air to his staple gun. He tapped the fuel tank with a screwdriver, but it echoed emptily. He wondered if the machine would ever work again after standing idle for so long. It was very old, and he doubted if they even made spare parts for it anymore.

A small movement attracted his attention. There were black shadows moving among some material in the corner. Vague and indistinct, they weaved in and out of the rolls. He walked across to the corner and crouched down, pulling the material aside. The shadows vanished, but the movement, vague and diaphanous remained, like an echo after a loud noise.

"Bastards!" he hissed under his breath, and suddenly years of containment and frustration boiled up and erupted.

He grabbed a wooden mallet from the bench, and with a cry started pulling the rolls of material away from the wall, chasing the shadows as they scurried for cover.

Finally he lashed out with the mallet. Dancing shadows showed an almost human instinct for escape, trying to find cover under the compressor.

"No, you don't." Czerwinski brought the mallet down again and again, and suddenly it wasn't the shadows he was striking out at. It was Helena. Helena lying there on the grubby floor of the workshop, her skull crushed, her face pulped beyond recognition. And still he kept smashing down with the mallet.

"Did you see them, Tomas?" voices whispered. *"Did you see the breathers?"*

"No!" Czerwinski yelled, and hurled the mallet against the wall. Gradually the images and shapes faded and Tomas sank to his knees, fearing the nightmares that had begun in prison were here to haunt him as a free man.

Pawel Wallenski drove slowly through the town, his eyes raking the pavement, looking for any sign of his oldest friend.

He was furious with Lucja for spiriting Tomas away from the reunion and made his feelings clear in a blazing, stand-up row with her, the ferocity of which made the other guests squirm with embarrassment. But then there were always issues with Lucja whenever they talked about Tomas Czerwinski.

Wallenski loved Czerwinski like a brother, but didn't trust either his wife or his best friend when they were alone together, and this simmering resentment always came to the surface during arguments, which were unfortunately increasing in frequency the longer the marriage survived.

His first stop on his search for his best friend was the workshop, Tomas's first love, and the reason he had spent the past few years languishing in prison. It was his fight to keep his upholstery business running when faced with the crippling credit card bills Helena had run up on her numerous spending sprees, that led him to seek other, less legitimate, ways of making money. Fraud, forgery, only ever at the expense of those who could afford it but illegal all the same.

When he reached the railway arches, he saw that the shutters were down and padlocked. Of Czerwinski there was no sign.

Czerwinski stood on the bank of the canal.

"What're you doing, Tomas?" Wallenski chuckled as he came up alongside his old friend. "I thought you were going to throw yourself in."

"Actually, I was," Czerwinski said under his breath and turned to him slowly.

Wallenski tried a half smile. "I should get you home. Julia's very pissed at you."

"Soon. Fancy a drink?"

Wallenski nodded and began to walk back to the road. Czerwinski stopped suddenly. "I think I'm going mad, Pawel," he said.

Wallenski hesitated for a moment, then said, "Well, you do seem a little overwrought."

Czerwinski laughed. "Overwrought! Oh yes, that's a good one. Overwrought, that's what I am." Still laughing, he climbed the steps to the road.

Czerwinski sat at a table and watched while Wallenski ordered the drinks at the bar. The barman was surly and seemed irritated at having his quiet afternoon ruined by the inconvenience of having to serve customers. The table was ringed with the stains of countless forgotten drinks and when Wallenski set two more glasses down, the marks from those joined the anonymity of the others.

Tomas picked up his beer and took a long pull, wiping the froth from his top lip with the back of his hand. The first normal alcohol he had touched for four years, and it soon left him light-headed. The homemade stuff inside was only any good for numbing the brain and most of the senses. His friend sat down opposite and stared at him over the rim of his glass as he greedily drank his beer. "It's been a long time since we shared a beer, Tomas," he said.

Czerwinski nodded and stubbed out his cigarette in the overflowing ashtray. "I keep having, I don't know, visions, Pawel."

Wallenski shook his head. "I don't believe in anything I can't see, hear, or touch. What sort of visions, religious?"

"No." Czerwinski shook his head impatiently. "I'm being followed, stalked, by the . . . I'm not sure what." Czerwinski watched his friend's face, ready to interpret his reaction. There was a slight tensing of the muscles around Wallenski's mouth, and a brief look of pity registered in his eyes. The reaction was transitory, replaced quickly with a smile and a laugh.

Tomas waited for the laughter to subside, then said, "I'm not joking."

The smile dropped from Wallenski's face. "Haunted?"

"Not actually haunted, but that's what it seems like. You know how they say that houses, the walls, can soak up bad things that happen inside them? Some houses feel happy, while others feel sad as soon as you walk into them. In prison there isn't much happiness, but there is an awful lot of sadness and despair. That must build up into something almost tangible. Sometimes inside there was a feeling, an atmosphere. We knew when something was going to happen; an inmate was going to knife another, or a minor riot was going to start. I was new to it all, but it was kind of explained to me once, in my first year, by a man I used to share a cell with."

Wallenski held his hands up and shook his head. "Hold on a minute, Tomas. Can you hear yourself?"

"Of course I know what I'm saying. And I'm saying it to you because you're my oldest friend, and you're the *only* person I thought I could tell this to who wouldn't think I was losing my mind. But obviously you do."

"I'm not saying that, Tomas . . . but, I mean . . ."

Czerwinski downed the remainder of his beer and got to his feet. "Thanks for the drink, Pawel. I'll see you around."

"Sit down. Don't take offense. But even you have to admit, it's not exactly . . . normal, is it?"

"No, it's not *normal*, but that's the whole point. My life has been anything but normal these past four years. Inside you can't play by the normal rules or you go under. This . . . feeling I've brought out with me was something I've lived with every hour of every day for years."

Wallenski stared down at the table, avoiding his friend's eyes, embarrassed. "I don't know what to say."

"I don't want you to say anything. Just hear me out. You were always good at that, a good listener. Listen to me now, because if I don't tell somebody about this, if I don't unload it, I think I *am* going to go mad."

Wallenski shrugged and checked his watch. He supposed

it was the least he could do; after all, they had been friends for years.

Lucja took the steps down to the towpath. Since Pawel had taken the car and Julia had indicated, none too politely, that she would prefer if Lucja leave, she had no alternative but to walk home, and the canal route was the quickest. She had really screwed up this time—only because she wanted to help Tomas out. When she had seen him in the garden he had looked so . . . so desperate. As though the world were closing in on him.

She felt a pang deep inside, a resonance of what might have been had circumstances been different. She loved Tomas, had always loved him, and in a way marrying Pawel had been a way to stay close to Tomas Czerwinski and at least see him on a regular basis. Not for one moment did she think that Pawel would see through her plan, but he was more perceptive than she could have imagined, and their marriage had suffered the repercussions ever since.

She caught a glimpse of something moving in the bracken ahead of her. At first she thought it was a cat, and then *cats* because there was more than one thing moving. Something rustled the ferns behind her, and she turned sharply. She could see nothing.

She walked on, quickening her pace. She had done this walk countless times before, and it had never bothered her. The bracken was low growing, and there were no trees for anyone to hide behind. A stout, chain-link fence bordered one side of the path while the canal edged the other. There was nobody else around and no reason whatsoever to feel nervous. But she did. The hairs on her arms and on the back of her neck were prickling, and she kept seeing shapes flitting around ahead of her—dark shadowy shapes with no form, like ragged, half-transparent pieces of black cloth, eddying in an unfelt breeze.

* * *

"Leon Eile was a killer. I was put in his cell when I first arrived at the prison. Of course, if the prison authorities had known the extent of his crimes, he would have been in solitary in some high-security block or other. But as far as they knew, he was inside on a manslaughter charge. The other killings he told me about later. Nine in all: men, women, and children. He didn't care—he didn't discriminate. He had a lust for killing, and because the killings were *so* random, so indiscriminate, the police really didn't have a hope of catching him."

"But he *was* in prison," Pawel observed.

"Killing a pedestrian while drunk at the wheel. He used to laugh about that. His one unplanned, accidental killing and he was banged up for it. It was he who told me about the shadows on the prison walls and how they got there."

Wallenski swallowed some beer and decided not to interrupt.

"He called them breathers," Czerwinski said. "He described them as living shadows and said he could see them and hear them, and they were marking all those people for death, telling him who the next victim would be. He had been in prison for most of his life, and he had learned how to control them and use them."

Wallenski drained his glass. "Well, that's not so unusual. A lot of serial killers have claimed to hear voices telling them to commit their crimes. All bloody mad, the lot of them."

"Yes, I agree. The only problem is, *I've* seen them too."

Wallenski said, "I hoped you weren't going to say that. Another beer?"

Czerwinski nodded. The first had gone straight to his head, and his mind was swimming. He had hoped he would feel better unburdening himself like this, but the more he spoke, the more he told Pawel about the past few years, the more he felt that he was losing his mind.

Wallenski put the beer on the table and sat down heavily. "Describe them to me, what do they look like?" he said.

"The breathers?"

"Yeah. You say you've seen them—so describe them."

Czerwinski thought for a moment. "I can't," he said. "At least not with any clarity. They're black, shapeless. I don't know. It's like Eile said—they're living shadows. They seem to flit about on the periphery of your vision. Like seeing something out of the corner of your eye, but when you turn around to get a really good look, it's not there. He said they're the residue of all the bad things that happen in the cells and the badness the prisoners bring in with them. As they spend hour after hour locked up, the . . . well, evil, I suppose, seeps out of them and gets soaked into the floors and the walls." Czerwinski sniffed as if trying to make light of it. "Of course, it's all probably old cons' stories, and Eile was winding up a new boy. None of it's real."

"Nor are the breathers, Tomas. They're not there at all. It's like I said earlier: you're overwrought. I know it made you laugh, but I truly believe you are. And I believe you need to seek help. A doctor . . . Even talking to Julia would be a start. You've had a terrible time of it. You've had four years of your life snatched away from you. Helena has left you. These things are bound to leave scars. You wouldn't be human if you weren't deeply affected in some way by it. But really, all this talk of shadows . . . and these *breathers* . . ." He gave a snort of derision.

The sense of danger was becoming oppressive, and Lucja quickened her pace. The bracken seemed alive now. There were black shapes everywhere, dancing on the path in front of her, skimming across the water of the canal, making the undergrowth rustle and move. She took one more look behind her, and a cry burst from her lips. Not more than three paces behind her was a man; at least it looked like a man, but most of his face and body were in shadow.

The heels of her shoes were hampering her flight and as she ran she kicked them off, ignoring the pain of the sharp gravel as it drove into the soles of her feet. Her breath was coming in short stabbing gasps, and her lungs were on fire. She glanced back. The figure was still behind her, at exactly the same distance—it hadn't gained ground or receded. She could see a gate in the fence ahead. Beyond the gate was the road and comparative safety. The road was busy, and it was only early evening. There had to be *somebody* around.

She was about to veer toward the gate when the flitting shadows came at her, rushing at her legs, entangling themselves around her ankles. With a choking cry, she pitched forward into the freezing, filthy water of the canal.

Water poured into her mouth and down her throat, but she felt surprisingly calm. She was an excellent swimmer, and as she kicked out with her legs, her head broke the surface. She coughed and spat out the filthy canal water, gulped in air, and looked back at the towpath. It was deserted. Her confusion lasted only for a second before hands, infinitely colder than the water, grabbed her ankles and pulled her down to the canal bed.

"What happened to this Leon Eile? If he was the master criminal you portray him as, surely his whole aim would be to get out of prison and start killing again."

Tomas Czerwinski laughed bitterly. "It was, believe me, it was. Remember, I shared a cell with him for two years, and for one of those years it was just the two of us. He had plenty of time to tell me his plans. He believed that the only thing holding him back from true greatness—that's how he saw his killing spree—was his physical form. He told me time and time again that he longed to be free of his prison, and he wasn't talking about jail. He was talking about his body. He believed that his own death would liberate him, that he would become *one* with the breathers.

"I was the one who found him in the cell when he'd hanged himself. His face was blue, tongue lolling out, but his eyes were open, and I can only describe the look in them as triumphant."

Wallenski leaned forward in his chair. He was absorbed in the story now, despite his doubts about his friend's sanity. "All right, so he killed himself. Why does all this worry you now? You're out—he's dead. Start again, Tomas. Put all that behind you."

"I think the breathers got out with me. Whether it's Eile controlling them or not, I don't know, but I think they're following me."

Wallenski looked at his watch. "I think I'd better get you home," he said.

"Is that all you're going to say?" Czerwinski said, suddenly angry. "You don't believe me, do you?"

Wallenski rested his elbows on the table and leaned forward. "Tomas, if I had sat you down and told you a story like that, you'd be telephoning for the men in the white coats."

Czerwinski opened his mouth to protest.

Wallenski waved him down. "No, don't deny it, because you know it's true. Before you went inside, you were one of the most down-to-earth guys I knew. I could always come to you for sensible advice, for a well-reasoned argument. What you've been telling me here is neither sensible nor well-reasoned, and frankly I don't believe a word of it." He got to his feet. "Come on, I'm taking you home, and I want you to promise me you'll go and see a doctor."

Czerwinski stared up bleakly at his oldest friend and realized he had been wasting his time. He got to his feet and followed Wallenski out of the pub.

"You're probably right," Czerwinski said. "I probably *do* need to see someone about it."

"No doubt about it. I'm glad you're starting to see sense."

They were about a hundred yards away from Wallenski's car. Czerwinski stopped. "Look, Pawel, I owe Julia an apology. I'm going to walk home. I need to clear my head."

"Are you sure? I mean, of course you can do what you like, but . . ."

"What you were saying makes a lot of sense, but I need to get it straight in my mind. A walk will do me good."

Wallenski nodded. "Fair enough." He started back to his car alone. Czerwinski breathed a sigh of relief. He needed to get as far away from here as possible. He had said nothing to his old friend, but as they came out of the pub, there, on the other side of the street, standing in the shadow of a shop doorway, was the pale form of Leon Eile, a wide grin on his face, an evil glint in his eyes.

Czerwinski looked from Wallenski's departing form to the shop doorway. Eile had gone.

When he reached the car, Wallenski looked back and waved, then slipped inside and started the engine.

They came from nowhere and everywhere. Flitting across the road, seeping out from the shadows, the breathers moved toward the car. They looked like nothing more than scraps of black rag, though less substantial than cloth, but Tomas Czerwinski knew that these were the harbingers of his friend's death.

They were swooping on the car, passing straight through the bodywork, filling the interior with their shadows. And as Czerwinski stared at the departing car, a face appeared in the rear window staring back at him. A slow smile spread across Leon Eile's face as he flicked his hair back from his eyes.

Tomas opened his mouth, to scream out a warning, but before the words could even reach his lips, he knew it was too late. The petrol tanker was barreling down the road a hundred yards away from the car. If Pawel had only kept a straight course, he would have passed it safely. But just as the tanker reached him, he spun the steering wheel and hit it head-on. Czerwinski could see the look of horror etched on the tanker driver's face as the small hatchback disappeared under his wheels in a scream of twisting metal.

Czerwinski turned away from the carnage. Wallenski was dead. No one could have lived through that. The breathers had killed him. He knew he ought to stay, to offer help, but he couldn't face it. He couldn't bear to see his best friend's twisted and mangled body, knowing that he, Tomas Czerwinski, was responsible for it.

He started to walk, back past the pub, dropping down from the road to the canal towpath. Already he could hear the sirens as the emergency services raced to the scene. He tried to block out the sounds, lowering his head and quickening his pace. Finally, when he had walked half a mile or more, the sirens faded into the distance, and the only sound he heard was that of his feet crunching on the gravel path.

There was something on the path ahead of him, something white—a pair of shoes. He stopped walking and looked down at them. The shoes were Italian, well made, and expensive, and for some reason he couldn't quite understand why they were significant. He stood staring at the shoes for minutes before a movement ahead drew his attention. Three black, formless shapes slithered into the canal.

Seconds later something else broke the surface of the water. He took two paces and recoiled when he realized it was the body of Lucja, floating there, unnaturally faceup, dead eyes staring into infinity. He rammed his fist into his mouth and bit his knuckles, drawing blood, to stop himself screaming. First Pawel, now Lucja. *Was no one he knew safe?*

The answer came to him with shocking clarity. No, nobody he knew was safe, because somehow the breathers had been released with him. Julia, Jacek, Czerwinski's entire family and all his friends were potential targets. As he stared down at Lucja's strangely peaceful body floating on the torpid water of the canal, facedown now, he realized what he had to do. Burying his hands deep in his pockets, and keeping his head out of the freshening wind, he walked back to town.

The multistory car park was high and accessible. He slipped under the barrier, paused to let his eyes adjust to the gloom, then walked past the cars to the elevator at the back of the car park. Once inside he pressed the button for the roof.

The wind had picked up, and it cut through the thin cotton of his shirt as he crossed the tarmac and climbed onto the highest wall of the car park. He stood there looking down at the road below. Now he was here and staring death in the face, he wasn't certain he could go through with it. It should have been so easy to step off the wall into space and to drop like a stone, but it was as if he was paralyzed, frozen in this spot, never to move again.

He felt a cool breath on his neck and a voice whispered into his ear. "*Can you see them, Tomas? Can you see the breathers?*" And as he looked down, he could. They were pouring out onto the street, emerging from under parked cars, flying out from open windows, whirling and spinning through the air, black and shadowy, gathering below, calling him down.

The formless shape materialized beside him. "*Don't you want to join them, Tomas?*"

Czerwinski turned and thrust out his hand. It went deep inside the wavering figure, but eventually he felt something hard, and he gripped it tightly. The shadow shape shivered like a fish on a hook, trying to free itself. Czerwinski held on and tightened his grip. He had no death wish, but he wanted to ensure his family was safe. He wanted to guarantee the breathers returned to their prison home.

He pulled as hard as he could, and gradually he felt something inside the shape tear and his hand began to pull out.

As it did, the shadows on the tarmac behind them rushed forward and molded into the cloudlike shape, adding to its bulk. It towered over Czerwinski now, his whole body all but immersed into it as he struggled to pull the shifting center out. Then, suddenly, it was free and the emaciated figure of Leon Eile lay in front of Czerwinski. The shadow shape reared and opened up like a flower, a black pulsating mass of fleeting shadows and movement. Deep inside there seemed to be eyes, red, yellow, peering out wide and beckoning. Muted screams echoed from within the dark body.

Czerwinski grabbed the cold, slippery figure of Eile and hoisted it onto the wall. With one hard shove the body was in midair, shadows opening in greeting, and then the broken body on the road below was covered with a swarm of them.

The black shape behind Czerwinski billowed into the air, then folded in on itself, sinking into the ground where it soaked away like a black pool.

Czerwinski shook his head sadly. Then he opened his arms wide, stepped out onto the ledge, and called the breathers home as he launched himself into the air.

Pike excused himself and moved to the pavement to be alone. Jacek Czerwinski's tears were heartfelt and deep. It was only polite to let him grieve in peace. No one wanted an audience at such times.

When Pike sat again he said, "And Julia?"

Jacek looked at him, rubbing his eyes. "We held the funeral. Arrangements were made for people to come back to Tomas's house. We came, she did not. I have not seen her since. I've since learned that the boyfriend who lent her the car that day to collect Tomas from the prison was Wladyslaw Kaminski. A name I've become very familiar with over the past few years."

Chapter Eighteen

King's College Hospital, London, England

Crozier considered Jane to be one of the department's greatest assets. She'd earned a master's degree in psychology at Cambridge and possessed an astute and incisive mind. Intellectually, Jane could wipe the floor with the majority of the department—in fact, with most of the people Crozier knew, himself included.

Crozier's only reservation about her had been her tendency to let domesticity come between herself and her work. He'd known David, her husband, for years, and was indirectly responsible for bringing the two of them together, but he had grown to feel that David was the worst thing that could have happened to her. Being with David had softened her and dampened much of the fire that had previously enlivened her work.

So, much against his better judgment, he had been pleased when David left Jane and she in turn took up with Carter. Much as Crozier despised Carter, he somehow thought the two of them as a couple would enhance their work for the department.

Jane held on to Carter's hand. "Well, say something."

The pain he had felt when he was brought into hospital was immense, but it was physical. The pain that followed Jane's words was far deeper. He was going to lose her again. "When did you see him?"

"You know I see him. We've got the girls." Surely she didn't need to explain to him how it tore her apart seeing her daughters so upset that Mummy and Daddy didn't live together anymore.

Gemma and Amy did their best to put on a brave face when they were with David, but both he and Jane could see how hard it was for them. Neither of the girls wanted to take sides; they didn't see it as different sides. In their young way, they thought they must have done something wrong if their parents didn't want to be with them.

"Yes, I know. I'm sorry. What about David's girlfriend?"

Jane looked out the dusty window. That gesture told Carter all he needed to know. "She was never really a girlfriend. Just a fling."

Jane's mother had blamed her, of course. She had come to stay for a few weeks while Jane coped on her own. Brenda never missed an opportunity to let Jane know it was her fault her husband had left her. She would sympathize but in a *what a disappointment you are* tone of voice. Jane had heard that same tone so many times in her life it almost didn't affect her anymore. Almost, she told herself, almost.

"A fling? We know about those don't we, Jane?"

She hadn't thought David knew about her affair, but of course people always do know.

She had changed during and since, to the extent that he must have suspected something was happening. It wasn't planned; these things rarely were. Jane and Carter worked together. They saw each other, on and off, for a few months in London. Whenever they were in the capital together—a movie, sightseeing. Flirting, stolen kisses, but never stepping over the line; not until Paris.

An assignment in Europe that appeared on the face of it to concern the department. The trip concluded in Paris and a drunken meal in their hotel ended with only one of their rooms being used that night. In the morning, expecting embarrassment, she opened her eyes and was surprised to find Robert already awake. They made love again in the glistening dawn and found themselves speaking of feelings deeper than a mere work-trip coupling.

Jane found Carter to be far more sensitive than she expected, and her own emotions hoodwinked her as she told him things about herself and her life that she didn't even believe she had told her husband.

They had three more days and two more glorious nights in Paris. Room service in this romantic city didn't blink an eye as they delivered to one room one night and the other the next. It was on the last afternoon, as they talked about how they could continue when they returned home that Jane saw the darker side of Robert Carter.

In retrospect, as she settled back into some kind of normality with her husband and children, she told herself Carter was just being sensible, was even being a gentleman in allowing her to escape back to reality without any baggage. It hurt all the same.

That afternoon, with bags packed and clothes scattered around them, he told her he cared for her but they should end it now. He didn't use the clichés of not wanting to hurt her or it being for the best. He was economical with his words, careful but decisive. Apart from working assignments, Jane hadn't seen him since.

Until they were assigned to a case concerning ley lines and a Scottish island. Working together on Kulsay Island, they found the power of what they felt too great. That it coincided with David leaving was the catalyst.

Carter realized now that it was David leaving that had been the spur that enabled Jane to start up a relationship with him again. If David hadn't left, would he and Jane have got together again?

"Robert," she said. "Is that what you think we're doing? Having a fling?"

"Aren't we?"

"Paris was a fling. Those kisses on the London Eye were a

fling. Surely the last few months have meant more than a quick . . ."

"Quick what?"

"Fuck, a quick fuck and move on. Is that what you think?"

"So why are you going back to him?"

She picked up her bottle of water and drank some. She was careful to screw the cap back on. Carter couldn't believe what was happening, but he knew he had to.

"He's asked me. I haven't said yes."

"So what *about* the girlfriend?"

"She's taken a job in New York. Moved on."

"So he gets dumped and wants his wife back."

"It's not like that. It's complicated. The girls really miss him."

Carter took some of his water, spilling most down his front. "And you?"

"Me what?"

"Do you miss him?"

She burst into tears.

Carter rubbed her arm. There were goose bumps from her wrist to her elbow. Still sobbing, she flung herself onto him, ignoring the drips but managing to avoid them. He hugged her the best he could.

"I love you, Rob. I always have and I always will."

"Don't leave me." There were tears in his eyes now.

Jane stiffened in his arms, and he released his hold slightly.

She rubbed her eyes as she sat upright. "I have to. Just for a while. Just while I sort out the girls. Gemma has her new school, and Amy . . ."

"Jane. I love you."

The plastic chair made just a small clatter as it toppled over. Jane pushed away and ran from the room.

For breath is life, and if you breathe well you will live long on earth.
—Sanskrit Proverb

Chapter Nineteen

Dublin, Republic of Ireland

Clutching a fresh bottle of Jameson's Irish whiskey, Simon Crozier made his way up the tiled path to the Victorian ruin that was Harry Bailey's house. The house had been in decline since the mid-1980s, and Harry had done nothing to arrest the gradual decay. Crozier tugged at the bellpull, half-expecting it to come off in his hand.

"Just a minute!" Harry's voice sounded from somewhere deep in the house.

A full two minutes passed before Crozier heard the bolt being pulled back. Another key turned and then the door opened with a sound like a pig being slaughtered.

Cigarette smoke and alcohol fumes wafted into the still Irish night, washing over Crozier and making him take a step back. "Jesus, Harry, you just wiped ten years off my life expectancy. There's passive smoking and there's *passive smoking!*"

"Shut your mouth, you miserable old sod." Bailey swung his huge frame into the doorway, cigarette hanging defiantly from his grinning mouth, a glass of amber liquid clasped fiercely in his hand. "If you're going to stay, you'll keep your bloody health-conscious opinions to yourself."

Crozier stood back, his hands on his hips, shaking his head. "Remarkable. You haven't aged a jot. What's your secret?"

"If I told you, you wouldn't believe me."

"Try me."

Bailey shrugged. "Cigarettes, alcohol, and sex."

"The first two I get, but I thought you swore off women for life after your divorce."

The grin widened. "I have a couple of young ladies who come to the house to do for me . . . and I don't mean cleaning and making beds, though they sometimes perform those services as well."

"You old rogue. I don't believe a word of it."

Bailey shrugged again, more expansively this time. "Suit your bloody self," he said, then made a gap in the doorway. "Well, are you coming in, or are you going to stand there all night like an idiot?"

Crozier shook his head resignedly and followed Harry Bailey into the house.

"Have you eaten?" Bailey asked as he led Crozier through to the ramshackle lounge.

"On the plane."

"That's not food. I wouldn't give a dog the garbage they serve up. A pitiful excuse for a meal, and they have the bloody cheek to charge for it. I've got a lamb casserole in the oven. Interested?"

Crozier could smell the mouth-watering aroma eddying out from the kitchen.

"I could be tempted."

"Good," Bailey said. "Let's eat. Then you can tell me about your love life with the boys young enough to be your sons."

Later, with a full belly and more than his usual quota of alcohol inside him, Crozier collapsed onto the overstuffed couch in the lounge and kicked off his shoes. "That was good," he said. "When did you learn to cook like that?"

"I've had plenty of time on my hands since I left the department." Bailey sat on one of the armchairs adjacent to the couch and poured whiskey from the near-empty bottle of Jameson's. He offered the bottle to Crozier, who covered the top of his glass and shook his head.

"Lightweight," Bailey said disparagingly.

"I've got to drive to Dunkerry in the morning to see Michael Dylan."

"Dylan? He's over here?"

"On leave."

"Well he couldn't have chosen a nicer spot. Dunkerry's a quaint little village, typically Irish. It only needs its own leprechaun and it'd be perfect. Why are you making such an effort? I remember a time when you only had to snap your fingers and you'd have people falling over themselves to work with you."

"Times change," Crozier said. "A few of the recent operations have not worked out as intended. As a result, the department's lost people for the first time in its history."

"Kulsay?" Bailey asked.

Crozier looked startled. He was convinced that the department's work, at least the more serious cases, were strictly private. "Where did you hear that?"

"Whispers, Simon. Even stuck over here I hear whispers. Are they true?"

Crozier recovered himself and smiled slightly. "That would depend on what you've heard."

"I've heard enough. It would explain why you're over here breaking into Michael Dylan's leave. Is there anybody left in Whitehall?"

"McKinley's still there, along with a few of the others, and the backroom staff of course. Carter's bloody hospitalized. But you're right. The department's lacking in what I call the heavy artillery at the moment. I need to persuade Dylan to come back to work. Hence the trip to Dunkerry."

"So, are you going to tell me what it's all about?"

"All in good time," Crozier said.

"What does that mean?"

"It means I can't talk about it yet."

"Bullshit! Of course you can. It's me, remember? Harry Bailey. The best bloody psychic the department's ever seen."

"If you're so bloody good, you should know what it's all about," Crozier said.

"Don't get cute." He closed his eyes and moved his hand in front of his face. "I'm seeing a name," he said, with all the drama of a stage magician. "It begins with an H. Helsing . . . Humphrey . . . Holly!" He snapped his eyes open and grinned at Crozier.

Crozier's face registered no surprise at all. He'd known Bailey too long to be impressed by his powers. He clapped his hands slowly. "Very good, Harry," he said. "You could make a living at the end of a pier somewhere. All you need is a crystal ball and a turban."

Bailey skewered Crozier with a look. "So you're not going to tell me?"

"As I said, I can't talk about it yet," Crozier said. "I'm waiting for Martin Impey to send me some information. When I have more details I'll tell you. In fact I'll tell you when we get to Dunkerry and meet with Dylan. It'll save me going through it twice."

Bailey's eyes narrowed. "What do you mean, when *we* get to Dunkerry?"

"I was thinking about it on the flight over. I could really use you on this one."

Bailey said nothing for a moment. He dragged a fresh pack of cigarettes from his pocket, peeled it open, and popped a cigarette between his lips. As he flicked his Zippo, his eyes squinted and he stared down at the lighted end. "And what makes you think I'd be interested in taking on another case?" he said, blowing a thin trail of blue smoke at the ceiling and letting the rest trickle out through his nose.

"I can tell from the short time I've spent with you that you're bored out of your skull. Cooking, for Christ's sake!"

"I'm a good cook."

Crozier nodded. "Yes, yes you are, but, as you said yourself, you're also a bloody gifted *sensitive* and I think you miss the chase."

Bailey inhaled again and couldn't stop the smile spreading over his lips. "And you expect me to say yes, without giving me a clue what it's all about?"

"You've had your clue. Holly."

"Which tells me precisely nothing."

"Listen, Harry, come with me to Dunkerry. We'll meet with Dylan together. I'll brief him and then you can decide whether you're in or out. How's that?"

Harry Bailey considered it for a moment. Then he said, "It'll have to do." He lifted the bottle again. "Nightcap?"

Crozier shook his head. "No, I'm off to my bed. I need a clear head for tomorrow. Michael Dylan can be a tricky bugger, full on Irish blarney a lot of the time, but a very deep thinker and very sharp. I need to be on top of my game to handle him."

"Handle him?"

"Trying to pin him down is like wrestling with smoke, and I need him on this one, Harry."

"Almost as much as you need me?"

"Almost." Crozier swallowed the last of his whiskey and got to his feet. He swayed slightly and silently cursed Bailey's overgenerous measures, then walked to the door. "I'll see you in the morning," he said, and headed toward the stairs, leaving Bailey alone with his thoughts and the rest of the Jameson's.

Once in his room, Crozier pulled his PDA from his bag and checked for messages. Martin Impey hadn't let him down. There were pages of new information to wade through. He undressed quickly and slipped between the sheets, settling down to read.

He surprised himself by first reading the updated report on Carter's progress.

Chapter Twenty

Krakow, Poland

Jacek Czerwinski sat at the table overlooking the square for a long time after Jason Pike had taken his leave. The story Pike had told made some kind of sense. It confirmed some of the theories that had been forming in his mind for the last year, that he was up against forces so powerful, so far reaching, that one man working alone could not hope to defeat them.

He stared out across the square, watching people going about their daily lives, oblivious to the fact that to Pike's creatures they were nothing more than fodder.

"They're parasites," Pike told him. "Their continued existence is dependent on the human race. They need the human life force, your essence . . . your souls in order to survive. These creatures are the reality behind the myth of the vampire. Those who created and perpetuated that myth mistakenly believed it was human *blood* they thirsted for. And you can see why. Life blood, life force; it's easy to confuse the two. Your investigations have brought you very close to the truth, Jacek—in fact, you are *too* close to the truth for some—and yet you're finding it difficult to accept what I'm saying."

"I'm listening, aren't I?"

"Yes, but do you believe me?"

"I believe there's a conspiracy. That the majority of the disappearances are linked in some way. I'm certain of that."

Pike smiled. "And that's why you can't get anywhere with the police. You present them with your theories and they laugh in your face."

"I know I'm right," Jacek said, quietly, almost to himself.

"Yes, you are . . . to a degree. You also believe that those involved in this conspiracy are not only in the upper echelons of the police force, but also reaching higher, into government itself."

Jacek nodded.

"Which is why your investigations have foundered, quashed before you can do any real damage to the conspirators?"

"It's the only thing that makes sense," Jacek said.

"I agree, but what would you say if I told you that this conspiracy isn't just limited to Poland but encompasses the whole of Eastern Europe: Romania, Bulgaria, Serbia, Croatia. It even reaches deep into Russia."

Jacek looked at him sharply.

"It's true, my friend. In fact it's not just limited to Eastern Europe. In nearly every country of the world people are plucked from their lives, never to be seen again. And this isn't a recent phenomenon. It has been happening for years, for centuries. It's a conspiracy on a global scale."

Jacek paid his bill and took a slow, meandering walk back toward his apartment, his mind picking Pike's story apart, examining each aspect of it, and trying to dismiss it as the ramblings of a deranged mind. He was so lost in his thoughts he failed to notice the black Fiat with its lights off, crawling along the road a hundred yards back, tailing him.

A few minutes later he became aware of the car's engine. As he glanced back along the road, the car's lights came on, glaring into his eyes. The engine surged and before he could move, before he realized what was happening, the Fiat was beside him, the doors flying open.

Three men leaped from the car, two of them grabbing Jacek, twisting his arms behind his back. The third man had something hard and heavy in his hand. His arm swung, and the heavy object cracked down on Jacek's skull. There was a searing pain, a bright, flashing light, and then blackness as he was hauled into the back of the Fiat.

Focusing on the act of breathing clears the mind of all daily distractions and clears our energy enabling us to better connect with the Spirit within.
—Author Unknown

Chapter Twenty-one

King's College Hospital, London, England

It was quiet in Carter's room. The plastic chair vibrated for a short while after Jane had left, but that had long since gone still.

Carter wished his mind could also be still.

For all his abilities, all his precognition, awareness, and skill, this was something he hadn't seen coming. He loved Jane, and he knew—thought he knew—that she felt the same way.

He had treated her badly some time ago, immediately after the Paris trip, but he had done that to protect her. He didn't want her to feel obliged to him then, to have the guilt that would inevitably be part of the fallout of telling her husband. Then there were the two young children.

He had judged, rightly or wrongly, that he should end the affair before it began. He hadn't realized just how much that decision would affect him, how much he missed and needed her. Or how much she resented him for, in her eyes, using and dumping her.

When they were able to rekindle the relationship, on that cursed Scottish island, it felt so right that he knew it was the only thing to do.

A whisper in his ear did warn him that she had perhaps wanted the relationship again because David had left her and seemingly found someone else. But Robert was so pleased that they were together again that he pushed doubt to one side.

Now, as soon as David called, she was back with her husband again. Yet, "I love you, Rob." She had said it emphatically, no strings, no doubts, no uncertainties.

So why did he feel so uncertain now?

The door to his hospital room opened and Paula, the nurse on current shift, came in. She took his temperature, checked the monitors and the drips, and fussed with his pillows and bedcovers.

"How are we today, Robert?"

The *we* was their little joke, built up over a few visits. There was a doctor who always asked the patient how *we* were, never listening to the reply before plowing on with "good," "splendid," and other banalities.

Paula asked her question with a complicit grin.

"We are fine. How are we?"

"We, *I* am fine, but then I've not been beaten up, brought into A&E, then attacked in my room by God knows what."

"You should get out more."

Paula opened the window a little. "Was that your girlfriend I saw leaving? She looked nice."

Carter shut his eyes and sighed. Paula noticed. She also

noticed the guarded reply when he opened his eyes and looked at her. "Nice. Yes, she is."

Paula was not even thirty, but she had seen life. "Married?"

Carter nodded, impressed. "With children."

"It's you she wants, though."

Carter forced a smile; he wasn't so sure. "Female intuition?"

Paula snorted her derision. "Lot of twaddle, that is. Because we're female we're psychic, are we? I don't think so."

Carter resisted commenting on the psychic aspect, though it reminded him that Jane was not only battling with emotions about splitting with David, but was having to come to terms with rediscovering her psychic powers. She had been forced to admit them to herself after years of denial. That had taken a lot out of her. He also had to remember that only recently the Kulsay case had taken a huge physical and emotional toll.

"So if it's not because you're female, then how do you know?"

Paula ticked the chart at the foot of the bed. She produced some tablets from her pocket. "Here, take these." She held the glass of water to his lips, though once the neck brace had been removed he found he was able to move relatively freely. "Not because I'm female, no, but because I was in love with a doctor once, and he loved his wife, who in turn loved him. I did a lot of crying, just like your girlfriend as she left here today."

Carter guessed Jane would cry as she left; it was a hard thing she had decided.

Paula opened the door. "Sobbing she was. Your dinner won't be long. Try to rest."

Chapter Twenty-two

Krakow, Poland

As his senses came crawling back, Jacek became aware of the smell of warm vinyl. He was being held down, flat against the backseat of the Fiat. He didn't struggle. His head was aching so hard from the blow it felt as if his brain had been dislodged and was floating about in his skull. The driver seemed to be finding every pothole and bump in the road, and with each bump, brain crashed against bone, sending a new wave of pain scorching through his head.

He tried to keep count of the passing seconds but soon realized he was phasing in and out of consciousness. Eventually he stopped fighting it and let himself drift.

He was vaguely aware the car had stopped. He heard voices; then the door opened and hard hands pulled him from the vehicle. There was no strength in his legs, and when he tried to stand, his knees gave way and he crumpled to the ground.

"Get him on his feet!" someone snapped, and more hands grabbed him under the arms, hauling him upright and propping him against the side of the Fiat. Someone yanked his hair, forcing his head backward. A flashlight beam glared into his eyes, blinding him. He couldn't see who was holding the flashlight and could only make out the indistinct outlines of the people surrounding him.

"He's all right. Get him inside."

And then he was being half-carried, half-dragged across the stony ground. A house loomed in front of him, and he was pulled up a short flight of stone steps. A door opened, and someone pushed him through it. He lost his footing and fell again. This time he was left to get up by himself, encouraged by a well-aimed boot to the solar plexus. "On your feet!"

Jacek looked up at the man who had kicked him. He was quite small, but stocky, his muscles looking hard and toned, stretching the Metallica T-shirt he wore. The man kept smiling and pulled his foot back to kick again. Jacek swore under his breath and pushed himself to his feet. The man took his arm and led him across the flagstone hallway to another door. With his free hand, the man twisted the handle and pushed the door open. "Inside," he said and let go of Jacek's arm.

The room was dimly lit and heavily shadowed. He could make out two chairs, wingback and large, that faced a dying log fire surrounded by a marble fireplace.

"Don't stand there all night, Jacek. Come closer." A woman's voice came from the direction of the fireplace, speaking in English but with an American accent. The voice was husky, almost seductive. "I said come closer. I want to see you."

Jacek walked shakily across the worn rug toward the fire. When he reached the chairs, he hesitated for a moment before looking down at the woman who sat there. She was in her late twenties, possibly early thirties, and beautiful. Her blonde hair was cut into a long layered bob that framed delicate features: soft, full lips; a straight, perfectly proportioned nose; and the bluest eyes he had ever seen.

"Good evening," she said. "I must apologize for the manner of your arrival here, but I didn't think a simple invitation would have persuaded you to come."

Jacek continued to stare at her. She looked familiar, but he couldn't bring to mind where he'd seen her before.

She seemed amused by his interest. A slight smile played on her lips and traveled up to her eyes, making them glint in the firelight. "My name is Rachel Grey," she said, the amusement reaching her voice. "Sit down, Jacek." She indicated the vacant chair. "We have a lot to talk about."

What the hell, Jacek thought. If he didn't sit down soon, he'd fall down. He slumped into the chair next to her.

"You've become a thorn in the side of many people in this country. Did you realize that?"

Jacek said nothing.

"So much so that I have been asked to take care of you. And by that, I don't mean I'm here to look out for your welfare. They want me to eradicate you, to make you go away . . . permanently."

"So what are you waiting for? I assume you're waiting for something. Otherwise your thugs would have taken me somewhere private and killed me."

"That's very true. And I'm going out on a limb here by not following instructions. I just feel that, pain in the ass though you are, you're more useful to me alive than dead."

"Useful to you? How?" Jacek was intrigued, despite himself.

She smiled. It was a smile that lit up her face and made her even more beautiful. "I believe you met with Jason Pike tonight," she said.

For a moment Jacek said nothing. So they *were* watching him.

"He approached me, yes," Jacek said guardedly. His head was throbbing, and having to squint to see her clearly in the light from the fire was doing him no favors.

She nodded. "Quite. And I suspect he told you an amazing story, most of which was true."

His eyes widened slightly as he took this onboard.

"He told you about a race of beings living alongside humans like yourself, feeding off your life force. Tell me, did he use the charming phrase 'soul fuckers'? He probably did. It's a favorite of his."

"So what are you telling me? He's right? These creatures exist?"

Her smile widened. "Of course. You are in the company of one of them at this very moment."

Jacek started from his seat, but she quickly laid a hand across his arm. "Don't be alarmed. As I said, I don't intend to harm you."

He relaxed slightly, took a breath. "Was it you who ransacked my apartment?"

She laughed, a soft sound, like water flowing over stones. "No, Jacek. That wasn't us. Jason Pike broke into your apartment and trashed it. We've been watching him for weeks as well. That's how we found out he was interested in you. Jason is building an army to fight us. He's recruiting, and I think he sees you as a useful asset."

Jacek shook his head. "So why would he wreck my apartment? It doesn't make sense."

"In his mind it does. By blaming *us* for the break-in, it made you feel that you were in some kind of danger from us. I suspect it was a ploy to persuade you to join forces with him." She paused and reached over to the fireplace, picking up a poker from the hearth and stabbing at a dead-looking log in the grate, flipping it over. The log popped and hissed as new flames leapt up.

"You see," she said, pointing at the log with the poker and looking up at him. "With the right manipulation, it's easy to breathe fire into the most unpromising materials."

Jacek stared into the grate. "Okay, so what do *you* want from me?"

Rachel Grey ignored the question. "There's one very important thing you should know about Jason Pike," she said. "And that is, he is not quite what he seems."

"Really?" Jacek said, with the best attempt at disinterest he could manage.

"I don't mean his duplicity and manipulations. This is

something much more basic." She paused, weighing her next sentence carefully. "Jason Pike is not human. He is, in fact, one of us."

Jacek wasn't sure how to react. He should have been surprised at least, but with everything that had happened in the past twenty-four hours, he was beyond such a simple reaction.

"So why is he against you?"

"There's a power struggle going on at the moment," Rachel Grey said. "A little while ago, one of the elders of our race, a man called Abe Holly, was killed. He was our leader in North America, and his death left a vacuum. We, like nature, abhor a vacuum. Understand, this is not an elected post. Usually Holly's position would be filled by his next of kin, and that is what has happened. John Holly took over. But John Holly has ideas that many of us find difficult to accept. There are several disparate groups in the States, each with their own agenda and each with their own aspirant eager to fill Holly's shoes."

"Let me guess. You're one of them."

Amusement glowed in her eyes. "Yes, Jacek, I am. And the struggle for supremacy is now spreading worldwide."

Jacek was losing patience. "This is all very interesting, but you're not answering my questions. I'm dragged off the street, beaten up, and brought here, for what? A history lesson?"

She picked up the poker again and began prodding the log with short, stabbing movements. For all her apparent serenity, Jacek could tell there was a lot more going on beneath the surface. There was a reservoir of pent-up anger there, and aggression, well hidden by the demure facade.

"No, Jacek," she said. "It's much more than that. This power struggle has caused huge divisions. There is so much in-fighting and we are so fragmented, it's left us vulnerable to outside attack. Pike isn't interested in entering that arena, but he sees it as an opportunity to destroy us. He hates what he is. He hates *us*. I'm sure if the opportunity presented itself, he would wipe us all from the face of the earth."

"I still don't see where I fit into all this," Jacek said.

Rachel Grey smiled. "Well, as I said, Pike wants you to join his army."

"And you?"

"I want you to join his army as well. I want you to get close to him, let him confide in you."

"You want me to spy for you, is that it?"

"In a nutshell, yes. I need someone on the inside, giving me advance warning of his plans, telling me what his mindset is, what he's thinking."

It was Jacek's turn to laugh. "Why the hell should I help you? So you can continue to feed on us? You're out of your mind."

She laid a hand gently on his arm again, a sisterly gesture. "You *will* help me, Jacek. You'll join Pike's army and you'll tell me exactly what he's planning."

"And if I don't?"

Her features hardened, and for the first time the real Rachel Grey was visible. "If you don't, you'll never see your niece alive again."

Jacek was out of his chair before Rachel Grey could blink. His hands were at her throat. "Julia's alive? You know where she is?"

And then he was grabbed and hauled away from her. Three men emerged from the shadows of the room where they had been watching the exchange. Two held his arms while his assailant from earlier sank a hard fist into his stomach. He folded, all the air knocked out of him. Rachel Grey was on her feet, smoothing her immaculately bobbed hair, looking as serene as before.

"Yes, Jacek. Julia is alive and well. If you do as I ask, you will be reunited with her. If you don't then . . . Well, I don't think I need to spell it out."

Jacek hung there, supported by the men, and struggled to get his breath back. "Prove it," he gasped. "I want proof she's alive."

Rachel Grey sighed. "But of course you do." She turned to Jacek's assailant. "Carl, bring me the photographs." To the other two she said, "Put him back in the chair . . . but watch him carefully."

Without ceremony they dumped Jacek into the chair, then stood, flanking him.

"Sometimes we don't kill those we take," she said, resuming her seat. "Sometimes it amuses us to do more. Your kind can sometimes make excellent pets. As you would keep a cat or a dog, we keep some of the more appealing of your kind."

Jacek said nothing but glared at her furiously.

"There is a couple in England who were very taken with Julia, so much so that we flew her out of the country, a mere twelve hours after she was taken." She looked at Jacek with something like compassion. "Poor Jacek. All that fruitless effort of searching the length and breadth of Poland, and the girl wasn't even here."

Carl returned with a white envelope. He handed it to Rachel Grey and then went to stand behind Jacek's chair. Rachel Grey slid her finger under the flap of the envelope and pulled out a small sheaf of photographs. She handed them to Jacek.

"See for yourself. They're all date stamped. As you will see, the most recent was taken the day before yesterday."

Jacek took the photographs and started leafing through them.

There was no doubt the girl in the photographs was his brother's daughter, Julia. She had changed little in the time she'd been missing. She'd filled out a little; the hair was longer, the face a little fuller. Many of the photos depicted her in the garden of a large house. Julia sitting on a swing, Julia dangling her feet in a fishpond, Julia lying on the grass reading. In each of the pictures her expression was the same. She was smiling, but Jacek had grown to know his niece well. He had been her favorite uncle and had spent a lot of his free time doting on her, taking her on picnics, taking her sightseeing, or simply just spending hours in conversation. He nursed her through the beginning, middle, and end of her first romance. He dried her tears when it was all over and was more than happy to hear about the next boyfriend and the next. He had been at her wedding and at the birth of her child.

The young woman in the photographs was Julia, but it was not the Julia he knew. Where was the spark, the almost consciously defiant tilt of her chin as she prepared to take on the world? The Julia depicted was a shadow of the feisty girl he once knew; the smile was bland, almost vacant.

"What have you done to her?" he said.

"Nothing that can't be reversed. We just took certain steps to make her more docile, more manageable. After all, no one wants a pet that will turn around and bite them. But there's your proof. Julia is alive and well. If you do as I ask, I will return her to you and return her as she once was. Do we have a deal?"

Jacek looked from the photographs, to Rachel Grey, then back to the photographs. Slowly he nodded his head.

"Good," she said. "Now I want your word that there will be no further investigations into our affairs and certainly in the people you've currently had under the microscope. If that continues, then I can no longer guarantee your safety. Do you agree to back off?"

Again Jacek nodded. He didn't trust himself to speak. He felt defeated. He'd always known that he was up against formidable forces. Now he knew for certain.

"Excellent, I knew you'd take the most sensible path,"

Rachel Grey said, turning to Carl. "Our business here is done, Carl. Take Mr. Czerwinski back to his apartment now." She switched her attention back to Jacek. "Carl will also give you a cell phone and the details about how to contact me. Good night, Jacek." She glided across the room to the door and opened it. "Oh, and Jacek," she said, looking back at him. "Don't even think about double-crossing me. Not if you want to see Julia alive again."

"On your feet," Carl said after she'd left the room.

Jacek hauled himself out of the chair. As he rose, he swung his fist, catching Carl on the side of the head, knocking him to the floor. Carl rolled onto his back and sat up, a smile twisting his lips. "She needs you now," he said as he rubbed his already-swelling cheek. "But once she's finished with you, you're mine."

One of the other men stepped forward and wrapped an arm around Jacek's throat, cutting off his air supply.

"Get him out to the car," Carl said, springing to his feet.

They dragged him through the house and out into the chilly night air. Then a hood was place over his head, and he was bundled again into the backseat of the car. The engine sputtered to life, and they drove off into the night.

Love is a portion of the soul itself, and it is of the same nature as the celestial breathing of the atmosphere of paradise.
—Victor Hugo

Chapter Twenty-three

Faircroft Manor, Hertfordshire, England

Alice Spur stood in the doorway, watching Karolina as she slept. The poor girl was exhausted by the time they finally arrived at the manor. Exhausted and scared out of her wits. Alice tried to calm her, to reassure her, but the best she could do for the girl was to make sure she was as comfortable as possible. There had been a glimmer of gratitude in the girl's eyes, but Alice realized it would be a while before she could fully earn Karolina's trust.

Silently she closed the bedroom door and went downstairs. She found Holly in the study.

"Let her go," she said.

Holly didn't look up from the computer screen. "Rachel Grey," he said. "I might have known. It was that bitch who was behind Saul Goldberg's defection. He was supplying her cartel."

"John, I don't care. Let Karolina go."

Finally he looked up at her. "No," he said.

"Are you doing this to punish me?"

"Doing what? She was a gift, from me to you. How can that be construed as a punishment?"

She crossed the room and stood facing him across the

desk. "I don't need a pet, John. I'm not like you, and I'll never be like you. I'm human."

"However much you might wish to be, you're much more than that. Have you been down to the nursery today?"

Alice flinched and shook her head.

"Or yesterday? The day before? You're neglecting your child, Alice."

Anger flared in her eyes. "*Your* child, John. Not mine."

"You gave birth to her," he said reasonably.

She leaned forward, resting her knuckles on the desk. "And don't think I'll ever forgive you for that. But don't expect me to act like a mother to that . . . *freak*, because it's not going to happen."

He leaned back in his chair. "It's a shame. A child needs a mother's love."

"Screw you, John!" she said. She walked to the door and slammed it behind her.

She took the elevator down to the lower levels of the house. In the last few years, Faircroft Manor had been renovated with no expense spared. Basements and subbasements had been added, and it was one of the subbasements that had been designated the nursery.

The elevator stopped, and the doors hissed open. She stepped out into a glaringly lit corridor. Walls had been tiled in plain white, giving the space a cold, clinical atmosphere. At the end of the corridor, reinforced glass had been set into a steel door, and behind the door was the results of John Holly's first experiment: the memorial to his father. The continuance of Abe Holly's work.

She approached, walking lightly, not wanting to alert the nurses on the other side of the door, even though a camera set high on the wall close to the ceiling tracked her every move.

At the door she stopped and peered through the reinforced glass. There were two nurses today, dressed in sterile white, dividing their attention between the two banks of machines set against the far wall. They were unaware they were being watched. But then, why should they be suspicious? Faircroft Manor was equipped with a state-of-the-art security system, and should this fail—which was a remote possibility at best—then there was an eighteen-strong security force who could be summoned at the merest touch of the numerous panic buttons placed at regular intervals along the walls.

Between the two banks of machines and linked to them by snakes of cables was a Plexiglas box, similar in structure to a maternity-ward incubator but three times the size. Alice could see movement within the box. An arm was raised; long, tapering, gray fingers drumming a tattoo on the transparent wall.

The baby.

Her baby.

A testament to John Holly's failed experiment.

She shuddered at the thought that she had actually given birth to this monstrosity. This creature had been conceived by her, nurtured in her womb, and thrust into this world by the excruciating process of her labor.

As she stared into the room, a torrent of images rushed into her mind.

Faces.

Daniel Milton, John Holly, her parents.

After first arriving here, she'd spent months strapped down to a bed while a team of geneticists and fertility experts tried to impregnate her with John Holly's seed.

His grand plan, to build a super-race of hybrids, looked to be a success. When she eventually conceived, his optimism was almost tangible. And the optimism lasted for three months. For three months he played the attentive, almost loving father to be, visiting her at the clinic, taking her for walks in the sprawling grounds, speaking of his hopes for the future; his race and the human race living together in harmony, at peace with each other. She didn't believe him, of course. She knew only too well the fine words were only for her benefit, to help her to live with the fact that growing within her was a life that could well herald the end of humanity as she knew it.

It was at the three-month mark of her pregnancy that a routine test revealed that all was not well. It was then that John Holly backed away, and from that point until the birth she never saw him.

The baby was born and its appearance confirmed the fears of the doctors who had monitored the pregnancy. Holly's genes were too strong, too powerful, too dominant. The baby had very little human DNA in evidence. When she saw it for the first time, a scream died in her throat. She was beyond voicing her terror, her revulsion. The only thing she wished for at that moment was death. It was the only way out she could see, but Holly and his team were never going to let that happen. They needed her alive to continue the experiments, and to this day they were still harvesting her eggs for future research.

For all their initial disappointment, there was a significant difference with this newborn; a difference the scans had not been able to detect. It might have had its father's form—the scaly skin, the long predatory fingers, and the lizardlike features. But it had sufficient human DNA to give credence to the hybrid theory.

It would be some time before they would know if the infant possessed the shape-changing abilities of its father; and that would not be evident until it had feasted on its first human. Along with the life force, it would also be able to take the physical form of its first victim. This happened only once in their life cycle, which made choosing the first victim so important. But at the moment the child was kept isolated until a suitable host could be chosen. Until its first feeding, it would keep its original form.

As she glanced through the window again, a noise

erupted from the room. The Plexiglas box shook as the creature inside hurled itself against the wall. An eerie keening sound filled the air as the nurses rushed to the box, making soothing noises. But it was futile. The creature had sensed Alice's presence nearby and was trying to escape the box by crashing against the Plexiglas. It wanted its mother.

One of the nurses turned toward the door, and Alice ducked out of sight. And then she was running, back along the corridor to the elevator, the image seared into her mind of the gray scaly body with its reptilian head and green eyes that seemed to look into her soul.

Alice knew Karolina had not been given to her simply for fun. John had said something about the girl taking on some of Alice's duties.

Which made Alice wonder what *she* would be doing instead.

Chapter Twenty-four

Krakow, Poland

Rachel Grey entered the bedroom and closed the door behind her. "A satisfying evening's work," she said.

The girl lying on the bed smiled up at her. "He agreed?"

"Of course he agreed, to everything. The photographs clinched it. A brilliant idea of yours."

Julia rolled onto her side, wiping all expression from her face except for a bland smile, identical to the one she'd used in the photographs. Then the smile broke into a laugh and life rushed back to her eyes. "I knew he'd fall for it. He's so sentimental, especially where I'm concerned."

Rachel sat down on the bed next to the girl and stroked her hair. "He really loves you, you know."

"Oh I know, and between him and my parents they would have kept me trapped in this boring, godforsaken country for the rest of my life. The Grants taking me as a pet was the best thing that could have happened to me. They were kind. They taught me English, dressed me well, and only fed from me occasionally. I thought I could want for nothing more. And then you came into my life and everything changed again. I can't believe we've only been together a few months. It seems so much longer."

Julia reached up and wrapped her arms around Rachel Grey's neck, crushing the older woman's lips with her own. Rachel's tongue darted out, exploring the moist sweetness of her young lover's mouth. Julia's hands were at her breasts, stroking the nipples with her thumbs, feeling them harden. Finally the two women fell backward onto the bed, their bodies locked in a passionate embrace.

"Can we go back to America now?" Julia said, breaking off from the kiss. "I'm scared someone will see me here. The thought of having to come back . . ." She shuddered theatrically.

"You worry too much, my love." Rachel rolled over onto her back, her fingers deftly unbuttoned her blouse and shrugged it off. The navy blue skirt was next, followed by her bra and panties.

Julia took this as her cue and shrugged off her jeans and T-shirt.

Once naked they entwined again, their lips locked. Julia felt Rachel's tongue probing her mouth and tried to respond, but suddenly the tongue was snaking down her throat. She gagged and tried to pull away, but Rachel's hand was gripping her hair, forcing her head down onto the pillow.

Julia felt a sharp stabbing pain in her side, and made a small sound of resistance. It should have been a scream, but the long, black tongue of Rachel Grey was filling her throat. She kicked and struggled, but the woman was too strong. The pain in her side intensified as Rachel's fingers lengthened and sought the gaps in Julia's rib cage, burrowing deeper in search of the precious organs.

The more Julia fought the stronger Rachel Grey became, feeling the girl's essence draining into her through the small spiracle-like openings in her fingertips. She pushed deeper, sliding over the girl's sweating body, all the while her own body changing, reverting. Her tongue was now deep inside Julia, reaching the girl's stomach, savoring the digestive juices.

Julia was choking. She couldn't breathe. Her body was on fire, and she could feel Rachel's fingers moving inside her.

It will be over soon, she realized as her mind took refuge in another place, a soft place where death would come as a blissful release.

I thought you loved me.

I trusted you.

I gave you my body.

I gave all of me.

There's nothing left. Nothing left.

Rachel Grey felt the body beneath her grow limp. She withdrew her fingers and her tongue and let Julia slump back onto the bed. The girl was close to death. It would take hours, maybe even days for her to recover, but then that was the main purpose of a pet: a constant, reliable source of sustenance.

It had been so easy to seduce her. Rachel had a way with both men and women that made them malleable and suggestible. Persuading the Grants to let her go was more problematic. They were reluctant to part with such an amenable and grateful pet, but Carl Schwab and his men could be very persuasive.

Eventually Julia *would* die. One day Rachel Grey would go

too far, would take too much. But not yet. She stared down at her, watching the girl's chest rise and fall with painful, ragged breaths. Had she really only been with her a few months? The girl was right. It *did* seem longer. More like half a lifetime. She'd be glad to finally rid herself of the silly little bitch. With her whining and pleading and her innocent doe-eyes, Julia irritated the hell out of her, but she was useful, and while she still served a purpose Rachel wouldn't kill her.

She showered and dressed, feeling more alive than she had for weeks. With no more than a cursory glance at the naked, withered girl on the bed, Rachel Grey left the bedroom and made her way downstairs. She took her coat from the stand in the hallway and walked out into the night.

Thus breathing is a natural way to the heart.
—Nicephorus the Solitary

Chapter Twenty-five

Krakow, Poland

The four men were armed and dangerous.

They had witnessed the bizarre tableau that had just taken place between Grey and the girl. Although human themselves, they had been at Faircroft Manor when their employer, John Holly, held his "house parties." What went on there would make any rock star excesses seem like a church social.

They waited until the Grey woman had left the building,

then checked the basic equipment they had with them. Mobiles, Ketamine, handcuffs, and the keys to the minivan that would take them to the rural and isolated airfield where the private airplane was waiting to take them all back to England.

The men were keen to get back as soon as possible. The girl would not be so willing, hence the equipment.

They didn't know why they had to snatch her. They hadn't asked. That was not a need to know. In their business they rarely if ever asked why, just who, where, and when. Why was a luxury they couldn't afford.

All were ex-military and all had seen action in various parts of the world: Grenada, Iraq, Africa, all known conflicts widely reported. They had also seen plenty of conflict in actions not reported on the news. In Europe, the Middle East, South America.

The leader signaled they had waited long enough.

Using a digital listening probe, one of them scanned the bedroom for movement. There was none.

Another used a diamond-tipped blade to cut a perfectly symmetrical hole in the glass of the door from the bedroom balcony. Reaching through with gloved hand, he slipped the catch on the lock and opened the door to let them all in.

Like a rush of cool evening air, they moved silently into the room.

Julia lay on the bed like a discarded dress.

Her skin had the pallor of the terminally ill, although she would recover in time. Rachel had been careful not to damage any internal organs as she fed. She took just enough from the spirit of the girl to satisfy her needs. Often the breathers fed at such a frenzy that the human body was destroyed in the process. The soft internal organs were often ripped and devoured at the same time.

One of the men went across to Julia and felt for a pulse. There was one, faint but insistent. He gave a thumbs-up.

There would be no need for the drug. There was no real need for the handcuffs, but they used them anyway, just to be safe.

When two of them lifted her from the bed, she was so light one man could have picked her up with ease.

They maneuvered her into the sack they had brought for the purpose and secured the top. All of them were aware of her nakedness and appreciated it, but none of them let it disturb their professionalism. They had a job to do and the price of failure was too high to contemplate.

From the balcony it was easy to lower the sack to the ground, with two of them holding and two of them receiving.

The minivan engine started immediately and they drove the short distance to the airfield where transfer to the airplane was done wordlessly and efficiently.

Only when they were airborne did the leader make the call.

The connection was instantaneous, as if the call was eagerly awaited.

"It's in the bag."

A low sound that may have been a chuckle, but knowing the man was probably not. "Most amusing. I await delivery."

The flight passed without further comment.

Chapter Twenty-six

Krakow, Poland

Krakow is Poland's second largest city; it was the capital of Poland until 1596, when Warsaw took over. When Poland joined the European Union in 2004, there began a slow but steady increase in foreigners and tourists visiting and exploring. Even then, economic wealth was slow to materialize, and many Poles moved to other parts of Europe for work.

Visitors go to the Wawel Castle to hear tales of a dangerous dragon, or to the Market Square to listen to the famous *hejnal* bugle call. Many go farther afield to discover the Salt Mines and Ojcow National Park and the horrors of Auschwitz.

Few tourists choose the outskirts of the city where poverty and the past go hand in hand.

In the shadows of the car park opposite Jacek Czerwinski's apartment building, Jason Pike waited in his hired Audi. It had been more than two hours since he'd left Jacek at the restaurant, and there was still no sign of him. Something had happened. Where the hell was he?

When the black Fiat pulled up outside the block, Pike got his answer. Jacek stepped out, exchanged a few terse words with the driver, then turned away and walked up the steps to the apartments.

As the Fiat pulled away, Pike emerged from the shadows and crossed the street.

"Jacek," he called softly.

In the doorway Jacek turned, anger flashing in his eyes. "You knew, you son of a bitch. You knew Julia was still alive."

"Yes," Pike said quietly. "I knew."

"Son of a bitch!" Jacek said again, spinning around and punching the wall.

"We need to talk about this," Pike said.

"Fuck that! I'm through talking. Talking to *you*, talking to *her*. What's the difference? You're both liars."

"By *her*, I suppose you mean Rachel Grey?"

"You know damned well who I mean."

"Well, as it was Carl Schwab who dropped you off, it couldn't be anyone else. Schwab is Rachel's lieutenant. She never travels without him. It was also Schwab and his cronies who trashed your apartment earlier today."

Jacek was breathing hard. "That's funny. She said you did it."

Pike shrugged. "Well, she would, wouldn't she?"

"Would she? How the hell would I know? Though I know now what she wants from me. But what about you? Why me? Why have you come all the way to Poland to see me?"

"Shall we go inside?" Pike said. "This is a bit public."

Jacek looked beyond him. An elderly man out walking his dog had stopped a few yards away and was openly listening to their conversation. Jacek glared at him. "Okay. Come in."

The apartment building was surprisingly quiet as they made their way up the stone staircases. Even the cooking smells had abated. Jacek checked his watch. Just after midnight. The evening had passed by in a blur.

He unlocked his front door and ushered Pike inside. He then went to the old plywood desk in the corner and pulled open the drawer. When he turned back to Pike, he had the Beretta in his hand.

A look of surprise flashed in Pike's eyes, and then it was gone.

"Sit down," Jacek said. "There on the couch."

Pike frowned but sat obediently. "Is the gun really necessary?"

"If Rachel Grey was telling the truth, then yes, it is."

"But you've already said she was lying to you."

"She was. About Julia she was lying through her teeth."

"They're lovers, you know."

Something flickered in Jacek's eyes. Surprise? Pain? Even he wasn't sure what he felt.

"The woman showed me photographs of Julia. She said she'd been sedated in some way, and from the look on Julia's face I may have been convinced . . . if I didn't know her so well. But it was a look I recognized. She used to use the same expression when she was in trouble with her parents."

He rubbed a hand over his face and sat down heavily on the hard wooden chair.

"Understand, I love Julia as I would my own daughter, but I'm under no illusions about her. Julia is a vain, self-centered little bitch who made her parents' lives a misery. Do you know, when she first disappeared her husband spoke of his relief that she'd gone. That's a terrible thing for someone to say about his wife, but I couldn't really blame him. Julia danced to her own tune and, as far as everyone else was concerned . . . well, they could go to hell.

"Julia was play-acting in those photographs, which means not only was she there by choice, but also she did not want to be found. She'd always been looking for an escape, to get away from home, her family. From Poland. I think in Rachel Grey she found it."

"Well, let's hope she doesn't get more than she bargained for," Pike said shaking his head.

"Rachel Grey told me that if I ever want to see Julia alive again I have to drop my investigations. Apparently I'm getting too close to certain people."

"And will you?"

"Do I have a choice?"

"And do you believe she'll be true to her word?"

"I believe Julia is lost to me forever." Jacek lowered his head. Tears were pressing at his eyes, but he fought them back. The sad thing was that he believed what he had just said. There was a slim possibility that he might liberate his niece, but he knew that his relationship with her was over.

"I'm sorry," Pike said.

Jacek lapsed into silence. The pain was almost too much to bear. Months of searching had come to an end. He'd found Julia, and now he wished he hadn't. He looked across at Pike. "Rachel Grey told me about you. About what you are," he said.

Pike leaned back on the couch with a sigh. "What did she tell you?"

"That you're the same as her. Do you deny it?"

Pike shook his head. "I would have told you . . . eventually. But there is a difference between them and me. They were born as they are. I was born human. They made me this way. I was born in Africa, in a small shanty town just outside Nairobi, Kenya. These creatures came to my town. They killed my mother, and I was given to one of them as a pet. Did Grey tell you about pets?"

Jacek nodded.

"The one who took me was Abe Holly. In some ways he wasn't as bad as the others, but in some ways he was worse. He stole my humanity from me and turned me into the same kind of creature as him. Their main weakness is their hunger for the human soul. Keeping them from humans, preventing them from feeding, is one way you can kill them. You injure them and they often revert to their true selves. Not a pretty sight. The way they feed is not attractive either. Talons in their fingers can pierce the flesh easily. Usually they feed during the act of sex. It's the way they attract their prey."

"Why keep saying *they* and *them* if they're the same as you?"

"Abe changed my body, but he couldn't touch my mind . . . or my soul. I feel no affinity for them. The hunger that drives them to prey on humankind is controllable, it can be managed. They choose not to control it. I do. That is the difference."

Jacek moved the gun from hand to hand. "When you sent Cyril Adamczyk to see me, did you really think I could help him?"

"Karolina Adamczyk is no longer in Poland. They flew her to England the day after she was taken. But I believe she is still alive. My contacts tell me she's been taken as a pet for a woman called Alice Spur."

"Why didn't you tell Adamczyk this? Why send him to me?"

"Do you honestly think he would believe me? It would have only distressed him further. I sent him to you to pique your interest. So you might be more receptive to my request," Pike said candidly.

"So it's as I thought. You're playing me."

"Come to England with me, Jacek. There are people there who can help us destroy these bastards. Grey is dangerous, but she's a walk in the park compared to Abe's son. John Holly is the reason there is the infighting between his people and Grey's. Holly has perfected the trafficking of their food. He calls them *candidates*, and arranges places where his people can feed undisturbed, *restaurants* he calls them."

Jacek laid the gun down and looked at him steadily. There were still questions with no satisfactory answers. He wasn't going to get the answers here and now, but there was integrity about Pike. It emanated from him, radiating from his eyes, from his words.

Jacek reached into his pocket, took out a cell phone and tossed it across to Pike. The big man's expression begged the question.

"Rachel Grey's hired thug gave it to me. It's a direct line to her."

"And when were you to use it?"

"They wanted me to spy on you. That was the second part of the deal. I was to report your movements to them, tell them what you were planning."

Pike looked down at the phone nestled in the palm of his hand. "So you trust me," he said.

"I don't trust *her*."

"That's good enough."

"What do you think she'll do to Julia once she realizes I'm not going to play her game?"

Pike sighed. "You know the answer to that. She'll feed from her. She'll take too much."

"Can we stop her?"

"We can buy Julia some time. Call Rachel Grey and tell her I'm going to London. It will show her you're honoring your side of the deal. But, Jacek, don't kid yourself that Grey will ever let your niece go. She was lost to you the moment Rachel got her hands on her."

Jacek regarded him steadily for a moment, then reached out and took the cell phone back, and put in the number he'd been given.

He finished the call and handed the phone back to Pike.

"You sounded convincing enough," Pike said.

"I wasn't lying. You're going to London. I am going with you."

Day Two

These, as successive generations bloom,
New powers acquire and larger limbs assume;
Whence countless groups of vegetation spring,
And breathing realms of fin and feet and wing.
—Erasmus Darwin

Breath is Spirit. The act of breathing is Living.
—Author Unknown

Chapter Twenty-seven

Dunkerry, Republic of Ireland

The Republican Arms was on the main road running through the picturesque village of Dunkerry. It was nothing to look at from the outside, a fairly simple brick structure with a tiled roof and an ugly glass conservatory latched on to the side of it.

In fact it was the ugliest building in the entire village, but as he stepped through the door, Simon Crozier's spirits lifted. Inside was the epitome of an Irish pub.

The walls were lined with autographed photographs. Some of the faces and names he recognized—the Dubliners, Pierce Brosnan, The Corrs—some he didn't. All the photographs were dedicated to *Patrick and Aoife*; obviously the licensees. A set of *uilean* pipes hung above the bar, to the right of them an Irish drum, the *bodhran*. The brick-built fireplace was huge, and Crozier could imagine great blocks of peat burning there, while the jigs and reels of a *céilí* filled the smoky air.

Behind the bar hung a Republican flag, the orange, green, and white panels faded and stained, the edges slightly moth-eaten. What looked suspiciously like bloodstains in the corner. Standing in front of the flag was a large man with black curly hair, a ruddy complexion, and liquid blue eyes. He nodded at them as they entered. "And what'll you two gentlemen be having?" he asked in a lilting Irish brogue.

A few minutes later they were seated at a table in the far corner of the pub with two pints of Guinness. Crozier checked his watch. "We're early," he said.

As he said it, the door opened and Michael Dylan walked in. He stood no more than five foot six, slim but hard muscled with haunted green eyes set in a pale face. He saw them sitting there, swept a curtain of fair hair away from his forehead, nodded a greeting, and went to the bar. Crozier watched him order a drink from the barman and felt the usual wave of apprehension. There was something about Dylan that back-footed him. He was never quite sure how to take the man. He felt Bailey tug his sleeve.

"So that's Dylan, is it?"

"It is," Crozier responded.

And then Michael Dylan was walking across to where they sat. He put his orange juice down next to the pints of Guinness and sat.

"This had better be good to rouse me from my bed at this ungodly hour," he said to Crozier, inclining his head toward Bailey. "Who's this?"

"Harry Bailey," Bailey said, stretching out a hand.

Dylan shook the hand and sat back in his seat, giving Bailey a look of appraisal. "I've heard of you."

"And me you," Bailey said.

Dylan turned to Crozier. "If *he's* here, why do you need me?"

"I need you both," Crozier said. "When I explain what this is all about, you'll understand why."

"I'm listening," Dylan said.

Cozier moved Guinness around his mouth and swallowed it. "The night before last I had dinner at The Ivy. On the way out, I was approached by a young man . . ."

"Your lucky night," Bailey interrupted

Crozier was used to Harry's acidic barbs regarding his personal life and didn't bite, but he was slightly irritated to see a smile flicker briefly on Dylan's lips. *Common knowledge,* he thought. *Rise above it and move on.* He continued, "I thought he was a beggar. He was scruffy as hell, and he looked like he hadn't eaten for a week. He told me his name was Daniel Milton and had something to tell me. I don't know how he tracked me down or how he knew I'd be there that evening, but he'd obviously done his homework. He knew my name and knew about Department 18 and what we do. He even started quoting case files at me. I must admit, at first I thought he was a crank, but there was something about him, a kind of quiet desperation I found compelling. So I took him to my club and fed him, and for the next couple of hours he told me a story so extraordinary that I felt it warranted further investigation." He turned to Harry Bailey. "Does the name Jason Pike mean anything to you?"

Bailey's drink was an inch away from his lips, but he paused and set his glass back down on the table. "Now there's a name I haven't heard for a good many years. He was quite high profile, a kind of Uri Geller figure."

"Guru to the stars," Crozier put in.

Bailey continued, "I only crossed his path once, but it left a lasting impression. He immediately recognized me for what I was and started playing mind games with me. I realize now he was testing me, to see if I was any good. It took all I had to keep him out of my thoughts." Bailey sipped his drink. "Not that there was any malice there. Quite the contrary. He was enjoying playing with me, but only because I was enjoying the challenge myself. I'm sure he would have backed off if I hadn't been willing."

"He's genuine then," Michael Dylan said.

"Oh yes," Bailey said. "And one of the most extraordinary minds I've ever come across." He looked across at Crozier. "I'm just wondering how Pike figures in all this. Simon?"

"There was an incident in Cambridge, a car accident.

Daniel Milton's girlfriend, Alice Spur, was driving. A man called Abe Holly was killed. Nasty business. It was ruled an accident. Abe was the father of businessman John Holly."

"Holly Industries?" Dylan said.

"The same. Well, it happened that the girl, Alice, disappeared from her hospital bed and hasn't been seen since. Until recently, when a young woman called Alice Spur took a job as John Holly's PA."

"The purpose of all this is, of course, what you're going to tell us," Dylan said.

"You know Simon," Bailey said. "He knows how to spin out a story."

Crozier ignored him. "Daniel Milton's investigation into his girlfriend's disappearance took him to Hertfordshire, which is where John Holly has his country house, a place called Faircroft Manor. Holly had taken Alice Spur down there for reasons unknown. It was while he was in the area that he met Jason Pike." Crozier took a mouthful of Guinness and let the taste of the dark brown beer fill his mouth.

"So what's so dangerous about John Holly?" Dylan said.

"Well, for one, John Holly has very powerful psychic powers. It would seem he is a very advanced empath. According to Milton, he has the ability to bend the will of others to his own, making them do things to suit his own purpose. His other kink is sexual vampirism," Crozier said. "And we've come across that before."

"I haven't," Dylan said flatly.

"But Harry has. Which is why I want him in on this."

"Jay Cavanagh," Harry Bailey said.

"Indeed. One of the department's failures. Perhaps you could sketch it out for Dylan's benefit, Harry. After all, it was primarily your case."

Harry Bailey sighed. He wasn't one for reliving the past, and he was reluctant to revisit this particular case. "Okay," he said. "Jay Cavanagh was responsible for the deaths of at least eight women, back in the 1990s. He was a good-looking man, apparently in his thirties, the type to snap his fingers and have women panting for him. The department was called in when a young woman went missing after being on a date with him. Sally Bronson. Sally had no family, but she did have a wide circle of friends, and it was one of her friends, a girl called Jenny Marshall, who contacted us, albeit in a roundabout way. She'd tried the police and got nowhere. But then her story seemed so far-fetched it was totally reasonable for the police to dismiss it." Bailey paused to take a mouthful of his drink.

"What do you mean, 'in a roundabout way'?" Dylan said.

"The initial contact was through her uncle," Crozier said. "The Department had been going through a bit of a shake-up and we were only partly operational, and so it existed, more or less, under the radar. But this girl's uncle was a fairly important civil servant in the Ministry of Transport. Once she'd told him her story, he contacted me and introductions were made."

Bailey continued. "The last time Jenny Marshall saw Sally Bronson was at a party at the house of a mutual friend. Sally was excited, telling Jenny about this wonderful man she'd been seeing for the few weeks leading up to the party. Jay Cavanagh. She was even more high on the fact that he was coming to the party later. Well, to cut a long story short, Cavanagh arrived and within the hour he and Sally had disappeared upstairs.

"Toward the end of the party, Jenny decided to go and look for her. Sally had been gone for hours and Jenny was worried. She'd been introduced to Cavanagh and taken an instant dislike to him. She thought he was, in her words, creepy. She found Sally and Cavanagh in an upstairs room. They were naked and apparently making love. She was about to apologize and leave them to it when she noticed the look in her friend's eyes. 'Glazed but terrified,' was how she described it to me. And then she noticed Cavanagh's hands, well, his fingers to be more precise. They appeared to be burrowing into Sally's flesh. Jenny said, 'are you all right?' or words to that effect, and at that point Cavanagh leaped from the bed. What Jenny Marshall described next was why the police had a problem with her story.

"She described Cavanagh's body as 'barely human.'" Bailey closed his eyes, trying to recall her words. "His fingers were at least ten inches long, and tapered to points. They were covered in blood. His skin was gray and scaly, like a reptile's. His tongue was long and black, and flicked like a snake's." Bailey paused again and took another swig of his drink, then closed his eyes and carried on. "His penis was thin, twelve inches long, and barbed on both sides. It, was covered in blood, like his fingers.

"But it was his eyes that terrified her. They looked totally different from when she had seen him earlier. Whereas earlier in the evening they'd been a deep brown, now they were pale, almost white. 'Dead-fish eyes,' was how she described them."

"So what did she do next?" Dylan said, leaning forward in his seat, his curiosity piqued despite himself.

"That's another problem. She doesn't remember *what* happened next. One moment she was standing in the bedroom, with Cavanagh coming toward her, the next she was being helped up from the floor by one of the other party guests. When she checked her watch she realized she'd lost two hours. It was now a little after three in the morning. She'd begun her search for Sally a few minutes before one. Of Sally and Cavanagh there was no sign. She called the police and told them what she'd seen. A short while later a single constable came along, took a perfunctory look around and left again."

"But there must have been blood on the bed," Dylan said. "If, as you say, Cavanagh's fingers and dick were dripping with the stuff."

Bailey shrugged. "You'd think so, wouldn't you? But there was no evidence that anything had taken place. And that was the police position throughout."

"So what's to say this Jenny didn't imagine the whole thing?"

"Because her story was corroborated."

"Who did that?"

Bailey smiled slightly. "Jay Cavanagh."

"We tracked him down," Crozier said. "Actually, he was very easy to trace. It was almost as if he wanted us to find him."

"I think he did," Harry Bailey said. "He agreed to meet with me at a hotel in Bayswater."

"So you met this monster?" Dylan said incredulously.

"Oh yes, I met him," Bailey said. "He looked completely normal and was perfectly charming. Quietly spoken, polite, and very open. He admitted killing Sally and seven others."

"Did he say how he'd killed them?"

"Yes, he did. He told me he had drained the life force from their bodies. He said he belonged to a race that co-existed alongside our own, who needed the life force of we 'lesser mortals,' in order to survive. And he often did this during sex when, as he succinctly put it, 'the human essence is at its most vibrant.'"

"So he was mad," Dylan said.

Bailey frowned. "No, I don't think so. I believed him, and I think he was totally sane . . . and totally evil. He was playing with me. He was demonstrating his arrogance and his complete disdain for human life. He was saying, I *can take any life I want, and there's absolutely nothing you can do about it.*"

"So what *did* you do about it?"

Bailey took a breath. "Nothing," he said and drained his glass. "Another, I think." He stood and went to the bar.

"Understand, Dylan," Crozier said. "I'd only just become Director General of the department. I was still wet behind the ears and we simply didn't have the resources or the clout we have now. And although we had the blessing of the prime minister and several members of the cabinet, Whitehall in general treated us with scorn, suspicion, or amusement. We didn't have much of a voice to be able to influence the police or any of the security services for that matter. That all changed, of course, after the Balmoral incident. Then they had to take us more seriously."

Bailey returned with three more drinks. "I went back to the hotel to see him again," he said, taking his seat. "But he'd checked out. And after that he proved impossible to track down. Which makes me think he wanted to be found the first time round. I think he needed to gloat. He got his kicks, then disappeared."

Crozier reached down and lifted his briefcase onto the table. He pulled out the file Martin Impey had given him the day before. "So, I have your interest now?"

Harry Bailey said, "What do you think?"

"Go on," Dylan said neutrally.

"Okay. In here is a rough transcript of the conversation I had with Daniel Milton and some photographs of some of the key players. Plus there's a dossier compiled by Martin on the Holly family. According to Pike, the Hollys are not human."

"Like Cavanagh," Harry Bailey said.

"Indeed. Just like Cavanagh."

He opened the folder and spread the contents out on the table. The other two men started pulling pages out at random and scanning them quickly before putting them back and moving on to the next.

"So what happened after you left your club?" Bailey said. "What happened to Milton?"

"He vanished. Disappeared into the night like a ghost. He was scared. I could sense that. He told me that since the incident at Faircroft Manor, Holly's people had been on his tail. He'd given up his house and his job and was traveling the country living in various squats and doss-houses. He was running scared. We left the club, and I went to call a cab. When I looked round, he'd gone. I've seen neither hide nor hair of him since."

Dylan was reading the transcript of the conversation between Crozier and Daniel Milton.

"Then excuse me for asking a rather basic question," Bailey said. "How do you plan to stop . . ." He fell silent, reached out, and pulled one of the photographs toward him.

The other two watched him, noticing that Bailey's ruddy complexion had paled. He was sitting, unmoving, staring at an eight-by-ten glossy color shot.

"Everything all right, Harry?" Crozier said.

After a moment Bailey seemed to shake himself. He slid the photograph across the table to Crozier. "And who's this?"

Crozier glanced at the photograph. "That's John Holly."

Harry Bailey shook his head. "No, it's not," he said.

Dylan leaned over to look at the photo. "It is. I recognize him. I've seen his face in the *Financial Times* a number of times. As CEO of Holly Industries, he earns himself more than his fair share of column inches. Of course, it has nothing to do with the fact that he's as handsome and charismatic as a movie star," he added with heavy irony.

Bailey didn't smile, but took a breath. "Gentlemen," he said, prodding the photograph with his index finger. "That is Jay Cavanagh."

Chapter Twenty-eight

King's College Hospital, London, England

Carter had been awake for hours, barely slept in fact.

Despite that, he felt fresh and alive. He had done a lot of thinking; about Jane mostly, but also about his life, his work, his future.

His last two assignments hadn't gone well. Sian had paid for it with her life, and now several casualties from the apartment building. He didn't blame himself for the deaths of Baines, McCrory, and Black, but he couldn't ignore them either.

And with that job, he had been badly injured. Though the way he felt now, just a day later, he clearly wasn't as bad as he first thought.

His ribs ached, but the bandages were tight and held off much of the discomfort. Scratches and bruises he could live with. The test results had shown no concussion, so the worst he had from the head was a migraine-level ache that was being kept at bay by copious amounts of painkillers. The knee had been put back in and was sore but flexible enough.

What had woken him, and then kept him from sleeping was Jane. Not literally he was sad to say, though thoughts of their time together were spinning around in his brain and refused to stay still. He wanted to be able to think rationally about what was going to happen between them, but the more he tried to think it through, the more his mind spiraled out of control.

In the end he got out of bed, which took him longer than he expected, and sat in the chair for a couple of hours.

By the time morning came, he was back in bed but sitting up, resting on the pillows. He knew what he had to do.

He was a man of action rather than introspection. His psychic powers had never led to deep psychological reasoning, and personal as his thoughts were, the emotions they contained clouded any logic or thought patterns.

No, he decided, it was time for action.

He had been outfought at the apartment, and he needed to get back into the fight.

He knew that if he had led the investigation fully, without the inexperienced colleagues, things would have been different. But it was too late for that now. He needed to get some stuff from his apartment and get over to Whitehall and join the fun.

He pressed the buzzer for a nurse and waited a few moments. The nurse who answered wasn't Paula, but she was friendly enough. Until he requested his clothes. Then she argued, eventually leaving the room.

Carter was sure she would return with a doctor in tow rather than the clothes.

Sure enough the door opened and Bernard entered, this time without accompanying junior doctors.

"Well, I alluded to you not being with us much longer, but even I didn't think you'd be this impetuous."

"I just need my clothes."

"No witty response? No sarcasm intended to prick my supposed pomposity? You disappoint for once. Nurse, where are the results of the scans?"

The nurse handed him a manila folder and he quickly read the contents. "You must have the hide of a rhinoceros and a head made of steel, Mr. Carter. Congratulations, no lasting damage, and indeed nothing too major currently."

"I'll put it down to being in your expert care."

Bernard handed the folder back to the nurse. "That's better. Now I know you are fit enough to go home to the loving bosom of your family. Though judging by the look of determination on your face I would guess pipe and slippers and feet up in front of the TV for a few days don't fit in with your plans."

"Seriously, thanks for sorting me out."

Bernard nodded in acknowledgment. "Nurse, please find whatever garments our guest had with him when he arrived and discharge him, and you"—he pointed at Carter—"keep out of trouble."

Smile, breathe and go slowly.
—Thich Nhat Hanh

Chapter Twenty-nine

Dunkerry, Republic of Ireland

"Jay Cavanagh? Are you certain?" Crozier said, picking up the photograph and studying it hard.

"Oh yes." Harry Bailey nodded vigorously. "He hasn't changed a bit. Looks no older, the same supercilious expression. It's him."

"How come you haven't come across Holly before?" Dylan said. "He's always in the papers."

"Harry doesn't read newspapers, do you, Harry?" Crozier said.

"Or watch the news on television. Too depressing," Bailey said.

Crozier leaned back in his seat and folded his arms. "Well, that settles it then. The department *has* to get involved in this. Are you with me on it?"

"You can count me in," Bailey said. "I'd give my pension to nail this bastard."

"Dylan?"

"I don't know."

Crozier's face dropped. Bailey gave a deep sigh and settled back into his seat.

"Dylan, we really need you on this," Crozier said.

Dylan rested his elbows on the table, steepled his fingers, and blew across them. "I'm not sure I'm ready to come back."

"Look, I know you've had a tough few months. That poltergeist case in Burnley took a lot out of you. I know that, but . . ."

"It's not only that," Dylan cut in. "I'm tired. Not physically, but up here." He tapped the side of his head. "I'm tired of dealing with all the horrors in the world. Ask Harry what I mean." He looked across at Bailey. "You know, don't you, Harry?"

Bailey stared down at the drinks on the table, avoiding eye contact with either of them. "It's like looking into hell on a daily basis," he said. "Over the years it gets more and more difficult to shut the images out. You walk along a street and you know everything about those on the street with you. You recognize the ones who beat their partners, the ones who are planning theft or murder; you even know what they had for dinner and when they last took a crap! Blocking is the only way of shutting the images out, and over the years it becomes less and less effective. So you try to dull your senses, to anesthetize yourself. Why do you think I drink? I'm not an alcoholic, but I need the booze to blur the visions and to muffle the sounds. It's one way, my way. What's yours, Dylan?"

"My way is to get as far away from civilization as possible," Dylan said. "A place like this. I can go for days without seeing a soul . . . and I use that word deliberately."

"Or is it simply that the powers you possess force you to hold a mirror up to your own souls and examine what's there," Crozier said. "And neither of you like what you see."

"Bastard!" Bailey said under his breath.

Dylan glared at Crozier but said nothing.

"I see I've hit a nerve," Crozier said. "So there must be some truth in what I say."

"Some," Bailey said.

"And you, Dylan?"

Dylan nodded slightly, almost against his will.

"I thought so," Crozier said. "Dylan, I think it's time you stopped acting like a prima donna and got your ass in gear. We've got a job to do."

Dylan got to his feet angrily. "Go fuck yourself!" he said and walked to the door.

"I've booked three seats on a flight to London, leaving Shannon at two o'clock," Crozier called after him, but the door was already swinging shut.

Bailey looked at his old friend steadily. "Well you blew that. You were too harsh. It's one thing knowing the truth yourself without someone else beating you over the head with it."

"He'll be on the flight," Crozier said confidently. "His ego is too big for him *not* to be involved in this."

Bailey looked skeptical. "We'll see," he said.

"Another drink? My round, I think."

Chapter Thirty

Faircroft Manor, Hertfordshire, England

As soon as the flight from Poland landed in the private airfield, the Jeep was driven to the exit doors and the sack and its contents transferred to the trunk.

The four men had stripped out of their black clothing and masks on the flight and were dressed in standard dark jeans and sweatshirts. One took the keys from the airfield driver and swapped places with him in the driver's seat. The engine already running, he waited for all the passenger doors to click shut and then drove off into the morning light.

They were just a few miles from the manor, and the mist on the fields gave a surreal appearance to the passing scenery.

Soon they drove in through the iron gates at the front and went slowly along the winding gravel drive. Trees and bushes lined the way, in places overhanging the road so the weak sun trying to filter through the leaves and branches was beaten back.

Eventually they turned a corner, and Faircroft Manor came into view.

Built on the grounds of a former royal palace where Elizabeth I spent much of her childhood, it was beautifully preserved. Additions had been made through the years, but sympathetically, not detracting in any way from the overall look of the house.

The bricks were of mellow russet, lined with pale mortar pointing, and the mullioned windows were symmetrically positioned. Inside the house, most of the forty or more rooms were wood lined with tall ornate ceilings, many bearing tapestries and paintings from centuries past, depicting former owners and their families.

In front of the house, as the Jeep pulled to a halt in front of the pristine portico and vast oak front doors, topiary and flowerbeds gave a neat but friendly welcome.

There was nothing friendly about the way two of the men pulled the sack out of the Jeep and carried, half-dragged, it up the front steps and into the house. Perhaps they would have been more comfortable performing these tasks at the rear or side of the house, at the smaller servants' entrances that usually witnessed the mundane house tasks, but Mr. Holly had been insistent about "not hiding our guest away."

Holly was waiting in the black-and-white marble-tiled entrance hall.

He nodded to the leader of the group and followed the men as they took the sack into the library. Floor-to-ceiling bookshelves held thousands of leather-bound volumes, and along the top of the shelves, a gallery was reached by some wooden steps by the window.

The sack was dropped, roughly, onto the large rug in front of the huge stone fireplace. The rope tying the sack shut was loosened and the contents tumbled out onto the rug.

Julia opened her eyes sleepily, still very weak from the feeding.

Holly thanked the men and dismissed them.

He sat in a sixteenth-century armchair and watched Julia for several minutes.

She hardly stirred during that time, lying on her back and then moving onto her side. If she realized she was naked, she gave no indication.

Eventually Holly walked across to a small desk and pressed a concealed buzzer. Moments later Alice came into the room.

"Alice," Holly said. "This is our new breeder."

Alice tried to look at the girl without revealing any emotion, but she wasn't adept at concealment and Holly was prepared for her reactions.

"You should be pleased. I shan't need your womb anymore."

"Who is she?"

Holly ignored her for a while. "I want you to nurse her back to strength. She is not damaged, but she has been drained. There shouldn't be any physical injury, but she will need nourishment."

Alice knelt down and stroked the young woman's hair. The girl opened her eyes and looked up at Alice, fear and fascination in equal measures.

"I asked who she is."

"Forgive me, where are my manners? Alice Spur, human, meet Julia Czerwinski, half human."

"Half . . ."

". . . half . . . nonhuman. The perfect mix for the next stage of my research."

Alice coaxed Julia into a sitting position, though Julia was partially slumped against her shoulder.

"Tell Karolina to help you, but please take our guest to the blue room and get her washed and rested."

"Why can't you . . ."

Holly was at her side before the blink of an eye. He took hold of her hair and twisted. "I asked *you*, not anyone else." He released her hair. "This is a special job, Alice, and you're my special girl aren't you?"

Alice had always known she wasn't special to Holly; no one was. Now she didn't even know whether he needed her at all.

Who will tell whether one happy moment of love or the joy of breathing or walking on a bright morning and smelling the fresh air, is not worth all the suffering and effort which life implies.

—Erich Fromm

Chapter Thirty-one

Dunkerry, Republic of Ireland

Dylan climbed into the driver's seat of his hired Ford Focus and slammed his palm on the steering wheel.

Damn Simon Crozier!

He took a breath to calm his anger and turned the key in the ignition. It was only a short drive back to the cottage he was renting on the other side of the village, but instead of turning right out of the pub car park back to the cottage, he turned left and headed up to the hills that surrounded the area. He needed to think.

He had been with the department for nearly twelve years, and recently he'd started to consider leaving. His reasons were those he'd mentioned in the pub, but there was more to it than he'd let on. There were elements creeping into his life that he wasn't about to disclose to Crozier or anybody else for that matter.

He was aware of being watched, vague shadowy shapes glimpsed out of the corner of his eye. They plagued him constantly and were starting to make his life a misery.

Ever since childhood, he'd had the ability to see beyond the normal boundaries. Even as early as seven years old he was seeing and conversing with the recently deceased. His great-grandfather was the first spirit he communicated with. Not twenty-four hours in the ground, the old man was back at his bedside, telling the very young Michael Dylan exactly what it was like to be dead. But then his great-grandfather had always been a mischievous old bugger. A Dubliner to the core, he embraced the myths and legends of Eire and was eager to impart the stories to his grandson. And Michael had listened to the old man's stories with rapt attention, never questioning them or disputing them.

"You're different, Mikey," his great-grandfather told him. "Different from the herd. I knew it the moment you were born. You have the *eye*. It's a great gift to be sure, but you must use it wisely." And although Michael didn't really believe the old man, he never argued with him. If his great-grandfather thought him to be special, then who was he to disagree? "I'll prove to you that you have the *eye*, that you can see things others can't. When I die I'll come back and visit you, and I'll be as real to you then as I am to you now."

And he did. And he was. It was like having the old man, living and breathing, in the room with him once more.

The visits continued sporadically for the next seven years, until he hit puberty, and then they stopped. There was no long farewell or any explanation why. They just stopped, and Michael felt completely alone.

Until he started getting other visitors.

Throughout his teens and into his early twenties, visitations happened on a regular basis. They set him apart from his peers and made him something of an outcast at school where his fellow pupils were quick to recognize that there was something different, something otherworldly, about him. The visitations also hampered his relationships with the opposite sex, with one young woman in particular running screaming from his bed when he told her that her dead father was sitting in the corner of the room watching what his daughter was getting up to.

After that incident he became more circumspect, shutting himself off further from the rest of humanity. The *eye* was a curse, something that was ruining his life. Until he heard about Department 18, and suddenly there was an avenue open to him; a way to use the power to his advantage and be with people who had similar isolating powers.

He flourished in the department, quickly becoming one of its top investigators, up there with the likes of Robert Carter and John McKinley, taking on cases of paranormal phenomena and usually solving them. For a while he was overseeing the department's clean-up team, men and women handpicked for their resilience and their ability to go into virtually any situation and resolve them. He became friendly with Patrick Donovan, an ex-priest, Irish like himself, and an experienced exorcist. It was Father Donovan who first told him about breathers.

"You have to be very wary of them, Michael. They are souls with no conscience, stranded on earth as a result of their misdeeds during their lives and unable to cross over to the afterlife. They are very angry, very bitter and, once they get their hooks into you, it's the devil's own job to get rid of them. They will haunt you, follow you, invade your life and make it a total misery. And the worst of it is that you'll never really see them. They're dark and elusive and will always be just there hovering, dancing on the edge of your perception."

He later learned that Father Donovan was speaking from bitter experience. He had spent years being tormented by the breathers, and just six months after Dylan's conversation with him, Patrick Donovan walked into a local meat-processing factory and threw himself into an industrial grinder used for mincing the beef into hamburger.

Once departed, Donovan never came back to visit, but Dylan always believed that it was the breathers who were responsible for the ex-priest's grisly end, that they literally tormented him to death.

And now he had his own breathers to contend with and was terrified he would end up the same way as Patrick Donovan. Only he knew what they were. Not the souls trapped in limbo that the Catholic priest had conjured up to explain his own demons. Dylan knew they were a race apart, knew they were probably the most dangerous foe Department 18 would face. In their unformed state, they may appear as shadows, floating black shapes that sometimes swooped in packs, seeking hosts for food. Their true form usually remained hidden away.

He parked the car halfway up a hill and sat there looking out across the landscape. He could see Dunkerry and the pub. There were a few cars in the car park. Probably one of them belonged to Bailey or Crozier. He needed to think long and hard about this. The case intrigued him, and he was itching to get back to work, despite what he had told his boss. At the moment he was hiding himself away and vegetating. He could almost feel his brain ossifying through lack of activity.

But going back, getting involved with the department, was risky. Not just for him, but for whomever he was teamed up with. While the breathers were a problem, and one he was struggling to contain, he couldn't be sure that they wouldn't latch on to someone he was associated with, and that would be catastrophic. It would sit on his conscience for the rest of his life.

His last case, the poltergeist in Burnley, had very nearly been compromised when he'd lost concentration at a crucial point. Something glimpsed out of the corner of his eye caught his attention and he let his mind wander, leaving him vulnerable. With his defenses down, the attack came swiftly and brutally. One moment he was sitting at the table in the prosaic little kitchen of the house; the next he was flying across the room, propelled by unseen hands that crashed him face-first into the far wall.

He wasn't badly hurt physically—a cut forehead and two broken teeth, but the damage to his confidence and his pride was incalculable.

Sitting on the floor wiping the blood from his brow and his mouth, he realized he would have to deal with the breathers once and for all. The only problem he had was just *how* he was going to deal with them.

Coming back home to Ireland seemed like a good enough place to start. In familiar surroundings, in a place he felt safe, he tried to banish the breathers from his life, let them be someone else's problem. So far he'd had some success. It wasn't a complete rout, but, as he grew stronger, fortified by the home comforts, he felt better, and so far he had gone five days without seeing a single shadowy shape or hearing a malicious whisper in his ear.

He checked his watch. The flight to London was in two hours. He didn't have long to make his decision. He got out of the car and breathed in the crisp, fresh air, filling his lungs. Delving into his pocket he produced a coin. Heads or tails. He wagered with himself and tossed the coin, catching it deftly. Then he slapped it down onto the back of his other hand. *Heads I go, tails I stay.* He took his hand away to reveal the result, smiled grimly, and got back into the car.

Two hours later he was sitting aboard a Boeing 737 with Crozier and Bailey, headed for London.

Chapter Thirty-two

Department 18 Headquarters, Whitehall, London, England

There was a knock at the door and Trudy, Crozier's secretary, walked in with a tray of cups, saucers, and teapot. The reputation of the English government flourishing on a diet of afternoon tea and digestive biscuits was kept alive in this part of the establishment.

Crozier stood and walked to the windows. Looking out, he could see the traffic starting to build up. The roof of Buckingham Palace was visible a short distance away. The flag was flying, indicating the queen was in residence.

"Twenty-seven million," Martin Impey said, addressing the five people seated at one end of the large oval table in the Department's conference room. "That's the figure. The estimated number of people worldwide kept in one form of slavery or another."

A murmur rippled around the table.

"Are you sure that figure's right?" Simon Crozier said. The flight back had passed quickly enough, and they had all settled into the task ahead.

Martin flicked on the projector. The screen was filled with a PowerPoint slide showing a breakdown of the figures. "I checked and rechecked," he said. "I've used all the Internet data available, and that's the figure. Staggering, I know."

"And an indication of the difficulty of the task ahead." This from Alan Liskard, the Under-Secretary at the Home Office, whose job it was to oversee the running of Department 18. It was a job he hated, one that had been foisted upon him by the prime minister, who wanted a buffer between himself and a very suspect department. The notion that he was that buffer irked Liskard immeasurably.

"Twenty-seven million men, women, and children across the globe who have been taken from their homes and traded illegally. The UN estimated a figure for human trafficking at 800,000 a year. The amount of money generated by this business is off the scale; it runs into tens of billions. It's the third most profitable business for organized crime, after drugs and arms trafficking," Martin said. "The current price for a white newborn baby in the UK is ten thousand pounds. The price drops slightly if the baby is from an ethnic group, but only slightly. Adults fetch less again, but remember that many of those are actually selling themselves into slavery. Many have parted with their life savings to escape countries with oppressive regimes or poor economic structures, only to find themselves working for a pittance or, quite often, nothing at all, in wealthy countries. Trapped and unable to extricate themselves from the position they've been suckered into."

"So Holly and his kind take advantage of this illegal trade?" Harry Bailey said.

"The people they take for their own uses are part of an unmanageable statistic. These figures are no great secret, but few governments see human trafficking as a priority. Isn't that right, Under-Secretary?"

Liskard glared at him but said nothing.

Martin continued, "It's one of the reasons Holly and his kind have stayed undetected for so long. The poor souls who are traded are invisible, untraceable. And it's easier to leave them that way. There are groups in the UK, like the Salvation Army, that try to raise awareness, and there are charitable organizations in other countries with similar agendas. But faced with such a huge problem on a truly global scale, they might just as well be pissing in the sea for all the difference they make. It's the perfect environment for these creatures to operate."

"A bit melodramatic, isn't it?" Liskard said, his face sliding into a sneer. "*Creatures?* Surely they have a name."

Crozier said, "Not as far as I know, Alan."

"Breathers," Martin Impey said.

Crozier looked at him sharply. "Pardon?"

"I found a book in the British Library written by Professor Oliver Vance in the 1930s, dealing with the myths and legends of ancient Rome. Apparently these creatures were around at that time too. The Roman's called them *Spiracie*, from the word *spiraculum*. Which translates as *breathe* or *to breathe*. The creatures have small openings in their fingertips like spiracles, or breathing tubes, and the Romans believed the *Spiracie* killed their victims by burrowing into their lungs with their fingers and stealing their breath."

"Well, they weren't *that* far away from the truth, were they," Bailey said.

"No, I suppose not," Martin said. "Anyway, the colloquial name that seems to have stuck for the last few hundred years is *breathers*."

Alan Liskard clapped his hands together. "Okay, let's get on. We have a name for them. Not particularly accurate, I dare say, but it will do, I suppose. The question is, what are you going to do about them?"

Michael Dylan's thoughts were drifting. The words were sinking into his consciousness, but his mind was miles away in Dunkerry. This was the part of the job he hated. When the starched shirts got involved, the fun dissipated. And Liskard was so buttoned up he looked permanently constipated.

Dylan glanced across the table at the young woman sitting opposite him. He'd never seen her before and was curious. She looked to be in her early thirties with jet-black hair pulled severely back from an unmemorable face and held in place with a tortoiseshell clip. Her clothes were loose, baggy, seemingly chosen to hide the body beneath them. She was listening intently to the conversation, tapping the end of a pencil against her teeth and occasionally using her nicotine-stained index finger to push her heavy, black-framed glasses back from the tip of her nose.

She'd been introduced to the group as Dr. Miranda Payne, an Oxford-educated psychologist and, Dylan suspected, brought into the team as a last-minute replacement for Jane Talbot. He felt sorry for Jane and missed her at the table, but her absence was understandable. Her last assignment on the island of Kulsay was the talk of the office. For her, the experience had been nothing short of cataclysmic. According to Crozier, Jane was on indefinite sick leave and he had no idea when she would be back to work, if ever.

"Are you still with us, Dylan?" Crozier's voice broke into his thoughts.

Michael Dylan mentally shook himself. "Yes, sorry."

"The under-secretary was asking what we're going to do about the problem."

"Problem?"

Crozier glared at him.

Miranda Payne put down her pencil and pushed back her glasses. "I think we need to focus," she said. "You've researched this brilliantly . . . Martin, isn't it? But bandying about the figures for human trafficking is only going to muddy the waters. Slavery is not the issue here. It seems to me that we're dealing with ruthless predators that see the human race as nothing more than food. If, as you say, they've been around since Roman times, we have to assume that they are either very adept at living in the shadows or that their presence has infiltrated the highest levels of our society and they are being very well protected. I suspect the latter."

"That's quite an accusation, Ms. Payne," Liskard said.

"You surely don't believe that their influence could have reached as far as government." He sounded affronted, as if the mere suggestion that the government, *his government*, could have possibly been compromised.

"Why not?" Miranda said. "And it's Dr. Payne." She lifted her chin defiantly, as if daring him to challenge her.

"Sorry, *Dr.* Payne," Liskard said, a slight smile playing on his lips. "Please continue."

"John Holly is a player on the world stage. His company is a global success and when he's not taking up space on the financial pages, he's the darling of the world's gossip writers and scandal sheets. If he's one of these . . . these *breathers*, and *he* can reach such heights, I see no reason why some of our lowly politicians might not be all they seem."

Michael Dylan stared at Miranda Payne in admiration. She knew how to ruffle feathers. He liked that. He glanced across at Liskard. He could see the pompous little prick was bridling and about to refute her argument again, when the door to the conference room opened and Trudy, Crozier's secretary, slipped in. She went straight over to her boss and whispered in his ear.

"Right," Crozier responded. "Show them through."

A few seconds later the door opened again and two men walked into the room.

The first man through the door was tall and black, in his fifties with a shaven head. He was heavily muscled but lithe, and although he seemed to saunter into the room, Dylan could see the muscles of his shoulders bunching. The man was a tightly coiled spring.

His companion was smaller, but probably no less than six feet, early forties with cropped black hair and a neatly trimmed beard. The brown eyes looked tired and troubled, and they were set in a face that seemed to contain all the sadness of the world.

Crozier rose to greet them, shaking their hands. "Mr. Pike,

we meet at last. Please take a seat and I'll make the introductions."

Once they were seated, Crozier said, "Okay, clockwise, from the right. Alan Liskard, from the Home Office; next to him, Dr. Miranda Payne, a new recruit to the department. Miranda is one of our leading psychologists. Across the table, Michael Dylan, one of our top investigators, and next to him . . ."

"Harry Bailey," Pike said, grinning and stretching out his hand to Bailey. "Good to see you again. It's been a long time."

Bailey took the hand and shook it warmly. "I'm surprised you remembered."

"I'm hardly likely to forget after our last encounter. I heard you'd retired."

"I am retired. I'm just helping out here."

"Well, it's going to be a pleasure working alongside you."

"Shouldn't Daniel Milton be here as well?" Crozier said.

"That was the plan," Pike said. "But as yet I haven't been able to trace him."

Simon Crozier frowned. "A problem?"

"A serious one, I think," Pike said. "I can't reach him on his cell, and the way he lives his life, his cell phone is his lifeline. He's never without it, and no matter how dire his living conditions, he always finds a way to keep the phone charged."

Crozier shook his head. "I don't like the sound of that," he said, then turned suddenly to Pike's companion. "I'm sorry; I don't know who you are."

"This is Jacek Czerwinski," Pike said. "I brought him with me from Poland. His aims are common with our own, and he's had dealings with the vermin in the past. I can vouch for him."

Jacek looked at the faces around the table, feeling out of his depth but determined not to let it show.

"And does Mr. Czerwinski speak English, or should we hire

an interpreter?" Liskard said acidly. Nobody had mentioned Czerwinski's inclusion to him, and he was furious that protocol had been sidestepped yet again. He turned to Crozier. "Really, Simon, this is too much. Why don't you sell tickets?"

Crozier smiled at him blandly, then turned to Jacek. "Do you speak English, Mr. Czerwinski?"

"I do," Jacek said.

"There you are, Alan. He does. And if Mr. Pike thinks Mr. Czerwinski has a contribution to make, then that's good enough for me."

"The proper channels in future, Simon. *The proper channels*," Liskard said with barely contained anger. "Now, may we get on? I have a housing committee meeting scheduled, and I'm late for it already."

"Housing committee . . . or the future of the human race," Dylan said, making a balancing gesture with his hands. "Tough choice. I can see someone like you would have problems prioritizing."

"That's enough," Crozier said. "Let's get on."

•

For what is it to die but to stand naked in the wind and to melt into the sun? And what is it to cease breathing but to free the breath from its restless tides, that it may rise and expand and seek God unencumbered?
—Kkahlil Ggibran

Chapter Thirty-three

Clerkenwell, London, England

At the same time that Simon Crozier was chairing the meeting at Department 18's headquarters in Whitehall, rats found Daniel Milton in the abandoned office building, two miles away in Clerkenwell.

He was running a high fever and was lost in a deep delirium, so he didn't feel them as they first nibbled, then gnawed and finally tore at the material of his combats, exposing the flesh of his legs. His broken spine ensured that he felt no pain as sharp teeth ripped at his pale skin.

As his blood started to flow and pool underneath him, the rats became more excitable, more daring. There were only four of them, but they snapped at each other if one encroached on another's feeding ground. Eventually one of them broke away from the group and started exploring Daniel's body above the waist. It jumped up onto Daniel's chest and began poking its sharp, pointed nose into the gap where the zipper of his jacket had split in the fall. It could smell flesh beneath the thin material of his sports shirt and scrabbled at the cotton with its claws, all the while sniffing, whiskers twitching.

The first bite broke through Daniel's delirium; a searing

pain burning into the flesh of his chest like a white-hot nail. His body convulsed and the rat scurried off, pausing two feet away, watching him cautiously.

Seconds later it was back, joined this time by one of the others. They climbed up onto his body again, making for the fresh wound. As the first rat soaked its snout in the warm blood, the second ventured farther, licking delicately at the small pool of sweat gathered in the hollow of Daniel's throat.

He could feel them squirming over his body, getting closer and closer to his face. *My eyes*, he thought in a lucid moment. *Have to protect my eyes.*

Gathering all his strength he lifted his arm from the floor, and in a Herculean effort swung it over his face. The pain was beyond belief and he cried out, the scream echoing from the bare concrete walls like a ghost wail as the broken bones in his body ground against each other. *Why can't I just die?*

That had been the plan, to kill himself; to put himself out of their reach forever. So why had the plan failed? He wasn't religious. He hadn't prayed for salvation. He didn't really believe in the concept of God in any of its forms. But he was considering now that if there *was* a God then he had certainly pissed Him off.

Daniel had considered his own death in the past, picturing different scenarios. But even in his wildest imaginings, he'd never conjured a scenario like this. Lying on the cold hard floor of an abandoned office building, paralyzed from the waist down, unable to defend himself, and eaten alive by rats.

In his increasingly diminishing lucid moments he had been thinking about Alice Spur. They had been soul mates, though she was always headstrong. Their only argument had been when she took the personal assistant job at Holly Industries. Daniel knew instinctively that Abe Holly was bad news, and after Alice disappeared and Daniel came up against the son, he recognized that John Holly was even worse.

Daniel had wanted to spend the rest of his life with Alice, but now he guessed he had no life left.

He had only one hope, and it was a hope so slim, so . . . ridiculous, he could barely bring himself to do it. He had tried it once before and it didn't work, but, as he felt the rats creeping up his body again, he tried it anyway.

Concentrating furiously, he focused his mind, feeling his thoughts coalesce into one, building to a thrumming pulse in the center of his frontal lobe. When the pressure became almost unbearable, he released the thought, letting it fly. He could almost feel it leave his body, exploding into the air, into the unseen distance.

JASON! HELP ME!

And then, the effort of sending the message having drained him, he sank into oblivion while the rats fed.

Chapter Thirty-four

Department 18 Headquarters, Whitehall, London, England

Jason Pike suddenly covered his face with his hands and groaned. It felt as though an express train was barreling through his mind. He steadied his breathing, then took his hands away and stared at the faces around the table.

"Where's Clerkenwell?" he said to no one in particular.

Crozier paused midsentence. "Clerkenwell?" he said as Pike got to his feet.

"Daniel's made contact. He's in trouble. Serious trouble. In Clerkenwell. I have to go."

"I know where it is," Michael Dylan said. "Anything to escape this red-tape boredom. I'll take you. A pool car, Simon?"

"Speak to Trudy on your way out. There'll be a car waiting for you downstairs."

Harry Bailey was also getting to his feet.

"Are you going too?" Crozier said.

"Oh yes, I think so," Bailey said. "You know me, Simon. Straight into the thick of the action."

Liskard was watching all this with confusion in his eyes. He couldn't work out what had just happened. "Would somebody mind telling me what the hell's going on?"

Everyone ignored him.

"Jacek?" Pike said.

Czerwinski nodded and joined them at the door.

Miranda Payne pushed her glasses back up to the bridge of her nose, slipped her notepad back into her briefcase, and edged her chair away from her desk. "Do you mind if I observe?"

"Tell Trudy to make it a minivan," Crozier said with a wry smile.

"Simon?" Liskard said, absolute outrage channeled into one word.

"Sorry, Alan," Crozier said. "I'm afraid I shall have to conclude this meeting."

"But what's happening? Where are they all going?"

"Clerkenwell, apparently."

"But we haven't decided upon a plan of action yet." Liskard could barely contain himself. He silently cursed the minister for landing him with this bunch. They ignored protocol, barely paid lip service to his presence and looked, for all intents and purposes, to be totally unmanageable.

"The plan of action has been thrust upon us, Alan. As Sherlock Holmes once said, 'the game's afoot.'" He smiled and then he too left the conference room, leaving Alan Liskard to sulkily gather his paperwork together. "Is it always like this?" he said to Martin Impey, who was busy taking down the projection screen.

"More or less," Martin said. "Always something going off somewhere." He smiled. "You get used to it after a while."

Liskard shut his briefcase and got to his feet. As he walked to the door he said, "Tell Simon to keep me in the loop."

Martin didn't bother to look round at him. He'd seen many officers of government come and go over the years. He gave Liskard eighteen months. Tops.

"Did you hear me?" Liskard said impatiently.

"The loop. Yes. He's to keep you in the loop." Martin finally looked round and beamed at him. "Wilco. Roger and out."

Alan Liskard mumbled something obscene under his breath and stalked from the room.

Whenever I feel blue, I start breathing again.
—L. Frank Baum

Chapter Thirty-five

Embankment, River Thames, London, England

"So do we have an address in Clerkenwell?" Michael Dylan said as they turned onto the Embankment.

Pike shook his head. "No. But the message he sent was strong. I'm still picking up residual energy from it. I'll know for sure when we get there."

There was silence in the car as they drove down Ludgate Hill, then cut across the traffic lights onto Farringdon Road.

Pike was in the front passenger seat. Dylan was driving, but he could see Pike out of the corner of his eye. The big man was sitting with his eyes tightly closed, fingers drumming on the dashboard. There was a sense of containment about him, as if all his energy was being held inside, channeled, focused.

"Take the next left."

"That brings us onto Clerkenwell Road."

Pike nodded.

Dylan flicked the indicator. The traffic lights ahead switched to green, and he swung the Citroen Picasso's wheel.

"We're very close," Pike said, and then his eyes opened and he pointed to a large derelict building on the left-hand side of the road. It was surrounded by a rusting chain-link fence, its windows boarded with thick sheets of plywood. "There!" he said, "Daniel's in there."

Dylan didn't bother to ask him whether he was sure; there was such certainty in the man's voice.

In the back of the Picasso, Harry Bailey, Miranda Payne, and Jacek Czerwinski exchanged glances. None had said a word on the journey, all of them totally carried along on Pike's wave of intensity. Dylan pulled out his cell phone and hit speed dial.

In his office, Martin Impey picked up his phone, checked the caller display, and said, "Yes, Dylan, what can I do for you?"

"We're outside a building at 115 Clerkenwell Road. It's derelict and boarded up. Can you find a schematic for it?"

"I'm on it," Martin said, his fingers already flying over the keys of his computer. "Give me a couple of minutes. I'll call you when I have something."

Pike opened the car door.

"Wait!" Dylan said. "Let Martin do his job. We're not going in there blind."

"But Daniel—"

"Won't thank us if we fuck it up now, will he? Let's wait for Martin. He's very good, you know."

Pike sighed but relented and sank back into his seat, eyeing the building apprehensively.

A few moments later, Dylan's cell buzzed.

"We're in luck. A developer's got his hands on it. He's posted the original plans along with the new ones. I'll send the originals through to your PDA. Sending now."

"Thank you, Martin. Remind me to buy you a drink next time we meet up."

Martin Impey laughed. "Dylan, you say that every time I help you out. So far I haven't had so much as a beer off you."

"I mean it this time," Dylan said, the insincerity heavy in his voice.

"Sure. Good luck."

Dylan rang off and slipped the phone into his pocket. At the same time he took out his PDA and checked the floor plans of the building.

"Okay. Let's move."

The doors of the Picasso opened and the team poured out onto the street.

Chapter Thirty-six

Clerkenwell, London, England

Daniel Milton didn't realize it, but he was close to death. Exposure, the loss of blood, and the toxins from the rat bites already running rampant in his body were conspiring to kill him. He was vaguely aware of noises coming from the floors below and resigned himself to the fact that John Holly and some of his confederates had come back to finish him off. *So be it*, he thought, and lapsed into unconsciousness.

"Any idea where we should start looking?" Dylan asked Pike as they pushed aside the corrugated iron covering the doorway. The iron sheet offered very little in the way of security, and it was obvious that many feet had passed this way recently.

"Up, I think," Pike said. "It's difficult. I'm picking up nothing now."

"Which means?" Bailey said, pushing past them to stand in what was once the foyer of the building.

"We could be too late," Pike said grimly.

Miranda Payne followed Jacek Czerwinski through into the building, picking her way over rubble and assorted debris in her slightly-too-high-heeled shoes. "The place stinks," she said, wrinkling her nose in disgust.

"It smells like the apartment building where I live," Jacek said. "People use that as a toilet too."

"Charming," Miranda said. "And you're happy to live there?"

"I've resigned myself to it," Jacek said with a rueful smile.

They reached Dylan and the others. Dylan was checking his PDA, scrolling through the screens. "The stairs are this way," he said, pointing to a doorway to his left. "I think it's safe to assume the elevator won't be working."

"Best check each floor as we go up," Bailey said, marching toward the door. He was feeling good, invigorated. He hadn't realized it until now, but he missed this. Hiding himself away in the peaceful environs of Dublin might have been good for his health, but it did nothing for his spiritual well-being. He missed the game too much.

He pulled the heavy fire door open and ushered the others through into the stairwell.

Pike stood at the bottom of the stairs and called out. "Daniel!" His voice was deep and booming, and bounced off the concrete walls. He called again, listening intently.

Nothing.

His deepest fears seemed to be edging closer to reality. He

remembered the loss of so many others. Their deaths could have happened yesterday, and the pain he felt from them was acute, exacerbated by the fact that he blamed himself for putting their lives on the line.

He'd pulled them into his own private war, as he had with others in the past. And now there were still more people involved. He looked around at their faces. All eager, committed, with perhaps the exception of Miranda Payne, who was looking distinctly uncomfortable and out of her depth. How many of these people would survive the battle with Holly and his kind? He shuddered inwardly and forced his mind to focus on the task in hand—finding Daniel Milton.

As Pike and the others climbed the stairs and started searching, more bodies were pushing their way silently through the corrugated-iron-covered doorway. The ones who possessed a modicum of psychic ability were searching the place with their minds; others sniffed the air hungrily. One of them, a man, stood apart, speaking quietly into a cell phone. "Yes," he said. "Pike and Czerwinski are here. But they're not alone."

In his study at Faircroft Manor, John Holly cradled the telephone between his chin and his shoulder, his fingers dancing over the keys of his computer. "That's interesting. Who's with him?"

"There are three others. Two men and a woman. I don't recognize any of them. But Pike and Czerwinski were in Whitehall earlier."

Department 18, Holly thought. It was the only clear reason Pike would be in Whitehall. "I'm going to send a photo of someone through to your phone. Ring me again when you receive it and tell me if you recognize him and if he's there with Pike."

The man with the cell hung up and waited. The others were all staring at him, waiting for further instructions. "We wait," he said softly.

John Holly clicked a few more keys and opened a directory. He scrolled through the list of files, finally finding what he was looking for. He'd had dealings with Department 18 a long, long time ago, and one man in particular. He found the file he was looking for and downloaded a jpeg to his phone, then he punched in the number, and pressed SEND.

In the office building, the man's cell phone vibrated in his hand. He checked the picture Holly had sent to him, smiled, and hit 1 on speed dial.

"Well?" Holly said.

"Yes, that's one of them."

"Harry Bailey. Strange, I thought he'd retired." He leaned back in his chair and considered the latest shift in events for a moment. "Okay, go ahead with the plan, but you are going to have to play it very carefully. Bailey is almost as formidable an opponent as Pike. Very powerful. I'll leave it to you how you work it, but my advice would be to separate them, split them up. Just remember I want Pike and Czerwinski alive. The others are expendable."

He hung up and laced his fingers under his chin. Department 18 could pose a threat. He'd kept tabs on them since the early '90s and had always been a little puzzled why they hadn't featured in his life since the days of Jay Cavanagh.

He remembered meeting Harry Bailey in the small hotel in Bayswater and being impressed by him, impressed and slightly unnerved. There was a depth to Bailey's psychic abilities that made John Holly reluctant to engage with him in anything other than mild mental fencing. He got to his feet, went across to the small drinks cabinet in the corner of the room and poured himself a large gin.

And then he went back to his desk, and his phone, to wait.

Care I for the limb, the thews, the stature, bulk, and big assemblance of a man! Give me the spirit.
—William Shakespeare

Chapter Thirty-seven

Clerkenwell, London, England

Dylan had hung back from the others and beckoned Harry Bailey across to him. "We're not alone," he said quietly.

"I know," Bailey said. "They must have been here waiting for us. I sensed them a few minutes after we entered the building."

"Do you think Pike is aware of them?" Dylan said.

Yes, I am.

The words entered his thoughts. He looked across at Jason Pike, who acknowledged his attention with a slight bow of his head.

"He's good," Dylan said.

"Yes," Bailey said. "Yes, he is. Come on, let's move up a floor."

As they pushed through the fire door onto the fifth floor, Miranda Payne gave a small gasp. Daniel Milton was lying on his back in the center of the corridor, unmoving. She opened her mouth to speak, but Pike was already running past her. At the sound of his feet beating on the linoleum, the rats scattered, disappearing through various open doors along the corridor. When he reached Daniel's side, he crouched down and felt for a pulse in his neck. "He's still alive! Unconscious but alive!" he called to the others, who were moving more cautiously along, checking each room they came to.

Harry Bailey was the next to reach Daniel, squatting down beside him, lifting the side of his jacket and examining the ragged, bloody wound in his chest. He made a noise of disgust in his throat. "Christ! The rats were eating him alive." He turned to Dylan. "Call an ambulance."

Dylan pulled out his cell and started to dial 999.

"Wait!" Pike said.

Dylan paused with his thumb poised above the last 9. "He needs medical attention, urgently."

"I know. But we have something else to deal with first, before we bring more innocent souls here."

As he said it, the door to the stairwell opened and three men and two women stepped into the corridor. At the other end of the corridor, another door opened and six more men appeared.

"What's going on?" Miranda Payne said, an edge of panic in her voice.

"Holly laid a trap for me," Pike said calmly. "Daniel was the goat tethered to the stake. The bait."

Dylan looked from one end of the corridor to the other and felt a chill take a slow walk down his spine. The intruders were standing there unmoving, their faces impassive. They looked like they had come from their daily work. Three were dressed in suits. One had come from a building site and was still wearing his hard hat; at the back of the second group there was a young, uniformed police constable.

"Looks like we've been ambushed by the Village People," Bailey whispered in his ear.

Dylan gave a small snort of laughter, but the comment had an effect as he felt his spirits rallying.

Pushing himself up from the floor, Pike got to his feet. He turned to Jacek. "Take Dr. Payne into that room and shut the door. Do what you can to secure it."

"But I want to help," Jacek protested.

"You two are the most vulnerable. Do as I say." There was steel in his voice, steel and total conviction. "We can handle this," he added, more softly.

"If you say so," Jacek said and ushered Miranda Payne into the nearest office and closed the door. Pike listened and could hear the screech of a heavy steel filing cabinet as it was dragged across from the corner and set against the door.

"Jason Pike!" One of the men from the first group took a step forward. He was middle-aged, brown hair graying at the temples. Dressed in a sharply cut, expensive-looking suit, he was every inch the successful businessman. He was holding a cell phone.

Pike took a step toward him. "Who are you?"

"My name is not important. This is." He held up the phone. "John Holly would like to speak with you." He crouched down and slid the cell phone along the smooth linoleum. It skidded to a stop three feet from where Pike was standing.

For a moment Jason did nothing, just stood staring at the phone on the floor. Then he took a step forward, bent down, and scooped it up, pressing it to his ear. "Yes?"

"Hello, Jason," John Holly said. "You seem to have a little problem there."

"Nothing I can't handle."

"Ah, but at what cost? Haven't enough people lost their lives in all this? Look at poor Daniel there. Back broken. Even if he lives—which is doubtful—he'll never walk again. Why don't we call an end to this now?"

Pike stared down at Daniel Milton. The skin of his face was gray and waxy, and he was scarcely breathing. "What do you want?"

"You and Czerwinski go with my people. Leave the others there with Milton. Simple really."

"Nothing to do with you or your family is ever simple, John, so let's cut the bullshit. What do you really want?"

"I'll tell you that when we meet face to face."

"And you give me your word that the others will not be harmed and that you'll let them take Daniel to the hospital?"

"Of course."

"Then tell your people to leave, and I'll make my way to Faircroft Manor to meet with you later today," Pike said. "I give you my word." He counted the seconds of silence as Holly considered the deal being offered.

Finally John Holly spoke. "Agreed," he said. "Pass the phone back to Malcolm."

"The guy in the suit?"

"Is he wearing a suit? Malcolm O'Donnell? Must be in your honor, Jason. Yes, pass the phone to him."

Pike crouched and slid the phone back along the corridor.

Malcolm bent to retrieve it and pressed it against his ear, listening to the instructions coming from the other end of the line. Eventually he rang off and slipped the cell phone back in his jacket pocket. He raised his arm and signaled to the men at the far end of the corridor. As one, they turned and disappeared through the door from which they'd emerged.

Then Malcolm turned and said something to the group he was with. Within seconds Pike, Bailey, and Dylan were alone in the corridor with Daniel.

Harry Bailey was the first to speak. "So you're going to meet with him?"

"I said I would," Pike said.

"Now, is that such a good idea?" Dylan said.

"No," Pike said. "It's a lousy idea, but it was the best I could come up with on the spur of the moment."

Harry Bailey rubbed his chin. "It was too easy," he said, shaking his head. "Something's not right. Phone for the ambulance now. Let's get Milton to a hospital." He walked across to the office in which Jacek and Miranda Payne had barricaded themselves and banged on the door with his fist.

"You can come out now. They've gone." He waited to hear the filing cabinet being dragged away from the door.

He heard nothing.

He banged on the door again.

"The ambulance is on its way," Dylan said.

As Bailey called out again Dylan said, "Another problem?"

"Give me a hand here," Bailey said. His shoulder was against the door, and he was pushing with all his strength.

Dylan and Pike rushed across and added their weight to the effort. Gradually the door inched open. When the gap was wide enough Pike said, "Mr. Dylan, you're the smallest."

Dylan nodded and squeezed through the gap.

"Well?" Bailey said once Dylan was through.

"They're not here," Dylan called back.

Bailey's anger boiled to the surface, and he slammed his hand against door. "I said it was too easy."

Inside the room, Dylan put his shoulder against the filing cabinet and pushed it out of the way, opening the door for the others.

Bailey was first through. "How?" he said.

Dylan jerked his thumb in the direction of the window, which was open wide. Bailey walked across and looked through. The window opened onto a metal fire escape.

"There must have been more of them waiting out there," Dylan said.

"So why didn't we sense them?" Bailey said. "We got a sense of the others."

"Because Holly was blocking you," Pike said entering the room. "He was watching our every move. Look." He pointed to the corner of the room.

The object was spherical, white with a black dot in the center and about the size of a garden pea. It was tucked in the corner where two walls met the ceiling. You would have to be looking for it to see it. "A camera," Pike said. "There are more in the corridor, and I suspect all over the building. He was watching us the entire time, and we—I—played straight into his hands. I've been guilty of the sin of hubris. I believed Holly had set all this up in order to get his hands on me. I was wrong. He was after Jacek Czerwinski. Jacek was the target all along."

"But why?" Dylan said. "What's so important about him?"

Pike allowed himself a small smile. "Jacek Czerwinski, or rather his niece, Julia, could possibly be the last hope for the human race."

Chapter Thirty-eight

Faircroft Manor, Hertfordshire, England

John Holly rarely showed emotion—he thought it a weakness—but as he watched events at the Clerkenwell office building play out on the multiscreened wall in his study, he couldn't resist a smile of triumph. It had gone even better than he'd anticipated. From the moment he saw Czerwinski's face appear on the screens in front of him, Holly knew he would succeed, and he'd settled back to watch how his hastily arranged plan would play out. And it had gone like clockwork, beautiful clockwork.

The expression on their faces when they realized Czerwinski had gone was priceless. As for the woman? Taking her as well was a masterstroke, effectively clipping the wings of Department 18. If they interfered now they would have Dr. Miranda Payne's death on their collective conscience.

As he switched off the screens, the phone on his desk rang. He picked it up, listened for a few seconds, and said, "I saw it all. Well done. Get down here as soon as you can." He rang off and left the study, taking the flight of stairs down to the first floor where Alice had her rooms.

She was lying on the bed reading, her arm folded behind her head. She barely looked at him as he entered the room.

"Get up," he said. "We're expecting company."

"Who is it this time? Another of your cartel? Frankly, John, I'm getting tired of being shown off like a circus sideshow," she said and went back to her book.

"I assure you this is one person you are really going to want to meet."

She snorted derisively. "I doubt that."

He ignored her and looked about the room. "Where's the girl?"

"What girl?"

He crossed to the bed and knocked the book from her hand. She glared up at him. "Right, do I have your attention now? Where's Karolina?"

"Gone," she said, lifting her chin defiantly.

"Gone where?"

"I let her go, and by now she should be far, far away. Away from this place, away from you."

"That was a very foolish thing to do," he said calmly.

"Why? You said she was mine to do with as I chose. I chose to let her go. Get over it." She picked up her book from the bed where it had landed and continued reading.

Holly said nothing more. He turned and walked to the door. In the doorway he stopped and looked back at her. "Tidy yourself up," he said. "They'll be here in an hour or so, and I want you downstairs when they arrive."

He closed the door quietly as he left the room, controlling his anger with a supreme effort of will.

Back in his study, he picked up the phone again. "Masters, get some of the men together. I want you to make a search of the grounds."

The girl might, as Alice had said, be miles away, but then again . . .

It was irrelevant in the wider scheme of things. Julia was all that mattered now.

Abe Holly had recognized this immediately when she was born, all those years ago. She was outwardly normal, despite her heritage. Unlike the abomination born by Alice Spur from Holly. Even though she was half human and half breather, Julia seemed to be normal from the human perspective. What it was that made Julia so unique Abe Holly had never been able to find out. Whether she was able to demonstrate the breather characteristics he was never able to ascertain either.

Now John Holly had managed to find her, and, after all this time, he intended to get the answers.

The power of God is with you at all times; through the activities of mind, senses, breathing, and emotions; and is constantly doing all the work using you as a mere instrument.
—Bhagavad Gita

Chapter Thirty-nine

Department 18 Headquarters, Whitehall, London, England

"So how the hell did all this happen?" Simon Crozier said, flicking a stray piece of dust from his knee.

"It was a setup," Michael Dylan said. "Pike thinks it was planned by Holly to get his hands on Czerwinski."

"And did our Mr. Pike tell you why Czerwinski is so important that Holly would go to all this trouble?"

Dylan and Bailey exchanged looks. Both shook their head.

"He said something about Czerwinski's niece being the last hope for the human race," Dylan said. "But he never followed it up."

"Fantastic," Crozier said with heavy irony. "And where's Pike now?"

"He went in the ambulance with Daniel Milton," Dylan said.

Harry Bailey shifted uncomfortably in his seat. This had been a foul up of the first magnitude. Usually, when this kind of thing happened, Simon Crozier would be incandescent with rage. He always worked off a short fuse, and the fact that he was taking this news so calmly, so placidly, bothered Bailey more. "Jason said he'd hook up with us later."

Crozier looked at him bleakly. "Well I suppose we should be grateful for that. And Dr. Payne? Any ideas what Holly wants with her?"

"A lever," Bailey said. "To use against us."

"Do we know that for a fact?"

Again Dylan and Bailey glanced at each other.

"Not for a fact, no," Dylan said. "But it seems the most likely scenario."

Crozier leaned back in his seat and rubbed his eyes with his knuckles. "I brought Miranda Payne on board as a favor to her father," he said. "I take it you're aware who her father is?"

This drew blank looks from the pair of them.

"Miranda's father is Sir Nigel Foxton," Crozier said.

Michael Dylan's face took on the color of freshly kneaded dough. "Shit!" he said under his breath.

Harry Bailey looked nonplussed. "Am I missing something? Who's Nigel Foxton?"

Simon Crozier sighed. "Sir Nigel Foxton is a *very* senior civil servant, based at the Treasury, Harry," he said. "He's the man who holds our purse strings. The man who could close this department on a whim if he chose to do so."

Bailey grimaced. "So we're in the shit," he said.

"Succinctly put," Crozier said. "And now I have to go to our paymaster and tell him that his cherished daughter, his *only* daughter I might add, has been snatched by a psychic sexual vampire, responsible for the countless deaths of young women all about Miranda's age. I don't think he's going to take the news with equanimity, do you?"

He rose from his desk. "Find her. Find her and bring her back alive. And when you see Pike bring him to see me and we'll go through this again. That's all." He dismissed them with a wave of his hand.

Once they had left the office, Simon walked across to the small cabinet in the corner of the office and poured himself a large single malt. He took a mouthful and savored the flavor. He brought the drink back to his desk and sat down heavily in the chair, reaching across for the phone.

"Trudy, get Sir Nigel Foxton for me." He put the phone down. A few seconds later it began to ring.

He sipped another mouthful of whiskey and reached for the handset. Sometimes he hated this job.

Chapter Forty

The Barbican, London, England

Department 18 kept a number of apartments in the Barbican Centre. They were owned discreetly under a holding company, but they were used by operatives on active duty while in the capital. Some of them were occupied pretty much permanently by retired or resting personnel.

Carter was using one while he worked on the apartment building investigation. Before he was hospitalized, the plan had been to visit Jane and perhaps take her to dinner and a show. *So much for plans*, he thought.

There was no doubt he felt weak as he left the hospital. A taxi took him to the Barbican and as he paid the driver he looked around at the normality of the scene.

The building was looking a little tired from the outside, even a bit dated, and the road was permanently busy with traffic. As Carter stood there a few moments he watched cars, taxis, and motorbikes rushing to wherever they were headed, oblivious to anyone else's business, dealing with the issues of the day.

Carter let himself into the building, checked his box for

mail and took the elevator to his floor. Inside his apartment, everything was how he had left it. He dumped the clothes from the hospital in the laundry, ate a quick toasted cheese sandwich from the meager rations in the refrigerator and drank lashings of hot coffee.

The apartment had a small balcony, and he took more coffee with him while he smoked and thought. Had Jane really left him, or was she suffering guilt over her husband and especially her children? Carter wasn't sure. Paula was certain, and sometimes it took a stranger to see the truth between people more clearly than they did themselves.

Before Jane had visited him in hospital, Carter had no doubts they were set for life, or as good as could be at any rate. Now he thought he still knew how she felt but needed her to tell him. He thought about calling her but judged that would only make matters worse. She knew where he was.

He took a shower—very hot, then very cold—the contrasting temperatures soothing and invigorating. As he dried himself, he began to think about his next move with work. He realized a report into the apartment building investigation would have been written, but he needed to write one as well. Partly to ensure the full facts were reported and partly as an exorcism of what had happened.

He spent the next hour working at his laptop, a Word document gradually forming into a six-page report detailing all the events, when and where they happened and whom they affected. Whenever a death occurred during a department investigation, an independent team would look everything over in minute detail, ensuring compliance with regulations and that nothing criminal had taken place.

That was another reason Carter wanted to give a comprehensive report, to cover his back. He knew he had a reputation as a maverick, and it was not just Crozier who disliked him. Though Crozier was the main thorn in his side.

If he rang Jane, there was every chance the call would be picked up by David. He couldn't risk a text for the same reason. It was then that he noticed the e-mail icon flashing. He had mail in the inbox.

Making sure he had his report saved, he closed Word and went into Outlook. Among the various messages about people adding him on Facebook and confirmations of CD orders on Amazon, was a message from Jane.

He took the laptop onto the balcony, lit a cigarette, and opened the message.

Darling Rob,

Seeing you in hospital like that broke my heart. You looked so frail and helpless I just wanted to fling my arms around you and hug you and kiss you and tell you everything will be all right. Just like I do when Gemma or Amy hurt themselves.

I know I didn't do that. And I know that what I did do hurt you even more than your injuries. Please understand why I had to do it.

I can't hurt the girls any more than I have already. They are so confused about why Mummy and Daddy don't live together with them, and why they argue all the time.

You will probably say I am running away and perhaps I am. I know now that I ran away before when I denied my powers, but I couldn't handle my feelings then and I am struggling now.

I do love you, Rob. If you want to know if I love you more than David, the answer is I don't love him at all any more. But if you ask me if I love you more than the girls . . . well I know you too well to think you would even ask me that question.

I can't be with you right now. That doesn't mean I am with David.

You and I will be together. We are a couple.

A couple of what . . . ??

I love you, J.
BUT DO NOT REPLY AND DELETE
THIS MESSAGE!

Carter read the message twice more, searching for meanings that weren't there. What Jane said was clear enough. He smoked three more cigarettes. He had guessed Jane would equate her turmoil of emotions with the time she suppressed her psychic gifts. She hated not being in control of her feelings and found comfort only in denial.

He e-mailed his report as an attachment to Crozier, ending the brief note with a "see you soon."

He didn't reply to Jane. Again, he didn't know who would read it, but he knew she wouldn't expect a response. He considered for a moment seeing if she was online on MSN Messenger but decided against it as too public.

He locked the door to the balcony, stored the laptop, and washed up the mug and plate he had used.

Crozier would see him soon.

Freedom is strangely ephemeral. It is something like breathing; one only becomes acutely aware of its importance when one is choking.
—William E. Simon

Chapter Forty-one

The grounds of Faircroft Manor, Hertfordshire, England

Karolina felt as if she had been running for hours, and now she was hopelessly lost. It had all seemed so easy when Alice had been explaining the route, even to the point of sketching a map for her, but that had been rendered useless when the rain started to fall from an overcast sky, making the ink run on the paper, smearing the lines and turning the landmarks into incomprehensible blue smudges. Now she was wet and cold. Her feet were blistered and her hands were bleeding from where she had tripped on a hidden root and gone sprawling headfirst down a leaf-strewn incline.

She couldn't shake the feeling that she was being tracked through the woods. She had heard nothing and seen nothing to confirm the feeling, but it was there just the same, gnawing away at her, making her jump at shadows. She had no wristwatch, so she had no idea how long she'd been out here, but judging from the way the light was starting to fade away, it must be getting close to evening. Alice had told her to head west, but with the thick gray rain clouds covering the sun, it was impossible to get her bearings. She pressed on.

Thirty or so minutes later, she pushed through a stand of silver birch trees and found herself in a clearing. In the center of the clearing was a dilapidated shack. Built from wood with a cedar-shingled roof, it would at least provide some shelter from the increasingly heavy downpour.

She ran down a small slope to the shack and pushed at the door, which opened with a scream of rusting hinges and released a foul smell of something like mildew, rot, and decay. She threw a hand across her mouth and stepped inside. One step in and something crunched and rolled under her foot. She withdrew her foot quickly, staring down in disgust at the crushed dead body of a rat, its throat torn out, the fur around the wound black, matted with congealed blood.

She took a breath to steady her churning stomach and ventured farther into the gloom.

Gradually, as her eyes became accustomed to the dim illumination, she took stock of her surroundings. To her surprise, the place was still furnished. The first room she came to had a couch and two armchairs, although birds and animals had obviously been using them as nests and beds as the upholstery was ripped and torn and covered in droppings. There were a few pictures still on the walls; hunting scenes—red-jacketed men and black-jacketed women galloping over the countryside. Against one wall stood a bookcase with a few books, curled from the damp, lining its shelves. Her English wasn't good enough to read the titles, but judging from the dust jackets, they looked like popular novels.

A noise from the back of the shack made her freeze in her perusal of the bookcase. Something was moving about back there. She looked around the room for something to use as a weapon, and in the sooty, disused fireplace she spotted a long poker. She picked it up and weighed it in her hand. Wrought iron and heavy, with a thick pointed tip. She raised it, ready to lash out, and moved from the room and along the passage toward the noise.

She found herself in a room that would once have been

the kitchen, but it was only the porcelain sink mounted by two brass faucets that betrayed its purpose. There were spaces in the work surfaces that would have housed a stove and refrigerator, but the spaces were thick with dust and debris, so it looked like it had been some time since any culinary miracles had been performed in this room. But at least it was lighter in here as the last of the afternoon sun trickled in through a window above the sink. Treading carefully and silently, she ventured inside.

In the corner of the room, lying on a bed of soiled and dusty newspapers was a threadbare tabby cat, presumably the murderer of the rat at the front door. Oblivious to her presence, it was washing itself, licking its paw and wiping it over its face. She approached it cautiously, lowering the poker in a gesture to suggest to the animal that she meant it no harm. When she was within a yard of it, she crouched down and stretched out her free hand to let the cat sniff it. She murmured soft, soothing words in Polish.

"Touch my cat . . . harm my Maisie an' I'll kill you, I swear it."

The words, deep and gruff, came from behind her, and Karolina spun around. The sudden movement frightened the cat. It gave a yowl of alarm and skittered past her.

The speaker was an old man with long, stringy white hair and an equally unkempt beard. Bright eyes glittered in a filthy and wind-worn face. He spoke again, revealing a row of gappy, rotten teeth. "I've been watching you," he said. "Who are you an' what do you want with Maisie and me?"

The words came out in a flurry, so fast Karolina barely understood them, but she caught enough to get a glimmer of understanding.

"No harm," she said.

"Put it down then. The poker, put it down." The old man made a gesture with his hand to make his point.

Karolina shook her head, raising the poker slightly.

He grinned. "Fair enough. I don't blame you. After all, you don't know me from Adam." He wandered to the door. "Let's talk in the other room. At least we can sit down in there."

Warily she followed him through to the main room, still tightly clutching the poker, ready to lash out if he tried anything.

He swept a space on one of the couch cushions with his hand and pointed to it. "Look, cleaner now. Sit down."

Karolina shook her head and remained standing.

He shrugged. "Suit yourself," he said and flopped down onto the cushion he had just cleaned, rubbing his arthritic knees. "That's better. What are you? Slav? Pole?"

Karolina said. "From Poland."

A faint smile appeared on the old man's dirty lips. "Good crew, the Poles. My old man flew with some of your people during the war. Always singing their praises he was." He paused, stroking his chin thoughtfully. Then, *"Jak się nazywasz?"* he said in faultless Polish.

"Karolina," she replied. "Karolina Adamczyk. You speak my language," she said, then let fly with a torrent of words, explaining her plight from the moment she was abducted and brought to England by Kaminski.

The old man held up his hands. "Whoa, Nelly!" he said. "I'm not fluent. Just the odd phrase my father taught me when I was a boy. I haven't got a bloody clue what you're goin' on about."

She stopped midflow, confusion clouding her eyes as she realized she wasn't being understood.

"My name's Albert," he said, then tapped his chest and repeated it. "Albert Wellington. Wellington, like the Iron Duke."

She looked at him blankly, not understanding the association.

"Okay," he said, wiping his lips on the ragged sleeve of his grubby overcoat. "Looks like we're going to have to take things a little slower. Oh, sit down, for Christ's sake." He flapped his hands. "I'm getting a crick in my neck staring up at you."

Cautiously she lowered herself onto the arm of one of the chairs, laying the poker down beside her. "Do you . . . live . . . here?" she said haltingly.

"If you can call it living, then yes, I do. Me an' Maisie."

"The cat?"

"Aye, the cat."

"Run away," Karolina said, pointing at the door.

"She'll be back at dinner time. Dinner time," he said again, miming eating a meal.

Karolina nodded with relief. "She's your . . . your *pet*," she said, shuddering at the new meaning the word now had for her.

"She is," Albert said. "But don't tell her I said so. She'd be mortified if she knew I thought of her that way. That's the funny thing about people an' cats. Too many people who keep cats believe they own them. Even have the cheek to call themselves *cat owners*. Bloody fools. You don't own a cat. A cat owns you. It chooses to stay with you, that's all. An' that's the natural order of things . . ." He stopped himself. "Listen to me waffling. That's the problem. I don't see a soul from week to week. Just Maisie to talk to, an' let me tell you, she's not much of a conversationalist."

He could see from the expression in Karolina's eyes that she hadn't any idea what he was talking about. He wiped his lips again. "Right, young lady. Perhaps you'd like to tell me what you're doing tramping through the woods on your own, an' then breaking into my house. In English an' very slowly. I'll give you a head start. I know you've come from the manor, the big house. I've been following you since you left the main grounds. So you can start by telling me why you left the place like the devil was at your heels, an' where it is you're making for." He spoke slowly, deliberately, and smiled broadly when Karolina nodded her understanding. "Brilliant!" he said. "You an' me are going to get along just fine."

Chapter Forty-two

Department 18 Headquarters, Whitehall, London, England

"How about we start with you telling us what you know about Jacek Czerwinski? Who is he, and why has John Holly abducted him?" Simon Crozier said.

It was early evening and Harry Bailey and Michael Dylan had reconvened, with Jason Pike, in Crozier's office.

The three of them sat there, facing Crozier across the obsidian lake of his desk. As usual, there wasn't a speck of dust or even a thumbprint on the smooth glass surface. Even though he had sat here on many occasions over the years, Harry Bailey still found the surroundings intimidating. Which was, of course, just what Crozier intended. He glanced at Pike, whose face was placid, serene. He was staring back at Crozier, evaluating the man, getting his measure.

"Well?" Crozier prodded after several seconds.

"I thought your first concern would be Daniel Milton," Pike said, his voice a low rumble, the voice of a volcano biding its time before the eruption. "Had it not been for him laying his life on the line, you wouldn't know anything about this."

"On reflection," Crozier said quietly, "I'm regretting we ever got involved. Anyway, there's nothing we can do about that now. So how is Milton?"

"Not good," Pike said. "His back's broken, and he'll never walk again. His left arm is broken, as is his collar bone, and he's got a severe concussion, probably due to the fractured skull he suffered at Holly's hands. The rat bites looked worse than they were, but he'll still need skin grafts on his legs where the little bastards gnawed down to the bone. He'll live, but he'll never be the same again."

Crozier nodded slowly, then took a breath. "Okay, let's move on. I go back to my original questions," Crozier said. "Czerwinski?"

Pike's eyes narrowed. There was a rebuke there, but it remained unspoken.

"Look, Mr. Pike, I know you're concerned for your friend, but the fact remains that one of my staff, Miranda Payne, has also been taken by these breathers."

"Does *everyone* know about breathers?" Pike said quietly to Dylan who was sitting to his left.

"It's a name we coined for them. Speak to Martin Impey if you want the historical reasoning behind it." He was silenced by a fierce look from Simon Crozier.

"For all I know Dr. Payne could well be dead, but we'll go on the assumption that she's still alive, and that makes her my prime concern. Giving us this information could lead us to her. Surely you understand that."

Pike stared hard at him, weighing the decision in his mind. Finally he spoke. "We have to go back to Alice Spur, discuss her, and especially discuss Julia," he said.

"Who the hell is Julia?" Crozier demanded.

Pike sighed, and spoke slowly as if explaining the obvious to a slow pupil. "She is the daughter of Tomas Czerwinski—Tomas being Jacek's brother. What Jacek doesn't know is Tomas and his wife were her adoptive parents."

Pike waited to see whether he would get a reaction. Crozier kept his face neutral, as did Bailey and Dylan. They'd all seen too much of the paranormal, of life, to jump to the conclusion that Pike was finished.

"The true parents were unknown. The birth certificate was nonexistent and the details of her birth are not recorded."

Dylan was the first to voice impatience. "But you know who her parents are?"

Pike shook his head. "I have no real idea who the mother was. The father was Abe Holly." Pike paused and took a handkerchief from his pocket to wipe away the sweat beading on his brow. "Abe Holly impregnated a woman. The baby was born and to all intents and purposes was human. It was a girl, and she looked like any normal baby. The fact that it carried Holly's gene made it a vital breakthrough in the search for the breather-human hybrid. Somehow Abe Holly had stumbled on a perfect breeding fusion of the two species."

Crozier frowned. "So they have been able to create a mutation of themselves for years?"

Pike shook his head and a cold smile creased his mouth. "That was what Abe thought would happen. The human spirit proved too strong. The mother took the baby, *her* baby, and disappeared. For all Holly's extensive network and for all his powers, she managed to elude capture and the baby remained hidden away."

"Not hidden but adopted."

"Exactly. Adopted under strict secrecy. I have no idea what happened to the mother, but she ran away from Holly and ended up in Poland. The Czerwinskis were sworn to secrecy, never to reveal to the girl who her real parents were, and how could they? No one knew. So Julia grew up safe in Poland, never knowing she was adopted."

"But she knows now, right?" Michael Dylan said.

Pike shook his head. "I doubt it."

"Well, this is all very well, but what is the relevance to us?" Crozier said.

"I am certain Holly has Julia," Pike said. "Because of who her father was, her biological father, she has the breather gene. I'm guessing Holly wants to breed from her to further his *research*. Czerwinski will have been taken as leverage."

"And for all the secrecy, the plotting and the plans, you still managed to deliver him into the hands of the breathers," Crozier said. "Does John Holly know who Jacek Czerwinski is?"

"Yes," Pike said. "I don't think he does anything without a purpose."

"We don't seem to be getting very far, do we?" Dylan said. "Surely the question is, how do we get Czerwinski and Miranda Payne back?"

"I've been thinking about that," Pike said.

"Well, that's a start," Crozier said.

"Hear me out," Pike said, picking up on the sarcasm in Crozier's voice. "We haven't a hope in hell that we can pull this off unaided. Holly is too powerful, the network protecting him too widespread and too efficient. We're going to need help."

"Anyone in mind?" Dylan said.

Pike smiled humorlessly. "A deal with the devil, my friends." He took a cell phone from his pocket and dialed the only number in its address book.

There was a long pause before the phone at the other end picked up.

"Hello, Rachel," Pike said. "It's Jason. I think we need to talk."

The body is a device to calculate the astronomy of the spirit.
—Mevlana Rumi

Chapter Forty-three

Hertfordshire, England

The Lear jet was ready for takeoff at the private airstrip.

Holly was standing by the plane, talking to the pilot, a young fresh-faced man with a neat beard and a studious expression.

Alice Spur sat in the rear seat of the Mercedes, staring through the tinted window at the red disc of the dying sun as it slowly sank beneath the horizon. She was thinking about Karolina, wondering where she was now and hoping the girl had followed her instructions and got clean away. But her thoughts were tinged with pessimism, as memories of her own attempts to escape John Holly insinuated their way into her mind.

She had made three attempts to escape, two in Switzerland, one in England, and it was after the one in England failed so dismally that she conceded that any attempt to free herself from Holly was futile. He was tuned in to her. Her brain acted like a tracking beacon. All he had to do was to concentrate, and he could invade her mind and pinpoint exactly where she was.

She'd managed to conceal from him her plans for Karolina. That had taken him completely by surprise, and it was so satisfying to see confusion battling the anger in his eyes. But she could still feel him probing her mind occasionally;

an insidious intruder stealing her thoughts and feelings—mental rape.

Her attention was taken by a white Ford van trundling toward them across the grass that flanked the runway. It pulled up next to Holly, and a man jumped out of the passenger seat. She recognized him immediately. She'd seen him a number of times at Faircroft Manor and knew his name was Malcolm, but no more than that. Not even if Malcolm was his first or second name. She could tell from the way they spoke to each other they were fairly close, but she wasn't sure where Malcolm fitted into the hierarchy of John Holly's life.

The two men exchanged a few words, and then Malcolm slapped the side of the van. The back doors opened, and two more men jumped out. Both had cropped hair and tough-looking faces. Both were carrying guns. The bigger of the two leaned back into the van and said something, though his words were muffled. When he stepped away from the doors, two more people stepped out, a man and a woman.

The man was probably no less than six feet, early forties with cropped black hair and a neatly trimmed beard. He didn't look English. The woman looked terrified. She was quite plain, with baggy unflattering clothes. Her hair was pinned up, but several strands had worked loose and were being blown about her face by the wind that was gusting across the airfield. It was when the woman tried to brush the hair away from her face that Alice noticed her wrists were shackled by handcuffs.

At a barked order from Malcolm, the two thugs moved in and hurried the man and the woman toward the Lear, virtually pushing them the three steps leading up to the fuselage.

Holly walked across to the Mercedes and opened the door. "We're ready to leave," he said.

"Who are they?" Alice said.

"Guests," Holly said, tapping his foot impatiently as he waited for her to get out of the car.

"Guests or prisoners?" she said sliding from the backseat of the car. As she got out she was hit by a gust of wind, making her shiver.

"Don't even think about liberating these two," he said, taking her arm and steering her toward the plane.

Chapter Forty-four

Hampstead, London, England

Rachel Grey took the phone away from her ear and stared at it as if it were something alien. She gestured to Schwab to pick up the extension, waited until he had, then continued. "Jason, what a lovely surprise," she said. "But what on earth do you think there is to talk about?"

"Holly has Czerwinski."

"Czerwinski? Who's Czerwinski?"

"The owner of the phone I'm speaking on now. The phone you gave him. Or rather the phone Carl Schwab gave him. Hello, Carl."

Schwab shook his head and grinned. "Jason. Good to hear from you."

"So let's not play games, Rachel," Pike continued. "Okay?"

"Okay," she said lightly. "But I still don't see what there is to talk about."

"A truce."

Rachel looked across at Schwab, who shrugged his shoulders.

"We should meet," she said.

"I take it you're in London."

"I took the flight after yours out of Poland. I'm in Hampstead."

"I can be there in twenty minutes," Pike said.

"You'd come here, Jason? Isn't that a bit like walking into the lion's den?"

"I trust you, Rachel."

"Then you're a fool."

Pike chuckled softly. "We have a common enemy, Rachel. We need to decide how best to join forces to defeat him. Give me the address."

Rachel Grey thought for a moment and then gave it to him.

"Twenty minutes. And I'm bringing some friends."

"Do I know them?"

"No, I don't think you do. Michael Dylan and Harry Bailey. They work for the British government. I'll see you soon."

The line went dead.

Rachel turned to Schwab. "Well?"

"Never heard of them," he said, cradling the extension. "I don't like it. He must have an angle."

Rachel snaked her fingers through her hair, pushing it away from her face. She agreed with Schwab. But if Holly had taken Czerwinski, then he must be thinking along the same lines as she was—that there was something very special about this Polish man, very special indeed. Or rather there was definitely something special about Julia.

"Get your men ready, all fully armed, and position them in the grounds and around the house. Then prepare the dining room for a conference. We'll talk with them there."

"*We?*"

"Yes, Carl. I want you to be there."

"To watch your back?"

"My insurance policy."

"You realize this gives us a chance to remove Pike from the equation permanently?"

"Yes I do, and I'm sure Jason knows it too. That's why he's not coming alone." She walked across to the window and stared out at the manicured lawn of her Hampstead house.

A family of blackbirds had set up home in the branches of an ornamental cherry that occupied a spot in the center of the grass. She watched the comings and goings of the birds for a moment, her mind busy, working on the possible ramifications of this meeting.

The British government were now involved, she mused. That in itself was not too much of a problem. They'd infiltrated the British political system decades ago, and now several top-ranking positions of all three major political parties were filled by her kind. But why should the others in the government be taking such an active interest in things now?

Her feelings about Julia were ambiguous. She hadn't finished with her, and if her assumptions were right, then a man she hated had taken the girl from her. That was an irritation. She certainly had no emotional reaction beyond losing something she wanted for a while longer.

There were a number of questions to which she needed answers. The next few hours should prove interesting.

To one who has been long in city pent,
'tis very sweet to look into the fair
And open face of heaven,—to breathe a prayer
Full in the smile of the blue firmament.
—John Keats

Chapter Forty-five

Zurich, Switzerland

A sharp crosswind rattled the Lear as it swept in at the private airfield, but the pilot was equal to it and made a perfect landing. Two black limousines with tinted windows were already gliding across the tarmac toward the runway, and they arrived alongside the jet just as the doors opened.

Jacek and Miranda were hustled down the steps of the Lear and into the backseat of the first limo; Holly and Alice Spur took the rear of the second. Without a pause, the two cars swept away into the night.

"Where do you think they're taking us?" Miranda said quietly, almost a whisper. There was a glass partition between themselves and the driver, but she was taking no chances. She was more frightened than she had ever been in her life and was looking to Jacek for some kind of comfort.

"No idea," Jacek said, flattening her hopes. He stared through the tinted glass at the passing scenery. He'd always thought of Switzerland as a land of mountains and snow, of picturesque landscapes and deep, mysterious lakes, but what he was seeing bore no resemblance to his mental image of the country. Factories, residential housing, automobile showrooms and warehouses. For a while they ran parallel to the railway line. A train passed them going the opposite way. The double-decked carriages were blazing with light and packed with passengers.

As they left the industrial area of the town behind, the landscape gradually changed, but by now it was too dark to make out many details. Jacek could discern a mountain but only from the twinkling lights of the chalets that dotted the side of it. When the car turned sharply left at the next junction and started to climb, he realized that the mountain was their destination.

"It's ironic really," Miranda said. "When my husband, Jeremy, left me, I was desperate to have a more thrilling life. Ten years spent in the university faculty, lecturing to terminally bored students and then going home to a man whose idea of excitement was buying a new piece of rolling stock for his model railway. That and banging his secretary every chance he got. I was determined to break out, to stretch my wings. When Daddy told me about the opportunity at Department 18, I couldn't wait to get involved. Now it looks like my first case is going to be my last." A tear trickled down her cheek. She wiped it away impatiently with the back of her hand. "They're going to kill us, aren't they?"

"If they were, they would have done so by now. They have had plenty of opportunity," Jacek said. He reached out awkwardly and covered her manacled hands with his own.

"So what do they want with us?"

"I don't know."

"I'm scared."

"Yes," he said. "So am I."

She leaned back in her seat and closed her eyes. Then her eyes sprang open, and she sat forward again. "Passport control," she said.

"Sorry?"

"How did we get into the country without showing our passports?"

Jacek smiled to himself. She was really quite naive. "There are different rules for people like John Holly. He has enough money to make such inconveniences go away."

"No," she said, shaking her head impatiently. "You're missing the point. There's no record of us entering Switzerland. Nobody will be able to find us. No one knows we're here." There was an edge of panic to her voice.

"No," Jacek said. "No, they don't."

Her mouth worked, opening and closing as if trying to catch words that refused to be caught. Finally she said, "Then we're screwed."

"Yes," Jacek said. "We are."

Chapter Forty-six

Department 18 Headquarters, Whitehall, London, England

"A Lear jet departed Hunsdon airfield at 1900 hours heading for Zurich," Martin Impey said.

Crozier leaned back in his desk chair, crossing his legs. "Do we know if Holly was on it?"

"We know the jet belongs to Holly industries, and it tends to be for his private use, so it's a fair assumption. He's certainly not at Faircroft Manor. I've had people checking it out. They saw him leave with a young woman just after six, and Hunsdon's only a thirty-minute drive away from the manor."

"Did anyone think to follow him?" Crozier said tiredly, knowing what the answer would be.

Martin shook his head. "Limited resources," he said. "We didn't have the manpower to watch the manor *and* follow Holly."

"And no one thought that maybe following Holly would be the better call?"

"They were under instructions to watch Faircroft Manor."

"Christ! Doesn't anyone act on their initiative anymore?" Crozier said, his patience finally evaporating. He took a breath. "Miranda Payne? Czerwinski? Are they with Holly?"

Martin shrugged. "They weren't in the car that left the manor, but they may have been taken to the airfield to rendezvous with Holly there."

Crozier thought for a moment. "Okay, why would Holly want to take Czerwinski and Dr. Payne to Zurich?"

"Holly is on the list of directors of a private clinic over there. The Spree Clinic. Situated halfway up a mountain overlooking the town."

"What kind of clinic?"

"The very exclusive kind. The people who check in are the types with enough money to keep their reasons for being there strictly confidential."

"Could it be a fertility clinic? That would tie in with what Pike told us about Holly."

"Could be," Martin said. "But then again, it could be a cosmetic surgery clinic for all I know. I've dug as deep as I can, but I can't find anything else out about it."

They were interrupted by the phone on Crozier's desk.

Crozier sat forward and picked it up. "What is it, Trudy?"

"Sir Nigel Foxton on the line, sir."

Crozier groaned inwardly. "Okay, put him through."

There was a pause, a click, and then Sir Nigel Foxton's voice boomed down the line at him.

Crozier glanced across at Martin, raised his eyebrows, and swiveled his chair around 180 degrees, lowering his voice so Martin Impey had to strain to hear what he was saying.

"We're doing all we can, sir . . . Yes, sir . . . We think Switzerland . . . Of course, as soon as there's any news at all . . . Yes, sir. I understand."

He swiveled back and slammed the phone down on its cradle.

Martin Impey looked at him expectantly.

"Miranda Payne's father."

"Sir Nigel."

"Quite. We need to get her back, Martin. It's imperative if the department is to survive. He just threatened me with a complete withdrawal of funding."

"Can he do that?"

"Oh yes, *he* can do that. I need more, Martin. Call in all the favors owed to you. I need to know for certain that Dr. Payne's with Holly in Switzerland."

Martin got to his feet. "It will cost," he said.

Crozier nodded his head slowly. "Yes," he said. "Of course it will. Grease as many palms as you have to, but get me that information. Don't let me down, Martin."

As Impey left the office, Crozier picked up the phone again.

"Harry, how's it going?"

"We're nearly there. Traffic through Hampstead was deadly but we're on schedule."

"Good. Listen, there's a possibility Holly may have taken them to Switzerland. Run it by Pike. See if he knows anything about the Spree Clinic in Zurich."

"The Spree Clinic. Okay."

As Harry Bailey rang off, the door to Crozier's office opened, and Trudy entered carrying a large mug of very black coffee. From her pocket she took a cardboard coaster and placed it on the glass desk, then set the mug down on it. "I thought you may need this," she said.

He looked up at her and smiled bleakly. "Trudy, you're a life saver," he said. He lifted the mug and drew in the aroma. "Brandy?"

Trudy smiled. "Of course."

Crozier smiled and blew her a kiss. Then he had a thought. "Wait a second. I've been here all day. I could do with a quick break. I'm going to go home for a couple of hours and freshen up."

"Sure. Do you want me to organize a car?"

"No, I'll take a cab. There'll be plenty at this time of night. I'll be back in a few hours, and, of course, I'm contactable at all times. You go home now though."

Trudy smiled. "I was hoping you'd say that."

Once outside in the street, Simon Crozier took a deep lungful of London air. The night was humid. Along Regent Street, cars were bumper to bumper, their exhausts blowing out clouds of pollution that gathered in a haze above the city. He pulled a handkerchief from his pocket and wiped the sweat from his brow, then waved the handkerchief in the air to hail a taxi. "Beaumont Place," he said to the driver, took a seat in the back of the cab, and opened his briefcase.

As the taxi pulled up outside the apartment building on Beaumont Place, Crozier paid the cab driver and let himself into the building, taking the elevator up to the fourth floor where his apartment was situated.

With its view over the Thames and desirable postcode, the apartment cost him a small fortune each month, but he wouldn't choose to live anywhere else. He opened the door onto the balcony and looked out over the water. There were cars on the nearby Tower Bridge, nose to tail, making snail-like progress across the river. A pleasure boat, lit up like a Christmas tree, was meandering its way west, music from an onboard disco wafting up to him on a thermal of torpid air. Farther down the river a police launch was cruising past a line of houseboats, a regular patrol to reassure the boats' inhabitants.

He went back inside and poured himself a malt whiskey,

which he brought back to the balcony. He slumped down on a steel-mesh chair and lifted his feet onto the balcony railing. As he took his first sip of Macallan, the telephone rang.

"Crozier," he said. He hoped it might be one of his regular companions, inviting him out for dinner and afterward some mutually pleasurable entertainment.

The best things in life are nearest: Breath in your nostrils, light in your eyes, flowers at your feet, duties at your hand, the path of right just before you. Then do not grasp at the stars, but do life's plain, common work as it comes, certain that daily duties and daily bread are the sweetest things in life.

—Robert Louis Stevenson

Chapter Forty-seven

Hampstead, London, England

"This is it," Dylan said as they drew up alongside a pair of heavy steel gates protecting a black asphalt drive.

The drive snaked through a garden dressed like heavy woodland with long stands of beech and dark green rhododendron bushes. Just visible through the bushes was a house, built in the late 1960s and designed by one of the more forward-looking architects of the day. All sleek lines and huge windows, it appeared at once futuristic and yet, in a strange way, curiously dated, very much a product of its time when all eyes were on the future but still bound by contemporary design and technology.

There was an intercom fixed to one of the gate posts. Pike got out of the car, pressed a button and spoke into the box.

There was a click and a hiss, and the gates swung inward.

Pike climbed back into the car. "Okay, we're in," he said.

As they reached the front of the house, the main door opened and Carl Schwab stepped out. He was holding a compact machine pistol and pointed it at Pike as the three men got out of the car.

"Not a very friendly welcome, Carl," Pike said, gesturing to the pistol.

Schwab grinned. "What did you expect, Jason? Flags and a marching band?" He stepped to one side. "Go into the house."

The three men climbed the steps to the door and walked past Schwab into the brightly lit interior of the house.

The greeting Jason Pike received from Rachel Grey seemed cordial enough, but Harry Bailey was watching the woman's eyes. *Like flint*, he thought. *Dead eyes*. Dylan was hanging back from the others. Bailey reversed and came alongside him. "Why didn't you tell me you weren't traveling alone?" he said in a whisper.

Dylan looked at him guardedly. "What do you mean?"

"Your shadowy traveling companions. They've been with us ever since we left London."

"The breathers? You can see them?"

"As clear as I can see you. Nasty buggers, aren't they?"

Dylan shrugged. "I don't know. I never get to see them properly. They're always flitting out of sight. I thought I'd got rid of them, thought they'd gone," he said tiredly. "I knew it was a mistake coming back to England."

They stopped speaking as Carl Schwab came up behind them, took Bailey's arm and steered them into the dining room.

"I suggest you let go of my arm," Bailey said. He kept his voice low, but there was steel in the tone.

For a second Schwab dug his fingers in tighter and then

released his hold. "Of course," he said smoothly. "Just trying to be of assistance."

"While holding us at gunpoint. Whose book on etiquette are you working from? Osama bin Laden's?"

Schwab smiled without humor and ushered them to their seats.

When Bailey and Dylan were seated Bailey leaned across to Dylan. "We'll talk about your little problem later," he whispered as the others took their places around the mahogany dining table.

Rachel Grey looked immaculate; a very beautiful woman, her hair sleek and shining, her makeup applied flawlessly. "Let's cut to the chase, shall we, Jason? What does Holly want with Czerwinski?"

Pike folded his hands on the table in front of him. "Jacek Czerwinski is Julia's uncle," he said in a flat tone, without emotion or emphasis. "Holly wants to breed from Julia, so Jacek is a bargaining chip."

Rachel Grey shrugged. "John is using Alice Spur as his sow. His revenge for her being the driver when Abe died. I don't believe it."

Schwab was looking at her curiously. "What's the problem either way?" he said.

Rachel ignored the question and sat forward in her seat resting her elbows on the table. "You may be right, though," she said to Pike. "Julia was taken quite forcibly. I was tired of her, so it was of little concern. But why would John want to use her?"

Pike wondered whether she was playing games, but decided she didn't know. "Julia is Abe Holly's daughter."

Rachel nodded. "She has the gene. No, wait. The mother was human?"

Pike nodded.

"So she may be the new beginning Holly has been after."

Chapter Forty-eight

The grounds of Faircroft Manor, Hertfordshire, England

"They keep a monster up at the manor," Albert Wellington said, his voice conspiratorial.

"A monster?" Karolina said.

"I've seen it. All gray skin and scales. Ugly brute. They keep it in the basement."

Karolina looked confused. She'd spent the last hour telling Albert Wellington her story, in halting English and with a surfeit of hand gestures, and now he was telling her about monsters. She was beginning to doubt his sanity.

"No," he said. "You're well out of there. The Hollys are evil, pure evil. I've seen things . . . heard things . . . Well, I'd better not say. You'll be having nightmares."

Karolina struggled to her feet. "I go now," she said.

"Go? Go where?"

She rummaged in the pocket of her jeans and produced a crumpled, slightly soggy piece of paper. "I go here," she said and handed it to him.

Albert unfolded the paper carefully and squinted at the smudged and blurred writing. "I can't read this," he said. "Wait a minute." He went across to the bookcase and moved a few of the books out of the way. He returned with a stub of candle and a book of matches. He set the candle down on the arm of the battered couch and lit the wick. The candle sputtered for a second and then caught. From the pocket of his coat he produced a pair of glasses, missing one lens, and slipped them on. Again he squinted at the paper.

"Cambridge," he said. "Who's Daniel Milton?"

Karolina shook her head and shrugged. "Alice . . . she give me. Said I should find him. He look after me."

"Well, you're not going there tonight. It's dark out there. How do you expect to find your . . ." He stopped speaking suddenly and spun round, cocking his head to one side. Then he crouched down, snuffed out the candle and put a sooty finger to his lips. "Ssshhh! Not a word. There's someone outside. Nod if you understand."

Karolina nodded hesitantly, opened her mouth to speak, then shut it again.

A flashlight beam cut through the gloom of the room. It missed them by a yard, but that didn't stop Albert grabbing Karolina's arm and dragging her down behind the couch.

The flashlight beam shone in through the window. A man's voice sounded from outside. "We'd better go in and take a look around."

"Come off it," another male voice said. "It's too dark to carry on with this nonsense. Anyway, who *is* this girl and why is she so important? It's not as if others haven't run away. He's always caught them in the end."

"It's not for us to ask. Mr. Holly said search the grounds for her and that's what we're going to do."

The flashlight moved away from the window. Seconds later Albert heard the scrape of the front door against the floor as it was pushed open. He looked about him frantically. Two feet away, still lying on the chair, where Karolina had put it, was the poker. He reached out and curled his fingers around the handle, pulling it toward him. He could hear Karolina breathing beside him. With his free hand he reached back and patted her arm. *It's going to be all right*, the gesture said, but she flinched back as if receiving an electric shock. He peeked over the top of the couch and saw the flashlight beam dancing off the walls.

"Smells like shit in here," one of the men said.

"Don't breathe then. Just through here, then we're done."

They had nearly reached the lounge. Albert ducked down out of sight and tried to hold his breath, wishing the girl would do the same. Her breathing was so loud he was convinced they'd hear her.

Another few seconds and the men were in the room with them. The light washed over the ceiling, sliding from the walls to the couch where it hovered for what seemed an eternity before moving on.

"See, I told you. There's nothing here," the first man said.

"I'm not so sure. Be quiet. Listen."

Whether Karolina understood what the man had just said, or whether it was pure instinct she took in a breath and held it. Whatever the reason, Wellington sighed inwardly with relief.

The second man took a step forward and prodded at the couch with his muddied boot, pushing it back a few inches. As he bent forward to yank it aside the crash of breaking glass split the silence making both men jump.

"What the fu—"

"Kitchen."

From behind the couch Albert Wellington let the air out of his lungs in a controlled, silent stream. He could hear the men's heavy footfalls as they ran back to the kitchen, but didn't dare poke his head over the couch to see what was going on. He glanced around at the girl. She looked terrified. Fat tears were trickling down her cheeks, and she was visibly shaking. He put an arm around her shoulder and pulled her close. She winced at first, gagging at the smell of his perspiration, but then relaxed and allowed herself to be held, taking comfort from the old man's body warmth and strong arms.

"Bloody cat knocked a beer bottle over! That's all." The exclamation came from the kitchen. "I've had enough. I'm going back to the house. Are you coming?"

There was a long pause before the second man said, "Okay. We've done all we can. Let's go."

Albert waited ten minutes before emerging from behind the couch. He wanted to make sure they were gone. As he got to his feet his knees cracked like gunshots, sending a spasm of pain all the way up to the lumbar region of his spine. His body was going to pay him back for keeping it in such an uncomfortable position for so long. He swore silently, and then reached out to help Karolina to her feet.

As she stood she rubbed her arms to try to get the circulation flowing again. She felt cold, icy cold, and it was beginning to make her nauseous.

"Are you okay?" he asked her.

She nodded but bit her bottom lip to keep herself from crying.

"It's all right," he said. "They've gone. You're safe now."

"Think again, granddad."

The voice came from the hallway. Albert spun around to face it and was immediately blinded by the powerful beam of the flashlight. He ran forward, charging at the man holding the flashlight, raising the poker above his head, wielding it like a sword. He brought it crashing down on the man's wrist.

The man squealed with pain and dropped the flashlight. "You've broken my arm, you old bastard!" he yelled.

The other man moved in. He aimed a kick at the side of Albert's knee, connecting solidly. Albert let out a hiss of pain and collapsed to the floor. Another kick landed in the middle of his stomach, knocking the air out of him and leaving him winded. As Albert lay there gasping for breath, the man grabbed Karolina by the arm and hauled her toward the door while his colleague leaned against the wall, nursing his damaged wrist, tears coursing down his face.

"Come on, let's get out of here. We've got what we came

for," the man holding Karolina said. She was struggling, trying to yank her arm away. He slapped her hard across the face with the back of his hand, his heavy gold signet ring opening a gash on her cheek. The blow subdued her instantly.

"What about him?" The voice was more a whine now, and he'd started to rock back and forth, holding his wrist.

"Leave him."

"But he broke my fucking arm."

"I said leave him. Come on."

And then they were gone, leaving Albert Wellington sprawled on the floor, close to unconsciousness.

Soul shadows you everywhere.
—Anda Fiori

Chapter Forty-nine

Hampstead, London, England

"Does the Spree Clinic in Switzerland mean anything to you?" Pike said.

Rachel Grey smiled. "Oh, yes. My people tried to infiltrate it months ago. No one survived. It's set into the side of a mountain. The part you see is exactly what it claims to be: a private clinic tackling things like eating disorders, alcohol and drug addiction, general rehabilitation. Very expensive, very exclusive. Think Betty Ford or the Priory, then crank them up several notches. But that is only the public facade, the tip of the iceberg. It extends deep into the mountain. The public only sees about a tenth of it."

"So what goes on there?" Bailey said.

"It's the hub of Holly's genetic research program. We wanted to get in there and destroy it. Jason, you know our feelings about hybrid research. We see it as the end of our race as we know it and, quite honestly, the end of the human race as well. If Julia is who you say she is, then Holly's program is about to take a huge leap forward. He's come a long way with only Alice Spur's eggs to work with. Can you imagine how far he can take it using Julia? In theory he could impregnate dozens of eggs in a very short space of time. If he used sperm from any number of chosen males, he could produce a dominant gene in less than a year. We could be overrun with hybrids. A few hundred years down the line, they could become the dominant species on the planet. It's like a Hitler Master Race."

"You like to think ahead," Dylan said with sarcasm.

Rachel shook her head. "For us it's not thinking ahead. You must remember, our life span is about five times that of the average human. For us this is a very immediate problem. John Holly must be stopped."

"I agree," Pike said. "Any ideas how to do that?"

Rachel shook her head. "There are others I need to speak to, to tell them the situation. But you know what this means, Jason, don't you?"

"At a guess, I'd say civil war."

Rachel nodded slowly. "Holly has his followers. The unrest in the States at the moment is caused by the divide between his people, who see this as the only way forward, and my group, who want to maintain things just the way they are."

"As I see it," Harry Bailey said, "whatever happens, we, the human race, lose."

"I disagree," Rachel said. "We have coexisted with you for centuries. When did you first learn of our existence?"

Harry shifted uncomfortably in his seat. "Only a few days ago."

"Exactly!" Rachel said. "Up until then, you, like the rest of the human race, were unaware of us. It was a perfect symbiosis."

"The people you've killed over the centuries would probably take issue with that," Dylan said, and spun round in his seat as he heard a sound behind him, a soft hissing whisper. He saw them then, crouched in the corners of the room, black amorphous shapes that looked like small clouds, twisting and eddying, advancing and retreating.

"Dylan?" Bailey said, but there was no need for an answer; the expression on Dylan's face said it all. Bailey followed Dylan's eye line and stood abruptly. "I think we need to get out of here," he said.

Carl Schwab was on his feet instantly. "Not so fast," he said, reaching for the machine pistol that he'd placed on the table in front of him.

Rachel Grey turned to Pike. "Jason?"

Pike was watching Dylan, and then he too looked to the corners of the room.

The breathers were writhing and growing, some breaking away from their groups and starting to move toward them.

"I think Harry's right," he said. "We need to get out of here." He stood and hauled Dylan to his feet.

Michael Dylan's face had drained of color, and he was starting to shake. "Get them away from me," he said quietly.

"Jason! What's going on?" Rachel pushed herself out of her seat, in time for one of the shadowy creatures to fly at her. For an instant the dark shape covered her features, making her look as if she'd thrown a black towel over her head. She cried out and rubbed frantically at her face, trying to brush it away. She knew what they were and who had sent them.

At the sound of her cry, the rest of the breathers took to the air, swooping at them in a shadow flight. Dylan was knocked to the floor and quickly engulfed. He stared at them wide-eyed, seeing faces in the shadows; hideous faces with bulging eyes and gaping mouths lined with needle-sharp teeth. "Get them off me!" he screamed as he felt bony spindle-fingers raking at his clothes, ripping the material to expose his flesh. He bucked and twisted, but the shadows were embracing him, impossible to dislodge. The stench of them was overwhelming, the smell of rotting flesh making him gag. He stretched out a hand and felt strong fingers encircle it.

"On your feet!" Pike shouted at him. "You've got to get to your feet."

Schwab was heading toward the door. He'd seen enough.

As he gripped the handle, two of the breathers hauled him backward into the room. The machine pistol was plucked from his grasp and spun slowly, hovering in the air in front of his eyes. Mesmerized he watched the trigger being slowly depressed, but at the last second he jerked his head aside and a hail of bullets spurted from the barrel, splintering the parquet flooring behind him. He scrabbled backward, but the breathers were on him again in an instant, pinning his hands to the floor, making it impossible to move.

Again the pistol was hanging in front of his face, but this time it spun in the air until the barrel was pointing directly away from him. His relief was short-lived as the stock slammed into his mouth, splitting his lips and shattering his front teeth. Mouth bloody and mewling with pain, he crawled away again, looking for Rachel, willing her to rescue him.

But Rachel Grey was pinned against the wall by the shadows and couldn't breathe. It felt as if a heavy weight was compressing her chest, crushing her lungs. Her mouth gaped open as she tried to suck in air and her eyes were bulging in their sockets.

Harry Bailey was struggling to open the window. Every time he raised it a few inches, it was slammed back down again. A breather had draped itself over his head and shoulders like a damp black shawl, and he too was struggling to breathe. He could feel consciousness starting to slip away, but he fought it, forcing himself to concentrate, to keep his eyes open.

He prized the window open once more, raising it higher this time, almost high enough to climb through. As he lowered his head to duck through the open window he felt freezing fingers encircle his throat and haul him away from his escape route. He was lifted off his feet and thrown backward, landing on the table and skidding across its polished surface to fall in a heap on the far side of it.

Chapter Fifty

Department 18 Headquarters, Whitehall, London, England

It was a relatively short walk from the Barbican Centre to the Whitehall building. Carter was in need of fresh air and some exercise to help him blow away the cobwebs and collect his thoughts.

His ribs ached, but the strapping that had been applied was firm and tight. The painkillers were still keeping the worst of the discomfort at bay and as he strode along the street, the cool evening weather was just what he needed. The knee ached a bit but otherwise was holding up just fine.

The Embankment by the River Thames was less than crowded, though the usual tourists with cameras and videos were still busy taking shots of the Houses of Parliament, with the Big Ben clock tower, as well as other varied landmarks such as the London Eye, the bridges, and the Tower of London. Centuries of history encapsulated into a digital slide show that would be watched less than a couple of times back home.

The architecture around Whitehall was formal and quite grand. Offices of the great and good, as well as the more mundane and less than good, were cloaked in a veneer of respectability behind the smart stone facades.

Carter used his security pass to enter the discreet front door; there were no signs or nameplates to advertise the building's use. At reception a new girl he didn't know checked his ID, got him to sign in, and told him Simon Crozier was busy.

Carter thanked her but took the two flights of stairs up to Crozier's office anyway.

Crozier's office was empty. Carter went inside and shut the door behind him. The window was open a fraction, and outside the streets were empty of vehicles and people. There was nothing on the desk, as there never was even when the man was seated behind it. Carter had never visited Crozier's home, and doubted he ever would, but he guessed it would be just as minimalistic as this office.

The door opened without a knock.

"Robert?"

"Martin," Carter said as Martin Impey walked in, leaving the door open.

"He's gone home to change. Looks like we're in for a long night of it."

Carter sat in Crozier's chair and put his feet up on the desk.

Impey smiled. "He'll notice the marks straightaway, you know that."

"Trudy still in?"

Impey sat down on the small leather couch. "No, it's pretty much just us."

"Well let's brew up some coffee while you tell me what's been happening."

What can we do but keep on breathing in and out,
modest and willing, and in our places?
—Mary Oliver

Chapter Fifty-one

Hampstead, London, England

Rachel Grey pushed out at the shadows. Some had burrowed beneath her clothes and were biting at her skin with small sharp teeth.

She knew what they were; she was one of them. That they had attacked her in this way, in her own home, was unforgivable. She had no doubts that John Holly was behind the assault. He would dress it up as a necessary move due to the presence of the government people with her, but she knew the truth.

Holly wanted to destroy her and the breathers that were loyal to her and her vision of their future. Sometimes she believed Holly wanted to destroy the breathers completely.

Harry Bailey was lying on the floor. The table he had fallen from stood over him as if threatening with its height. He had far more to be concerned about. The breather that had enveloped his neck and shoulders was still attached, and Bailey could feel the fingers digging into his side, opening and closing as if tiny mouths.

He raised his arms and tried to grasp the creature's back, but it was like trying to hold onto smoke. As solid as it felt as it swathed his head, it felt ephemeral to the touch.

Clouds of breathers were still in the air, rising and falling on invisible airwaves. Dylan had been knocked to the floor and quickly engulfed. He was using his powers to hold them at bay, but he seemed to lack the resolve to fight them off. He was hallucinating, seeing faces in the shadows; faces from his past, distorted versions of faces from his present.

The breathers were massing over and on top of him, mouths lined with needle-sharp teeth. Bony spindle-fingers raked his clothes, tearing his flesh. He remembered Father Donovan and realized his words were coming true. He had prophesied what would become of Michael Dylan.

As the breathers grew stronger on top of him, he felt the sharp insertion of fingers into his body. Faces were distinguishable in the mass now; he saw his father and his mother, their features distorted into lustful urging. The creatures were crawling over his entire body, scurrying under his clothes, piercing his skin. The stench of them was overwhelming; the smell of rotting flesh making him think about dead things and redemption.

"We have to get out," Pike shouted, but no one was listening; no one was able to respond.

Carl Schwab was on his knees, his mouth hanging open, blood and torn lip dripping onto his chin. The machine pistol was hovering in the air in front of his face. First the barrel was toward him, and then it was reversed and the stock was there. He tried to move his head out of the way, but hands gripped his shoulders and movement was not easy.

Without warning the pistol fired, and bullets passed through his ear. He screamed at the pain, aware of the burning sensation as blood trickled down his cheek.

Rachel Grey was sinking beneath the weight of the shadows and couldn't move or even breathe properly. It felt as if a truck was parked on her chest, pushing her ribs into her lungs. Her mouth opened, then closed as she gasped for air. She was fighting for control, but she was fighting for her life. There were so many of the breathers, and they were not just young unformed creatures; these were a well-disciplined force that seemed to know exactly what it was doing.

Schwab was knocked to the floor as the stock of the pistol cracked against his jaw. The impact propelled his body backward, his arms flailing for something to slow his fall. There was nothing. His shoulder took the brunt of the reverberation as his whole weight bounced off the wood floor. Sharp teeth and talons ripped at him.

Pike had, for the most part, kept the breathers at bay. As soon as he recognized what was happening, he shut his mind down so that in effect he created a force field of energy around him. As long as he stayed where he was, kept as still as he could, he would be able to keep the attack away from him.

His problem was that keeping himself safe did nothing to help the others.

He watched as Rachel began to dissolve into a black lake unable to break free. Schwab was all but unconscious on the floor. Bailey looked as if a blanket was shrouding his head. Dylan had not moved for minutes, although his eyes were wide open, staring at the ceiling and the walls as if he could see things there that Pike was unaware of.

Pike could not hesitate any longer.

He pushed out with his mind, finding resistance, solid at first, then wavering, a little uncertain, liquid at the edges, fraying as a shape, the seams starting to strain. He shut down entirely. Felt the shock, then opened. Not completely open, not fully vulnerable, keeping enough in reserve for preservation.

Freed, even if temporarily, he rushed across to Rachel. Her eyes were wide open, in obvious pain. The source of the physical pain was clear to see. Her chest and upper body were coated as if by thick oil paint. He could only guess at the mental strain she was under.

He probed her mind. He and Rachel were from the same species as their attackers, both possessed powers. Pike was devoid of emotion about the attack; he had experienced persecution by Holly for years and was under no illusions about him. Grey, though, had a romantic notion about the nobility of the breathers. For her, the attack by her own kind, even a rival faction, was a treason far more painful than the physical threat.

He sent waves of energy into her mind. She responded with surprise; then, quickly realizing what was happening, her thoughts gripped his with grateful enthusiasm.

Force

Pike insinuated words into her brain.

Force your strength

Force your strength into your neck

Almost immediately Pike felt his own mind lurch downward as if he was physically linked to Rachel. As her thoughts focused on freeing her neck and shoulders so his mind and his power were transmitted there.

It was like aiming a jet-wash hose at her. The black cloak of breathers began to fall away until her body was clear. The effect was like watching an Etch A Sketch being erased.

She fell forward when she was finally free, but Pike was ready and caught her.

"Are you strong enough?"

She looked at him, and a ghost of a smile caressed her lips. "The weaker sex?"

He helped her to stand upright. "Weak isn't a word I associate with you, Rachel."

Gunshots distracted them.

Schwab was clutching his left arm. Blood poured from a jagged hole in it, and his hand was doing nothing to stem the flow.

Rachel Grey ran to him.

Pike closed his eyes.

He concentrated on the machine pistol.

Gradually it began to change shape. The end compressed until the barrel squashed toward the magazine. The stock enlarged, and then the whole thing exploded. A shower of metal and plastic flew over Schwab, who looked half dead. Blood coated his face and his arm hung, useless, by his side.

Pike opened his eyes. Rachel was kneeling beside Schwab, trying to comfort him.

"Bailey," Pike shouted to her. "We must help Bailey."

Rachel stood and looked over at Bailey. He was like the Elephant Man. A huge misshapen mass of black clung to his head and was folding over his shoulders and chest. It was as if discolored skin had grown out of the top of his skull and was seeping downward, intent on covering his entire body. It was amazing he was still standing.

Pike probed into Bailey's mind and found huge concentration. Clearly Bailey was using all his strength and power to resist the breathers. Only it looked as if they were winning.

Pike felt a hand grasp his. "Don't get any ideas, Jason," Rachel said. "Purely professional."

Pike smiled. "I won't order the engagement ring just yet."

Rachel's grip tightened in his, and they both threw their thoughts at Bailey. Trying to penetrate the barrier of the breathers was difficult. Resistance was strong.

Pike and Rachel released hands. "Will you do it or me?" she asked.

"You are purer than I am. It has to be you."

"Buy me some time," she said as she turned away.

Pike renewed the mental battle inside Bailey's mind. Occasionally he glanced across at Rachel, who had moved over to the window to take off her clothes. Her body was toned and beautiful. High, firm breasts; flat, smooth stomach; long, tapering legs.

That was her human shape.

Her true body began to reveal itself.

The hands were first to change, elongating and sharpening at the nails. The ends turning into small openings, which flicked and twitched in the air seemingly seeking food. Her head lolled back as if the neck muscles weren't strong enough to support the enlarged skull. The shape of the head changed completely, the forehead swollen, the skin taut with sinews and veins throbbing at the temples. The skin over the body was gray, darker in places to an almost black color. The texture was dry like flaking cement. The feet were clawed and wide.

Rachel Grey was now in her natural form.

She launched herself at Bailey. Her fingers thrust into the black cloud over his head, pulling and ripping. Her mouth closed over the clothlike shape and bit down hard. Holes started to appear in the shadows coating Bailey, and Pike felt the change in his brain. Bailey was getting stronger.

Rachel continued her assault. Her anger and betrayal were feeding her energy, giving her a strength even she was not familiar with. She was like a lioness hanging on to its prey. Her feet scrabbled at the figures covering Bailey, scratching and tearing to make them release their grip. Her teeth and claws ripped at them to cause maximum damage.

It succeeded.

Pike felt Bailey suddenly open and his full force joined Pike's. Between them, and with Rachel still attacking like a thing demented, Bailey was free.

Schwab lay quietly licking his wounds.

That left Michael Dylan.

He lay motionless on the floor. His eyes were wide open, but they weren't blinking.

Pike looked around the room. There were no more black shadows, no shapes.

"I think they've gone," Pike said.

Rachel barely registered his words. She was still enjoying the high level of bursting energy that always came with the kill.

He left Rachel to revert to human form, and knelt down beside Dylan.

He was still, and he was cold.

Chapter Fifty-two

Zurich, Switzerland

The Spree Clinic was all Swiss efficiency and respectability from the outside.

Inside the illusion was maintained. Glass and chrome predominated, with swirling abstract paintings on the walls and polished ash flooring.

The reception desk was peopled by three young men and a slightly older woman. As soon as she saw Holly, the woman spoke quietly to one of the men, and he slipped away through a side door.

"Mr. Holly." The woman extended her hand and suppressed the natural shudder when Holly grasped it. "I trust you had a good trip?"

Holly ignored the question. "Is everything ready?"

The woman nodded. "I have just sent Klaus downstairs to ensure your vehicles are safely parked and the contents transferred. Will you be with us long?"

"A couple of hours at most. I have urgent business to

attend to in England. Oh . . ." he added as if it was an afterthought. "There will be one less . . . *content* . . . on the flight back."

The woman turned away. Another administrative task for her to sort out before she could go home for the night.

In the basement the second limousine was parked and the driver gestured for Alice to get out. Annoyed but without choice, she stood by the elevator and waited.

The first limo sat silent by another elevator, the occupants still seated in the back.

Alice had no idea why Holly had brought them. This trip was a regular event, and it was usually just the two of them plus the driver. She was suspicious of change, concerned whenever Holly didn't operate to his usual routine. He liked order in his life, and bringing those two here was a break in the pattern.

Just then the elevator doors opened and Holly appeared.

"John—" Alice began, but he cut her off with a gesture. He walked across to the other limo, where he gave whispered instructions to the driver.

The rear door of the limo was opened, and Jacek and Miranda, still handcuffed together, were pulled out and bundled to the elevator. The driver pressed the down button, and within seconds they had left the basement.

Holly turned to the other driver. "Toby, please escort Miss Spur to the visitor suite on the second floor."

"John?" Alice said. "Visitor suite? What's going on?"

Holly smiled. "Nothing for you to worry yourself about, my sweet. I want to show our guests the facilities. Then I have a surprise for you. There are drinks and food in the suite until I join you. I won't be long."

Worry.

Surprise.

Neither were words she wanted to hear John Holly say to her.

Jacek and Miranda were taken from the elevator through a maze of white sterile corridors until they were in a laboratory.

"Are they going to experiment on us?" Miranda asked Jacek.

Jacek shook his head. "I did wonder, but now we're here I doubt it. I think he wants to show us something."

"What?"

Before Jacek could answer, the driver told them to be quiet. Neither had the courage or the opportunity to argue.

While they waited and Miranda worried, Jacek tried to make sense of their surroundings. The lighting was bright and white, from ceiling strip lights to under-desk up lighters. On clean white surfaces computer equipment buzzed gently. Next to each computer was a white plastic box about two feet square, and in each box were test tubes, some with lids and some without. Beyond the room, connected by thick glass screens, was a smaller room.

In the other room were what looked like fermentation tanks for alcohol. They were smaller than that, but they had wires and tubes running into and out of them.

Before he could see much else Jacek was addressed by name. Holly had joined them. He indicated that the driver should unlock the handcuffs, and as they rubbed their sore wrists, both Jacek and Miranda realized how Holly was completely absorbed in the room.

After a few moments Holly gathered himself. "Forgive me," he said. "I always feel overwhelmed when I come here. To see the near culmination of my father's work and the fulfillment of his father's dream before him, is a true honor for me."

"Why are we here?" Miranda said.

"Come, let me show you what I have created. Here are the gestation tanks." He pointed to the room beyond the screens. "In there the new breed lies. Safe in the artificial wombs until their birth. In here"—he spread his arms in an expansive gesture to take in the whole room—"the eggs and sperm are mixed in perfect conditions so that each individual sperm is used. Not quite so wasteful as the human reproductive process you see."

Jacek looked him in the eye. "So this is your goal? An artificial strain of your kind."

"Far more than that, Mr. Czerwinski. A strain that can survive on its own terms without need for your kind."

"Except you need my kind. Miranda and me, for example. Otherwise why bring us here?"

"I need you as a failsafe. It is Julia I need, and Julia I have."

Jacek lunged at him, but the movement was anticipated and with one raised hand, Holly propelled Jacek against the cold metal edge of a work surface.

"If you behave, Julia will remain safe. If she does as I ask, you will remain alive. That is why you are both here. To show you how high are the stakes."

Holly pressed a button by the screen door and almost immediately a white-coated man appeared. Gray haired, bespectacled, with a distracted air.

"Herr Klimdt, you have the specimens ready for me?"

"Naturally."

He handed Holly a small refrigerated steel container.

Holly gave the container to the driver, ushered Miranda and Jacek to the elevator, and nodded a farewell to Klimdt.

In the basement, Jacek and Miranda were placed on the rear seats of the limousine. The container was secured in the trunk, and the driver stood by the hood.

Holly made a call on his cell phone, and moments later Toby, the second driver, came down.

"Wait here, both of you. We shall only need one limousine on the return home, so one of you can have a few days in Switzerland. I'll leave you to decide."

In the visitor suite, Alice hadn't had anything to eat or drink.

Something was very wrong, and she knew there was nothing she could do about it. Her chances of escaping this room before Holly returned were zero. Her likelihood of escape from the clinic was even less.

The door opened, and he walked in.

"You wonder," he began without preamble. "You worry and you speculate."

"Is this because of the auto crash, John?"

"I always admired your perception. You must believe that. If there could have been another way. Regrettably I no longer need either you or your artfully created double."

He was undressing.

Her mouth was dry. Her legs were trembling. It was fear, not excitement.

When he was naked, he punched her so hard in the stomach that she fell to the floor, unable to breathe.

Then he kicked her in the head.

"You killed my father. Killed. Killed. Killed."

With each word he kicked her. In the back, the ribs, then between her legs.

She curled into a ball and tried to regain her breath.

The attack ceased.

She lay still for a while, then raised her head to see what he was doing. Instantly she wished she had not.

The body was huge, bulging with muscle, the sinews and veins visible beneath the thin skin. In places on the stomach, small openings breathed as if they were mouths seeking air. The skin was gray and scaly, almost reptilian, with a translucent property that made the creature seem to shimmer in the moonlight.

When he grabbed her arms, the movement was almost graceful, the powerful legs economic but insistent.

He ripped the clothes from her body. Not caring whether he tore her flesh as well as the clothing, both were shredded with fingers that were long, at least ten inches, and tapered to points. They twitched, each moving independently of the others, as if with a life of its own.

When she was torn and bleeding, he pulled her legs into the air and thrust inside her. The penis was thin but long, about twelve inches, and barbed on both sides; and she bled where it tore her until it too was covered in blood.

He reached for her mouth and pushed his tongue deep inside. The tongue probed and pummeled until it had forced itself down her throat, farther still until it blocked her airway. Then it continued on until it began to burrow out of the back of her neck.

When he removed his mouth from what was left of hers, there was blood smeared around the bloated lips. The tongue was long and black, and flicked back into his mouth. It was split, like a snake's tongue, but covered in tiny, sharp points, each facing toward the mouth so if it caught on something it would grip it and tear it. As it had with Alice's throat.

As the penis pulled out of her, it felt as if her insides were being ripped out with it.

Alice was barely alive.

Holly fell upon her, his talons burrowing deep beneath her skin, seeking out the vital organs, the fullness of her.

By the time he was dressed, back into human form, and driving away in the limousine, Alice was a jumble of limbs and flesh, strewn about the room as if she were a model for the abstract paintings in the lobby.

Who will tell whether one happy moment of love or the joy of breathing or walking on a bright morning and smelling the fresh air, is not worth all the suffering and effort which life implies.
—Erich Fromm

Chapter Fifty-three

Faircroft Manor, Hertfordshire, England

"Time for some fun."

Holly had made a call to the security men at Faircroft. "You can have the girl," was all he said.

The man who took the call wasn't known for his kindness. A bully at school, he had survived in the world by using threats of violence backed up by a knowledge of how to inflict pain when it was needed. All he had to decide now was how much pain to inflict and how many of the other men he would share that pleasure with.

Holly had made it very clear that the girl he had groomed as an exact replica of Alice Spur should die a painful and violent death.

The man decided there should be four of them. He made a call on the internal system and went to tell the other chosen ones.

"Time for some fun."

By the time they reached the concrete windowless room in the basement, Karolina was already there.

When she saw the four men and the looks on their faces, she backed against the rough unpainted wall. There would be no escape.

The four men fanned out as if hunting prey.

One grabbed her left arm, another her right. They hoisted her arms against the wall, twisting the joints, making her cry out in pain.

Her breasts were seized and roughly groped, the material of her shirt ripped and pulled away, exposing her bra.

Hands pulled at her skirt, lifting it to her waist as hungry fingers scratched her thighs.

The men holding her arms let them go. One of them punched her in the right temple, the other punched her on the left. Both hit her hard in the face, breaking her nose, closing an eye, splitting her lip as teeth broke.

Her bra was cut away with a knife and the blade was used to cut tiny nicks in her nipples, the breasts then kneaded and pulled. A mouth grasped a torn nipple and teeth bit and chewed at the flesh.

Her skirt was cut off and she was forced to her knees by repeated kicks to her shins. When she was kneeling, the kicks were aimed at her back and stomach until she fell to the floor.

Like a pack of hyenas they fell upon her. Her panties were torn away and thick fingers inserted into her dry vagina. They pushed and opened inside her until one had four fingers hurting her.

She was lifted like a doll and fingers were thrust into her anus.

Momentarily the attack paused, but then the fingers in her vagina were replaced by a penis. Another pushed at her lips and she was forced to open and take it as her hair was pulled so hard tufts came out at the roots.

She was lifted upward and thrust upon an erect penis that penetrated her anus. Shoved backward her legs were forced wider as another penis forced itself into her vagina. Yet another pushed itself down her throat until she choked.

One by one the men satisfied themselves.

Karolina lay on the floor.

The four men stood over her.

They urinated over her.

Three of them began to kick her while the fourth stuck the knife in at random parts of her body.

Death was a relief.

Chapter Fifty-four

Department 18 Headquarters, Whitehall, London, England

Carter was sitting with Martin Impey, their third pot of strong coffee on the desk beside them.

Impey had spent nearly two hours filling Carter in on everything that had happened. Impey read from his notes and consulted the computer files when he needed to.

Carter made no notes. He had already thought long and hard about what they were up against, and he was convinced he had the answer.

"Shall we get some more coffee?" Martin Impey asked.

Carter shook his head. "No, I'm all coffeed-out. Does Crozier still keep that single malt in his bottom drawer?" He stood and started fiddling with the lock of the discreet filing cabinet against the wall.

"Robert, he won't like it."

"Won't like what?"

Martin Impey and Carter both stared into the doorway as Simon Crozier entered.

Carter moved away from the cabinet slightly, one hand still resting on its top. "We've run out of coffee and thought a drop of the hard stuff would help us with our research."

Crozier looked immaculate. He had changed into a blue pinstripe suit, with wine red tie and cuff links. He had showered and although it was the middle of the night, he looked as if he had rested for a week. He made a show of pulling the chair out from behind his desk and brushing the seat; almost as if he knew Carter had been sitting there before him and wanted to remove all traces. He leaned over and rubbed at an imaginary mark on the desktop.

He looked hard at Carter and came to a decision. He opened a drawer in his desk and threw a small key at Carter. "Careful, it's a Macallan." He said the word reverentially.

"I'll treat it as if it's my own," Carter said as he pulled open the bottom drawer.

"That's my concern."

Carter arranged three crystal glasses on the desk and poured generous measures into each.

"Good health," Martin said.

Crozier breathed in the aroma before sipping delicately. "Speaking of health. I thought you were in hospital, Robert?" From his lips the name sounded like an insult.

"I'm touched by your concern, Simon."

"Don't mistake professional necessity for personal interest in your health. I've had to bring in people who probably weren't ready because you've been laid up."

"Injured on department business, Crozier, not on a rest break. That team at Dunster House were ill prepared, and that's down to you."

Martin sipped his drink. "None of us knew, to be fair, Robert, what we were walking into there. It's what we've been discussing for the last couple of hours, Simon."

His intervention slowed the natural antagonism between the other two men. Both looked into their drinks before locking eyes.

Crozier broke the link first. "All right. Are you fit for duty, Carter?"

Carter noted the change from first to last name. "I am back at work. The question is what the next step is going to be."

Crozier let out a gentle sigh. That was about as much emotion he allowed to be visible, outside his disagreements with Carter. "I have to assess the current situation. Martin, what developments have there been with Dylan and the team in Hampstead?"

"They made initial contact with the Grey woman. Using Jason Pike as the conduit proved important as he and Grey have a certain respect for one another. Dylan and Bailey haven't reported in for over two hours. I am worried."

Carter poured himself some more whiskey without being asked, though he did lift the bottle to Crozier, who accepted some more, and to Impey, who declined. "Putting Holly's two rivals in one place at the same time might be a mistake."

"In what way?" Crozier said.

"It might give Holly too big a target, make him strike to try to take out the leaders. If he was able to kill Pike and Grey, it would make his aim of taking over that much more achievable."

Crozier steepled his fingers over his glass. Carter, he was reluctant to admit, had a good point. He was concerned Bailey or Dylan had not been in touch. It might be they were busy with the Grey business, but it might also mean they were in trouble. After the Clerkenwell ambush, there was no telling which route Holly was taking.

"Robert," Crozier said, all too aware he was back to the first name, and was inveigling. "Is there anything you can do to locate Harry and Michael?"

"They've gone to Grey's house in Hampstead?"

Martin Impey nodded. "With Pike to cut a deal with Rachel Grey."

"That's not how I would describe the activity of two department operatives," Crozier said. "Investigating the possibilities of an alliance of need rather than choice."

"However we put it," Carter said, "we don't know what, if anything, has happened. Martin has brought me up to speed, so I know how we got where we are."

"We just don't quite know where that is, do we?" Crozier said, and raised his glass in a silent salute.

Carter drained his glass, ignoring Crozier's wince at his lax etiquette with such a delicate whiskey. "I'll try to locate Bailey and Dylan."

He walked to the window and pulled it down a little. The night air was crisp rather than cold. He looked out at the dark discreet buildings in Whitehall. An up market part of London, all was quiet at this time of night.

As he stared out he let his mind relax. There was no danger here, he sensed that, so he was free to open completely.

Pain.

He felt it immediately.

Familiar faces.

Head, aches, tearing at my eyes.

It was both Bailey and Dylan. He didn't know either man that well, but he could feel the two different emotional wavelengths. Both were under attack.

"They're in trouble," Carter said quietly.

Crozier picked up the telephone. "The Hampstead address. Get a team over there immediately. Code Red. Three of ours."

"Three?" Impey queried.

Crozier wrote something on a pad. "I'm counting Jason Pike in for the purpose."

Carter let his mind close down again. There was nothing to be gained by sharing the suffering. He had enough of his own to manage.

It was getting crowded in Crozier's usually neat and sterile office.

Martin Impey had left to coordinate the assault team and

the administration afterward, leaving Crozier and Carter with the others.

Jason Pike looked old and drained. His eyes were bloodshot and his skin sallow and drawn. The efforts he had used in defending Rachel and the others had left him exhausted. After the attack on Milton, he wasn't surprised at the lengths Holly would go to achieve his aims, but to attack two senior breathers as he had spoke of an ego out of control.

Bailey had been examined by a doctor at the scene and been pronounced in no serious danger. The cuts to his neck and shoulders were deep, but they weren't infected. Tufts of hair had been pulled from his scalp but the skin where broken was disinfected and bandaged so he could heal quickly. He too was tired.

Michael Dylan was dead.

The assault team had fanned out around the property, gaining access at various points and sweeping each room and each floor to ensure all was clear. By the time they reached the interior of the house, all that remained from the attack was broken furniture, blood, and the dead and injured.

Schwab was taken away in an ambulance, his gunshot wounds needing surgery.

Dylan was worked on by the paramedics, but there was nothing they could do. His heart had stopped some time ago and there was no brain activity. The hundreds of puncture wounds on his body were septic already, but it wasn't those that had killed him. He seemed to have died from severe shock to the nervous system. He had just shut down like a bank of lights in a power wipeout.

While formalities were taken, his body was removed to a local funeral director the department used occasionally.

There had been no sign of Rachel Grey.

"Harry, here, drink this." Crozier had poured a large

measure of whiskey into another glass and pressed it into Bailey's trembling fingers.

"There were too many of them," Bailey said.

"You can file a report later. Don't worry for now," Crozier said.

"The Grey woman . . . she became . . ."

Pike put his hand on Bailey's shoulder. "I asked Rachel Grey to fight fire with fire. She reverted to . . . well, let's just say she changed so she could fight them better."

"She turned into a breather," Carter said.

Pike looked at him. "She *is* a breather, Mr. Carter. She cannot *turn* into one. She took her natural form so we could defeat them."

"How did you achieve that?" Crozier asked.

"By a mixture of mind and body. Brain and brawn. Also Rachel and I have the advantage of being like our attackers. It helped."

Carter held out his glass for some more Macallan. "Where is she now?"

"She left before your team arrived. She has to go through a metamorphosis process before she can re-enter her human body."

"She'll be joining us?" Crozier said.

Pike shrugged. "I'm not her keeper, or her friend."

Crozier knew it was time to assume command. Setting his emotions about Dylan and Bailey to one side, he drew upon his reserves of strength and addressed the room. "What we have to do now is decide on our next move. What dangers does the country face from Holly specifically and from breathers in general? What does the department need to do?" He felt the effects of the whiskey as his head began to fuzz, but this was no time for weakness or resting.

Carter was the first to speak. "Let me tell you what I know."

But friendship is the breathing rose, with sweets in every fold.
—Oliver Wendell Holmes

Chapter Fifty-five

The grounds of Faircroft Manor, Hertfordshire, England

What looked like an owl floated softly on a gentle downwind, its ghostly white under feathers reflected in the half moon that was suspended in a flawless dark night sky. So silent was its flight that it might have been the only wave in an otherwise smooth black sea.

It swooped and rose, as the breeze and its hunger dictated. It cried out just once, as it plunged into a wild meadow on the edge of some trees, its plaintive sound ending abruptly as it gripped its victim. Then the creature it believed it had captured turned and became the captor.

John Holly rose from the meadow, the blood of the owl staining his lips and his clothes in ragged splatters.

He had flown back from Zurich almost moments after killing Alice. He regretted having to kill her, but the death of his father had to be avenged and that was all there was to it. He felt slight regret but nothing more.

Centuries of life had modified what emotions he may once have possessed.

He stripped his ruined jacket off and threw it to one side. One of his people would collect it tomorrow. As he undid his tie, he was thinking of the lives he had led, the places he had been, the oceans crossed, the people known.

He could tell stories of his life, but few would believe

them. His kind had existed since prehistoric times when man first learned to walk. Breathers had invented evil, though were adept enough to allow others to take the glory or the blame.

He dropped his tie to the ground and began tearing at shirt buttons in his haste.

There was excitement at the plans that were progressing well. The specimens he had brought back from Switzerland were perfect and would just about complete the embryo phase. Amidst the success, though, was a new and nagging feeling that was unfamiliar.

Constantly these days his thoughts were tending to veer to the past. He understood the death of his father was part of the reason, and he hoped that now he had dealt with that he could move on. Somehow he knew it was more than that.

He kicked away his shoes and pulled off his socks, enjoying the cool grass beneath his bare feet. Payne and Czerwinski had been brought back safe and sound, and were carefully locked away within the basement of the manor.

He could tell stories of his life, but most of it would be sad. There was a melancholy about him recently that he was finding hard to shake off. That worried him, as it made him vulnerable.

The night was a fine one, with a slight wind rustling the tops of the oaks and beeches. He could see the roof of Faircroft Manor ahead of him, though he had delved deep enough into the grounds that he knew he couldn't be seen from the house.

It felt good to walk on the damp grass and smell the night air. He was attuned to the sounds of the night. The small animals out foraging, the fox, badger, stoat. Each one hunting for something.

Which was exactly what Holly was doing. Hunting.

Myths and legends about his kind populated every

culture. At many battles throughout human history reports were heard of black shadows seeming to inhabit soldiers of one side, and those soldiers being infused with a strength and a ferocity for fighting that was supernatural.

In some primitive cultures when the thirteenth child was born in a community it was left outside the perimeter as an offering to the creatures. Though few had seen them, no one dared disbelieve.

Some thought they were vampires, the ferocious feeding of the soul through the fingertips misleading many, so that the myth of drinking blood through fangs was born. Because of the shadow appearance some had mistaken them for ghosts and believed they were haunted. Werewolves, once a dominant tribe in parts of the world, had been wiped out by breathers as they were becoming a threat to the food supply.

Although the prime reason for feeding from humans was the sustenance of the soul, many breathers had evolved over the centuries to enjoy the taste of the human body. Many enjoyed this sexually, in a kind of ultimate auto-eroticism, while others feasted on the flesh itself, especially the delicate internal organs.

Young breathers were primarily in shadow form, often acting in groups, swooping like bats, which was another reason for the vampire connection. These often ill-disciplined groups would inhabit buildings, existing until they were able to feed. Many reverted to shadow form at the end of their life span.

Once feeding had taken place, many breathers, but not all, would take the form of the human from which they had fed. That allowed them to live among people, unrecognized. In their natural state they would be too terrifying.

Holly dropped to his knees as the moon fell behind a cloud. His father was in his head. Memories and images crowded his mind, forcing out all thought. His brain was overloading, filled with a history he wasn't certain he had lived or learned.

There was movement, but it was uncertain, and then he was swimming. There was a vast desolate landscape where mountains soared in the distance, marking the horizon of this yellow barren land and the dark troubled sky above it. Smoke rose from small campfires over the prairie, showing the locations of the few wandering tribes of nomadic peoples that were the human race. In the hills a large tribe of men and women lived, hunting by day the wild herds of pigs, setting traps for the giant mammoths that grew scarcer with the passing of each snow. The women were coarsely clothed in bearskin or pig-hide, their faces painted with the colored dyes they made from the berries they pulled from withered trees higher in the hills. The men dressed in bearskins like their women, except for a handful of fierce warriors who clothed their apelike bodies in the dried skins of the long-toothed tigers they had fought and killed single-handed, armed only with the flint axes and the short throwing spears they used.

The tribe quarreled and fought with the neighboring peoples over the rights to drink at the solitary water hole that bound them all to this wasteland. Arguments were settled with grunts and scuffles, with the hill people allowing the others access. They were a wild and primitive early people who killed the game for food and shared what comforts they could with the other tribes. Mostly they kept to their own territory in the hills. When nightfall came they huddled around the fires, cooking the fresh meat from the kill, drinking the berry juice they made in scooped out wooden bowls. It was a time of fear when the huge fire in the sky hid behind the mountains far away, and the cold pale light of different shapes came in its place. The night had sounds of its own that even the bravest of the tribes warriors flinched from facing. There were cries and howls that were not heard by day, and the women moved closer to their menfolk and waited for morning.

One morning when the false dawn brought the first light into the hills the warrior on lookout at the highest point of the camp called out in the primitive language they understood that there was movement in the desert. Other tribes were moving toward the hills in a single group, and at their head was a stranger. The women took the young ones into the caves where the food and clothing was stored. The men armed themselves with the weapons they used to kill game and went to the lower slopes to meet the men of the other tribes. Although the combined plains tribes outnumbered the hill tribesmen, the peaceable settlements they had made before had been reached with ease, and they had no fear.

The stranger at the head of the tribesmen could have been from a different race compared to the shambling hair-covered men. He walked erect on his two hind legs, not using his arms for support as the ape-men did. His hair was black and swept back from his white forehead; his skin was smooth and pale, not darkened by the sun and the wind. They could not see his face. Even when he and the tribesmen reached the massed hills-people his face was shielded by shadow, or by shafts of sunlight. He took a rock from the barren ground and handed it to the leader of the plains tribesmen. Without words he indicated that the man should throw the rock. With as much force as he could the tribe leader threw the rock at the nearest of the hills tribesmen.

It was the first act of war the men had ever known. The rock struck the head of the man, and he fell to the ground, while his companions drew back startled. The stranger motioned with his arms and the other tribesmen fell upon the fallen warrior and beat him with rocks and axes until the blood flowed into the dust. The stranger turned away from the sun, his face clear of shadow . . .

Holly tore off the rest of his clothes and lay prostrate on the ground. The coolness of the earth, the damp grass and wild flowers did nothing to stem the hot flame of unrest that was flooding his mind. His thoughts were in turmoil, uncontrollable, as if someone else was plugged into his brain and was feeding him limitless supplies of other people's thoughts and memories.

He surfaced in a clear blue sea with water lapping around him, his eyes blinded by a fierce white heat and his throat burning. His limbs were heavy in the swell of the sea and his brain screamed to him that he was drowning, floating into unconsciousness. There was feasting at the gates of Rome as the legions were returned from the sacking of the cities of Arabia and the treasures were glorious; gold and silver and precious stones as large as a fist so it was rumored. Cloths woven in every color, slaves brought into the city blacker than any shadow; they had to be clothed in white togas so they could be seen in the darkness of the night. There were horses with fine intelligent faces, with spirit and strength that would pull the chariots of the racers in the next games. The wild animals in the cages were proud, fierce with anger at their capture; lions that would rip the flesh from the captives in the show ring. The young girls were light brown and soft, with dark flitting eyes that promised passionate fire. That night there would be celebrations throughout the city as the soldiers drank and sated, shouting their pleasure to be home again to mother Rome after the battles. They would shaft their women folk until their thighs dripped blood and the wine and the meats drugged them into coma.

In the Caesar's palace the commanders of the forces were taken before Caesar to report the final victory that added to the glory that was Rome. Shadows entered the palace with them, seeming to follow them through the scented gardens, past the open courtyards into the interior of Caesar's private rooms. The man on the throne was Caesar, but there was someone with him, whispering into his ear; it was a man but his face was diverted. He leaned into Caesar as if he was becoming part of him. Caesar's voice held scorn despite their brave news, his voice selfish, mocking, holding no praise for the commanders for their victories, no interest in their prizes. The men searched his eyes for understanding but there was none; the cold blue eyes were like the vastness of the ocean, deep and unforgiving. The commanders shuffled their feet in their confusion and longed to get to their wives who had waited for them through the six long months of the campaign. Still Caesar would not release them from their torment; he began to berate them for cowardice, threatening them with punishment for their behavior. As the man at his side continued his whispering so Caesar escalated the catalog of imagined crimes and the irrational insults grew in bile.

Suddenly Caesar stood from his throne, seemingly propelled off it by the whispering man, and moved to a side of the room where red velvet drapes were pulled across an archway. Caesar pulled the drapes aside and the men wept when they saw what lay inside. Their wives were tied upside down on immense stakes thrust into the ground, their skin flayed from their bodies and left hanging down from their torn and bleeding shoulders, falling over their faces like strands of pink raw hair. Their voices were the exhausted mews of drowned kittens. The commanders turned to Caesar and began to exact revenge. They did not notice the whispering man slip away unseen, his face hidden behind a jester's mask. For a moment it seemed the mask would slip, but it stayed firmly in place, until the man got to the edge of the room when he tore off the mask . . .

Holly could not cope with the montage of images filling his mind. He knew he was seeing breathers at work, whispering in the ear of Caesar, corrupting his thoughts, causing the first death in a peaceful world. He tried to drag himself to his feet. He hated being out of control. But he was drowning.

And then he was swimming. He struggled for air, but there was none below the surface. The clear blue waters closed over his head and he fought the pressure on his lungs; there were lights above the surface, but he was falling into darkness. He opened his mouth to cry for help, but there was only water; he swallowed and felt the cold enter his mouth like a release. Ahead his blinded eyes saw a single beam of light, and he pushed his tired limbs toward it.

There was a train moving over rusted tracks, and he was on it. There was a cattle car enclosed on all sides, and he was wedged against a rough wooden door. The stench of the car was appalling, crowding into his senses. The car was filled with men and women and children huddled together in mute despair, clothed in tattered rags, some even naked. They mumbled incoherently to one another in a language he couldn't understand. Some stood, but most sat or lay where space allowed, pressed shoulder-to-shoulder, unable to move. Eventually the train rocked to a halt and the wooden door was flung open revealing the harsh sunlight of the day outside.

Soldiers in gray uniforms herded the people from the train, into lines along the track, separating the sexes and the ages. Then they were loaded onto open trucks and driven into a bleak countryside, along roads pitted with craters and strewn with the debris of bombed vehicles. The trucks pulled up outside the gates of a large wire-fenced compound where armed guards stood alert in watchtowers, and shabby wooden huts awaited their next occupants. As he stepped from the back of the truck, Holly realized where he was. The gates were open, and the soldiers marched the prisoners into the compound where they stood in ragged lines for inspection. Holly was in the front row. He watched the soldiers stand at attention as the camp commandant approached, the bristle of fear and respect apparent in each of them.

Holly had no wish to meet the cold blue eyes, or even to see the face. How did he know the eyes were blue? Would he see the face at last? He broke ranks and began running. Shouts echoed in his ears as he ran, he heard shots fired and dogs began to bark, but he ran until the blood pounded in his head and his legs began to falter. Then he saw the water ahead, the clear blue sea. He ran to it and dived in. As the water enveloped him, the shouting and the pursuit stopped. He surfaced moments later and felt the relief of floating on crystal-clear water. He closed his eyes and breathed in the sweet air; he floated for hours it seemed.

When he awoke, there was the stench of decaying flesh in his nostrils. He looked around and saw with surprise but little fear, that the water was crowded with floating bodies; as far as he could see the dead and moldering corpses bobbed up and down on the waves, the whole surface of the sea covered with bodies, each one facedown. In the distance a thick black cloud was rolling over the waves, moving with the grace of a bird in flight, but he knew that the smoke held . . .

The black cloud was filled with breathers. He knew. He was tired. The events of the past few days had been important, but he was under immense pressure.

Suddenly the cloud lifted and the moon lit up the meadow as if Holly was under spotlights. He knew he had to complete the work his father had started. It was a risk; there were many who opposed him. He would deal with them in time.

Tonight he had an irritation to deal with.

It was just the kind of diversion he needed to relax him.

Chapter Fifty-six

The grounds of Faircroft Manor, Hertfordshire, England

Albert Wellington dragged himself carefully to his feet.

There had been a time when young thugs like that wouldn't have gotten the better of him, but those days were long gone. Now he was tired and bruised as well as scared for the girl.

If what he knew about the manor was anything to go by, she would not be well treated.

He had become used to the strange comings and goings

over the months since he had started living rough on the estate. Often he told himself he would leave, find somewhere else to live, perhaps go back to his native Devon. There would be plenty of work on the farms or nature reserves for a man with his skills. Then reality kicked in and he knew he was tied to this place for good or ill.

He wasn't certain they would allow him to leave.

Once, not so long ago, he had been head gamekeeper at the manor. That was under Lord Solsbury. A fine man, a real and proper English gentleman who could trace his family tree back before Henry VIII.

After the lord died, his wife and family had to sell the house and grounds to pay the Death Duties. Albert thought it was a real shame.

Built in the seventeenth century, the Jacobean house had seen much history during Elizabethan and Victorian times. In the grounds, an oak tree marked the spot where Princess Elizabeth heard she was to be queen.

The new owner was a businessman from London the staff were told. At the first staff meeting most were told they would not be needed any longer, even people who had been there all their lives. One day they were there, the next, gone.

Albert lasted about a month. He watched some guests of the new owner, Mr. Holly, hunt and catch a deer. Instead of shooting it, as was expected, they formed a circle around it, so it couldn't escape, and then they took turns to press their hands into its side. Albert was not a superstitious man, but it looked to him as if the hands actually went into the deer's body. It took a long time for the poor animal to die, and when it did the group fell onto the body like a pack of hyenas.

When Albert protested, he was dismissed.

He had no idea what to do or where to go. He had a crazy idea if he stayed around, Holly would realize his worth and reinstate him. That had been months ago, and if Holly knew he was still hanging around he had given no sign of it.

There wasn't a lot to do. The shack was barely habitable. He caught rabbits and fished in the river, and he knew how to skin and gut and cook over an open fire. He existed.

His scheme took up most of his time.

While he worked the estate, he had begun to make a detailed plan of every aspect of the manor and the grounds. Each field and copse, each animal sighting. Back in the days when he had access to the manor itself, he made notes and drawings of every room, every entrance and exit, every hidden passage and priest hole. It had become quite an extensive piece of work. He had hopes he might sell the idea to Lord Solsbury and they might publish a book that would help the coffers. It never happened of course.

Nowadays he spent most of his time filling in the gaps so his work was as complete as possible.

Under cover of darkness he would get as close to the house as he could and note and sketch doors and windows, paths and walls. He noted where animals trekked and what flowers grew during which season.

He kept it hidden in the shack.

Vaguely he wondered whether it might be possible to interest Holly and get his old job back by giving Holly the book.

He flexed his legs. Stiff but not too much damage. His head ached but a good night's sleep would cure that. Maisie was sleeping curled on the floor beneath a window.

A noise.

What was that?

Again, there it was again.

He raised his head over the couch to see if there was anyone there.

Then the front door crashed open.

In an underdeveloped country, don't drink the water;
in a developed country, don't breathe the air.
—Changing Times Magazine

Chapter Fifty-seven

The grounds of Faircroft Manor, Hertfordshire, England

Albert watched the wood of the poorly fitting door to the shack splinter as something heavy smashed it open.

Then he saw what it was.

Maisie made an odd sound that would have been a scream in a human and hid under the couch.

Albert's legs felt unsteady beneath him and all he could do was move slightly backward, though he knew the shack was so small that no amount of distance would be any help to him.

Nothing would help against what was standing in the doorway.

The monster he had seen that time at the manor left him in no doubt that there was evil existing there. The creature facing him had just one intention, although the eyes looked like those of a shark, black but dead, staring without recognition or emotion. Staring with one purpose, to kill Albert.

The wall of the shack was rough and greasy. Albert backed against it and felt the wood with his hands. His mind was racing. He realized he was speaking, jumbled words tumbling out of his mouth as the fear took hold.

It was dark with just enough light from the moon to let

him see clearly enough, too clearly. He would have preferred it if he couldn't see anything.

He briefly wondered if he shut his eyes whether he would wake and find himself alone, like every other night. Then he heard the grunts, smelled the fetid odor, saw the huge misshapen body, and knew this was not like any other night.

He knew it was also his last.

The creature shifted in the entrance to the shack.

There was blood smeared around the bloated lips.

Albert heard a piercing scream disturb the night and realized after a few moments that it was his scream.

The creature thrust itself at him. He felt the sharp talons tear his skin, then felt the agony as they burrowed deep within him, seeking out the soft organs, and began to feed. The breath was foul, as if corpses had been consumed and were trying to escape. The tongue was lolling over the mouth, moving cobralike, waiting to strike. Up close the head was immense. It was on a thick solid neck, wide powerful shoulders. The features were jumbled, as if a waxwork had been too close to a fire. Forehead dripped over eyes, a nose that was squat and hoglike, molten cheeks, and a skull of tufts and bone.

As it fed, the black eyes began to change. From a deep night black they began to lighten, so by the time Albert was so weak he could no longer stand, the eyes were a bright and brilliant blue.

When he used to skin rabbits, there was a moment when the final piece of fur was ripped from the body. He could never describe the sound that last tearing made, but it was ingrained in his senses. As the last vestige of his life was ripped from him, he sensed that was the noise his body was making.

He died, but the creature stayed a long time after that, devouring and mutilating.

Day Three

A hunter of shadows, himself a shade.
—Homer

Chapter Fifty-eight

The Home Office, Whitehall, London, England

Robert Carter had been speaking uninterrupted for almost half an hour.

"To summarize," he said. "There is a race of vampirelike creatures. The race is called *Spiraci,* from the Latin *to breathe.* Colloquially they are known as breathers, and they feed on human souls. They also consume their bodies and use them as sex pets. They've existed since before man walked the Earth, evolving over centuries and, in the twenty-first, they are split into three factions.

"John Holly leads a global business that has franchised the feeding. He's organized and ruthless and wants to genetically modify the creatures' DNA so they are no longer dependent on humans. If his plan works, the breathers will have no need for us. We would, in effect, become redundant, and the breathers will become the dominant species on the planet.

"Rachel Grey runs the second faction. She and others like her want to destroy Holly and stop his research, want to maintain the status quo, so they can carry on as her forefathers did—in the traditional manner."

"So they'll continue to use us like cattle?" the home secretary said.

Carter nodded.

"Unacceptable," he said, as if dismissing a proposal for an inner road route.

"I agree," Carter said. "Both groups are a threat to humanity and have to be stopped."

"And the third group?" Crozier said, prompting Carter. He'd noticed the home secretary surreptitiously checking his wristwatch.

"The third group is less organized, barely a group at all, more a collection of disparate individuals led by Jason Pike, who want to stop both Grey and Holly. Pike and his people want a complete end to the feeding."

"Surely that will mean they die out completely?"

Carter nodded grimly. "I believe Jason Pike is aware of that."

A silence hung in the air.

"Is Pike here?" the home secretary said eventually.

"He's downstairs, waiting for us to reach a decision."

"But surely this is all conjecture," Alan Liskard butted in. In setting up this meeting with the home secretary, Crozier had effectively gone over his head, and the under-secretary was furious about the breach of protocol. "You haven't offered us any proof of your findings."

"How many more people have to die before you have the proof you need, Alan?" Crozier said.

Liskard flushed and turned to his boss. "Home Secretary?"

Richard Reid had been home secretary since the last cabinet reshuffle three months ago. It was a job he'd coveted since his first entry into politics fifteen years before. Now he was starting to wonder why he had wanted the job so badly. Riots on the streets of Hoxton, illegal immigrants swarming in from Eastern Europe via the Channel Tunnel, the Metropolitan Police threatening to strike over pay and working conditions, and now this.

Carter's scenario was a nightmare. Even before he became home secretary, Reid had long been uneasy about Department 18's existence and had actually chaired a select committee a couple of years ago that looked into the running of the department and the results it had achieved. It was his opinion then that Simon Crozier and his team of *gifted* people should be shut down, but the vote went against him, and now he was home secretary.

Department 18 was very much *his* responsibility. This was exactly why he had employed Alan Liskard to oversee it, effectively putting another layer of bureaucracy between the department and his office. He was thinking now that he should have found someone tougher and more experienced than Liskard for the role. He looked at the expectant faces around the table, all waiting for his decision, then reached into his briefcase and took out a thick manila folder.

The folder was old, curled at the edges, the ink on the title label faded with the passage of time. Reid rested his hands on it and cleared his throat. "This is an unfortunate sequence of events," he said. "However, they are not without precedent." He looked across the table at Simon Crozier. "One of your predecessors found himself in a very similar position to the one you find yourself in today. Unfortunately, at that time, no action was taken. Had it been, we might not be sitting here having this conversation." He glanced down at the file and slid it across the desk to Crozier, who flicked it open and started scanning pages.

"This is dated 1951," Crozier said, not looking up.

"Quite," Reid said. "And the year is significant. You'll notice that the report was compiled by Henry Manners, the director of your department at the time. By '51 Manners was about to be replaced. His credibility was wearing thin with the government of the day and, to be frank, the minister responsible for the department at that time had lost all faith in him. If you read the entire file you'll see that Manners recommended that action be taken against a group of individuals who displayed very similar characteristics to these breathers. Unfortunately there was no one left to take him seriously and so the file was buried. Not long afterward, Manners was replaced."

"So in effect you're saying that successive governments have known about the breathers and have done nothing about them," Robert Carter said incredulously.

"That's about the size of it," Reid said.

"That's despicable," Carter said. "Have you any idea how many people have died at the hands of these creatures since 1951?"

"No," Reid said bluntly. "But then I'm sure that you don't either, so climb down from your high horse. Posturing will get us nowhere." He poured himself a glass of water from the carafe in front of him. He took a sip and turned to Crozier. "So what you're proposing . . . your solution . . . is a surgical strike against Holly."

Crozier nodded.

"We believe it's the only way," Carter said, interrupting again. "We need to rescue our people."

"Czerwinski and Dr. Payne."

"Of course."

Reid leaned back in his seat and steepled his fingers, blowing lightly across the tips.

"I'd hardly call Czerwinski one of *our people*," Alan Liskard said.

Carter had his mouth open, ready to slap Liskard down, but Reid beat him to the punch.

"Alan, stop being such an ass. The department brought Czerwinski on board, so he counts as one of ours. And as far as Dr. Payne is concerned . . . If you want to go see Sir Nigel Foxton to tell him we're abandoning his little girl and leaving her to the mercies of these monsters, then please be my guest."

"I didn't mean that," Liskard blustered, but the home secretary waved him away, turning instead to Simon Crozier. "Okay, Simon. I'm going to authorize this." He checked his watch again and got to his feet. "I've got a meeting with the PM in five minutes, so I have to draw this to a close. Tell Alan here what you need in the way of support. Alan," he said, glancing at Liskard. "Accommodate the department in any way they feel is necessary. Let's bring this to a satisfactory conclusion, gentlemen, and do it as quickly as possible."

The meeting was over.

Nutrimentum Spiritus (food for the soul)
—Berlin Royal Library inscription

Chapter Fifty-nine

The Home Office, Whitehall, London, England

Pike was pacing the lobby.

"You're making me nervous," Rachel Grey said. She had arrived a little over an hour ago and was now sitting on one of the green leather visitor's benches clutching a plastic cup of watery coffee.

"This is taking too long," Pike said. "We need to strike against Holly sooner rather than later."

Rachel crossed her long legs and sat back on the bench. "Patience was never your strong suit, Jason, was it?"

He scowled at her. The alliance with Rachel Grey was born out of necessity. Given the chance, he would have ripped out her throat. Instead he was killing time in an ancient building belonging to the British government making small talk with the woman.

He gave an audible sigh of relief when he heard voices from the top of the long, curved staircase and Robert Carter and the others came into view.

By the time they had reached the lobby, Pike was standing at the foot of the stairs, Grey at his side. "Well?" he said.

"We have a green light," Carter said.

Pike sighed with relief. Even Grey allowed herself a moment, shutting her eyes for a second and imagining what it would be like to tear John Holly apart; she could almost feel her fingers burying themselves in his flesh, ripping, rending.

"We go this evening," Crozier said. "Now I suggest we get back to the department. We need to plan this very carefully."

Pike shook his head. "Rachel and I will meet you at Faircroft Manor later. There are things we have to do first."

Crozier looked taken aback. "I thought we were joining forces on this."

Pike gave an easy smile. "And so we are. But you shouldn't underestimate Holly's powers. He would be aware of our presence before we got within a mile of the manor, and it would take very little for him to turn us against one another."

"He needs distracting," Grey said. "And Jason and I will provide that distraction."

Pike turned to Carter. "We'll coordinate by cell phone. You can let us know your progress and we, in turn, will tell you when it's safe to strike. Are you happy with that?"

"It makes sense," Carter said.

Simon Crozier looked uncomfortable but said nothing.

"Okay. That's settled. We'll see you at the manor."

As they watched Pike and Rachel Grey leave, Harry Bailey said, "I don't trust them."

"My thoughts exactly," Crozier said.

Robert Carter said, "They don't trust each other, those

two. I'm amazed they're able to work together, especially considering where this strike against Holly will eventually lead them."

"What do you mean?" Crozier said.

"Civil war among the breathers is what I mean. This afternoon we are going to set a chain of events in motion that will inevitably lead to carnage."

"And how do you feel about that?" Bailey said.

Carter smiled grimly. "Well, I won't lose any sleep about it, if that's what you mean."

Crozier buttoned up his coat. "Come on. We've work to do."

Chapter Sixty

Department 18 Headquarters, Whitehall, London, England

Martin Impey sat at the conference table flanked by the two senior members of the assault team who were going to spearhead the attack on Faircroft Manor.

Captain Frank Allen and Lieutenant Ian Fulbright had worked with the department a number of times in the past. Both ex-SAS, but now employed by the government and used for projects where conventional methods were deemed inappropriate. They were hard men with many years of active and dangerous duty under their belts. A map of the manor and its surroundings was spread on the table in front of them.

Carter, Bailey, and Crozier had been joined by McKinley and were standing, two each side of the table, staring down at the map.

"So, Martin," Crozier said. "What's the plan?"

"I'll leave it to Captain Allen to explain. This is very much a military operation."

Frank Allen cleared his throat and got to his feet. "As I understand it, the purpose of this operation is to liberate Dr. Payne, Mr. Czerwinski, and the girl, Czerwinski's niece, Julia. Before we go any further, I need to know how much collateral damage is acceptable."

Crozier considered the question for a moment. "I think the question is now moot. Of course the safety of Payne, Czerwinski, and his niece is primary, but it's been decided that Holly and his people pose a significant threat, and as such they should be treated with extreme prejudice."

"In other words, we take them out," Fulbright said.

"Quite," Crozier said.

Allen and Fulbright exchanged looks.

"Do you have a problem with that?" Carter said. "John Holly is pure evil. If he gets a chance to kill you, or any of us, he will."

"No problem," Allen said with a smile. "I just like to know what the etiquette is, that's all."

"Nice turn of phrase," Harry Bailey muttered under his breath.

"So, just to be clear," Fulbright said. "I can tell my men that anyone at the manor other than Payne, Czerwinski, and the girl is a legitimate target?"

"Sanctioned by the home secretary himself," Crozier lied.

"That's good enough for me."

"Right. Can we move forward to the plan itself?"

"We think the best way to attack the place is to come in through the woods, here." Allen swept his hand over a green-shaded area on the map to the east of Faircroft Manor.

"We have a couple of sources stationed there already," Martin Impey said. "And the intelligence we've received from them tells us the trees are dense enough to give us cover until the last possible moment."

"If I can interrupt," Carter said. "Tree cover in itself won't be enough, Captain. John Holly is a very powerful psychic. He will pick up on you and your men before you're halfway through the woods. His telekinetic powers are extraordinary. He could have your men blowing one anothers' balls off in the blink of an eye."

Allen didn't question it. He'd worked too many operations with the department to be fazed by the more outlandish elements involved. "Interesting," he said. "So how do I protect my men?"

"You don't. We do," Carter said. "Harry, McKinley, and I will set up a psychic screen. Call it running interference if you like. We can block any signals you and your men give off. If Holly tries any kind of psychic probe he'll be met with what is effectively white noise. He'll know something's going on but won't be able to determine what it is. If Jason Pike and Rachel Grey are true to their word, he'll have his hands full dealing with the diversion they're planning."

"Which is what, precisely?" Crozier said.

Carter shook his head. "I don't know the details. But when I spoke to Pike just before we came in here, he suggested it would be something that will totally focus John Holly's energies."

"Well, let's hope he's right," Bailey said. "Otherwise this could turn into a nightmare."

"Well, we'll try to look on the bright side, shall we," Crozier said. "Carry on, Captain."

This is the ultimate end of man, to find the One which is in him; which is his truth, which is his soul; the key with which he opens the gate of the spiritual life, the heavenly kingdom.
—Rabindranath Tagore

Chapter Sixty-one

Malcolm O'Donnell's apartment, Holborn, London, England

Malcolm O'Donnell threw the sheet aside and swung his legs to the floor, turning to smile at the girl on the bed beside him. Sophia was extraordinarily pretty with clear skin, rich pink lips, and the greenest eyes he had ever seen. Her fair hair was long, hanging halfway down her flawless back. He knew when he'd seen her at the club the evening before that she would be his next victim. She was young, barely above the age of consent, but that only enticed him further. He was longing to sink his fingers into her, to savor her youthful organs, to extract her young and vibrant life force. That he hadn't dispatched her already said much for his iron will and much-prided self-control, but it would happen soon now; he could not contain himself much longer.

"Coffee?" he said.

"Oh yes." Sophia licked her lips and flopped back down onto the pillow, her hair fanning out like a silver cape. "Don't be long," she said.

Malcolm stared down at her long, lithe body; his gaze dwelling on the small but perfectly formed breasts and traveling down to the neatly trimmed mound of pubic hair. There were tiny droplets of moisture trapped in the curls. He felt himself swelling again. Perhaps one last fuck before he fed, but first the coffee.

When he returned to the bedroom, the bed was empty. There was a momentary pulse of panic before he heard the water running in the en suite shower room. He relaxed, set the coffee mugs on the bedside cabinet, and lay back down on the bed.

When the door to the shower room opened and Sophia emerged, still dripping but wrapped in a towel, he was nursing the largest erection he could ever remember having.

"My word," she said, admiration in her voice, and dropped the towel to the floor. She slid onto the bed and straddled him, taking his erection, and inserting it inside her, making a small groaning noise in her throat. She leaned over him, letting the wet strands of her silver hair glide over his chest, making him shiver. She started to move rhythmically in time with his breathing, then reached down and traced a line on his chest with her fingernail.

"Does that feel good, honey?" she said breathlessly.

"Oh Jesus, yes," Malcolm said and closed his eyes to block out any distractions and to intensify the sensation.

Suddenly there was pain, indescribable pain.

He opened his eyes.

Sophia was smiling down at him. Her fingers were buried knuckle deep in the soft skin under his rib cage. He felt the fingers curling inside him, closing around his ribs.

"Bye, Malcolm," she said sensually, and wrenched at his rib cage, ripping the skin, splitting his sternum and opening him up like a clam.

As Malcolm screamed, Sophia fell on him, burying her face in the soft tissue of his lungs, liver, spleen, and heart; tearing at them with her razor-sharp teeth.

Malcolm died before his mind could comprehend how things could have gone so terribly, terribly wrong.

Sophia climbed from the body and wiped the blood from

her mouth with the damp towel, padded across the bedroom and picked up the telephone. It was answered on the first ring.

"It's done," she said.

On the other end of the line, Jason Pike said, "Good girl. I knew you wouldn't let me down." There was a smile in his voice.

Chapter Sixty-two

Faircroft Manor, Hertfordshire, England.

Holly felt Malcolm's death as a ripple through his mind. Malcolm was his most trusted aide. Holly was sitting in front of his computer screen, trying to take onboard the reports coming in from various contacts around the world.

His empire was coming under attack.

There had been arson attacks on three of his "restaurants" in the US. The two in New York had been burned to the ground; the one in Seattle was still burning, but looked likely to go the same way. Many of his people had been attacked in their homes, and there had even been random gang attacks on the street. In Spain three of his people had been hunted down and stoned to death in the Mijas bullring.

On their own the incidents were slight—minor inconveniences. But together they were taking on a much greater significance. They were being orchestrated.

And now Malcolm, his trusted aide, dead. He searched with his mind, trying to concentrate on Malcolm's last moments, but the images he was getting were jumbled, confused. He slammed his hand on the desk, furious with himself for not being able to focus. When the telephone rang he snatched up the receiver. "Yes!"

"It's Klimdt. We have a situation here."

Your own soul is nourished when you are kind;
it is destroyed when you are cruel.
—King Solomon

Chapter Sixty-three

The Spree Clinic, Zurich, Switzerland

Wolfgang Klimdt had just finished his morning rounds when the security alarm sounded. The wailing siren was deafening, and Klimdt threw his hands over his ears as he ran to the nearest security station.

The guard was sitting at his post, watching the bank of CCTV screens with openmouthed astonishment. Klimdt pushed him out of the way and took his seat, punching buttons and checking each screen in turn. Each screen told the same story. The clinic was under attack.

Paramilitaries armed with semiautomatic weapons were rampaging through the complex. There seemed to be forty or fifty of them. It was similar to the raid that had occurred several years ago, but there was a difference this time. In the last attack the clinic's security staff had been able to put up a big enough show of force to deter the attackers and drive them back, eventually overpowering and killing them all. This time the attack force was like a hydra. For every one of the raiders who fell, there seemed to be two more to take his place. The raiders were behaving like fanatics, disregarding their own lives. It had all the hallmarks of a suicide mission.

While Klimdt was trying to find the confidence that his own people would prevail once again, a niggling doubt was beginning to insinuate its way into his mind. He picked up the phone and punched in the number to Faircroft Manor.

Chapter Sixty-four

Faircroft Manor, Hertfordshire, England

Holly listened while Klimdt described what was happening at the clinic. When the man finished speaking, Holly was silent for a moment as he tried to assess the situation.

Finally he took a breath. "Salvage what you can and get out of there. Go to the emergency tunnel. I'll have someone there to meet you at the other end. He'll take you to the airport. There will be a plane waiting for you. It's imperative you get yourself and the remaining specimens to England. You can carry on your work here at the manor. We will not let this incident stop the project. Understood?"

"But what about the staff? *What about the new breed?*"

"Anything you can't carry is expendable. You have the code for the self-destruct?"

Klimdt hesitated. "Yes, but . . ."

"No buts," Holly said. "Get out of there, and before you do, set the self-destruct. Blow the place to hell. Understood?"

"Yes, sir. Understood."

Holly severed the connection and dialed another number.

And what is it to cease breathing, but to free the breath from its restless tides, that it may rise and expand and seek God unencumbered?
—Kahlil Gibran

Chapter Sixty-five

The Spree Clinic, Zurich, Switzerland

Klimdt checked the screens again. The raiders were still two floors above him, and the specimens and the papers he needed were in a laboratory three floors below, deep in the heart of the mountain. Two floors below that was the emergency tunnel. He ran out into the corridor and hit the elevator button.

He waited for the car to descend, checking his watch. "Come on," he muttered, but after a full minute it became obvious the elevator would not be coming. Somewhere above him elevator doors had been wedged open, immobilizing the system. The door to the stairs was at the end of the corridor. He ran to it and pulled it open, hitting the stairs still running, taking them two at a time. Above him he could hear people shouting and the sound of sporadic gunfire. He didn't look back.

By the time he reached the laboratory, he was panting for breath; a sedentary lifestyle, forty-a-day cigarette habit, and advancing years were doing him no favors.

The two technicians working in the lab looked at him curiously as he bustled in.

"Is everything okay?" one of them said. "We thought we heard shots."

Klimdt appeared flustered. "It's an attack on the clinic. You're not safe here. Go up to the tenth floor. Our people are there. They'll protect you."

"What about you?"

"I'll join you there shortly," Klimdt lied. "Go now . . . while there's still time."

The technicians looked at each other for a moment, then ran to the door.

"Take the stairs. The elevator isn't working." *Expendable.*

He waited until the lab was empty, then went to the cold store and removed the phials he needed, nestling them down in a cold box. Once they were safely packed, he downloaded the files he needed onto a memory stick and logged in the password sequence for the self-destruct. As he hit the enter key, an alarm siren began to wail throughout the complex. With the memory stick in his pocket and the cold box tucked under his arm, he rushed back to the stairs and started his descent. He had ten minutes before the entire complex exploded. He was praying he had enough time.

There were safety lights set every ten yards along the walls of the tunnel. He used them as markers to chart his progress. He was continually glancing at his wristwatch, counting off the seconds. With less than a minute to go, he reached the reinforced steel door that led to the outside world and safety. There was a lever and bar mechanism to open it. He carefully put the cold box down on the floor and gripped the lever with both hands, using all his weight to push it down. After a moment's resistance, the lever moved and the bar securing the door slid aside. He pulled and the door opened easily.

Fresh air hit him in the face and he sucked it in greedily. The sun was blazing down and glared into his eyes. He put his hand up to shield them. He could make out the outline of a man standing by a limousine parked on the mountain road.

"Quick," he said. "We have to get out of here. The whole complex is going to explode."

The man was walking toward him slowly, with no sense of urgency. Klimdt could see enough now to recognize him. It was one of Holly's drivers. Toby? Was that his name?

The man, Toby, was smiling.

"I said quickly, goddammit!"

Toby put his fingers to his lips. "Shhh. Listen," he said.

"What?"

"Listen."

In the still Swiss morning air there was silence. Klimdt blinked, trying to understand the significance of the peace and stillness. Then he realized what was wrong. The self-destruct's warning system. The siren. He couldn't hear it.

Toby's smile widened. "We switched it off," he said. "No explosion. No kaboom. Understand now?"

Klimdt shook his head.

"How about now?"

Suddenly a gun appeared in Toby's right hand. The gun coughed twice.

Klimdt didn't feel the bullets enter his chest. He stared down at himself, watching the blood spreading across the front of his shirt like a red flower blooming in the morning sun. He sank to his knees. His mouth opened. A question formed on his lips, but it remained unasked as Klimdt toppled forward onto the tarmac and died.

Toby punched in a number on his cell phone. "Klimdt's dead."

"And the clinic?" Rachel Grey said.

"Under our control."

"Good," Rachel said. "Good."

Chapter Sixty-six

Department 18 Headquarters, Whitehall, London, England

Harry Bailey dropped the sixty-year-old file onto Crozier's desk. "So why did Reid wait until now to produce this?"

Crozier looked up at the cuts and contusions on his old friend's face. "You look dreadful. Are you sure you're up to this?"

"I'm fine. The file?"

"You've read it?"

"Cover to cover." Bailey pulled up a chair and sat, stifling a groan. He'd lied. He wasn't fine at all. His body felt as if it had tumbled over a cliff and hit every rock on the way down.

"Henry Manners was a good man, but he ruffled too many feathers while he was director here. I think the government of the day used this report as a lever to oust him from his position. In letting me have the file, Reid was handing me my own poisoned chalice."

"But why?"

"Reid's no friend to the department. Hasn't been for years. If he had his way, he'd close us down."

Bailey frowned. "So why is he giving us the go-ahead for this operation?"

Crozier smiled. "What's the phrase? Give them enough rope . . ."

"So you think Reid wants you out and he'll use this to persuade his buddies in the cabinet to replace you?"

"That's my take on it."

"Why give you advanced warning by letting you see the file?"

"Politics," Crozier said. "There are enough people in government who know of the file's existence. If Reid hadn't handed it over, questions would have been asked. Why let us go into this operation without all the known facts? But now, with the file in our possession, we have all the known facts, so we go in with our eyes open."

"So what does all this mean?" Bailey said, genuinely baffled.

"It means, Harry old friend, that we have to succeed. We don't have a choice."

"And Reid doesn't think we will?"

"No, I don't think he does."

Harry Bailey shook his head. "Politicians," he said. "I hate the bloody lot of them."

"Amen to that," Crozier said.

"I'd better get going."

"Take care, Harry. Carter has a habit of losing people."

"You should cut him some slack, Simon. I've read the reports of all of his missions. He's in the clear, and he's bloody effective."

"So you've no problem having him beside you on this?"

"I couldn't ask for anyone better."

"Let's hope, for your sake, you're right," Crozier said.

Bailey smiled wryly. "So do I, Simon. So do I."

Prayer is as natural an expression of faith as breathing is of life.
—John Edwards

Chapter Sixty-seven

The grounds of Faircroft Manor, Hertfordshire, England

Fulbright ducked down behind an old oak tree stump and pulled out his radio. "We've come across a structure, sir. Looks like some kind of dwelling."

Frank Allen responded immediately. "Does it look occupied?"

"It looks as if it's about to fall down. It's little more than a shack. Whether or not there's anyone in there I can't tell. All I know is it's not on the map."

"Okay," Allen said. "What are your coordinates?"

Fulbright checked the map and relayed them.

Allen looked at his own map. "Right, Ian, hold your position. We're about five minutes away."

"Shall I move in and check it out?"

"No. Not until we've ascertained what the place is."

Ian Fulbright retreated back to the tree cover, plucked a long stem of grass and set about systematically shredding it into one-millimeter strips with his thumbnail.

"Something wrong?" Carter said to Allen.

"I sent Fulbright on ahead to check on the security. Seems he's found a building smack in the middle of the wood. Any ideas?"

"There's been nothing in our intelligence. Could be an old gamekeeper's hut, something like that."

"Hmm. I was thinking much the same. Still, we'd better take precautions." He went across to his Land Rover and opened the back door. He returned holding something that looked like a large video camera with a small screen mounted on the top of the sturdy rubber casing. "Thermal-imaging camera," he said. "We'll be able to see if anyone's in the place without getting too close. We don't need any unpleasant surprises this early in the game."

He checked his compass and turned to his men. "This way," he said. There were eight in each of the six assault squads, as well as Allen and Fulbright, all of them carrying semiautomatic weapons and dressed in camouflage gear. To Carter's eyes they looked a formidable force, but he was very aware that their safety was dependent on him, Harry Bailey, and John McKinley. If Holly got so much as a sniff of what they were intending, he could use his telekinetic powers to make the men turn their weapons on each other. The thought of the carnage that might ensue from such a scenario made him shudder.

McKinley came up beside him. "Why is this starting to feel like a Boy Scout nature ramble?" he said.

"I know what you mean, but try not to lose concentration. It's up to us to block any stray thought probes Holly might send out."

"I thought Pike was going to be keeping him occupied."

"Both he and Rachel Grey, but I'm not too sure how they're going to achieve that. So we have to be vigilant."

McKinley glanced back at Harry Bailey, who was bringing up the rear of the group. Bailey was perspiring freely, dabbing at his damaged face with a white cotton handkerchief. "I have my doubts about him. He doesn't look fit enough for a mission like this."

"Harry's one of the best," Carter said. "He's had his problems in the past, but he seems to have them in check."

"The booze you mean?"

"Since he's been in on this I haven't seen him touch a drop. He seems to be on top of his game."

"Well, only time will tell."

"You're a cynic."

"And you're telling me you're not?"

"Don't worry about Harry. I have my eye on him."

"Just don't spread yourself too thin. That's all I'm saying."

"I won't, but it's important to remember that Harry's been up against Holly before. That experience could be invaluable."

"Point taken," McKinley said.

Carter let him walk on, hanging back to hook up with Bailey.

"If Simon told you to babysit me you can forget it. I can look after myself," Bailey said.

"I'm sure you can. But that's not what I want to talk about. Is there anything you know about John Holly that might give us some kind of edge?"

"An Achilles' heel, you mean?" Bailey shook his head. "Apart from his arrogance, I'd say not. But then my contact with him was slight. All I know is that he's the most evil individual I've ever come across. When he was describing the killing of those young women, there was a look in his eyes that chilled me to the core. I couldn't wait to get out of his presence, and it wasn't that I was scared for my own safety. It was more that I was convinced prolonged contact with him would be dangerous. He was just so damned charming."

Carter raised his eyebrows. "Charming?"

"How do you think he got all those young women into bed with him? He's got an innate animal magnetism. For someone, man or woman, coming to him without any knowledge of what he is, I should think he'd be irresistible."

"That doesn't really help us," Carter said.

"Sorry. Just telling you what I know."

Ahead of them Frank Allen had stopped walking and raised his hand to stop the rest of them. Ian Fulbright ducked out from behind the bole of a large oak. "It's just through here," he said.

"Okay," Allen said. "Let's check it out."

"Well," Allen said. "Something's alive in there. See." He pointed to the camera's screen. There was a small, colorful image in the center—blue, yellow, and red swirls forming the shape of a small animal.

"What is it?" Carter said. "Fox?"

"Too small. Probably a cat. Let's check it out."

He led them through the trees to the clearing where Albert Wellington's shack stood.

"It's derelict," Fulbright said.

"We still need to check it out, Lieutenant."

Fulbright saluted. "Very good, sir." He turned to the others in the group, picking out two of the men. "Harris, Langton, you two with me," he said. "The rest of you make sure you're ready to give covering fire if necessary. It may be a trap."

A few minutes later Fulbright's voice crackled over the radio. "All clear, but I think you should get in here and take a look at what we've found."

"Roger," Allen said, then turned to Carter. "Well, let's go and take a look then."

Carter felt a sick dread building in the pit of his stomach. Something in Fulbright's voice told him that whatever was in the shack wouldn't be very pleasant.

The first thing they saw as they pushed through the door was Langton, one of the two men who had accompanied Fulbright, leaning against the wall, a pool of vomit at his feet.

"In here," Fulbright called.

Fulbright was crouching down in the center of the floor.

"Was there a cat?" Allen said.

"Yeah. It ran for it when we arrived. It was eating . . . this."

He moved aside slightly so they could see. There was something pink and wet on the floor.

Allen moved forward, peering down at the object on the floor. "What is it?" he said. Then, "Oh, good God! Is that . . . ?"

"Part of someone's face. Yes, sir," Fulbright said.

Carter looked over the lieutenant's shoulder. It was part of a cheek, bewhiskered, still with most of the nose attached. The edges were raw and bloody, and if you looked closely, you could see where it had been nibbled by the cat.

"The rest of the body is over there," Fulbright said, pointing across the room. "Behind the couch."

Harry Bailey walked across and looked over the back of the couch. He winced and turned his head away. "Well, I'll tell you something—it wasn't a bloody cat that did this. A lion or tiger, maybe."

McKinley was at his side, staring down at the dismembered body, which lay like a heap of bloody rags on the floor. "He looks like he could have been a tramp. Look at the clothes," McKinley said.

"There's an arm missing. What the hell could have done this?" Bailey said.

"Holly did it."

At the sound of the voice they all turned to see Jason Pike's large frame filling the doorway.

"How the hell did you find us?" Carter said.

"I've been tracking you for the last few miles," Pike said, stepping into the room.

"And Grey?"

"No idea. We split up shortly after we left you. She's been busy, though. From the reports that have been filtering through, I think we can safely say that she and Holly and their associated factions are now at war with each other."

"Then you must be a very happy man," Carter said.

Pike gave a tight smile. "Yes, I am."

"How do you know Holly's responsible for this?" Bailey said.

"I can smell him." Pike sniffed the air. "I can taste his stench."

"But why kill him?" McKinley said. "I can't see how an old vagrant like this would pose a threat to Holly's empire."

"He did it for sport. I've seen him do much worse. The one thing you have to understand about Holly is that he has zero regard for human life. To him you are little more than vermin. He'll snuff out a human life with as much thought as you'd give to swatting a fly."

"Time to move on to the house, I think," Carter said. "Captain Allen?"

Allen moved to the door. "Right, outside everyone." He spotted one of his men standing in the corner, leafing through some kind of notebook. "Corporal Harris, what have you got there?"

Harris snapped the notebook shut. "Found it, sir, under the couch. Looks like some kind of journal."

Allen went across and took it from him. He opened the battered cardboard cover and read the first page. "Albert Wellington," he said. "Could be our victim." He flicked through the pages, not really taking in the contents. He closed the book and tossed it onto the couch. "We haven't got time for this. Outside. There's nothing we can do in here."

Chapter Sixty-eight

Faircroft Manor, Hertfordshire, England

It was a fine, clear night.

The kind of night, someone commented, that when it was all over was made for lovers walking hand in hand.

Three men were standing by a small clump or trees, holding hands, but they weren't lovers. Far from it. They were fighters. At that precise moment they were fighting with their minds. Fighting any attempts Holly might make to intercept the assault teams.

Carter, Bailey, and McKinley stood, eyes closed, sending blocking waves of thought across an imaginary line in front of the manor. The house was not completely in darkness; in a few rooms lights could be seen. But the effect was more spooky than comforting; the lights diffused as if viewed through a fog.

Pike stood a little way from the Department 18 group, watching their concentration, envying the closeness of the comrades. He could feel the residual essence of the forces they were conveying, but he stood in isolation, as he so often did these days.

The assault teams had been split into three forces. One was approaching from the rear of the house. Using walls and vehicles as cover, they were going to go in through four separate downstairs windows. Another group was the surprise element that was working its way up to the top floor. They planned to rappel in, "just like the SAS in that Iranian Embassy siege," one of the soldiers had said. The main team was simply a full frontal attack; hit the front door, stun grenades, machine rifles, maximum damage.

Frank Allen checked with Fulbright and both men nodded. The teams were in position. Allen walked across to Carter, attracted his attention and waited while Carter disengaged from the other two.

"We're keeping up a kind of blocking wall, but to honest there isn't a lot to block," Carter said. He motioned for Pike to join them. "Whatever diversion you've created seems to have worked wonders. There's little sign of activity from Holly."

Pike let a small ghost of a smile touch his lips. "It's been a pleasure." He didn't offer that Rachel Grey was also involved. Not that he minded sharing any glory, just that so far she had not made contact and so he was ignorant of what she was actually doing. That made him very worried.

Allen pulled his night-vision goggles down over his eyes. "Right," he said. "We're going in."

Carter didn't see a signal but immediately the front of the house was lit by floodlights. Explosions were heard from the rear of the house. Dark shapes rushed the front door as the assault team moved quickly into attack mode. The front door was heavy and thick. Under the targeted explosion it crumbled like hope.

Harry Bailey opened his eyes to see Carter frantically beckoning him. Bailey dropped McKinley's hand. "No offense, but I don't want to get used to that kind of thing."

"Holding hands? I was planning my wedding cake," McKinley said.

Both men moved across to Carter, and all of them ran as fast as they could behind the final team of soldiers. They heard muffled gunfire from the back of the house. Over the heads of the running men, bullet tracers were leveled almost continuously toward the front windows.

Breaking glass echoed through the ruined front door as the upstairs floors were invaded by the team at the back.

Standing in the doorway, Carter watched as Allen and Fulbright wordlessly directed the men in different directions, checking each door and alcove. Rooms were entered and a fierce battle soon developed as the security guards defended for all they were worth.

"This is going to take a while," Pike said.

Carter nodded. "We need to find Julia, Payne, and Czerwinski while the army keeps security busy."

"Find Holly and we find them," Pike said.

"I'm not so sure." McKinley was tuning out the noise of the battle. He was searching for Holly with his powers. "I can feel him, only him, through there." He pointed to a wide oak door to the left.

All four men instinctively dropped to the floor as stun grenades were thrown up the winding staircase to combat the machine-gun-carrying men rushing down. The soldiers took up firing positions and shredded the stairwell and walls with thousands of rounds.

"Come on," Carter said.

In a crouched run, they reached the oak door and pushed it open.

The room they entered was calm, almost serene. Music was playing from hidden speakers, "Fingal's Cave" from Mendelssohn's *Scottish Symphony*. Despite the warmth of the evening, a log fire burned brightly in the huge stone hearth; small cracking sounds as logs popped and glowed provided a gentle backdrop to the music.

Floor-to-ceiling bookshelves held thousands of leather-bound volumes. By the fire a wing-backed chair in maroon leather was pulled close so that it had its back to the door. Wafts of cigar smoke indicated the chair was occupied.

McKinley suddenly groaned in pain and sank to his knees.

Carter and Bailey immediately constructed their mental barricades.

"I trust Mr. McKinley won't vomit on my newly laid oak-paneled flooring."

"Are you going to show your face, Holly?" Carter said.

An elegant arm laid the cigar in the onyx ashtray on a small occasional table, and the chair was pushed round so that John Holly could be seen.

Carter took his chance. While performing even small tasks like moving the chair or laying down the cigar, a tiny chink of concentration faded. Carter probed, opened his thoughts, and disconnected the hold Holly had over McKinley.

McKinley rubbed the side of his left temple and slowly stood. "I'm okay."

Holly clapped his hands together silently. "Of course you are. Jason, I see you have joined the British government. They have a decent pension scheme I hear, not that you will live long enough to be concerned about annuities or dividend yields."

"I've come to take back what you've stolen from me, John."

Holly put a look of mock uncertainty on his features. "Stolen? Yours? I can't think what you have in mind."

"Not what, John, but who. I trust they are well, especially poor Julia." Pike was keeping his voice polite and level. All the time his brain was protected as well as he could manage.

"Oh," Holly said, as if what he had been trying to remember had just come to mind. "The womb."

The barb worked. Pike was angry, and his anger weakened his resolve. He felt the razorlike cuts into his mind straightaway. Holly was in.

Then, even before any damage could be done Carter was there, and Bailey. Like fumbling fingers being firmly lifted from an arm, Holly's thoughts were removed.

If he was annoyed or concerned, no one would have known it from his face. Holly continued with the confident, slightly arrogant smile he had worn from the beginning.

McKinley had checked out the room's perimeters. The library was clear. There was no one else there. They had all searched the corners of the room with their eyes as soon as they entered. They were looking for shadows that moved and dark patches where there shouldn't be darkness. The room was empty of anything sinister.

Anything apart from John Holly.

Holly stood. He closed his eyes, held his arms out with palms up and immediately all four men felt pulsing in their heads. Holly was sending wave after wave of concentrated power at all of them at once. Carter had never felt such a force.

He looked at Bailey, who was nearest to him. The look in Bailey's eyes was not encouraging.

Carter summoned the very peak of his powers and began to push back. It was as if he was pushing at soft rubber. The more he pushed, the more his mind was sucked in. It seemed as if the greater the force they applied to resist Holly the more Holly grew stronger.

Then Holly sat down and the fierce heat in their brains dropped.

"I never liked this suit," Holly said. He lifted his legs out in front of him and the men stared as the feet began to expand, the shoes lasting only seconds before the expensive leather and stitching split open. The legs of the pants ripped along the seams as throbbing leg muscles bulged out, the legs lengthening with gray rippling flesh.

"Jesus," Bailey said.

"*Spiraci*," Carter said.

Holly stretched his arms over his head as if invigorating himself after a sleep. The arms were getting longer, the biceps bunching into an impossible size as the gray skin rippled with vessels and muscle. The suit jacket tore like paper as the chest expanded and the shirt disintegrated. Hairless and adorned with small openings that seemed to be breathing independently of Holly, the chest became huge. At the ends of the hands, the fingers were curled into vicious claws, talons flicking in the air, each dancing to its own tune as the ends opened and closed as if singing.

The creature stood, dwarfing the men who backed against the closed door.

Then a window crashed open as a shape broke through it. Holly turned, the massive head lolling on the shoulders like a boulder at the start of an avalanche.

Standing in the room, oblivious to the broken glass, was another creature, as big as the one Holly had become.

Snarling like an angry beast, Holly launched himself at the new entrant.

They locked arms around each other in a parody of love, but there was no romance in the way their teeth tore at throats. No caress in the claws ripping at chests, no tenderness as the feet scrabbled to rip at legs and at flesh.

The noise was so loud the gun battles still ensuing outside the room were all but drowned out.

Both creatures were huge and powerful. Injuries were being inflicted but ignored. This was a fight to the death.

Carter took hold of Bailey's hand.

"What the . . ."

"We'll never have a better chance."

Bailey realized what Carter had in mind. So did McKinley as he held on to Bailey's other hand. Carter looked to his side as he felt Pike take his hand and they completed a circle.

Together they sent out layer after layer of pulses, probing into the Holly creature. It was hard to keep track of which one was Holly, as the fight spun round and round, but once locked in on the target, their minds were as one, fixed like a heat-seeking missile.

Gradually, over nearly an hour, one beast began to weaken. The hour was long and grueling, and the concentration of effort was draining. Carter was exhausted, but he could see both

Pike and Bailey become ashen under the strain. This was going to seriously damage their health for a while.

Then it was over.

With a triumphant roar, one of the creatures locked its jaw over the throat of the other and ripped and tore and bit and chewed. Blood spurted like a fountain, coating the floor with the color of victory.

Holly was dead.

The winning creature was badly injured. Huge, standing for a moment before lowering itself to the floor, panting for breath.

"Should we . . ."

Pike shook his head. "Leave her to revert. Let's find what we came for."

Victory at all costs, victory in spite of all terror,
victory however long and hard the road may be;
for without victory there is no survival.
—Winston Churchill

Chapter Sixty-nine

Faircroft Manor, Hertfordshire, England

Outside of the library the house was relatively quiet.

Frank Allen in the hallway talking into a mobile device. "Outer perimeter secure? Upstairs all cleaned out? Ground floor is friendly, so that leaves the basement. Two detachments down there. Thermal imaging doesn't reveal many

large shapes so it may be little resistance, but keep the guard up."

Carter brought him up to speed on what had happened with Holly. Allen was concerned about having a creature on the loose, but Pike explained, as best he could, that fairly soon a bloodied, battered, but ostensibly human figure would walk out through the doorway.

"Can we go with your men to find the others?" Carter said.

Allen watched as the first of his men went down the stairs to the floors below ground level. "You and Mr. Pike can go. I'd prefer to keep some of your expertise aboveground if you don't mind."

Carter turned to Bailey and McKinley. "You both okay with that?"

Bailey and McKinley were both drained by their efforts; they had no energy left to argue.

Carter and Pike followed the soldiers down the steps to the basement. They had decided to use the old entrance rather than trust the elevators. The stone-flagged steps were worn smooth from the countless feet that had walked them over the centuries. But no one was in the mood to appreciate the history of their surroundings. Everyone was tense. The soldiers walked with guns poised, treating every turn in the corridor as a potential trap, a death trap.

The rough-hewn walls of the original building gave way to a newer part of the basement where the surfaces were flat and painted white, with discreet lights set into the plaster walls. Later the walls were smoothly tiled in clinical white.

At each doorway the soldiers performed their search ritual. Two would stand at each side of the entrance while a third used an electronic device to listen for sound inside the room. When they were ready, all three pushed open the door and would enter in a low crouch, guns ready.

In two of the rooms they found security guards, but each

time the soldiers swamped the room with gunfire and resistance was quickly extinguished.

Gradually they reached the end of the corridor, where one door remained before there was a corner.

The soldiers went through their check and the opinion was the room was occupied.

They tried the handle.

The door wasn't locked. Inside the room were two forlorn and defeated-looking figures.

"Jacek," Pike said, and embraced the bewildered Pole.

Carter took hold of both the hands of the woman. "Dr. Payne. Are you hurt?"

Payne shook her head, tears in her eyes. "I thought they were going to . . ." She dissolved into sobbing. Carter held her close.

Farther along the corridor they could hear machine-gun fire and a tumultuous noise like a million birds taking flight together.

"Jacek," Pike said gently. "Where is Julia?"

Jacek seemed confused by the question, and Pike had to repeat it. Even then it was Miranda who answered.

"Unless they've moved her, she'll be in the nursery at the end of the corridor."

"Nursery?" Carter said.

The noise of the birds was getting louder. Only they weren't birds.

Pike stayed with Jacek and Miranda. Carter followed the noise.

The white-tiled corridor ended in reinforced glass that had been set into a steel door. Behind the glass, thousands of black shapes were spinning and weaving in the air, crashing against the transparent surface in a futile attempt at escape. The incubation room that had given them birth was now the coffin of the young breathers.

The sergeant of the assault force was taking orders from a

cell phone, a grim look on his face. He put the cell phone into a webbed pocket in his tunic. "Destroy them all."

Carter watched as two of the men set explosives into the hinges of the door. Working silently and quickly, they seemed to give the thumbs-up signal almost before they began.

A button was pressed and the door was blown away. Grenades, machine-gun fire, and incendiary devices obliterated the breathers, the nurses in the room, and all the furniture that had been there.

All but the Plexiglas box.

Tentatively the soldiers went to it.

It began to shake.

Gray fingers, long and curled, gripped the top of the box.

"Help me."

The words were spoken in a whisper, an echo, but they came from the box.

The fingers disappeared from view and a long groan of pain was heard. It was a female voice.

The men circled the box. Close up, the box was transparent. While they got into position, Carter was able to confirm what he already knew; there were two life forces in the box. One was human, and one most definitely was not.

When they were next to the box, they could see clearly what was inside. They wished they hadn't.

As Carter had realized, it was Julia in there. The baby creature that Holly had created with Alice Spur was suckling at her naked breast. The breast was ripped and torn. If milk was being produced, there was no sign; the breather seemed to be drinking blood.

Julia's eyes were closed. She opened them, but they didn't see anything. Then they glazed over and her body went limp. The creature continued to gnaw for a few more seconds before instinct made it realize it was feeding from a corpse.

Without warning, and with a speed that surprised them all, it launched itself upward and leaped from the box. It slipped a little on landing and fell onto all fours as it turned and faced the group of men. Although still young, it was large and misshapen.

It roared and jumped at the group. It managed to kill two soldiers before a hail of machine-gun fire ended its doomed existence.

Everything was quiet. Smoke wafted across the silent room.

The soldiers busied themselves with a brief search of the rest of the basement area, but there was nothing else to be found.

Carter went back to Pike and the others.

"I'm sorry, Jacek," he said.

"I think I always knew she would not live a long life, but I would have wished her a happier one."

"I know there are other considerations," Pike said. "But I don't trust Rachel Grey."

"We couldn't have beaten Holly without her," Carter reminded him.

"I know that, but killing him was as much to her advantage as it was ours. More so in fact."

"You think she has a wider agenda?"

"Don't we all?"

Allen and Fulbright were as organized in victory as they had been in attack. The house was secure, the remaining security guards disarmed and restrained.

The library, with the body of Holly inside, was sealed and guarded. Instructions had been received from the upper echelons of the government that the body would be removed shortly. Analysis would be carried out at a hidden, unmarked location by scientists sworn to silence under the Official Secrets Act. Each of the scientists would die in apparent accidents within months of the research being concluded.

A strategy would at long last be put in place for future dealings with the breathers.

A breather was still among them.

Rachel Grey had reverted to human shape and was smartly dressed in a loose-fitting summer dress of reds and yellows. She looked ready for an elegant garden party at a country house. Only the deep bruises and tears in her skin showed otherwise. She was seated in a drawing room with McKinley and Bailey.

Carter handed Jacek and Miranda over to Allen and ensured they were taken away in one of the ambulances that had been waiting for casualties.

Pike seemed reluctant to go with Carter to join the others. "What's wrong, Jason?"

"I don't trust her."

"And she probably doesn't trust you either. But with Holly gone, you two are going to have to work together." Carter didn't add, in fact he had been deliberately building a complex layer to conceal the fact, that the department was already at work on a plan to wipe out the *Spiraci* wherever they could locate them.

In the drawing room three couches had been pulled in front of the windows, and Grey, McKinley, and Bailey were seated on separate couches, all staring silently out into the night, even though it was pitch-black outside. It was like the awkward first moments at a party where no one knows the others.

As soon as Pike entered the room, Rachel Grey stood and walked across to him.

Carter thought they might embrace. He was wrong.

Rachel slapped him so hard across the face that Pike took two steps backward.

"I didn't realize you were so full of hatred," she said.

Pike stroked his cheek, feeling the skin start to burn. "I

hate you and all your kind. It has been my life's work to destroy you all."

"Was it worth so many lives?"

"Those and thousands more if that is what it takes."

Bailey looked at Carter, but neither knew what was going on. "Care to tell us what the hell you are talking about?"

Rachel looked at Carter as if suddenly remembering there were others in the room besides Pike and her. She took a pace back from Pike and turned to Carter.

"Him." She pointed at Pike. "He has orchestrated all of this. Daniel Milton, Julia, Alice Spur, all his own people who died before. He has sacrificed all of them."

"And I would willingly do it all over again."

"He let Holly know where Milton was. He led Holly to Julia in Poland. He arranged the abduction of Czerwinski and Dr. Payne. All of it suited his purpose."

"Which was what?" Carter said.

It was Pike who answered. "To pit breather against breather. Holly against Grey. A civil war between them so that every last one would be wiped out. Destroyed and cleansed from the world forever."

"Instead . . ." Rachel never got to finish what she was saying.

From within his jacket pocket, Pike produced a small pistol and shot her once through the eye. The second shot, which took out the second eye, wasn't needed.

Pike turned to Carter, the gun hanging limply in his fingers.

At the periphery of his vision, Carter saw movement at the window. He shouted to Bailey and McKinley, and each of them managed to throw themselves to the floor before a volley of automatic weapons fire blew out the windowpanes, the light fittings, and ripped into Jason Pike.

He was dead before his body hit the floor.

In the seconds that followed, Carter scanned the windows. Whoever had killed Pike had vanished; it had to be men Grey had positioned in the woods, ready for any eventuality.

When they guessed the danger had passed, those in the room got to their feet and looked at one another.

The door opened and three soldiers rushed in, weapons scanning the room.

Allen walked in a pace or two behind. He barely glanced at the bodies. "More work for the hired help."

Carter gave him a quick recap of what had happened in the last few moments.

Bailey, typically, had found a decanter of whiskey. He was pouring large measures into three crystal tumblers.

McKinley took one, Carter the other, and Bailey jealously guarded the third.

They raised their glasses and clinked them together in a toast.

Carter broke the silence as they drank. "I suppose I had better report events to Crozier."

Bailey poured another measure without asking the others if they needed a refill. "Yes, let's wake the bastard up and spoil his beauty sleep."

Robert Carter reached into his pocket for his cell phone.

For they have sown the wind,
and they shall reap the whirlwind.
—The Bible

www.maynard-sims.com

www.dept18.com

"Gagliani has brought bite back to the werewolf novel."
—James Argendeli, CNN Headline News

W. D. Gagliani

Homicide cop—and werewolf—Nick Lupo has battled other werewolves before, killers who unlike Nick have no problem hunting human prey. So when a new series of savage animal attacks terrifies the area, Nick already has a suspect in mind. And he knows that if he's right it'll be up to him to destroy her. But even as he begins his surveillance, someone else is out there, watching them both. Someone with a very deadly plan. Someone who knows just what it takes to kill a werewolf.

WOLF'S BLUFF

"The best werewolf novel since *The Howling*!"
—J. A. Konrath, Author of *Whiskey Sour*, on *Wolf's Trap*

ISBN 13: 978-0-8439-6348-9